DECEPTION

A HOLLYWOOD MYSTERY

BRITT LIND

Paperback ISBN: 978-1-64704-085-7
Hardcover ISBN: 978-1-64704-087-1
eBook ISBN: 978-1-64704-088-8

Author Photograph by Michael Roud
Cover Design and Distribution by Bublish, Inc.

Praise for *Deception*

A thrilling page-turner about a group of flawed, yet compelling characters caught in a cesspool of greed and ruthless ambition behind the scenes in Hollywood. I couldn't wait to find out the ending while simultaneously wishing the book wouldn't end.

—Lara Wickman, Writer, Producer, Actress

...the story takes some refreshingly unexpected turns, picking a path through genre clichés and keeping readers guessing. The author has an easy writing style and a cinematic grasp of pace. Fans of silver screen crime should approve, as, in many respects, this reads like the novelization of a movie.

—Kirkus

If you want to read a book that offers romance, suspense, detective work, intrigue, and feels like you're watching a movie, then this is your book. I highly recommend it.

—Andreas Michaelides, Writer, Reviewer,
Blogger and Natural Health Educator

Deception is a gritty rendering of the classic battle between good and evil played out in the milieu of Hollywood. As an actor herself, Britt is ably qualified to explore and articulate the disappointment and heartache of fame-obsessed performers as they struggle to "make it" in an unforgiving industry where fame is illusive and disappointment can lead to murder,

—Tony Eldridge, Executive Producer, *The Equalizer I & II*

Praise for *Learning How to Fly*

(Beverly Hills Book Award Winner)

Learning How to Fly *is the inspiring story of a fellow activist who has hung in there through thick and thin for all of the 32 years I've known her. Fighting vivisection is a hard road and it takes both courage and incredible patience to stay in the battle. But Britt found a way to stay on course and still fulfill her passion for acting. Readers will find this book entertaining and humorous, but it's also her journey that provides guidance on how one can find their own way to a meaningful life.*

—Chris DeRose, Founder and President of *Last Chance for Animals* and author of his autobiography, *In Your Face*

As a young starlet, Britt Lind was a beauty who was cast in a Clint Eastwood movie and found happiness being married to a television producer and acting and raising a baby girl. But in a flash, her marriage ended, riches vanished, the house was foreclosed on, and her career crumbled. Britt's story of disappearing success is poignant and unforgettable, and by the time she is beaten down in Hollywood and heads for New York with visions of Broadway, you cannot help but cheer for her and the animals she has dedicated her life to saving. This is a heartfelt, timeless story of shining on to create a life filled with love, beauty, and triumph.

—Janette Turner, Writer, director and author of the forthcoming memoir *Magazine Crush: My Life as a Cosmo Addict.*

These are the adventures of an innocent young girl from Norway, thrust into American culture, driven by a passionate ambition to be an actress in a ruthlessly unpredictable and sexist industry. Britt navigated through a life of obstacles, betrayals, and disappointments with courageous resolve, a resolve deeply rooted in a firm moral foundation and strengthened by a deep compassion and a fiery desire to end the suffering of animals.

—Captain Paul Watson, Founder of *The Sea Shepherd Conservation Society* and author of several books including, *Sea Shepherd: My Fight for Whales and Seals, Seal Wars, Twenty-Five Years on the Front Lines with the Harp Seals* and *Ocean Warrior: My Battle to End the Illegal Slaughter on the High Seas.*

Dedication

To my best friend, Maude, who moved with me from place to place to place with nary a whimper. Since the moment I first saw her at the L.A. downtown animal shelter as a tiny black kitten, where she made it clear she expected me to get her the heck out of there, she was in charge. There was a lot of Noor in her and vice versa. She was a pint-sized black panther with a heart that beat with love and loyalty until the day she crossed the rainbow bridge.

"So lightly I played with those dark memories,
Just as a child, beneath the summer skies,
Plays hour by hour with a strange shining stone,
For which (he knows not) towns were fire of old,
And love has been betrayed, and murder done,
And great kings turned to a little bitter mould."

— Rupert Brooke

"…I have hunted you under my thoughts,
I have broken down under the wind
And into the roses looking for you.
I shall never find any greater than you."

— Carl Sandburg

"True evil cannot endure.
It preys upon light,
then consumes itself."

—Anon

NEW YORK

The homeless man, hunched over and shivering, pulls his thin, tattered coat tight against the icy wind that ignores the brilliance of the November sun. He walks slowly up Broadway, head down, lost in thought, his lips moving in silent conversation with himself.

As if by miracle, the masses flowing up and down the sidewalk part and make room for the pathetic creature, abhorring and avoiding him at all cost. He is seen by them but never acknowledged, his ravaged face reminding them too much of someone they know or might become. It makes them move faster, try even harder, not to see him. He's not there. It can't happen to them.

The man picks up his pace as he crosses Central Park South and enters the park. He takes the path to the lake, slips behind the benches, and climbs through the bushes, making his way to the edge of the water. Protected from the cold breeze by the trees and rocks, he takes off his cap and smiles. Enjoying the solitude, he stares off into the distance for a while, into another place and time, but then, as quickly as it came, the smile disappears. A half-forgotten nightmare intrudes on his thoughts. His body begins to tremble and sweat stands out on his forehead. He remembers the strangled cry, the eyes staring up at him in terror and surprise, and finally, touching the cold, dead hand—dead because of him. He scrambles to his feet and wipes the image from his mind. He has learned to live with his demons. This is just a temporary lapse. The man climbs back up the path and, with renewed purpose, strides out of the park. He passes a news stand, and as his eyes run over the magazines and papers on display, he reaches *into his pocket and takes a long swallow from a bottle wrapped in a plain paper bag. The touch of a feminine hand on his arm startles him.*

"Is that you?"

The familiar voice is ever so hesitant. His heart in his throat, he turns and faces the woman. She cries out before she embraces him, full of shock and pity.

"My God! It is you!"

They cling to each other tightly, as if letting go will make the other disappear forever.

The man's stubbly face is wet with tears, but his bright blue eyes are laughing.

His luck has changed, and he knows he is close to winning everything.

CHAPTER ONE

MARYSVILLE, WISCONSIN

"Hey, you two, hold on a second!" Ellie's words rang out sassy and cheerful. She leaned up against the cotton candy wagon to steady herself so she could slip off a shoe and shake out the sawdust. She blew a stray blond curl, sticky with perspiration, out of her eyes and sighed with contentment. Even though it was hot enough to fry an egg on the white line running down Main Street, Ellie loved the beginning of summer when the carnival came to town. It was the place that made her remember best how it felt to be young. All the sights and smells and sounds invaded her senses and carried her back to a time when life held nothing but possibilities, and unimaginable adventures were waiting somewhere, out there, to be experienced.

Only nineteen years had passed since she was the age of her son Josh, but it seemed a lifetime ago, before fear replaced anticipation and self-doubt replaced the longing for discovery. With the death of her parents in a car crash on the eve of her high school graduation, Ellie's perception of the world had undergone a drastic change. The world was a dangerous place and life was short. She moved without hesitation from the protection of her loving, supportive, parents to the protection of a husband. George Sibley was alone, without a family, just like her, but he never talked about his parents or what had happened to them and Ellie was not one to pry. They found comfort in each other, at least for a while, in the beginning.

Contrary to what people thought, Ellie knew she wasn't very smart. This was made plain as day to her as she struggled to get through school, barely graduating with her class. Deep down, she had always known that whatever worlds there were to conquer outside of Marysville, Wisconsin, they would be too overwhelming for someone with her limited capacities. Besides, she loved her part-time job at the beauty parlor, and the chores she had to do around their small farm weren't all that hard. She'd been doing almost as many since she was ten years old and living there with her parents. She figured she'd be living and working there till the day she died, and that was fine with her. At least she would always be safe and secure.

She stopped her daydreaming and hurried to catch up with her young son and husband. Her seven-year-old had something on his mind today, that was for sure, and she intended to keep an eye on him. He hadn't pestered her at all today to see the Egyptian belly dancer, or even to see the real live snakes in the jungle show. That had been his favorite since he was five years old. He was acting strange, all right, and she had a feeling she'd find out real soon what it was.

She caught up with them at a booth where Josh was staring with narrowed eyes at a heavyset, florid-faced man who was spinning a huge wheel set on a table. Her husband was looking around restlessly, bored to tears and, Ellie figured, already thinking about his poker game tonight. She took George's hand. It lay limply in hers.

"So, what do you two want to see now?" She hoped her enthusiasm would infect her husband, but his answer was flat and indifferent.

"Doesn't matter to me."

Josh spoke without taking his eyes off the game. "Is it okay if we waited here just a few minutes?"

My Lord. She thought her kid was so polite and solemn sometimes it scared her. "Why sure, baby, we just want you to have a good time today." She looked up at her husband for affirmation, but he ignored her and took a healthy swig from his pocket flask.

"Too damn hot to be walkin' around."

Ellie hated his drinking like crazy, but she knew better than to say a word about it, and she wasn't going to let anything ruin Josh's day at the carnival.

Her son was still staring intently at the wheel. It was divided into twelve sections, each of which had a hole at the edge with an attached can underneath. The man would spin the wheel, throw a white rat onto the wheel as it spun, put a whistle into his mouth, and lean down and blow a piercing scream at the rat. In total panic and terror, the rat would scramble around on top of the wheel looking for safety. Finally finding it, it would jump into one of the holes, thereby deciding the winner of the game. Then the man would take the rat out of the can and spin the wheel again. Two other rats were in a cage on the ground, awaiting their turn.

The whole scene made Ellie uncomfortable. She didn't especially like to see any animal used like that, even a rat.

"Come on, Josh. Let's not stay here. George, I don't think I care to see this anymore. Doesn't seem right to me."

George misread her completely. "Yeah, hard to win on this one—just takes dumb luck."

Ellie and George started to walk away, but Josh stayed glued to the spot. Ellie was getting impatient. "Josh, come on, sweetheart." He still didn't move a hair. "Josh!" His intensity was starting to frighten her.

Before she could grab his hand and pull him away, Josh made a flying leap at the spinning wheel and grabbed the rat who had just jumped for safety into a can. He bent down and swooped up the cage holding the other two rats and accidentally backed into the flimsy wall holding all the stuffed animal prizes, sending it crashing down on top of the wheel and the fat man. Josh jumped over the falling debris and took off running through the crowd.

Ellie looked after her fleeing son in amazement and then at her husband. He was as stunned as she was, but she thought she saw a flicker of approval in his eyes.

The fat man was hollering and blustering in a fit of rage. "Somebody stop that little son-of-a-bitch!"

Fat chance, Ellie thought, with everybody's grocery money in his pocket. They're having too good a time laughin' at his expense. Exasperated, the man stopped shouting and started shoving through the crowd. A feminine foot reached out and tripped him as he passed, and he fell flat on his face into a mound of sawdust. He looked up at the crowd angrily and glared suspiciously at Ellie, but her face was all innocence as her husband shot her a look and steered her away from the unfortunate man shaking sawdust out of his hair and shouting obscenities.

Josh raced through the meadow so fast that he felt as though he was almost flying. All three rats were in the cage swinging at his side. He thought he would burst with satisfaction. For a year, he had waited for the fat man to come back so he could rescue the poor, scared rats. Last year, he had been too afraid and had walked away feeling like a crummy little coward. For a year, he had lived with his guilt, knowing he would never be able to stop thinking about it until he had the courage to do what was right.

Now he had done it! And it felt great. The animals were free, and he would make sure they stayed that way. Even if his parents screamed at him. Even if the police put him in jail and tortured him, they would stay that way. He would *never* act like a coward again.

CHAPTER TWO

LOS ANGELES

TWENTY-FIVE YEARS LATER

I t was 10:30 a.m. on the Hollywood freeway and unusually clear sailing for Josh and his beat-up old blue Mustang as he headed over Cahuenga Pass. He wished he could say as much for his perpetually stalled career. He hadn't done a commercial for over six months and his bank account was dangerously low. His regular, part-time job offered more therapy than profit and he had to start thinking realistically about paying some bills. A lot hinged on this morning's audition.

But even more important was the possibility of Joell, the most famous pop singer in the country, recording a song he had written for a feature about to go into production. If it became a hit, it could turn his whole life around. Maybe she would record more of his songs, maybe they all would be hits and advertising execs would beg for him to do their commercials. Ah well, he could dream. Meanwhile, he was late, and Jennie would be pissed.

Spending the night with a dental hygienist he had picked up in Donte's had been a big mistake. First woman he had ever met who could match him drink for drink and stay conscious, and he didn't even get laid. He vaguely remembered her dumping every problem she had ever had since age six on him till about 3:00 a.m., when he had mercifully passed out. He hated himself for sneaking out of her apartment this morning without even having the nerve to look at her and see her face in the cold, hard light of day. This wasn't the morning to test his strong stomach and he was known to relax his standards in the wee hours of the morning when he was feeling lonely.

He wouldn't bet on how he would sound trying to sing the commercial he had written. His mouth felt like all the smog in Los Angeles had found a permanent home there, and his head like every car on the Ventura freeway was crammed inside his brain, crashing against his skull trying to get out. What were the damn lyrics? He struggled to remember. No time to go home and dig through his notes. Raking through all that chaos could take days. Why couldn't they just have hired him from the demo tape? But no, they didn't think it was quite what they were looking for, wanted a different approach.

He was disgusted with himself. He needed this job and had worked for hours on his presentation. But more important, he didn't want to let Jennie down. She was the one who had pushed for this audition and constantly praised his work to Ken and all the clients at the agency. Not that Ken needed any convincing, but the clients could be brutal in their criticism.

He turned right at the Cahuenga exit, and pressed down on the accelerator. If he hurried, he would only be forty-five minutes late.

* * * *

Jennie Seger looked at her watch and then double-checked it against the time shown on her computer for about the hundredth time in the last thirty-five minutes. She was so nervous she couldn't concentrate on typing the letter Ken had asked her to be sure to get out with the morning mail. She didn't know why she became so anxious every time Josh did this to her. Ever since she had known him, he had yet to be on time for an appointment. She should be used to it by now.

Ten years ago, in San Jose, she had loaded up her faithful Toyota Corolla, waved good-bye to family and friends, and headed for Hollywood to become a star without the slightest idea of how to become one. With her junior college degree in hand, she had assaulted the studios, but they had withstood her every attack effortlessly. She soon found out that there was an overflow of blonds with big brown eyes who were willing to go to greater lengths to succeed than she. A few bit parts had come her way now and then, but mainly she was grateful she had taken all those computer classes in college, along with the acting classes that didn't mean didley squat to casting directors who wanted you to already have made it before they hired you.

Even though she had done some things in Hollywood she wasn't especially proud of (hadn't most people?), she figured she lacked the chutzpah, the killer instinct, necessary to screw over your best friend or go to bed with producers who were usually a cross between Godzilla and the Pillsbury dough boy, in order to get a job.

Anyway, her receptionist job at Jordan Advertising wasn't complete torture. She wasn't one of those actresses who only felt alive while on stage. She knew her meager talent would never set the world on fire, but being an actress was what she wanted, and she would keep working at it till she died or got old and senile trying. Sooner or later, her friends would come through for her. She knew they would. It was only a matter of time, and she had to be patient. She tried not to think about possible failure, but sometimes she had to admit she wanted success as desperately as any aging ingenue who would go to bed with the ugliest man in town for a bit part.

She would have liked to have met and married a successful producer or director by now, but that hadn't happened either. It seemed almost impossible to make attractive, successful men take her seriously. Inside, she knew she wasn't just another flakey, dumb bimbo, so why did they always make her feel like one? Except Stan, but he was married and had other glaring faults besides that one. Jennie sighed deeply. A future with him was just wishful thinking.

She half-heartedly went back to her computer and tried to concentrate on the letter, but her thoughts drifted back to Josh. She looked at her watch again. He was now forty-five minutes late. She hoped he could sing with damaged vocal cords because she had every intention of strangling him the minute he walked through the door.

Josh's financial situation was too unreliable for her to take him seriously as a potential boyfriend, not to mention his world-class drinking habits, so she had kept their relationship strictly platonic. He hadn't really tried too hard to turn it into anything else.

Josh's talent filled Jennie with awe. The first time she heard him sing at a demo session, she had gushed over him so profusely, he was convinced that she was a complete phony. Gradually, as she kept sitting in on his recording sessions and they became friends, he realized that her admiration was sincere.

Jennie found it difficult to believe that anyone who possessed such a beautiful voice and wrote songs so sensitive and heartfelt that they made her cry, could find it almost impossible to accept any praise.

The intercom buzzed, and she cringed before reluctantly picking up the receiver. "Yes?" She waited while Ken asked again for Josh, then looked up gratefully as Andy Saber walked through the door. "No, not yet, but Andy's here and he's ready right now." Andy nodded at her in confirmation. Jennie's aggravation with Josh was growing. Through tight lips she said to Ken, "I'll send him right in," then accidently slammed down the phone in her fury.

As soon as Andy disappeared into the other office, she hissed out loud, "I'm going to kill him! This time I'm really going to kill him!" She attacked her computer keys with a vengeance.

"So the bastards are finally getting to you, I see." Josh stuck his head in the door and flashed his best Brad Pitt grin. It usually succeeded in melting her wrath, but not this time.

"Josh, God damn you!" Jennie shot out of her chair and stomped around to the front of her desk to face him.

"Don't I even get a chance to defend myself?" He closed the door and tried to give her the usual hug, but Jennie wasn't having any.

"You're forty-five minutes late! Why can't you be on time just once, just one lousy time?"

He laid his guitar on the couch and shrugged. "Sorry, honey, but freeway traffic was brutal."

"Liar!"

She walked back around behind her desk and did a double take. "Freeway? You only live a couple of blocks from here. Where were you coming from?" She could see Josh's brain whirring to come up with a good one. "Never mind, never mind." She sank down into her chair, resigned. "Why do I go through this every time. Why? Can you tell me?" Josh was smiling at her affectionately, as he watched her scowl. What's the use? She might as well give up. "Forget I asked, okay?"

He sat down and leaned forward on his elbows. "Works for me."

He hesitated before asking, "Any word from Stan?"

"Not yet."

Josh nodded and breathed out heavily.

Jennie busied herself shuffling papers to avoid looking at him. The least she had to do was impress upon him the importance of the audition. "These people liked your Datsun commercial and even though the demo wasn't quite right, they're very open to your ideas. Do you realize if this goes national, it could support you for a year?"

He picked up his guitar and strummed a couple of chords. "Don't worry, Jennie, I won't let you down."

She dropped the papers on her desk in exasperation. "Me? Don't do it for *me*. Do it for *yourself*." She was beginning to think he was hopeless. There didn't seem to be anything she could do or say to make him care. She had decided to launch one more time into her speech on wasting one's God-given talent when the intercom stopped her short. It was just as well. The speech only wore her out and put him to sleep. Ken asked for Josh again, and she was relieved to have a positive answer this time.

Andy came out of the inner office stone-faced, passed Jennie's desk, and went out without a word to either one of them.

Jennie looked at Josh gleefully. "He wasn't in there for more than two minutes! They must have *hated* him. I know this makes me a terrible person, but I'm glad. Now go in and knock 'em dead!" She gave him a thumbs-up gesture and her most determined expression. He returned the sign gratefully and went in.

They were all seated at the conference table waiting for him. The amenities were over quickly. As always, Josh ignored the piano at the far end of the large room, pulled out a chair from the table, and made himself comfortable. Time was money and Bernie Braverman, the owner of Hoffman Bread and about sixty other companies, only had a few hundred million to play with. He and Joe Hines, his vice president of marketing, sat across the table from Ken.

"Go ahead. Let's hear it." Bernie smiled at him like a Jewish Santa Claus. His white teeth gleamed behind his short black beard and his brown eyes twinkled benevolently. A total stranger could be in a room with Bernie for two minutes and find himself reciting his life story and revealing his deepest, darkest secrets, confident that they would be safe with this warm, caring human being.

Josh knew better than to be deceived by the friendly grandfather act. He liked Bernie all right but he had worked for him in the past and had learned the hard way that, underneath that pudgy bundle of warmth, beat the heart of a shrewd businessman who had never been known to go out on a limb for anyone. He was brilliant at both taking credit and avoiding blame.

The personality of his new vice president of marketing, on the other hand, was so cold it would have to heat up to reach freezing level. Joe Hine's handsome forty-year-old face was framed by an immaculately styled helmet of salt and pepper hair. It was either arrogance or a healthy acceptance of the inevitable that kept him from coloring it, and even though Josh had never met the man before, he was pretty sure he knew which description fit him.

Josh sat down at the far end of the table and strummed a few chords.

"You sure you don't want to use the piano?" Hines asked in an overtly disparaging tone.

"No, I'll play my guitar," Josh answered softly.

"Most people use the piano. Never had anybody audition with a guitar before," Hines almost sneered. "Of course, we usually make our decision from the demo, but Ken convinced us you could do better."

"Whenever you're ready," a friendly voice interjected.

Josh glanced up from tuning his guitar and caught Ken Jordan's encouraging nod. He could always count on Ken. He still looked like a remnant of the flower-child era he had caught the tail end of, with his longish blond hair that was starting to thin on top, and light blue eyes that peered out through rimless glasses. His agency was small, but Ken liked it that way. Being able to spend time with his wife Julie and his teenage son Kevin was more important to him than setting the advertising world on fire and that wasn't where his heart was anyway. His dream of producing movies had dimmed as one script after another that he had optioned failed to find financing, but Josh had a feeling his dream would never completely die. That was how it was in this merciless town that kept stabbing you in the heart while enticing you to come back for more.

Josh began his presentation. "The familiar jingle that you've been using for several years now has been effective in getting the brand name out there, but I was thinking of ingraining your product not only in the minds of the public, but in their hearts. Emotions play such a huge part in what people buy. So, I was thinking of the set as a country kitchen—warm, homey, family gathered there, that kind of thing—and the music could reflect a softer mood. Well, let me show you." As he sang, he was relieved to find the words come back to him.

"Through the years, home is forever,
Love shines through in many ways.
All the memories that we treasure,
Will remain and fill our days."

He tried to read their faces as he sang but discovered nothing in Bernie's perpetual smile or Joe's aloof mask. He resumed his explanation. "Then, after the announcer copy, we go back—"

Hines interrupted abruptly. "Ken, this is shit. Talk about retro. It's nothing like we had in mind. It's worse than the demo." He looked at Josh. "No offense to you. I'm sure you're a very sensitive, talented guy. Right, Bernie?" He looked across the table at Bernie, who was noncommittally examining his manicure, and then at Ken, who seemed at a loss for words. "We need some pizzazz, something edgy. All this homey love crap doesn't make it." His cruel words were made more so by their nonchalant delivery.

Ken said something but his words were drowned out by the blood pounding in Josh's ears. He realized he was gripping the neck of his guitar so tightly the strings were cutting into his fingers. Josh numbly got to his feet and with a cursory glance at Ken, he made his exit. His mouth had turned into a desert and needed intensive watering down.

Jennie had kept her fingers crossed the whole time Josh was auditioning but when she saw his face as he came out, she knew it hadn't done any good. She had enough sense not to ask any questions, but all was not lost. Stan had just called.

"Be at Universal in half an hour," she said, handing Josh a piece of paper. "Stan's office. Drive in the third gate off Lankershim."

A glimmer of hope faintly crossed his face.

CHAPTER THREE
MARYSVILLE, WISCONSIN

The musty aroma of hay and manure permeated the air in the half-lit barn, surrounding Josh with a warmth and security he felt nowhere else. He was seated on a bale of hay with Sullivan, his Golden Retriever pup, snoring softly at his feet and the rats in their cage by his side, munching on carrot sticks and lettuce. The secondhand guitar that his mother had saved up a whole year for out of her small salary at the beauty shop to buy him for Christmas was cradled in his lap.

It was funny how he could express his feelings so much better by singing and playing his guitar than by talking to anybody. He knew he would go to a big city some day and become famous, although nobody had heard his songs yet. But for now, it made the pain he felt sometimes when his parents argued hurt less.

He was surprised that they hadn't been mad at all about the rats and had pretended that nothing out of the ordinary had happened that day. He looked around at his animals and at Lottie, Bessie, and Gertrude standing in their stalls contentedly chewing their cuds. He sighed with a contentment of his own, and before his father came out to take his after-dinner swig from the bottle he kept behind a loose plank in the barn, Josh felt the beginnings of a new song coming on.

CHAPTER FOUR

LOS ANGELES

"**G**in! You owe me six thousand dollars!" Fifty-seven-year-old, silver-haired Olga Mostad slapped her cards down on the coffee table and placed her plump white hand palm up in front of her boss, who was seated on the couch opposite her in the small reception office of Stan Levy's bungalow at Universal. Glasses filled with ice cubes and Coke sat on the table. Olga picked up a glass and drank hers down.

Stan tried to weasel out. "You cheat," he accused half-heartedly.

But his secretary couldn't be dissuaded. "Six thousand dollars!" She waggled her fingers in front of his nose.

Stan decided to get devious. "How about a part in my new picture instead, baby?"

Olga looked like she was considering the offer. "Can we do the casting couch bit?"

Stan shook his head. "No way! You and your female activist friends would have me tarred and feathered and thrown off the lot. I'm on to you, lady."

Olga sat back in her chair and folded her arms. It was clear she would show him no mercy. "Then forget it. That'll be six thousand dollars."

"All right, all right. You'll get it all, with interest, as soon as my feature grosses its first five million."

Olga was not excited by the offer. "Sure, boss. Bring it to me out at the motion picture home, if I'm still alive by then."

Stan shook his head sadly. "Oh, ye of little faith. And I thought you believed in me."

"Oh, I do, boss." She was gathering the cards off the table. "But as they say, money talks and bullshit you-know-what."

He picked up his drink and took a couple of short sips. "It's broads like you who give grannies a bad name. You know that?"

The opening of the front door cut short their sparring and the man they had been expecting walked in, out of breath, and smiling diffidently. He was tall and blond and already going to seed in his thirties. His blood-shot eyes and the dark circles underneath them detracted from what had once been a very handsome face. Probably booze, possibly drugs. Stan was all too familiar with the signs of self-abuse.

He and Olga stood up and Stan offered his hand. "You must be Josh. I've heard a lot of nice things about you…really liked the demo Jennie sent me." Josh nodded and thanked him. Stan's handshake was firm and his manner confident despite his modest demeanor. He wrapped an arm around Olga's waist. "And this is Olga, my secretary. Hang on to your wallet around her. She's dangerous."

Olga pooh-poohed and pushed him away affectionately. "I'll go see if Howard is still on the phone." She disappeared down the hallway.

Stan indicated a chair. "Sit down, relax. I've got to return a call. Won't take a second."

As soon as Stan stepped into his office, he closed the door and headed for the bathroom, then closed the door and locked it. Olga would kill him if she knew about this. As for Lila, God only knew what she would do. If she found out he hadn't stopped using, she'd probably leave him. He knew Olga had heard the rumors about him being an occasional party user but she hadn't confronted him about it yet. His habit was no worse than some of his friends. Kicking it would be easy. As soon as he finished production on *Run for the Money*, he would check himself in somewhere, tell Lila he was fishing with his buddies, or come up with some better excuse. If Howard had been able to do it, he sure as hell could.

He patted his shirt pocket and felt the familiar packet. It had only been a half hour since his last hit, but he figured he deserved to indulge himself. His regular supplier from Vegas had cut him off since the big blowout with Lila, when she caught the guy slipping a packet of coke into Stan's pocket at a party. She had gone berserk and screamed obscenities in a house full of people, including his supplier, who was now terrified of being exposed by her. Stan had been frantic to make a connection for two days. Then, this morning, peace, lovely peace. Chuck Barenhaus, an out-of-work key grip, had stopped by with a fresh supply and had left with a promise of a job on the feature.

He dug his spoon out of his wallet and took the cocaine from his pocket. He inhaled deeply of the pure white powder and leaned against the sink to enjoy the rush. He knew it wouldn't last long. It was taking more and more hits to get him to the same place. But that was cool; after production, he'd get right.

He studied the face staring back at him in the mirror. He looked at least ten years older than his thirty years and the brown hair was sprinkled heavily with grey. But looking old didn't bother him. It was getting old and dying that filled him with dread and gave him nightmares. Ever since he was five and his father had taken him to his mother's funeral and forced him to kiss her cold, waxy face, the inevitable black, pitiless specter of death had never been far from his mind. Even now, he still couldn't sleep without the flickering light of the television being on. It had driven Lila crazy, until someone suggested she wear a sleep mask (she discovered it made her feel like a thirties movie star); but then, most things about him drove Lila crazy. Maybe the movie would appease her for a while.

Josh was relieved to have a few minutes to himself. He sat down and took his guitar out of the case with shaking hands. The piece of crap he called a car had broken down again and he'd had to run the last several blocks to the studio. Even when he started out early, he ended up late.

Stan seemed a nice enough guy, and if the plush furnishings in his bungalow were any indication of his success, then he had to be one of the most important directors on the lot. Jennie had told him that Stan and Howard Grossman, the producer, had both loved the *Never on My Mind* demo. Joell had been willing to listen to it because not only would it offer her a chance to sing the theme song for a major motion picture, she was also considering doing a cameo as a band singer in the movie. Now, Josh had a chance to get two songs into the movie sung by the hottest singer in the business. But he didn't get his hopes up for any of it. After ten years in this town, his optimism wasn't what it used to be.

Stan and Olga came back into the room, followed by a heavyset man in his forties. He sat heavily into one of the overstuffed chairs and raised a hand in greeting. "I'm Howard Grossman, nice to meet ya." Before Josh could respond, he went on wearily. "I don't want to pressure you, kid, but we've got two weeks to prep before we start shooting, so this better be good."

Stan laughed. "So, scare him half to death, why don't you, Howard?" Then to Josh, "This song will be sung in a small, classy club by a beautiful lady right after our hero has found out the love of his life has left him. So, he's at a table by himself, drinking club soda, trying to stay sober, and finds himself mesmerized by the singer and the song. We need something moody and bluesy, but not too depressing."

Josh immediately knew the song he would sing—one he had just finished. But suddenly, he had the crazy feeling he didn't want to share this song with them. All the memories he'd forced himself to dig up, and the despair and resentment he had wrestled with to get the words and melody into a form and structure that expressed his feelings, were of incidental interest to them. Now he was supposed to expose his soul to people who didn't give a crap about him and most likely would never even get to know him.

The three other people in the room were still looking at him in various stages of expectancy and hopefulness. He knew he was being totally irrational. He wondered if this was the beginning of losing his mind. Songwriting was his job, for Christ's sake. He had to get himself out of this crazy mood and remember why he was there—bills, food, rent. The threat of eviction was a powerful incentive, and Josh began to sing.

"I'm walkin' down a road to nowhere.
I lost you long ago.
And dreams of tangled memories
Whisper soft and low.
I wander down the path where only
Fading secrets sing
Wondering how I'll face the night
And what the dark will bring.
The road to nowhere,
The road to nowhere,
Why can't it bring...
Why can't it bring...
Why can't it bring me back to you?

Why can't it bring...

Why can't it bring…

Why can't it bring me back to you?"

He finished and all three were staring at him as if they were slightly hypnotized. He hoped it was because they liked it. Olga spoke first.

"Wow. You are really good."

Stan nodded, "I second that opinion."

Howard stood up. "I like it. Too bad you're not a woman, or you could record it yourself." After a friendly salute, he went out the door.

Josh followed him with his eyes and turned back to Stan and Olga. "Does that mean he wants my songs in the movie?"

Stan smiled broadly. "I think you're in, kid."

All the air left Josh's body and he slumped down in his chair. For once—for *once*—something had gone right! He was on the verge of having two hit singles with Joell. Life was sweet and every bit of rejection he had ever suffered was worth this moment.

"Will I be able to help produce the songs with Joell?"

Stan looked uncomfortable and looked at Olga, who shrugged and stood up. "I think it's time for me to go to lunch." She gave Josh a fond smile. "You are amazing, Josh. Don't ever let anybody tell you otherwise. You'll make it big, sure as I'm the best gin player in this room." She tossed a wry look at Stan before grabbing her purse off her desk and going out.

Josh was uncertain about what just happened. "Is something wrong?"

"No, your songs are in the movie, no question, but Joell will be singing just the theme song. The other song will be sung by my wife, who will play the band singer."

Not the end of the world. One hit record was better than none. "Is your wife an actress?"

"Actually, she wants to be a singer and an actress but right now she's neither. This will be her debut."

"I see..."

"Yes, it's awkward. But Howard has agreed to give her a shot. She has to prove herself first, and if she can learn the song and the recording is decent, it will be her voice. If it turns out she's less than adequate, we'll teach her how to lip-sync to a professional singer's voice and hopefully she'll look the part, at least."

"So, I'll be working with Joell and the other singer whose voice you might use?"

"Actually, that comes later."

"Later?"

"I'm asking you to work with my wife first. I'll pay you extra, of course, but Jennie tells me you work well producing singers so...will you do it?"

Josh hesitated for about a second before agreeing. Money was speaking to him and it was a language his landlady understood. "Sure. Just tell me where and when."

He walked out of the office and down the streets of Universal with a huge grin on his face. He smiled at everybody and they smiled back. He imagined that somehow, they knew that, finally, he was a part of what they were doing. His mood was infectious, and he had someone special to share it with.

* * * *

The large black panther, sleek muscles rippling, saw her prey seated on a rock only a few yards away. He was a large white man, partially hidden by brush, but she could see he was soft and fleshy with little or no muscle tone, mentally distracted, and totally unprepared for her attack. The ground was moist and giving beneath her paws as she inched her way forward. His back was toward her, bent over something in his hand that he was looking at, still oblivious to her presence. She stopped only inches away from the man and hesitated for a split second to gather her strength before the final leap. With a roar that echoed off the hillsides, she attacked, knocking the man sideways and then flat on the ground. She whirled back around and faced him, crouching low as she inched forward, and snarling dangerously.

Josh pushed himself up and sat back on the rock and picked up his tablet and pen from the ground. He smiled at the black panther, "Noor, if you'll stop playing for a minute, I have great news to tell you! I sold a song!"

Noor would not be put off. She wanted to play. She placed two giant paws on his chest to make her point. Josh fell back on the ground from the pressure. "Jeez, you're getting heavy. It's time to put you on a diet." Noor wasn't sure of what he said, but it didn't sound pleasant. She hoped he wasn't upset with her. Sometimes, he just wasn't in the mood to roughhouse. She took her paws off his chest and crouched down beside him.

He sat up cross-legged and scratched Noor's head absently. She closed her eyes and enjoyed the sensation. Next to naps in the warm sun, this was her favorite thing.

"I could be making a lot of money soon and I'll have more time to work on getting you out of here. The people who run the zoo don't want it to happen, but I promise you, it will. You'll be free to run and play and climb trees. It will almost be like being in the jungle...almost."

He cleared his throat." Listen to this. I've been working on it while you were sleeping. It's a song for my musical. It's different from my other songs—Broadway's different from pop. Anyway, here it is. I only have the first few lines.

You overwhelm my senses,
So, I can't speak my mind.
You share your secret dreams with me,
And never act unkind.
But I am like the air you breathe,
Unnoticed and unseen..."

"That's where I'm stuck, Noor. I don't know, maybe it's too sentimental, maybe the whole musical is too sentimental. I've been told that more than once and maybe they're right. The forties and fifties were more my style, but what can I do? This is where I am." He looked up at the blue sky, contemplating his words, "See, it's about a limo driver who falls in love with the daughter of his very wealthy client. They're worlds apart. The whole thing's hopeless but they end up falling in love anyway."

Noor yawned, lay her head on her paws, and closed her eyes.

Josh looked at her. "Am I boring you? What do you know? You're a cat. You should become an ad exec. Anyway, I'd like another opinion. Don't tell me, I'm also ugly." Josh laughed at the hackneyed old joke and stopped suddenly and stared into space. "I think I'm losin' it, Noor. I'm telling myself these great old jokes and giving you the credit." He stroked Noor's back and leaned close to her. "I'm badly in need of some quality female companionship."

Overwhelmed by love, Noor slurped her tongue across one side of his face.

Josh cried out in pain. "That's not exactly what I had in mind!"

Noor lowered her head back down on her paws and closed her eyes. Nothing seemed to please him today.

Josh patted his cheek tenderly. "I think I can forget about shaving this side of my face for a couple of days."

Noor suddenly lifted her head. A man was yelling at them from outside the compound. Growling, she followed Josh over to the fence and looked out. The man was running down the path towards them, exhausted, younger than Josh, wearing the same khaki uniform, but his was wrinkled and stained with dirt and sweat. He leaned heavily on the railing and forced his words out between gasps of air. "Josh, you see Jerry? He's not answering his cell."

"He had surgery out at the wild animal park this morning. What the hell's the matter, Alan?"

Alan's breath started coming easier but the worry was intense. "Katy's foaling but she's having a bad time. I think the head's trapped and she won't let anybody near her!"

"Get back to her! I'll meet you there!"

Noor watched Josh run up the hill and out the gate. She longed to run beside him and protect him from whatever was causing him distress, but she was trapped in her prison and there was nothing she could do. She jumped up on the highest ledge with the best vantage point and settled down to wait. She knew he would be back before he left for the night.

Josh saw the zebra, her stomach swollen with her baby, lying in a far corner of her compound, surrounded by brush. She was jerking her head around in panic and her eyes twitched nervously as she saw the two men approach. Josh moved toward her slowly, murmuring softly, then stroking her neck.

"Hold her head, Alan."

He stripped off his shirt and patted her back, moving down to her hindquarters, still reassuring and comforting her. He could see the baby's twisted neck through the opening of the vagina, where Katy's flesh was straining and starting to tear from the pressure. He remembered the same thing had happened to a mare owned by his best friend Jimmy back in Wisconsin and he felt the same pain wrench his gut now as he had then, watching the animal's suffering.

Moving swiftly, he reached in, found the baby's head, turned it around and moved it toward the vaginal opening. He used both hands to pull the baby free, the final expansion causing Katy to moan in agony. The foal landed in his lap, slippery and bloody but alive and, as far as he could tell, in good health. He hadn't had time to think, but he felt pretty good about what he had just done. He shook his head at Alan, who was grinning from ear to ear, and Josh laughed out loud with relief. He heard a voice behind him.

"Not bad for an amateur." A conservative-looking man in his late twenties with short dark hair and horn-rimmed glasses was looking down at them.

Zoo veterinarian Dr. Jerry Widel had missed the excitement by thirty seconds.

CHAPTER FIVE
MARYSVILLE, WISCONSIN

Josh huddled against the wall in the corner of his bed and drew the covers tight under his chin. He was trying hard not to cry and would have liked to clamp his hands over his ears and drown out the sounds coming from the next room. But his father's drunken words were coming out much uglier and louder than Josh had ever heard before, and he had no choice but to listen in case his mother needed him.

For an hour, he sat without moving and listened until the quarreling died down. He tried to go to sleep but anger kept his thoughts churning. It was so unfair! Couldn't his father see any more how wonderful his mother was, how she would rather die than hurt anybody? She wasn't very good at helping him with his homework like some of the other parents, and she wasn't much on cooking and cleaning house, but she loved to joke around and have fun, more like a friend than just a mother.

Sullivan had buried his nose in Josh's armpit and was sound asleep, with no worries or bad thoughts interrupting his dreams. It had been a long time since Josh had felt like that and he wondered if he ever would again. He was trying not to hate his father, but it was getting hard, very hard. Tomorrow he would be nine years old. The only present he wanted was that his parents would never argue again.

CHAPTER SIX

LOS ANGELES

The Universal Grill at Universal Studios was crowded, and Stan was fifteen minutes early. Erik, the maître 'd, had been kind enough to seat him anyway and the wait was made more tolerable by the companionship of a vodka on the rocks. He nodded now and then to familiar faces, willing them not come over to the table. He was in no mood to have a forced conversation.

The only person he wanted to talk to now was Jennie, the one person who would understand—a fact that would sound strange to anyone who knew him for the dyed-in-the-wool chauvinist that he was. He wasn't sure if the film business bred them, or if chauvinists were attracted to the business because the multitude of beautiful, untalented, ambitious, so-called actresses made it easy for men to use and discard them like so much soiled toilet paper. On second thought, it was undoubtedly the same in any business.

If women thought they could get what they wanted by making themselves available for their boss or forced themselves to put up with unwanted advances out of fear of losing their jobs, then that's what some women were going to do. They would make it rough for decent, hardworking women like Jennie. Of course, he could never reveal that kind of traitorous thinking to Sonny and Maury and the rest of the New York contingent at the studio. With those guys, the only accepted mode of behavior was getting loaded after work, hitting on barhops, and talking macho bullshit all evening before going home to the wife and passing out. Bedding down an occasional actress who wanted her SAG-AFTRA card in the worst way was par for the course. He himself had enjoyed introducing several actresses to the Screen Actors Guild—a practice he had cut down on drastically since he married Lila.

No, having a meaningful discussion about your fears and insecurities was not something you did with Sonny and the rest of them unless you wanted to become the butt of jokes for the next ten years. Better to talk to Jennie, who he knew would understand and care. He smiled to himself. If his best friend was a woman, maybe he wasn't the chauvinist they thought he was or used to be. The slim possibility was there.

As an actress, Jennie was mediocre; as a friend, there was no one better. She would do a lot better in the business if she would just concentrate on her behind-the-camera skills and forget about acting but she wanted too badly to perform, and he had stopped trying to dissuade her. He wanted her to be happy, so whenever a small, undemanding role came up, he would let her audition and hope she wasn't too disappointed that he never considered her for the larger parts she craved.

Stan glanced anxiously at his watch. He had to be back on the set in an hour and a half. They were shooting the last few location scenes of the season of his cop show, *Tanner,* in a nightclub downtown and traffic on the Hollywood freeway would be murder. Moe Tayler, his transportation captain, had volunteered to take him back to the studio to look at dailies and have lunch. Moe could give you a heart attack the way he wove in and out of traffic, but you knew you would get where you were going on time and this way he could spend more time with Jennie.

Moe had also witnessed the ugly scene in Stan's trailer this morning when Howard had caught Stan taking a hit. The self-righteous bastard had exploded and threatened to fire Stan off the feature and reveal the reason why, if he had to. Howard was making a big deal out of nothing. Stan had made sure there was no one around before taking out the cocaine. It had just been bad luck that Howard had chosen that moment to look for him and had seen him slip surreptitiously into his mobile home. Moe had been following Stan to ask a question about one of his drivers and had heard every word. But he was no problem since, up until last week, it had been one of Moe's relatives from Las Vegas who was his main supplier. This was before Lila went ballistic in front of everybody. Howard, however, had the power to destroy him, and Stan had to beg and plead and call on all their years of friendship to get him to agree for Stan to stay on. On top of that, he had to promise to lay off cocaine as long as they were in production, and Stan knew that was impossible. He would just have to be a lot more discreet and not get caught next time.

For a guy who used to have a habit ten times worse than Stan, Howard had turned into a real narrow-minded prick, but the two of them had worked together on a lot of TV shows. Howard knew Stan had made a lot of shitty shows and scripts better because he knew how to get the best out of their writers. Together, they were going to finally get the break they had been waiting for. Stan could hardly wait to find out if the actors he wanted would accept the offers that had already gone out. The two stars were set, but Stan loved getting the most out of character actors who usually were the heart of the movie. The only iffy part about the whole deal was Lila. He'd heard her practicing her song and it was pathetic. He only hoped that Josh could work with her and then Stan would have the impossible job of making her look like a band singer. If Howard nixed her, Lila would raise holy hell and probably leave him—not a bad outcome, actually.

Lila. He needed to find out what Jennie knew about Lila. He had suspected for months that she was seeing someone and toyed with the idea of hiring a private detective to find out. But that seemed too pathetic and insecure, so he dismissed the thought immediately. Maybe Jennie's friend, Vanessa, had told her who it was. Vanessa knew Lila from acting class and you never knew what women might talk about. But first, he needed to talk to Jennie about this morning. She would know how to reassure him and lay his fears to rest, if only for a few moments.

He finally saw her approach the maître 'd, who directed her in Stan's direction. Her face lit up with genuine pleasure when she saw him wave to her. It was this sweetness in Jennie that had drawn him to her, not just her pretty face…the sweetness he had thought that Lila possessed in the beginning, but which had proved to be a short-lived cover-up for her all-consuming ambition.

He stood up and hugged her in greeting, longer and harder than he usually did, and she looked at him questioningly when he released her. He took her hand and didn't let go, even as they sat down. Soon, he would tell her how he felt about her, but right now, there was too much to be resolved.

* * * *

Josh muttered a curse at himself. He always felt the sense of failure so strongly driving through this part of town and he didn't like feeling that way. He didn't want bitterness to poison his feelings and creep into his music and his lyrics. At least, so far, he had kept that from happening. But there was just no way to avoid the sharp contrast between the splendors of Bel-Air and his one-bedroom apartment on Cherokee in Hollywood. As a matter of fact, nowhere else did the reality of his dying dreams hit him so hard—so hard it could start his head pounding and his body shaking with frustration. It wasn't the houses and the cars he wanted; they had never been important to him. It was the success they represented and that he desperately needed, the knowledge that his work had found its audience and was respected, instead of mired in oblivion. He wished he'd had time for a drink.

Fuck it all. It was a job. And Stan was paying him $200 an hour to work with Lila. It was a way to stay alive until Joell turned his song into a hit and doors he'd been knocking on would finally open. He glanced down at the scrap of paper on the seat beside him and compared it to the address on the mailbox just ahead. At least some of these houses at the very top of Bel-Air weren't as opulent as those massive monuments to greed down below. He turned up a steep, tree-lined driveway and parked in the circular driveway in front of the house.

"Let's hope she can carry a tune," Josh prayed under his breath. He left his guitar in the backseat. He had a feeling Lila would need help with her intonation and it was easier to help singers find their notes on the piano. He didn't play piano well, but good enough for this job.

He got out of the car and admired the modest Spanish-style house that was surrounded by trees and flowering shrubs, which gave it a cozy feel. A young Latina girl in her late teens answered his knock with a cheerful smile. Her mood was so infectious, Josh couldn't help but smile.

"My name is Josh Sibley. I'm here to see Mrs. Levy."

The girl opened the door wider and gestured in the direction of the living room. She spoke with a heavy Spanish accent. "Oh, yes. Please come in. The misses is expecting you."

Josh walked through the small, white-tiled foyer and found himself in a room facing a breathtaking view of rustic hills and an uncommon blue sky.

The girl started up the steps leading from the foyer. "I go get the misses." She laughed as if they shared a secret.

Josh smiled in acknowledgment, enjoying her refreshing good nature. He looked around the room. It was decorated with heavy, light-wood Spanish furniture; a tan, suede-like couch; rustic oil paintings; and a grand piano that dominated a corner of the room. There was a profusion of cut flowers in vases on tables and sideboards. He decided he could definitely feel at home here. Scattered around the room were pictures of a stunning brunette, which he assumed was Lila. He decided even if she couldn't sing a note, this would not be as painful an experience as he had thought it would be.

He stepped closer to the open windows to look out beyond the wooded hills to the city spread out below. It was a rare, smog-free day and he took advantage of it by breathing in deeply and letting the air out with a sigh. Just living up here could make a man feel powerful, as if he's the center of the universe and everyone down below is at his feet. Josh laughed out loud. He hadn't had a thought like that in years. Basic survival—that's what life was all about now, but maybe that was about to change.

A soft, throaty hello caused him to turn around. Lila Levy walked towards him smiling, holding out her hand. Josh stopped breathing. The photographs were an insult to the real Lila. They deserved to be shredded and thrown in the trash for failing to come anywhere near capturing the lady who stood in front of him: smooth, dark, silky hair that fell to her shoulders, green eyes framed by long black lashes, skin that shunned makeup, full lips that were all hers, and a body he was already undressing in his dreams. He was a goner. Lightning had struck. No other woman he might ever happen to meet for the rest of his life would ever live up to this one. She was the one and there was no point in living if Lila was not in his life. And she was married.

"I'm Lila. Glad to meet you." She gave him her hand briefly, brushed by him, and continued speaking without giving him a chance to respond. "I just had the piano tuned, so it will be perfect for us. Can we get started right away? I'm really nervous."

He watched her rifle through some sheet music on the piano. She looked to be about 24, medium height, and had an attitude that announced she knew exactly the effect she had on a man. She was wearing a silky red blouse that clung to her breasts and tight blue jeans that were molded to her hips and backside.

"How about singing something for me," he managed to get out.

She indicated the sheet music. "I mostly have old standards," she apologized. "How about *Since I Fell for You?*"

Her insecurity was so palpable, Josh had to fight with every fiber of his being the impulse to put his arms around her and calm her fears.

"Sure," he said instead, and made himself comfortable on the piano bench as he ran his fingers over the keys. He looked at the music. "Key of C okay?"

She nodded and stood in the curve of the piano, facing him. He gave her the first note and then a chord and she began to sing. Whatever God had given her in the way of physical attributes, he had failed to extend to her singing voice. Her breathy, barely audible sound was killing one of his favorite songs. Josh agonized all the way through but at least she sang in key. When she finished, she looked at him expectantly, and he searched for the right words. Any performer, amateur or professional, could be easily undermined by the slightest criticism. It would stay in his or her brain for a lifetime unless the person was one of the gifted few with an ego that was unassailable. Lila was not one of those few. She was not even a natural singer. Getting her voice ready to record would be next to impossible.

"Very nice, uh...very nice. Actually, I have an idea of how to approach this song."

Amazingly, Lila seemed to believe the compliment and relaxed for a split second against the piano. Then she leaned forward, her eyes lighting up, "You do? Tell me. I'll practice really hard. This means everything to me."

Josh searched desperately for an answer as he kept running his fingers over the keys. What singer sang in a low, breathy voice that she could imitate? Who could he imagine singing his song that way, so far from the way Joell would have sung it?

Her vulnerability as she searched his face touched a long-forgotten part of him as he contemplated working with this woman for long hours in order to get her ready for the recording session. No matter what the outcome, being with her would be worth it.

"Do you really have an idea, or did you make that up to make me feel better?"

"No, no, I'm just trying to imagine what you would sound like if..." Then an idea struck him. "...if we worked to have you emulate Julie London. She has the perfect voice for this song and with your own unique quality added to hers, I think we'll end up with something really special."

"Who?"

Yikes, she was young. "Julie London. She was a jazz singer before your time, but ageless. No one will ever sing *Cry Me a River* the way she did, no one."

"Okay, I'm more than willing to give it a go."

"We'll buy some CDs of hers, if we can find them, and next time I come we'll start turning you into a jazz singer with some blues thrown in."

Her whole face was lit up with enthusiasm. "I'll have them next time you come. Give me a couple of days!" She stepped away from the piano and he stood up. "Ingrid just made some lemonade. I'll ask her to bring us some." She leaned close to him. "I'm so grateful to you for doing this for me. No matter what you say, I know I'm not very good, but I won't let you down, I promise."

She smiled at him and he was surprised to see an invitation that was hard to miss. For a split second, he thought he saw something else in those emerald eyes. A foreboding swept through him that he shook off, almost unnoticed. His eyes followed her closely as she left the room.

****

Josh was seated on the couch across from Lila, who was perched on the edge of the coffee table near the boombox. Julie London was singing *Cry Me a River* and Lila was doing her best to sound like her. Again, Josh marveled at how someone with Lila's face and body could be so totally devoid of musical talent. He wondered if he would ever listen to that song again with any enjoyment. Lila came to the end and looked at him, ready for his critique.

"You're doing a lot better. I can tell you've been practicing."

She preened at his praise. "You're completely on pitch, which is extremely important, but we need to work on your breathing to get more sound coming out. Remember what I said about breathing from your diaphragm?"

She jumped to her feet and performed the exercises he had shown her. He nodded his approval as she went through them.

"That's good. But, Lila, you know, you really need a proper voice teacher to help you with this."

"No! I want you! They don't know about this kind of singing. I already had a voice teacher and he didn't help me at all."

"Then, after I leave, I need you to go over the song, note by note, trying to sound exactly like Julie, breathing where she breathes. I know you can do it. If you've made enough progress, we'll start on my song."

"Great! I'll do it. Want something to drink before you go, Coke, 7-Up, sparkling water?"

"Have anything a little stronger?"

"No. I don't allow alcohol in this house."

"That's okay. I better get going anyway."

"I'm sorry, I just don't like any kind of harmful substance in the house. Stan has a problem."

Josh stood up and walked around the table towards the doorway. Lila caught up to him and grabbed his arm. He turned to face her.

"I'll work on it all night, and when you come back tomorrow, I'll be perfect." She gazed up at him as if searching his face for approval.

"You already are perfect," Josh answered, wincing internally at having said something that sounded so trite. But his heart was pounding, and forbidden thoughts raced wildly around his brain. He wanted to put his hands on her shoulders and pull her close. They had been building up to this moment for hours and they both knew it…barely brushing arms and knees, her hand casually touching him when adjusting the boombox. He had an overwhelming urge to sweep her up into his arms, like Rhett Butler did to Scarlett O'Hara, and carry her up the staircase into her bedroom and ravish her body all night long. But, unlike Scarlett, Lila seemed more than willing. Annoying reminders forced their way up from the murky depths of his conscience. She was married to Stan and Josh wasn't about to ruin the best chance he had ever had of finally making it as a songwriter. With a will power he didn't know he had, he backed away from her. "I've got to get out of here. I'll call tomorrow before I come over."

But Lila wasn't ready to let him go. She moved close to him and kissed him softly on the cheek and whispered, "You know it's inevitable."

He backed out the door and welcomed the unexpected cold breeze, hoping it could penetrate the sexual haze that had been building all afternoon and blow some sense into him. Her eyes stayed on his as he mumbled his good-byes and she slowly closed the door.

He walked to his car with shaking legs. He wanted her so badly he could've pounded nails with his dick. What did he do now? He had met the girl he had been dreaming of all his life and she was married to the guy he was working for. Shit, shit, shit. He jumped in the Mustang and cursed his fate, but when he turned the key and the engine to old unfaithful started the first time, without any coaxing, he was sure it was a sign that something extraordinary was soon going to happen in his life.

CHAPTER SEVEN

LOS ANGELES

Martha hummed to herself as she pushed her shopping cart along Hollywood Boulevard. She had just found an entire cheese pizza in the trash behind Dominic's Pizza Place and it was still hot! Must've been too well done for one of its snooty customers. Just because it was a little burnt around the edge, that didn't hurt nothin'. She could hardly wait to get back to her place and eat it while reading yesterday's sports page that she had found in the same trash bin. No one had discovered her little room at the abandoned car wash yet and if she was careful sneaking in and out, she could very well have her cozy hideaway for many more months to come. A hand on her shoulder broke her concentration.

"Hey, Martha, when you comin' up again?"

It was that nice boy, Josh, who didn't know how to care for his plants properly. With animals, he was a wonder. He could nurse any hurt animal back to health, but plants turned brown and died at the very sight of him. He was lucky she was willing to help him out.

"I've been very busy lately. You're not my only customer, you know."

"You've got to help me out, Martha. They can't survive much longer without you."

The poor boy was desperate. He reached into his pocket and pulled out a couple of bills. "Maybe tomorrow?"

She drummed her fingers on the handle of the shopping cart and considered his request.

"You're the only thing that keeps them alive, Martha."

She grabbed the bills and put them safely in her blouse pocket, underneath her coat and her sweater. She shoved off down the street and he yelled after her.

"Tomorrow?!"

She waved without looking back. "I'll be there!"

Josh watched the old lady make her way across the street to whatever hovel she was living in now. Her clothes were nothing but rags and her brain had to have been pickled in vodka long ago, but something kept her going—pride, stubbornness…he had no idea. He just knew he wanted to help the poor old broad stay alive since, for whatever reason, that's what she wanted to do.

Martha was ecstatic. Now she would be able to buy some beer to have with her pizza! Pizza and beer—nothing like it. It reminded her of happy times long ago, with somebody, somewhere…but never mind that. Better not to wallow through hazy memories and come up with things that would only depress her. Tonight, it was pizza and beer and the sports pages. Yesterday didn't matter and she didn't have to think about tomorrow till it came.

* * * *

"Susie!"

Josh slammed through the door and flopped down on the couch, barely aware of the piles of sheet music and scraps of lyric scribblings that littered the floor and the couch and were crushed by the weight of his body. He was not entirely oblivious to the labyrinth of litter that passed for a two-bedroom apartment. Once, a long time ago, he had considered cleaning it up and trying to keep it that way, but considering his steady stream of temporary visitors, what was the point?

"Hey, Gilbert, come out here!"

The words were hardly out of his mouth before a grey and white bundle of fur bounded out of the bedroom and made himself at home on Josh's chest. He looked at the mountain lion cub accusingly. "What have you done with Susie? Did you take another bite outa her?" He laughed as Gilbert covered his face with kisses. "I don't smell feathers on your breath. You two staying apart, like I told you?"

On cue, the cockatoo landed on the arm of the couch beside his head in perfectly good health. "Guess you been behaving yourself, Gil."

He took his cell phone out of his shirt pocket and, before listening to his messages, examined the healing cut on Gilbert's leg. "I hate to tell you this buddy, but you're getting too healthy to stay around here much longer." He dialed up his voice mail and a woman's voice reminded him, "Gower Towing calling again, Josh. We'd like your payment before we have to send the bill to a collection agency. Please call." It was great how having money in your pocket could make even a bill collector's voice sound friendly. He'd stopped by Stan's bungalow that morning to update him on Lila's progress and Stan had handed him an envelope with five hundred dollars in it. "Make it work, pal. Make my life easier." Josh assured him he would and took himself and his money out of there, hoping against hope he wasn't lying.

The next voice hit him like a punch in the solar plexus. "I'm working on one of Julie's songs, Josh. I think you're going to be proud of me." He closed his eyes and indulged himself in the pleasure of remembering the softness of Lila's lips on his cheek. The memory started the juices flowing and his mind racing with possibilities. Her wedding ring obviously didn't mean a hell of a lot to her and just the sound of her voice tempted him to forget all his good intentions. But no way was he going to self-destruct this time, no way. Not for Lila, not for anybody.

He looked at the landline phone, saw that the message light wasn't blinking, and scooted forward on the couch. "Excuse me, guys." He lifted Gilbert off his lap and headed for the bathroom. He hoped that the Department of Water and Power hadn't made good on its threat, because right now the only thing that could cool down his fiery imagination was a cold shower.

* * * *

At first, he thought the pounding was coming from inside his own brain and was just the usual consequence of an evening spent draining half a bottle of vodka, but the faint female voice calling his name was not in his head. He kicked off the green army blanket that had settled around his ankles and stumbled out of the bedroom. He leaned his ear into the door, his eyes half-closed.

"Yeah, who is it?"

"Josh, it's me." Lila's voice was weak and plaintive and the battered face and huddled form that greeted him when he opened the door chilled him to the marrow.

"Lila!"

He pulled her inside and supported her around the waist as he helped her over to the couch. She sat down hunched over and he could see her struggling to maintain control. Then the effort overwhelmed her, and she covered her face with her hands and began to cry. Josh took her in his arms and felt the uncontrollable sobs wrack her entire body. Finally, he had to ask. "Who did this to you, Lila?" She shook her head and clung harder to him, quivering like a wounded bird. He could feel the sharp outline of her shoulder blades protruding like broken wings.

"Who was it, Lila?"

She dug a tissue out of her jacket pocket and blew her nose. "It was Stan." She kept the tissue by her face and avoided looking at him.

Josh sat upright, stunned.

"Your husband?"

She sat quietly for a moment then turned her face to Josh. There was only defeat in her voice. "What am I going to do?"

He couldn't hide his agitation any longer. He stood up and began to pace. "Is he still at home?"

Lila leaped to her feet and almost lunged at him. "No!" There was fear and panic in her voice. "You can't go over there!"

Her vehement outburst startled him.

"It's the cocaine. That's what makes him like that!" She hung on to his arm as she pleaded with him. "Don't go over there. You'll only make it worse!"

"All right, all right," he soothed her and pulled her into his chest. He smoothed down her hair and held the back of her head in his hand. It felt small and vulnerable to his touch. "You can't go back there, Lila."

"I have to."

"You can stay here until you find another place."

She reached for another tissue in her pocket and carefully and deliberately started wiping the mascara that stained her face. Her response to his offer was wooden. "I'll deal with it. It was my fault."

Josh stood up as he exploded into a fury and kicked the wooden chair near the front door, sending it flying against the opposite wall. "That's horseshit!"

Lila cringed at the harshness of his outburst and bent over, whimpering, on the couch.

Josh regretted his insensitivity instantly. "I'm sorry, I'm sorry. I'm a jerk. Listen, I know this apartment isn't much, but you're—"

Lila cut in adamantly. "It makes him crazy when I get on his case for coming home drunk. It was partly my fault."

It was hard for him not to show the impatience he felt. "You were right the first time, Lila. It's the cocaine and the alcohol, not you. A normal man doesn't beat up a woman because she complains that he comes home drunk."

A sleepy-eyed Gilbert took that opportunity to wander out of the bedroom and Josh gently swooped him up into his arms. He reassured a startled Lila. "He won't hurt you. He cut his leg on a piece of broken glass in the zoo nursery and came to stay with me for a while." He up-righted the chair he had kicked over and sat down, cradling Gilbert. "I need to know why you want to go back there."

She sat mute and stony, refusing to answer.

Josh released Gilbert, who was struggling to get down to his water bowl. He moved closer to Lila and cupped her chin in his hand, forcing her to look at him.

"Why?"

She fixed his eyes with a cold hard stare. "Because without him I have *nothing*."

Josh stared back at her, taking in the whole of her, not being able to comprehend why someone like her would say something so obviously untrue.

* * * *

After leaving Noor's compound and spending as much quality time with her as his job would allow, Josh stood outside the elephant enclosure looking at Sammy, the lonely bull elephant, and his heart ached for him. He needed to be in a sanctuary, wandering for miles, knocking over trees, and maybe having another young male to be friends with. He had been suffering at the zoo for a long time and people had been trying to move him to a sanctuary for decades. Josh watched Sammy bobbing his head up and down, slowly going insane. He wished there was something he could do to help him, but his priority now was Noor. After she was free, he would work on the others.

He headed for the maintenance building and unlocked the door. He started loading feed bags onto one of the small trucks parked inside but it was hard concentrating on work after what had happened to Lila. She had insisted on going home before dawn, and nothing he had said could change her mind. She seemed confident that Stan would have passed out long ago and would be asleep by then, and that he would be apologetic and contrite the next day. She pleaded with Josh to act like nothing had changed and made him promise that they would keep working together and he would say nothing to Stan. That last part was hard; how do you be friendly with a guy whose face you want to smash in? But for her he would. And, he had to admit, for himself as well.

He drove to the zebra compound where he found Jerry finishing up his examination of Katy. Her foal lay in the straw in the same stall. "Katy's a little shaky but the baby's just fine."

The zebra started nuzzling Josh's neck and the tickling sensation forced him to laugh despite all his worries. "I think she's already back to her feisty self."

Jerry stuffed his instruments into his case. There was no resentment in his attitude. "What is it with you and animals anyway? I've never seen zebras take much to anybody. With you, she's almost obscene."

Josh gave Katy a final pat. "Don't know, Jer, but I've got a delivery to make to a couple of hungry bison and then go over and see Noor again before I leave. Her appetite's been off."

"You and Noor. Now there's a real romance. She sending out invitations soon?"

Josh got in the truck. "You're just jealous, Jer. You're the doc but I'm the one who feeds them…except for Noor, of course. That's pure love."

CHAPTER EIGHT

LOS ANGELES

"I like her reaction here. Keep that, but cut the pause before his speech. He gets a little self-indulgent building up to his angry outburst."

Stan was in Doug Meyer's editing room looking at the day's shoot. Doug was his best and most trusted editor. Stan had made sure he would have him on the feature.

"Don's going to shit when he sees it."

"Let me worry about that half-baked ham. The network forced him on me and now the rest of us have to live with him. If they only knew what we go through every week to make him look like he's not doing a poor man's Brando. He fights me on the set but there's nothing he can do about what happens in this room."

"Just sayin."

Stan knew that Doug was right, but he could always handle actors, even Don Lazlo, who was the worst actor he had ever been forced to deal with. What he couldn't handle was remembering last night and what he had done to Lila. It was unforgivable. He was relieved that Howard was meeting with investors today. He was alone with Doug, so he didn't have to put up with any superfluous comments, objections, or casual bantering that only extended editing time and rarely improved the show. Doug had little or no ego and just made the cuts as he was told, which was why Stan hired him whenever he was available.

Last night had been a nightmare. Stan had hoped that that was all it had been, but one look at Lila's battered face this morning shattered that illusion. He stood silently by her bed in one of the spare bedrooms where she had chosen to spend the night and could not fathom how he could have lost control so completely. He had always thought of himself as not having a violent bone in his body—good old Stan, full of jokes, the life of the party, and always able to inspire a fierce loyalty in his crew. So what the hell was he doing pounding his fists into a helpless, hundred and ten-pound woman? Thinking back on it sickened him, and he felt the bile rising from his stomach into his throat.

"What did you think of the cut just before the pan down the beach?" Doug was asking him. "I wasn't sure if the hair matched the close-up."

"No, it was fine...just fine." He was barely aware of what he was seeing on the monitor.

He had heard that cocaine could lower your boiling point a little, but he didn't see how the small amount he had snorted last night could change the entire makeup of his personality. And when he really thought about it, if Lila hadn't started screaming at him, he wouldn't have become aggravated enough to hit her. Any man would have had a hard time restraining himself.

Yesterday, after a great deal of thought and soul-searching, he had come to the conclusion that as much as he loved Lila, as much as her beauty still fascinated and excited him, there wasn't much left of their marriage. They hadn't had sex in months and any warmth that she had sparingly shared with him in the beginning had slowly died down into barely tolerant indifference. He didn't want to live like that anymore. Coming home and looking at that face used to be a joy. Now he looked for any excuse to avoid it. He admitted to himself now that he may have been too blunt with her last night, but he was sick of the playacting that went on between them. He was up to his eyeballs in that at work and he didn't need it from his own wife. But hitting her after she started screaming at him, that wasn't who he was. After he finished the feature, the booze, cocaine, and Lila would all have to go. Meanwhile, he would placate her and keep her off his back so he could work with a clear head.

Stan's cell phone rang. Still distracted, he took it out of his pocket and answered. He heard Moe's voice. "He'll be in from Vegas tomorrow. If you can promise that there won't be any blowback from the bruhaha with Lila, he'll be happy to start accommodating you again."

"Tell him he's got it and ask him where he wants to meet."

He hung up, happy that at least one of his problems had been solved. "Doug, let me see that last cut again."

Doug made a few clicks on his computer and brought up the scene. Stan relaxed and concentrated on his work. Everything was under control, he assured himself. He finally felt like his life was headed in the right direction.

* * * *

Lila hated not being perfect. She had been perfect ever since she could remember. No matter what else she had lacked in her life, perfection of face and body was not among them.

She examined herself in her bedroom dressing table mirror with the seasoned eye of a veteran nitpicker and was appalled at what she saw. Several layers of foundation, concealer, and powder were beginning to cake on her face, but heavy makeup was the only way to hide the yellow and blue discolorations. But there was no time to take it all off and start over again. Josh was due any second. She hadn't wanted to see anyone until her face returned to its natural, flawless beauty, but the recording session had been scheduled for next Monday and every day of rehearsal was important. Missing one day was all she could afford.

At least the swelling had finally gone down. She looked closer at the skin around her eyes. Thank God, no wrinkles yet but as soon as the first one appeared, she would immediately have a laser peel to get rid of the offending crevices. Having a face that looked old and wrinkled was such a terrifying prospect, it turned her cold with fear if she allowed her mind to dwell on it. The doorbell mercifully ended her dark ruminations and she smiled as Ingrid opened the door and she heard Josh's footsteps coming down the hall.

* * * *

"Just remember what I told you; try to draw the words out smoothly and don't enunciate so clearly. Think lazy and feel free to add the curly-cues like I did on the demo."

She was standing in front of the piano near the boom box while he sat on the bench facing her.

Lila laughed. "I feel like a real jazz singer when I add extra notes. Do I really sound okay?"

"Like Ella Fitzgerald." Forgive me Ella, Josh thought.

She poked him in the chest with her finger. "Don't bullshit me, mister...I'm not quite there yet, but close!"

Lila's voice had sounded a lot better than he had expected. She must have been working her ass off all day yesterday despite the pain from the bruises on her face. When he had looked at her more closely and seen the patchwork she had done to cover up the evidence from something they were both pretending never happened, the rage that he had had to keep suppressed threatened to boil to the surface again. But he knew he had to stay calm for her sake. She needed acclamation now, not more harsh rhetoric.

"You'll do fine on Monday. You've got your own soft, sexy sound."

She sat next to him on the piano bench and they looked at each other intently, not sharing their thoughts. Josh felt her thigh pressing close to his and he knew if he stayed one second longer, it would be a terrible mistake. He stood up and pulled her up into a friendly hug, then held her at arm's length. "Keep doing the exercises, practice breathing, and trust yourself that you know the song backwards and forwards. We'll be recording it several times and take the best cuts, so you have nothing to worry about. I won't let you out of the studio until I have what I need. Okay? Trust me?"

"Like nobody else, ever."

He released her with a quick smile and walked quickly down the hall.

* * * *

"Sing that last phrase again, just one more time, and then ad lib as we fade out. I'll let you know when to stop. I promise, this is the last time."

Lila had felt the wetness starting in her armpits as soon as she began to sing. Her back was damp and tiny rivulets of perspiration were flowing between her breasts. In her anxiety to perform well, she had uncharacteristically disregarded her physical appearance and given her total concentration to the song. Now that she was almost finished, she was mortified to notice the stains on her blouse. There was nothing she could do about it now. She put her earphones back on and heard the music start a couple of measures before the last phrase. She cleared her throat and started tapping out the beat with her foot, keeping her eye on Josh for her cue. She saw him hold up his hand, then point his finger to cue her. She started to sing.

To Josh, her nervousness had been palpable as she sat in the booth with him and watched the musicians lay down the music track. He had reached over to give her hand a gentle pat and it had been as cold as ice.

He looked at her now, putting every ounce of energy and concentration into the last phrase. He thought he had never seen anyone so determined and driven to succeed. He looked over at his engineer, Carl Wheatley, who nodded his approval. He pressed the speaker button and called her into the booth.

"Tell me the truth. Did I do all right?" Lila was as tense and anxious as when she had first arrived. Josh knew she wouldn't be convinced until she heard the results for herself.

"Your assignment now is to go to the commissary and get yourself some lunch and hang out for at least two hours while Carl and I mix the song."

"I can't stay?"

He gently propelled her out the door. "You're outta here."

She had no choice but to give in to his insistence, and reluctantly trudged off to the commissary. Josh was determined that she would have the pleasure of hearing her own voice for the first time coming through the speakers—sensuous, soft, and perfectly mixed and balanced.

As always, Josh was meticulous in producing every recording he ever did, and Carl was practically obsessive-compulsive, so they made a great team. They had just finished when Lila returned, still wound up like a spring and hands clenched into tight fists. He sat her down on the couch in the control room and gave Carl the nod to start.

The transformation of her mood as her voice came through the speakers was almost enough reward for the job.

"Is that me? Is that really me?" she asked, her face lit up with astonishment and pleasure.

The three of them sat back and listened to the song in silence. As many times as Josh had heard her sing it in rehearsal, he had never been aware of the melancholy sound in her voice that the microphone had picked up. It was almost as if the music and her voice had melded together to produce a song that had been written just for her.

CHAPTER NINE

MARYSVILLE, WISCONSIN

I t had been hotter than heck and sticky-muggy all day long and the mosquitoes had declared all-out war on every exposed part of Josh's body. Whack! he slapped his thigh and another bug met his maker, but the mosquitoes were winning, no contest. He was covered with bites and scratching like crazy.

He'd been sitting on the porch for most of the day, with his eyes glued to the spot where the road met the horizon, miles away, before it dipped down the other side of the hill out of sight. Any minute, his father's old Ford truck was sure to appear like a brown speck at the top of the hill, carrying its precious cargo of his mother and brand-new baby brother.

It had been a week since his mother had felt the pains in her stomach and had to go to the hospital in Leroy. It was over fifty miles away, but it was the closest one to their farm. When his father had first come back from the hospital, he had been as proud as a peacock and crowing like a rooster at having a new son. His mother had had to stay in the hospital an extra day or two. Then came a phone call from the doctor that had changed everything. His father's mood turned foul, and his drinking became so heavy some nights, he didn't even come home. That part didn't bother Josh because he was ten years old and could take care of himself. He always got most of the chores done before going to school in the morning, but he was still worried sick. There was something terribly wrong with his brother. He wasn't sure what it was, but there was something. His mother's phone calls were received by his father with indifferent grunts or all-out, red-faced anger.

When they had first heard about his mother's pregnancy, Josh had been the only one in the family who had been happy at the prospect of a new brother or sister. His mother had tried not to seem depressed, but he could tell she was very unhappy, and his father had snarled every time the subject came up. When the baby was born, everything had miraculously changed, but only for a couple of days, until the telephone call came, and things were now worse than ever.

He wished he were grown up so he could take his mother and brother far away to live in a beautiful city where they would be safe forever from this crazy man who was his father.

Today, he had finished the chores bright and early and had begun his vigil. His father had left the night before and they all should have been home long ago. New apprehension hit Josh in the stomach. Would his whole life be like this—uncertainty and fear and nowhere to run? In his anxiety and restlessness, he picked up his basketball and shot baskets through the hoop over the garage.

He heard the truck before he saw it. He dropped his basketball and ran out to the road to wait, his heart beating like crazy. His father turned the truck up the gravel driveway and Josh ran alongside, grinning and waving to his beautiful, smiling mother. His hopes rose. If she was smiling, then everything must be alright, but he would feel better when he saw for himself. He helped his mother out of the truck and she gave him a hug while still holding the baby. He was wrapped in a fluffy white blanket and held close to her chest. She drew the blanket aside and held the baby down to let Josh take a peek.

"Meet your little brother, Scott, honey," she said softly.

The tinge of sadness in her voice had to be in his imagination because when he looked into the smooth sweet face of Scott Sibley, all he saw was a perfect, healthy little boy. He breathed a sigh of relief and held out his arms so he could carry his brother inside.

CHAPTER TEN

LOS ANGELES

Los Angeles had an aggravating way of heating up at the end of the year, reaching a peak on Christmas Day, when the temperatures invariably shot up into the nineties. The heat melted the plastic wreaths strung up between palm trees and withered joggers who were out exercising in their shorts. L.A. would never be portrayed as a Hallmark Christmas card, that's for sure..

But autumn brought chilly desert nights, and on this particular night, Josh was freezing as he walked by the deserted animal compounds on his way to check on Katy and her foal before he left for the night. He hadn't kept as close an eye on them as he should have the last few days because he had been spending most of his spare time with Noor. He was worried sick over her refusal to eat and intended to move her to the hospital tomorrow if her condition didn't change. Her weight was getting dangerously low.

He was startled to hear laughter up ahead and hurried his stride. No one had any business being here this late. Another burst of laughter made him break into a run. He was sure the sounds were coming from the zebra compound and he had a queasy feeling in the pit of his stomach that something unpleasant was about to happen.

He saw three teenage boys, all with gang tattoos covering every square inch of exposed skin. One of them, white, about fifteen or sixteen years old, was chasing Katy's foal towards the far end of the enclosure. The other two boys, Latinos, who were a few years older, were standing outside the fence, baiting Katy while she held them at bay. The sound of her baby's cry caused her to whirl around and charge after the younger boy who was beating her foal's hindquarters with a tree branch. Katy, in her concern and fury, lost her footing and stumbled, which the boys found hilariously funny.

A righteous anger rose up in Josh that could find satisfaction in only one direction. He was upon them so fast that the first slimy bastard didn't even see the fist that exploded in the center of his face. But the second one had plenty of time to slip a knife out of his pocket, eyes gleaming with both fear and excitement as he went into a half crouch and moved back and forth in front of Josh on the balls of his feet. Josh ripped off his jacket and wrapped it around his right forearm, never taking his eyes off the boy, who he could now see was in his late teens or early twenties. The sheer force of his anger couldn't overcome a knife and he regretted all his failed attempts to get into shape. But the basic Army training that he had embraced so intensely many years ago and thought he'd forgotten, came flooding back into his body and senses. He knew exactly what he had to do.

The boy lunged forward and swung the knife past Josh's face. Josh avoided it easily and the boy retreated with a nervous laugh. They circled each other slowly and Josh waited for that split second when the boy would lose concentration and leave himself vulnerable. He didn't notice the younger boy slipping over the fence, but his peripheral vision picked him up as he leaped at him from one side. Josh's arm struck out and caught him dead center in his chest, sending him sprawling into the bushes. The older boy saw this as his chance and suddenly lunged forward again, aiming the knife at Josh's chest. Josh sidestepped, grabbed the boy's arm, and brought it down on his thigh. The knife dropped on the ground and Josh grabbed it. At the sight of the boy rolling on the ground and moaning in agony, the anger that had boiled over was giving way to more rational thinking, now that he knew Katy and her foal were safe. He knelt beside the boy to check his arm and never saw the rock that came smashing down on his head, hurtling him into oblivion.

* * * *

Hari Suma wondered how many pots of coffee he had made since he started working in the twenty-four-hour market, and how many more he would have to make before one of the hotshot movie dudes who came in the store discovered him and starred him in a picture. He was twenty years old and not getting any younger. He had busted his ass to get this job. He hadn't bothered with acting classes. To become a success in show business, two things mattered: who you know and who you blow. Everything else is bullshit. But after eight months of waiting patiently for his big break, Hari's enthusiasm for show business was waning. He had even changed his name from Harry O'Shaughnessy to Hari Suma to get some good karma going in his direction.

One of his dates, Hilda, a girl from Sweden who worked for some big network honcho, had dragged him out to Woodland Hills to talk to some old lady who said she was a god from five thousand years ago in China and could talk to dead people. She looked like a plain old ordinary housewife to Harry, but if it made his date happy, he would go along with it. She had promised him that the next time he came to pick her up, he could meet the network honcho and who knew where that could lead.

So, on hopes of furthering his non-existent career, he had let the old broad in Woodland Hills connect with his brother, even though he had never listened to his drunken bum brother when he was alive and didn't see how dying could make Rob any smarter or worth listening to. Anybody who drove off a cliff on Mulholland, stinking drunk, was not somebody who should be handing out advice.

Hilda got excited as all hell when his brother started talking through the old lady's mouth but to him, it didn't sound at all like Rob to him. He listened anyway and the upshot of the whole thing, as far as he could see, was that his karma was bad, and he was taking the chance of coming back as a cockroach and getting stomped on if he didn't change his aura. The name change was his own idea—might as well start with a fresh slate. Lou Alcindor had done it and look what happened to him. You can't argue with success. That had all happened two months ago and still, nothing had happened to further his career. Hilda wanted him to join her chanting group but sitting in a room making noises seemed a little too passive, even for him. He'd give the name change karma a few more weeks to work and then he might consider changing it back.

He flipped the switch on the coffee machine and went back behind the cash register. He leaned his elbows on the counter and gazed out the window at the mansions of Bel Air in the hills above the store and wondered what it would be like to live in one of them. With all the time and effort he was putting out to become a success, it shouldn't be long before he found out.

He was giving serious consideration to whether he should project a Zac Efron or Robert Pattinson image when a red Mercedes SLK came tearing into the parking lot so fast, he was scared shitless that it wouldn't come to a stop until it reached the dairy case at the back of the store. The car screeched to a stop by a pump and a woman wearing sunglasses and a dark scarf wrapped around her head and neck jumped out of the car, fumbling with her wallet. She ran into the store and handed Hari a twenty-dollar bill. "On three," she yelled, pulling at the scarf to conceal her face, and ran back to her car, yanked out the pump and waited, shifting impatiently from one foot to the other.

Hari stuck the bill into the cash register and punched pump three. The woman saw it was ready and started pumping gas into her tank. Hari strolled over to the window and casually straightened out the newspapers on the news stand and gave the lady a once-over as she waited for the tank to fill. Despite the getup, he recognized her as a regular customer, the wife of a producer, according to his boss, Rham. But he'd never seen her look such a wreck. Usually, she was a classy dresser but tonight she was wearing flip-flops and a shirt hanging halfway out of an old pair of jeans. She looked so upset, he thought he'd better go out and see if there was anything he could do. He opened the door and started walking towards her, but she didn't even glance up at him as she jammed the gas pump back into its slot, jumped back in the car, and sped up the street.

He walked back into the store, disgusted. Truth be told, he hated the rich people who came into the store. What did they have to get uptight about anyway? They treated people like shit and any trouble they got into, they could buy their way out of. He would handle success differently…with grace and consideration to those still struggling. He decided to pour himself a cup of coffee and contemplate either chanting or changing careers.

* * * *

With a great deal of effort, Noor raised her eyelids and surveyed her surroundings. She was still lying on a table in a small room where the heat was so intense it was making her feel tired and dizzy. Josh's friend in the white coat was stroking her head and speaking softly. "You've got to get better, Noor. You can't do this to him now."

She wanted to get outside into the cool air, but her legs wouldn't move. She needed to breathe but her lungs felt tight and heavy.

The man's voice was fading, and she became frightened. A chill passed through her. She wanted to stay awake till Josh came but she couldn't keep her eyes open any longer.

* * * *

Jerry fell back on his bed exhausted, too tired to take off his clothes or pull back the spread. But, even though it was three o'clock in the morning, he was wide awake. Maybe an old movie could lull him to sleep. He started flipping through the endless number of cable channels and let his mind drift back over the unbelievable events of the past evening.

Jerry hadn't seen Josh at the zoo that entire previous day. Because the Mustang, which could have been an awesome classic in more appreciative, loving hands, was in the shop, Josh had taken the bus to work and Jerry had offered to take him home. When Josh hadn't shown up at Jerry's car at the agreed upon time, Jerry had first set out for Noor's enclosure, where he didn't find Josh but saw that Noor's condition had worsened. He had called the zoo clinic to send an ambulance and two attendants. Noor was completely limp and didn't struggle as they moved her into the ambulance and to the hospital. He examined her quickly, then gave her continuous intravenous medication to stabilize her vitals. He stayed with her, calling Josh on his cell every few minutes. Dr. Jensen, who worked at the zoo on a part-time basis, agreed to come in and cover for him. He filled Dr. Jensen in on what Noor was experiencing and set out to see if Josh was somewhere on the grounds. A security guard ran past him at full speed and he called out. "Hey, what's going on!" He didn't respond, so Jerry followed him at a run, fearing the worst.

He caught up to the guard, who was standing over an unconscious form laying in a ditch by the side of the path. Josh! He started to move to Josh's side, but the guard stopped him.

"I work at the hospital here! I can help him!" The guard stepped aside while speaking urgently into his cell phone.

Jerry knelt and checked Josh's pulse. He had a lot of blood loss from a crack on the back of his head and his blood pressure was dangerously low. He tore off his shirt and held it tight on Josh's wound and tried to stay positive as they waited for the ambulance. Within minutes, they were on their way to St. Joseph's Hospital, only a few miles away in Burbank.

As it turned out, Josh had a concussion but no subdural hematoma, thank God, and some bruised ribs where he must have been kicked after being knocked out. The surprising news was that the three boys had already been apprehended. They had been spotted by two security guards as two of the boys half dragged, half carried their injured cohort towards the front entrance. When the guards approached, the two doing the carrying didn't waste much time deciding that being your brother's keeper wasn't all that it was cracked up to be. In perfect unison, they dropped their friend like a discarded refuse bag and ran. Unfortunately for them, the two guards only worked at the zoo to supplement their athletic scholarships to the University of California at Northridge. The rotten little bastards didn't stand a chance.

But the worst part of it all was that the parents of the kid with the bloodied face and broken nose had wasted no time in bringing assault and battery charges against Josh, which meant immediate suspension from his job.

Jerry kept clicking his remote, unable to find anything that held his interest. He settled on a local news show that was expanding on a bulletin he had heard on the car radio on the way home. Jerry groaned aloud. How would Josh deal with *this*? He watched until the weather report came on and his eyes closed, the remote slipping out of his hand. His last thoughts before he drifted into a dreamless sleep were of dread. Tomorrow, he would have to go to the hospital and tell Josh about Noor, the charges against him, his suspension, and now, this incredible disaster. It was almost too much for one person to take.

CHAPTER ELEVEN
LOS ANGELES

Jerry hesitated outside of Josh's hospital room, not wanting to be the bearer of bad news, but there was no way out of it. He heard a female voice. "I can't get anything on here. I think your cable's out. I'll go check."

Josh replied, slurring from the heavy medication, "Damn, I wanted to watch *The Young and the Restless*. I missed a whole week."

"I didn't like how Neuman was treating his daughter, so I stopped watching."

"They made up weeks ago. You can watch again."

Jerry walked in as a pretty nurse somewhere in her twenties was gathering up her equipment. She gave him a smile. "Don't stay too long. Don't want to wear him out." Then to Josh, "I'll bring my DVD in tomorrow before I start my shift. You really think your friend Ken will listen?"

"No promises."

"Good enough."

After she flounced out, Jerry asked curiously, "Was that about what I thought it was about?"

"She's a singer. She asked me to help her."

"I don't believe it. Even your nurse. Is anybody in this town not in show business?"

"You're not."

"Yeah, well, I've been meaning to get your opinion of my John Wayne impression."

Josh looked at him blankly, his eyes half closed, too sleepy to appreciate his feeble joke. Jerry knew he better tell Josh what he had come to say before he fell asleep.

Josh spoke first. "I'm checking out of here tomorrow."

Jerry pulled a chair up to Josh's bed and sat down. He leaned forward concerned. "You can't do that. You have to stay in here least a week."

"No can do, Jer. I've got to get back to work, so I can pay for these deluxe accommodations."

"You've got insurance."

"It won't pay my other bills."

"You can't go back to work for a while. You'll have to live off your residuals."

"Not enough. I'm supposed to start working with Joell in the studio in a week. I'll get some money up front for that. I'll do some easy work around the compounds till then. How's Noor?"

There was no way to avoid it. "Noor's worse."

Josh strained to lift his head off the pillow and shook it as if to clear his brain of the drugs that were threatening to put him to sleep again.

"Do you know what it is?"

"We think it's Feline Enteritis."

"Diarrhea and vomiting?"

"Her white cell count is below 5,000. We've got her on IV fluids, antibiotics, and antiserum. All we can do now is wait."

Josh clawed feebly at his bed covers. "I've got to get to her."

Jerry pushed him back on his pillow easily. "You couldn't even make it to the door, pal."

"She'll think I've deserted her."

Jerry figured it was as good a time as any to give him the bad news. "Look, Josh, besides bringing charges against you, the kid with the broken nose is suing the city. You've been suspended."

"That's not fair! They broke into the zoo and were harassing Katy and the baby!"

"I agree, but the lawyers will have to sort that out. Meanwhile, you're not allowed on the grounds."

"Tomorrow, take me there."

"They'll haul you off if you try."

Josh reached up and grabbed the edge of Jerry's jacket and pulled him forward with surprising strength. "You've got to help me on this, Jer. Please!"

Jerry reassured him, sounding more confident than he felt. "All right, all right. I'll do what I can."

Josh loosened his grip and fell back on the pillow. He was starting to fade. "Gilbert...Susie?

"They're taken care of. They're fine."

Josh made a noise that sounded vaguely like thanks.

Jerry stood up and walked to the foot of the bed and saw that Josh was sound asleep. He didn't envy Josh the mess that faced him as soon as he checked out of here. And he didn't even get a chance to tell him the worst of it.

* * * *

Josh hung up the phone, satisfied that he would be checking out of the hospital the next afternoon. The doctors and nurses had given him holy hell about it, but he had been adamant. Jerry had just cautioned and clucked like an old mother hen but had reluctantly agreed to pick him up.

His first order of business was to get in and see Noor without getting Jerry fired. If he went charging in there, he'd just get hauled out by the guards, as Jerry had said. Not that he had the ability to charge in anywhere. He had stopped taking the pain medication after he woke up last evening, but he was still weak and dizzy and had his right arm in a sling and it was hard to walk without help. After he knew how Noor was doing, he would worry about getting himself a lawyer.

"Hello." Jennie appeared in the doorway. He'd never seen her look so haggard and miserable.

"I'm sorry, Josh. I should have come to see you yesterday." She dragged herself over to his side and pecked his cheek before sagging into the chair by his bed.

Josh made a simple statement of fact. "You look like hell."

"Well, considering what's happened," she paused and put her head in her hands and rubbed her face. "Anyway, that was supposed to be my line. You don't look too swift either."

"Forget my looks. What's going on with you?"

"There's a lot I never told you, Josh."

"For instance?"

Jennie's shoulders drooped. She looked too defeated to cry. "It doesn't matter anymore. He's dead."

"Who's dead?" Josh hadn't meant for such a hard edge to creep into his voice but the pain throbbing in his skull was making him impatient. "Who's dead?" he repeated to Jennie's blank face.

"You don't know?"

"Don't know what?"

"Don't you watch TV? No one's called you or told you?"

Josh couldn't take any more of this unintelligible runaround. He exploded. "No, I don't have TV and I don't know why I don't know but I know one thing for damn sure, I don't know!"

Jennie's eyes widened and began to tear.

"Come on." He patted her hand awkwardly. "Don't cry."

But once the crack appeared, there was no holding back the dam. She answered Josh's question between sobs.

"Stan was shot."

"Stan Levy?"

"He's dead. They think Lila had something to do with it."

Josh grabbed the phone off the nightstand and dialed.

"She's not home. She's disappeared."

He almost couldn't hear the phone ringing for the blood pounding in his ears.

"She's not home, Josh, and nobody can reach her on her cell."

He let the receiver fall back in the cradle and put the phone back on the nightstand. The wretched hospital breakfast he had just consumed was in the back of his throat threatening to make a reappearance. He was completely disoriented.

Jennie gripped his arm. "Do you think she could have done it? Do you think she could've?"

Josh was too stunned to respond. Right now, he didn't even know the questions, let alone have any answers.

* * * *

Lila didn't like admitting it, but for the first time in her life, she was really scared. She sat down on the edge of the bed and stared at her reflection in the mirror hanging above the dresser. She had just stood in a hot shower for twenty minutes, trying to decide what to do, and her hair and body were still wrapped in the thin, cheap, white towels that belonged to the tacky little motel in Oxnard, where she had checked in an hour ago.

What was the best thing to do now?

She could say that she and Stan had had another fight and she took a drive up the coast two days ago and slept in her car in a rest area and then checked into the motel today. It sounded strange even to her but, oh well... then she'd say she had been too depressed and tired today to watch TV, so she had no idea of what had happened. That would have to do. It was plausible. Josh and Ingrid could back up Stan's history of abuse, and Ingrid hadn't been working two nights ago. The only catch was that Neanderthal at the all-night market. But he wouldn't connect her with anything. People who worked at jobs like that couldn't have fully functioning brains anyway.

So that would be her story.

She looked at her face devoid of all makeup. She was one of those women who looked almost as good without makeup as with it. Yes, she was very lucky to have what she had, and she would make it work for her, as always. This was an incredible fuckup, but she wouldn't allow herself to feel helpless and trapped. There was a way out of this, and she would do whatever she had to do. She had let her emotions run away with her. Now was the time for clear thinking.

Lila took the towel off her head and shook her damp hair free. One thought nagged at her constantly. Where was he? He hadn't answered his cell or shown up at the motel where he usually stayed when he was in town. She had stomped on her prepaid phone and thrown it in a dumpster at a gas station, but she couldn't use the motel phone in case they traced it later. She'd have to buy another prepaid phone later. She picked up a brush and ran it through her hair carefully and steadily. It would all work out. She could handle whatever happened.

CHAPTER TWELVE
LOS ANGELES

"Would you get your ass off my paperwork, Coleman? I'd like to get out of here!"

Larry Coleman, the self-appointed lothario of the Beverly Hills Detective Division had just made himself comfortable on Rosemaria Baker's desk. She was dog-tired from a three-day stakeout with no suspect in sight and was not in the mood for his pathetic advances. She stopped typing on the computer as one half of his rear end was situated on her notes and reassessed the creature on her desk in amazement. It never failed to astound her how such a tall, dark, attractive, dream of a guy could be such an unadulterated creep.

A month ago, when he first came into the division (and it was a puzzle to her how he ever made detective in the first place), she had responded with initial enthusiasm, but after ten seconds of conversation, it was evident that all the brains he had were below the waist, which meant he was probably limited in that department, too. He didn't know the meaning of rejection and the words, "get lost" or "leave me the hell alone," seemed to work like aphrodisiacs on him. She decided if she couldn't come up with more successful tactics, he would drive her completely nuts and she might as well check into the nearest mental hospital. She smiled at him.

Encouraged, he brought his face close to hers. "I love it when you talk dirty. Where we going tonight?"

She steeled herself and managed to hang on to her smile. "I'm meeting my father for dinner at Antonio's. Care to join us?"

He looked like he didn't know whether to be excited or suspicious. "Are you serious?"

Rosemaria wished she didn't find so much pleasure in pulling the wings off this particular fly. She liked to think she had more character than that. "I told him all about you," she gushed.

Larry looked dubious. This sudden change in her personality was throwing him off. "Yeah?"

Rosemaria went back to her computer. Larry inched his way off the desk and into the chair next to it.

"I always hated having a cop for a father," Rosemaria said. She could see Larry's enthusiasm wane.

"Your father's a cop?"

Her fingers skipped over the keys. "Too protective. He'd always greet my dates with his gun halfway out of his shoulder holster." She stopped typing and looked sadly off into the distance. "Poor Chester."

Larry furrowed his brow. "Who's Chester?"

"Just one of my dates."

Larry was not going to let this go. "Why poor Chester?"

Rosemaria causally looked over her notes. He was hanging on her every word. "Oh...nothing to worry about. He recovered quite nicely."

"Recovered?" He was clearly alarmed.

She picked up her coffee cup and chuckled. "You know how fathers are about their daughters, and I gotta tell you, old habits die hard."

"You're putting me on, right? You're making this shit up to put me off?"

Rosemaria took a sip of her coffee. "So, you think you can be there?"

He eased out of the chair, not sure if he should be skeptical or wary. "Maybe some other time. I have a lot of work to do on the computer myself."

Her phone buzzed but she couldn't resist a final, "You're sure?" before answering.

He nodded vigorously in response and backed away to his desk, where he became immediately engrossed in something on his computer.

She stifled a laugh, but the voice of Lieutenant Mandel on the other end sobered her up. "Be right in, lieutenant."

"Now what?" She wondered apprehensively. Her bar exam was coming up and the last thing she needed was another assignment. Sergeant Harvey was in charge of the Levy case, so she couldn't get stuck with that. Even though Bel-Air was not in their jurisdiction, downtown had their hands full with two serial killers and had offered the case to Beverly Hills.

"Come in," Lieutenant Mandel responded to her knock. The dapper, silver-haired man still looked more like a successful banker to her than a cop.

"Ask Sergeant Coleman to come in, too, please." His quiet, almost whispered voice was edged with steel. There was no mistaking it for weakness or escaping the respect it commanded.

"Yes, sir," Rosemaria looked over at Larry at his desk in their shared cubicle, suddenly busy on his computer. "Hey, Coleman, the Lieutenant wants to see us." She didn't wait for him to follow her as she walked up the aisle. Every step of the way, she prayed she wasn't about to be assigned to a new time-consuming case.

She was still praying down to the very last moment when she and Larry stood before the Lieutenant's desk and he announced, "I'm giving you two the Levy homicide. Sergeant Harvey has to go out of town for a few weeks on a family matter. I'll have someone else take over the stakeout."

Rosemaria visualized her hopes of passing the bar exam fly out the window.

Larry sounded excited. "The director in Bel-Air?"

"That's right. Sergeant Harvey will fill you in before he leaves." He looked at Rosemaria's crestfallen face. "Something wrong, Sergeant?"

"No... no. We'll get right on it."

"The media's all over this and they'll be hard to ignore, but the usual 'can't comment on an ongoing investigation,' will suffice for now. You'll have Waite and Osborne on your team. Harvey will walk you through the crime scene and give you his take on the case, such as it is so far. He'd like to do it this afternoon. That work for you two?"

Rosemaria and Larry nodded, "Yes sir," they said in unison.

"Three o'clock. He'll meet you there."

Larry had to nudge Rosemaria to get her moving from her frozen position and she followed him out the door. She was so frustrated, she wanted to put her fist through a wall and inadvertently slammed the door as she left the office. Larry shot her a look and shrugged, palms up, like asking "What the hell?" It was an agonizing walk to her desk, waiting for a reaction from the Lieutenant, but it never came. She had to get out of the office and cool down before she did something else stupid.

She walked over to Coleman's desk as he was sitting down. "I'll meet you back here in twenty minutes." She grabbed her purse and barreled angrily past a perplexed Coleman, out the door of the detective bureau. She punched the buttons to the elevator and, when the door opened, ran right into the thickly muscled arms of Ernie Kowalski, the veteran uniformed cop and now desk officer who had been her father's partner and friend for fifteen years. He held her at arm's length, refusing to let her pass. "Hey, what's eatin' you?"

Rosemaria looked down at the floor and muttered, "Piranha and horseflies."

Ernie laughed heartily. "Ve-e-e-ry feminine."

"Oh, Christ, Ernie. I'm a cop, not a Miss America contestant."

"Which makes your father happy and your mother roll over in her grave, and you don't intimidate me one bit, young lady."

"I'm sorry Ernie." She gave in to his no-nonsense good nature and hugged her friend. "I just had the Levy killing dumped on me with exams coming up right after Christmas."

Ernie patted her arm. "Levy, huh? Now I understand. The exams you can handle. It's having to deal with all those show businesspeople that's getting to you. Considerin' where you work, it was bound to happen sooner or later. You don't have no choice."

Rosemaria gave Ernie a jab on the forearm and jammed the down button as Ernie stepped out. "I will soon."

Ernie held the door open. "You're just mad 'cause they haven't discovered you yet," he joked good-naturedly.

"Huh!" she frowned back at him as he released the door and it closed on her grim face.

* * * *

Coleman was driving and enjoying himself tremendously. He wasn't overly impressed with the mansions he was driving by. But the prospect of a huge case drawing nation-wide interest and getting access to big shots in show-business, he had to admit that was what he dreamed of when he was transferred to Beverly Hills from Santa Monica. The only downside was working with the tight-ass bitch sitting beside him. She couldn't take a joke if her life depended on it. Did she really think he wanted in her pants? Forget it. Getting frostbite wasn't on his agenda. And that farkakteh story about her father was total bullshit. But just in case, he had decided to tone down the rhetoric a bit. Might as well try to get along. He wanted to solve this case and show everybody he belonged just as much as anybody else on the squad. Her annoying voice interrupted his thoughts.

"Turn at the next right."

"I can read the GPS, same as you."

Rosemaria counted to ten as her mother had instructed her when she was young. "I know you can. We're going to be working closely for a long time. Maybe we can be pleasant with each other?"

"I have no problem with that."

He turned right and up a fairly steep hill, then into the driveway of a nice but not ostentatious house. He pulled up near the front door behind another new Responder Hybrid cop car like their own. They got out and looked around, making note of the wooded surroundings and the distance to the nearest houses. No security cameras. Too bad. The front door was open.

Sergeant Harvey was in the living room when they walked inside. "Sorry to spring this on you, but my daughter had a car accident in Dallas, where she lives, and the wife and I are flying out in a few hours."

"Is it serious?" Rosemaria was immediately pulled out of her own selfish agenda.

"Could be. We'll know more as soon as we get there."

"I'm sorry," Rosemaria said, "I hope she'll be okay."

"Let's get to it then, so I can get back to my wife."

He walked them around the living room for half an hour, giving them as much as the criminalist and pathologist knew so far. Stan Levy had suffered a contact gunshot wound to the shoulder from a .38 special that passed through the muscle and fatty tissue of his underarm and ended up in the wall behind the piano. He fell or was knocked down and cracked his head open on the edge of the glass coffee table and bled out for maybe an hour. So, the bullet didn't kill him, it was the head wound that caused his death between approximately eight and ten p.m. If whoever shot him and or shoved him had called 911, he could probably have been saved. He had DNA under his fingernails that was checked in the various databases, but no match so far. Ditto for the fingerprints they had lifted.

The knocked-over vases, tchotchkes, lamps, and tables, and bruises on Stan's hands and arms showed there was a terrific fight before the shot. Stan had a Smith and Wesson revolver registered to him—it looked as if he kept it in a drawer that contained boxes of ammunition. The drawer was in the sideboard near the entrance to the living room. That could have been the weapon. Cadets and uniforms had searched the hillsides for the gun but hadn't found one. The neighbors were questioned and claimed they heard no shots. The maid, Ingrid, said Stan was sometimes abusive to his wife, who hasn't been heard of since the day of the murder.

"And that's what we have so far. You can look at the video yourself and see what we found when we got here and talk to the pathologist. She says she has more to tell us about Stan, but I leave that all to you."

Rosemaria smiled grimly at Harvey. "We appreciate your meeting with us. I know having to hang around waiting for us can't have been easy."

"Don't worry about it. The flight to Dallas isn't for a couple hours." He reached out and shook Rosemaria's hand.

Coleman patted Harvey's arm as he shook his hand. "Our thoughts and prayers are with your daughter."

"Thank you both." And Harvey headed for his car.

"What do we do now, boss?" Coleman said without a tinge of irony or sarcasm.

Rosemaria relaxed and thought maybe there was a smidgen of hope for this guy. That story about her father may have done the trick.

CHAPTER THIRTEEN
MARYSVILLE, WISCONSIN

He sat on the bed with Scott in the darkness and showed him how to clap his hands. "First, I sing two notes, then you clap once. Then I sing again, and you clap twice. Got it?"

Scott looked at him vaguely. At three years of age, he was more like ten months old, but Josh persisted.

The shouting in his parents' room got louder and he strummed his guitar harder in a futile attempt to cover the noise. He recoiled as he heard a slap, then a sickening thud, but even though he wanted, with every fiber of his being, to go help his mother, he couldn't leave his brother.

Scott looked uncertainly in the direction of the sounds. Even a baby could sense the brutality going on in the next room.

"Tell you what, buddy," Josh said. "Let's sneak out to see Sullivan for a while. We can sing louder in the barn."

Scott held out his chubby little arms to be picked up and Josh lifted his brother out of bed and carried him out of the house. As soon as Josh was old enough, he would carry Scott away and never bring him back.

CHAPTER FOURTEEN

LOS ANGELES

Vanessa Sheridan pushed open the glass door of the Producers Building and walked confidently out into the brisk sunshine. She had just given an inspired reading for the lead in a pilot and there was every reason to be optimistic. For once, it hadn't been necessary to pretend she was younger than she really was, and she'd been able to relax and concentrate on her performance.

It was almost lunchtime and people were milling around the courtyard between the Producers Building and the commissary. A couple of tourists smiled as they recognized her but were either too shy or too polite to ask her for her autograph. Jobs had been few and far between in the past couple of years, and she was grateful for the acknowledgment. Long live all those lovely reruns and the residuals they brought.

Vanessa decided to reward herself for her exceptional performance today and take herself to a matinee. She walked the few yards to the Coffee Bean to pick up a paper and sat at one of the tables outside of the commissary to see what was playing. An article on the front page caught her attention: "NO ARRESTS YET IN MOVIE DIRECTOR'S MURDER." Her hands trembled and shook the paper involuntarily as she read. The police had no leads but there would be an extensive investigation. Vanessa's mind reeled. She had been trying to forget about Stan's death ever since she had first heard about it on the news. Could Lila have had something to do it? She had never trusted the woman and suspected she was capable of anything, even murder. It was very possible that the police would want to question Vanessa, and she dreaded the thought. She had nothing to fear from them, but she did have a reason to hide from Lila. Vanessa was definitely afraid of her.

Vanessa forced herself to calm down. She caught a couple of worried glances aimed in her direction and knew she must do better at controlling her anxiety, especially if the police ever got around to her. She had no idea what happened that night, but she had her suspicions. Please, God, let them find the murderer without involving her…not now, when she finally had a shot at something good.

* * * *

Ingrid sat across the table from Rosemaria and Coleman in the interview room, wide-eyed with fear.

"We know you're undocumented, Ingrid, and we don't care. Really, we don't care." Coleman assured her. "We just want to ask you a few questions, that's all. We don't talk to ICE and they don't talk to us and that's how we like it, comprende?"

Ingrid looked at Rosemaria, who smiled and nodded her agreement.

"You told Sergeant Harvey that Mr. Levy sometimes hit his wife," Coleman continued. "Was that frequent? Had it happened recently?"

Ingrid spoke hesitantly, searching her English for the words, "Mister, he very nice man. I like him very much, but they argue a lot."

"And he hit her?"

"She scream at him sometimes and he get mad and he slap her face. He did that the week before…he was…very bad fight."

"But you weren't there the night he was killed, is that right?"

"No, I was not there since the day before. I go to a wedding and misses she say okay."

"What did the two of them fight about? Could you understand what they said?"

"Always the same thing, mister was drinking and taking cocaine. Always that."

"They never fought about anything else?"

Ingrid hesitated, then remembered something. "One time, maybe last month, he said she maybe seeing another man."

"Do you know who that was?"

"No, but I know it wasn't mister Josh."

"And who is mister Josh?"

"He the man who teach her how to sing. He very nice. She like him but he always gentleman. Never do anything he shouldn't do."

"And he came here a lot?"

"Yes."

"Do you know his last name?"

"No, but he a friend of mister's, too."

Rosemaria reached over the table and patted Ingrid's hand. "Please don't worry, Ingrid. Nothing bad will happen to you. We'll contact you if we have any more questions."

Ingrid pushed her chair out and stood up, still uncertain. Coleman took her arm and helped her to the door. She looked up at him gratefully. "Thank you."

Coleman waited in the doorway for Rosemaria, half expecting a sarcastic comment, but she was all business. "Good work, partner. Let's confab with our partners in crime."

"Confab? I believe that is a showbusiness term."

"Wash my mouth out with soap."

Detectives Coleman, Waite, and Osborne were seated around Rosemaria's desk and watched as she inserted a flash drive into her computer. As she waited for the download, she observed her team. She was happy with every one of them. Coleman, for whatever reason, had abruptly abandoned his annoying come-ons. Jimmy Waite was a young, red-headed, bandy rooster of a man who was meticulous in his investigations, sharp as a tack, and, like all young kids these days, a whiz on the computer.

Darryl Osborne, tall and skinny with hair already thinning in his early thirties, was insightful and diligent, would do whatever job he was assigned to without complaint, and knew his way around computers. The video came on and they watched without comment as the camera moved through the front door, down the hallway, and into the living room, where it scanned the upheaval that had taken place there. Stan was on the floor by the coffee table, the bullet hole in his shoulder visible. "Contact wound," Waite observed as they studied the close-up. "They fought over the gun."

"The M.E. confirmed that," Rosemaria said. "If it was an accident or self-defense, why run away and let him die?"

The blood under Stan's head was spread out underneath him like a big black halo. "Didn't have to die." Osborne said. "Heartless bastard, whoever he was."

They watched as the camera moved over the crime scene until the video ended. Rosemaria removed the flash drive. "Harvey compiled a short list of some of Levy's friends and people he worked with. It has come down from 'on high' that we are not to go rampaging around the studio like storm troopers and disrupt productions." They all laughed at the absurdity. "So, gauging from that comment, we know what the mayor—I mean, 'on high'—thinks of us. At any rate, be sweet, kind, and considerate to any and all murder suspects you may find in your travels, and act at all times like your typical, well-dressed, sophisticated Beverly Hills cops the public expects us to be." More guffaws.

"I talked to Levy's producer, Howard Grossman. He says this Josh guy's last name is Sibley. He was teaching Levy's wife to sing. Apparently, he's an aging, would-be song writer who does commercials. He could have a motive for getting rid of the husband if he and the wife got cozy."

She looked down at her list. "Osborne, I'd like you to start with Levy's secretary, Olga Mostad. She probably knew Levy better than anybody and where all the bodies are buried, no pun intended, secretaries usually do. Follow up on anything you find out from her. Levy's producer, Howard Grossman, is in the same office. Apparently, they've been friends and co-workers for years."

She made a few clicks on her computer and studied the screen. "The M.E. told me this morning that from the autopsy, it was clear that Levy was a heavy drug user, mostly cocaine, although there was alcohol in his system and amphetamines and other assorted drugs as well. His septum was close to perforating, he showed signs of heart disease and the beginnings of a stomach ulcer. In other words, he had been using for years and it wouldn't have been long before he became very, very sick. Harvey found no stashes in the house, which is amazing for such a heavy user. He had to have had a regular supplier among friends, or co-workers, or a stranger. All of you, see what you can come up with. Osborne, the secretary may know something about that as well."

"Waite, I need you to get on the computer and see if you can locate Mrs. Levy. She could have run away, could be a victim, could be dead, could be anywhere. We've got an APB out but she's nowhere to be found.

Check uses of credit cards and debit cards in every hotel in L.A., Orange and Ventura counties, and beyond. If you locate her, I don't want to bring her in before I know more about her and her husband. If she's found, have a car go to the location and, whatever happens, tell them not to lose her. My ass is grass if that should happen. Find out about Stan's financial records, any bad debts, any rough people he owed money to and that sort of thing."

"Coleman, I'd like you to interview Ken Jordan, who produced a couple of commercials Sibley wrote, and see if you can find out who his musician friends were. I don't like to assume and stereotype but maybe one of them can give us a lead on who Levy's supplier was. I'm going to track down Sibley who, incredible as it sounds, works at the zoo, of all places."

"Most performers have to take any kind of job they can get before they make it," Osborne observed kindly.

"I know that, believe me, I know that very well."

* * * *

Noor lay sleeping on the table in the bare hospital room, an IV inserted in her upper front right leg. Through the window that faced out into the hallway, Jerry could see Josh looking in at her with an expression torn between anger and helplessness. Jerry glanced at his watch, worried about Dr. Jensen coming back from lunch early.

Every time someone walked by, Josh pulled his hood tighter around his face, knowing if he stayed much longer, someone was bound to recognize him. He didn't dare go inside and risk being discovered. They were taking a big chance already and if Jerry was fired, neither one of them would be able to stay near Noor.

Jerry raised his hand to signal to Josh that it was time to go and hoped he wouldn't have to go out into the hallway and drag him away, but Josh sadly nodded his thanks and turned away.

Jerry stroked Noor's back gently and slowly, barely touching her, thinking how ironic it was that Ed Hahn, the zoo administrator, cared so little for the animals in his charge. He had tried to establish a primate "research" center on zoo grounds a couple of years ago until public outcry forced him to abandon the idea. Jerry and Josh had both fought him tooth and nail on the idea, enraged that a place that was supposedly built to protect and preserve animals was threatening to become a convenient place for sadistic, pseudo scientists to get their rocks off torturing animals.

Ed Hahn hadn't been able to fire Jerry and Josh then, because he had been put on suspension himself for his underhanded dealings with UC vivisectors and was suspected of getting kickbacks, but the guy hated their guts. Ever since he'd gotten his job back through plenty of political string-pulling, they had been at the top of his hate list. As soon as the parents of the young punk who attacked Josh filed their lawsuit, Hahn was on the phone to Jerry with orders to keep Josh off the grounds. As he put it so quaintly to his friends in the press, "We can't have a wild maniac running around attacking park visitors." What a joke. The only maniacs around the place were the zoo administrator and the board of directors. One thing he knew for sure, Ed Hahn was dancing around with glee at all of this and the thought revolted Jerry. Somehow, they would find a way around the vindictive bastard.

He wished that all the animals imprisoned at the zoo could be freed to sanctuaries, but for now, his main goal was making sure Noor recovered and then he and Josh would deal with Hahn and getting Noor and Gilbert out of there.

He heard the outer door of the clinic open and left Noor's side to find a red-headed woman standing a few feet away. She flashed her badge and said she was there to see Josh Sibley. Jerry had instinctively known Lila would bring Josh nothing but trouble and here it was, right on time.

* * * *

After finally prying the information out of Dr. Widel, Rosemaria hurried down the path in the direction he told her Josh was headed. She wanted to catch him before he made it to the taxi that was supposed to be waiting at the exit. If that happened, she would have to go to his apartment and wait, hoping he hadn't taken off to places unknown, like meeting with Lila Levy, wherever she might be. It had taken some heavy persuasion to convince Dr. Widel that she had no intention of arresting Sibley, but merely wanted to ask him a few questions. The turning point in winning his confidence had been when she showed an interest in the black panther who, apparently, was quite ill. When Dr. Widel had told her, with obvious heartfelt emotion, about Sibley's desire to be at the animal's side and the obstacles in his way, she had become quite sympathetic. Rosemaria sensed that they both felt quite a commitment toward the panther and that this was a way to win their trust. Not that she didn't sincerely wish the cat well, it was just that she had to take her opportunities where she found them.

Personally, she had never had much empathy with animals and had never felt the need for a pet. She had been too busy putting herself through UCLA and the academy, working her way up to detective sergeant in a chauvinistic atmosphere, and then working her butt off going to law school part-time to worry about having a fur ball underfoot. She remembered, with distaste, her mother's yappy pet poodle, Yvette, that her mother had carried with her everywhere. With her ribbons and bows and rhinestone collars, the damn dog had had a more expensive wardrobe than Rosemaria. Until her mother died when Rosemaria was ten years old, she had always felt her mother loved that dog more than her own daughter. And when Yvette had been given away to a distant relative, she hadn't been the least bit sorry.

Rosemaria hesitated as the path separated into two different directions and chose the one she thought headed toward the exit. She'd find out soon enough if she was wrong.

Why on earth was she thinking of Yvette and her mother now? She had more pressing concerns at the moment and getting some answers from this singer/songwriter, animal nut was her first order of business.

Up ahead, she saw a man who, according to Dr. Widel's description, had to be Sibley. He was hard to miss in that ridiculous getup: green plaid lumberman's jacket with a hood, one arm in a sling, faded jeans, sunglasses, and black wool cap. From what she knew of musicians, this outlandish disguise was probably how he usually dressed. He was walking with a limp, his head down, one hand in his coat pocket.

She caught up with him at the concession stand near the exit.

"Mr. Sibley?" Josh stiffened when he heard the woman's voice but managed to keep walking anyway. Maybe she'd figure she'd made a mistake and go away. But the woman was persistent. "Mr. Sibley, I need to talk to you." He decided it was better to deal with her quickly before the guards spotted him. He turned to face her.

He didn't recognize the attractive woman with the friendly expression on her face and concluded, with relief, that she must be a park visitor he had talked to before who remembered him.

"Yes, what can I do for you, ma'am?"

She flashed a badge with one hand and held out the other. She smiled as she said the words that sealed his fate and Jerry's. "Hello, I'm Detective Baker." Now, he'd managed to get Jerry fired, too.

He shook her hand despite the sinking feeling in his chest. "You've got a real friendly way of arresting somebody. And it wasn't Dr. Widel's fault. He didn't know I was coming."

She smiled sympathetically. "I'm not here about that. Your disguise is safe with me. I'd like to ask you about Stan Levy."

Josh had enjoyed his relief only for a split second before the alarm bells went off. This was one smooth cop. "I don't know how I can help you. I barely knew him, but he seemed like a nice guy to me. And, if you don't mind, I'd like to get out of here, for obvious reasons."

He turned and left her standing there as he went out the exit, but she caught up quickly due to his slow, limping gait.

"I hear you were a friend of Mrs. Levy's."

"I worked with her for a few weeks at her house. Her husband hired me to coach her on a song she was supposed to sing in his movie. I guess that won't happen now." His face registered deep disappointment. "Not that I'm not sad about what happened to Stan. I just thought that..." His voice trailed off.

"It was a chance for you to get your song in a movie."

"Yeah."

"What was your relationship with Lila? Were you close?"

"We were friends, that's all." Every step he took was painful, and he was having a hard time breathing, and his ribs were aching. Why couldn't she just leave him the hell alone?

"We heard that she was very fond of you."

"News to me."

"Did you have feelings for her?"

"She was married."

"And that makes a difference to you?"

"Yes."

"And to her?"

Josh ignored that one. People prying into his personal life had always annoyed him and this broad was relentless.

"Has she tried to contact you since the murder?"

"No." He looked toward the other side of the parking lot to where the cab would be pulling in. The distance may have only been the length of a short city block, but now, it looked wider than the Sahara Desert. He kept walking and she kept interrogating.

"Were you at the house that night?"

"I was busy."

His sarcasm didn't faze her. "That was later. The evidence indicates that Mr. Levy had quite a struggle with someone before he was shot. You could have picked a fight to cover your previous injuries."

"You're saying I knew ahead of time that those three gangbangers were going to attack Katy and her foal and I, on purpose, got myself beat up and knocked unconscious?"

"Sorry, when you put it like that..."

They walked in silence to the entrance of the parking lot. Josh looked anxiously down the road to check out the cars headed in their direction. He sure as hell didn't feel like getting stuck here, endlessly fielding Detective Baker's questions. Right now, she seemed to have temporarily exhausted her supply of them and was leaning against the hood of a parked car.

"I'm sorry about the panther. Dr. Widel told me you raised her from a cub when she first came to the zoo."

He shifted his gaze from the road to the detective and looked at her closely for the first time: short auburn hair, blue eyes, freckles across her nose. She looked more like a Wisconsin farm girl than a cop. But in a town of illusions, he wasn't fooled by such gross miscasting. A female cop pushing thirty had to have a lot of tough mileage on her. Now she was fattening him up for the kill and he resented her using Noor to do it.

"She's going through a rough time right now. She could die."

"It could make a difference if you were allowed to be with her; at least that's what Dr. Widel told me."

"Tell that to Ed Hahn."

"And he is...?"

"The zoo administrator. And if I were going to do bodily harm to someone, it would be him, not the man who was about to give me the biggest break of my life."

He saw the cab coming down the street and flagged it down. The cab stopped next to them, but before Josh could open the door, she was beside him, handing him a card.

"If you hear from Lila, call me. You know it's best for her."

He took the card and opened the door. "Don't worry. You can count on it."

"On what?"

"Doing what's best for Lila."

He slammed the door and the cab sped off. He glanced back at Detective Baker and saw that she had been forced to step back quickly and had caught her heel in a pothole and almost stumbled. Her vulnerability at that moment broke through his self-defensive, suspicious attitude and he regretted he had left so abruptly. He would apologize later. He was sure he'd see her again and he would make it clear he wanted to find Stan's killer as bad as anybody. But where was Lila? Was she alive? The thought that something might have happened to her sent a chill through his body. Meanwhile, he had to think of a way to get in to see Noor. Losing her was not an option.

CHAPTER FIFTEEN
MARYSVILLE, WISCONSIN

Josh planted his body firmly in front of the door, his arms outstretched. He directed a fierce burning gaze at his father, who was sitting in his favorite chair reading the paper.

"I won't let them take him away," Josh said with all the passion in his fourteen-year-old heart. "I won't!" he added with special emphasis.

"Don't be a brat. He's going." His father hardly bothered looking up from his paper.

Josh heard the two men climb the steps and walk to the front door. The doorbell rang.

"Open the door," his father ordered calmly.

"No." Josh had never felt so determined.

His father put down his paper. "Open the goddamn door!"

"He's not going!" Josh shouted back at him. He could see the rage building in his father as he got to his feet. It scared the heck out of him, but he wasn't about to back down now.

"Open the door before I tan your hide!"

The shouting brought his mother running into the room. "Stop all that yelling. You're upsetting Scott!" She stopped short at the sound of the doorbell.

"Oh, my. They're here." She wrung her hands and looked nervously back and forth between father and son. "Please," she begged, "I don't want them to hear us arguing. They might decide not to take him."

He didn't understand his mother at all anymore. How could she be doing this to her own son? It was all up to him. "They're not taking him, anyway." He glared at his father.

The discussion ended right there.

Josh's father took two steps toward him and gave him a blow to the side of his head that sent him flying across the room, then he calmly turned to his wife, who was staring at him, horrified. "What the hell are you waiting for? Go get the kid."

She looked helplessly at Josh, who was sprawled on the floor with blood trailing out of his mouth and down his chin. She wanted to come to him, but she wouldn't. He had come to expect very little of her in the past few years. She did as she was told, as Josh knew she would.

His mother went back into the bedroom and came out holding a small suitcase, leading Scott by the hand. His father opened the door.

"No!" Josh screamed and, gathering all his strength, flew across the room, trying to slam the door shut, but his father was too fast for him. In full view of the two men from the institute who had come to pick up Scott, he landed a punch in Josh's stomach that doubled him over with the worst pain he had ever felt in his life. He lay on the floor moaning and clutching his stomach and heard his father say, "Take him." Then the door closed, and his mother started crying softly.

The last thing he remembered before everything turned black was the creak in the springs of his father's chair and the rustling of the paper as his father continued reading as if nothing out of the ordinary had happened.

CHAPTER SIXTEEN

LOS ANGELES

"'m sorry...I'm so sorry...can't seem to get myself together." Olga put her hands to her face and started weeping uncontrollably. Osborne walked around the desk to where Olga was seated, bent over and overcome with grief. He helped her up and walked her toward the couch.

"No, I'm the one who's sorry. My questions came off too blunt. You're not ready for this yet." He sat her down and grabbed a tissue from the box on the coffee table and handed it to her.

Olga spoke through her tears, hoarse as if she had spent hours crying. "I came in to return phone calls, so many calls, and see if I could help Howard at all, but he decided to stay home and I'm not good for anything."

"That's to be expected." He sat on the couch a couple feet away from her. "He was your boss."

"Oh, no, so much more than that. Like a son, really." She snickered in spite of herself. "A naughty, outrageous, overgrown kid. No one was like him...I still keep hoping he's going to walk through that door any minute. A part of me can't accept that this isn't all some horrible nightmare...I'm just a stupid, stupid, old lady." The tears flowed down her face.

"No, not at all." Osborne looked around the office. "Can I get you something to drink? Anything at all?"

"Thank you, but I'm okay. No, that's wrong. I'll never be okay again. I haven't felt so alone and lost since my husband died. Then Stan hired me and my whole life changed for the better."

Osborne took out his cell phone, clicked record and placed it on the table. "Do you mind if I record our conversation?"

Olga sniffled a "no" through her tissue.

"He sounds like a great guy," Osbourne continued.

"The best." She started sobbing again and Osborne waited patiently until she was spent.

"I guess you must have been friends with his wife."

Olga stopped crying and blew her nose. "I hated that bitch."

The change in her was so abrupt, it took Osborne by surprise.

"Oh?"

"She went after Stan like there was no tomorrow, and he was too smitten blind to see what she really was."

"What was that?"

"A user. A typical, selfish, self-centered, Hollywood user who would do anything to get ahead."

"It must have been difficult for you to see that happen. Where did he meet her, do you know?"

"At a party. Lila was living with another actress at the time—nice girl, she worked on our show once. She was a real actress, not an empty vessel like Lila. She brought Lila with her to a wrap party at a restaurant in Beverly Hills. Lots of people from the studio, but Lila made a beeline for Stan. I know. I saw it happening and it was disgusting."

"Do you remember the name of the other actress?"

"No, I'm sorry. Howard would know."

"Mrs. Levy has disappeared. Do you think she could have had anything to do with...?"

"No...as much as I hate her, I know she could never kill him. He was her ticket to fame and that was the only reason she married him. She was going to appear in his feature, the break of a lifetime. No, she would not have killed him."

"I hear they argued, sometimes violently. Not even during an argument?"

"Not a chance."

"I suppose you know about his drug use?"

"It was never that bad! He had it under control!" Olga almost pleaded with him to believe her.

"I'm sure you're right about that. It's hard to avoid drugs when there's so much going around your industry."

"It was his friend's fault—Moe, his transportation captain. He was a bad influence."

"Anyone else you can think of?"

"Howard had an addiction problem five years ago. Went to rehab and became like a fanatic about drugs. He was on Stan like a mean nun with a ruler if he even *thought* he was anywhere near that stuff."

Osborne put his cell phone back in his pocket. "I appreciate your talking to me, Ms. Mostad."

"You need to talk to Howard. He might be able to help you."

"I will do that."

Olga leaned over and grabbed Osborne's arm. "Please find out who did this. I won't be able to think about anything else until you do."

Osborne patted her arm. "We'll do our best."

* * * *

"Any news on the fingerprints?" Rosemaria was at her desk on the phone with Diane in forensics, hoping for a break. She listened for a minute then replied, "I guess Ingrid wasn't much for polishing furniture, if you found that many. If we have a suspect, maybe one of them will match. Thanks, Diane."

Her cell rang and she picked it up off her desk. "Dad, what happened?" Waite came over and stood next to her desk. She gestured for him to sit, but he shook his head smiling as if he had won the lottery. "That's fantastic, Dad!" I love you!" She thanked her father and said to Waite, "Talk to me."

"I tracked down our girl to a motel in Oxnard. She used her real name and her debit card to pay."

"Drive up there first thing tomorrow morning and haul her ass in. I think we know enough about her now to give her a run for her money."

"Think she'll give us a snow job?"

"Are bears Catholic?"

* * * *

Osborne looked around Howard Grossman's living room and decided producing must be where the money is. His house was three times the size of Levy's and situated on a block of several very nice mansions in Holmby Hills. It was also decorated in the popular Mediterranean style, but the impressive pieces of furniture were definitely antiques, not reproductions like Levy's. Even he could see that. He heard footsteps coming down the tiled hallway and turned around and saw a man of medium height, overweight, thinning hair, and a face only a mother could love—Howard Grossman. "Sit, sit," he said, and waited until Osborne had made himself comfortable before walking over to the bar. "I only have pop and sparkling water, if you'd like some."

"Coke is fine with me."

Grossman poured and brought the glasses over to the very comfortable chair where Osborne sat and handed him a glass. He drank deeply of his own glass of water and sank into a chair across from Osborne.

"Is this fucked up or what?" He sighed deeply.

"Murder usually is."

"It had to happen. Where Stan was headed. Nothing good could come of it."

Osborne took out his cell phone and placed it on the table. "Do you mind?"

"Go ahead. I've got nothing to hide."

Osborne clicked the record button. "You mean the drugs."

"I'd been there. Not as bad as Stan, but I came to my senses, thank God. Stan was in denial. He didn't have any idea that I knew how bad it was. He was able to function on the set—crews loved him, actors loved him, he could settle any complications with a smile and a joke. He knew his craft up one side and down another. He would have directed the hell out of my feature."

"Will that still go ahead?"

"There will be a bit of a delay while I try to find another director who's as good as Stan and who's available. The studio and the investors don't care that somebody dies; hire somebody else and stay on schedule. But that's not going to happen. I'm not going to hire just anybody just to make the studio happy."

"Will Lila still be in the movie?"

"She worked really hard on her song and I thought it was great. But no, I had to tell Stan, I think it was the day before he died, that Lila was out. Joell decided she wanted to sing in the bar scene after all and once the studio heard that, Lila was history. A shame, too. She worked her ass off."

"Did she find that out the day Levy was killed?"

"You think she was angry enough to kill him? I doubt it. There would always be more shows, more movies, more parts. Lila knew Stan was the best thing that ever happened to her, drugs or no drugs."

"Know where the drugs came from?"

"Ask his transportation captain. It's an open secret that he has relatives in Vegas who supply a lot of celebrities with a wide assortment of drugs. Stan was one of their best customers."

* * * *

Josh had told the cab driver who picked him up at the zoo to drop him off at Ken's office. He wanted to make sure that Ken knew as soon as Noor was well (and he refused to believe she wouldn't be) he was available for any and all auditions Ken could scrape up for him. But after taking two steps into the reception office he promptly collapsed on the couch. He woke up a few minutes later to find Jennie seated in a chair next to him, her hand on his shoulder and a worried look on her face. Josh had pulled himself upright and, against Jennie's protestations, insisted on calling another cab to take him the few blocks to his apartment. Now, as the cab pulled up in front of Josh's building, he handed the driver his last dollar. Jennie had informed him that a residual check was on its way, so he shouldn't worry, but now his head was pounding like a sledgehammer and he needed so badly to lay down that even being broke seemed an insignificant problem. His whole body ached, and he wobbled unsteadily on his feet. An old homeless man with his hat and coat covered in military medals blocked his way to the front door. He was one of the regulars in the neighborhood.

"How you doin', General?"

"Yes, I'm ready," the General intoned in a sing-song voice.

"Good for you," Josh said, stepping around him to go in.

"Yes, I'm ready," the General repeated.

"That's fine."

He didn't have the strength to try to carry on a conversation with the General. Visions of sinking into his bed upstairs for a couple of hours were all that kept him on his feet.

He put his hand on the door handle and felt a tap on his shoulder.

"Joshua Sibley?"

The voice belonged to a uniformed cop about twice his size. Another cop, a little less intimidating, stood beside a squad car parked a few feet away.

"Yeah?"

"Come with us, please."

The cop standing at the curb opened the back door and waited.

"Am I under arrest?"

The other cop took his arm and led him to the car. "Escort service."

"Wait a minute." Josh resisted being pushed into the back seat. Something wasn't kosher about all of this.

"I talked to Sergeant Baker. She said I wasn't under arrest."

"Sergeant Baker's orders."

The cops maneuvered him easily into the car and then got in the front seat.

He didn't understand what Sergeant Baker would want with him now. He had said he would call her if he had anything more to say. Josh let his head fall back on the seat. He was too tired to think straight so he might as well get a little shut eye on the way to the station. He didn't notice they were headed in the opposite direction.

"Mr. Sibley."

The cop was shaking him awake, forcing him out of his coma-like sleep. He looked around groggily. They were parked at the front entrance of the zoo.

"What are we doing here?"

"Our orders are to escort you to your friend, Noor. Sergeant Baker said it was a matter of life and death."

Relief flooded though Josh as tears filled his eyes.

"I guess this Noor must be a pretty close friend of yours," one of the cops added.

"Yes, yes. Very close."

With a policeman on either side, he walked toward the hospital as fast as his wobbly legs would carry him. He wished Ed Hahn could see him now.

* * * *

The middle-aged receptionist at the recording studio was so snotty, you'd think she was working for Quincy Jones instead of in a tiny recording dump like this. Coleman's badge didn't impress her and his attempts to charm her fell flat, so he went with blatant intimidation, which brought him to the door of the studio where Ken Jordan was recording a commercial.

Coleman opened the door slowly and walked in. Four people were in the control room. On the other side of the glass, a black singer was singing or rapping or whatever the hell it was that Coleman thought sounded like the worst thing he had ever heard. Rapping about bread?! All heads turned in his direction when he came in. One man gave him a "shhh" and then turned back to listen to the man behind the glass. Coleman sat down in a rickety old chair that looked like it was on its last legs and waited for the redundant noise to end. When it finally did, he noticed the dour-faced expression on one of the older men in the room. Apparently, the rap was not much of a hit with him. A younger man with gray hair that looked like a Raider's football helmet sitting next to him tried to persuade him that this is what they needed for the newer generation of bread buyers. The older man got up and stalked out of the room without a backward glance. The younger man followed him, and he had to assume the man left sitting there with the engineer was Ken Jordan. Ken clicked on the mike and told the singer, or whatever the hell you called somebody who recited bad poetry to music, "You can take a break." The singer nodded, came out, barely glanced at the two of them, and left the room. Ken turned around and stared at Coleman. "What can I do for you?"

Coleman brought out his badge. "Detective Coleman. If you're Ken Jordan, I need to ask you a few questions about Stan Levy."

*　*　*　*

Josh walked into the surgical room and was surprised to see Detective Baker standing next to Jerry. Noor was lying on a gurney with tubes coming in and out of her and his heart stopped as he saw how emaciated she had become. He approached her hesitantly, fighting back tears, then looked down on her sleeping form. He put his hand on her shoulder, gently stroking her fur. "I'm here, Noor. You're going to be fine...just fine...but you have to wake up, okay? Stop worrying me like this...I promise you, soon you'll be climbing real trees and running free in tall grass and I'll come visit so often you'll get sick of me." His tears were flowing now, and he didn't care that Jerry and the detective could see he was crying.

Rosemaria walked toward him.

Josh could only choke out a single word, "How?"

She spoke softly. "My dad went to the academy with the mayor. They've been friends ever since."

"He got me in here?"

"Yes."

"Thank him for me."

"Be happy to."

He rubbed Noor's forehead gently.

"Do you mind if I stay here with you awhile? No questions. I promise."

"You've earned the right."

"Thank you."

Jerry handed Josh a handkerchief and Josh accepted it gratefully and wiped his face and blew his nose, never taking his eyes off Noor.

"The way the cops picked me up. That was your idea?"

"Who, me?"

"I think you must have inherited a dramatic streak."

"Curse the thought."

Jerry brought two chairs over so they could both sit next to Noor. For almost an hour, they sat together, barely speaking. Rosemaria watched him murmur words of encouragement into the cat's ear and stroke her tirelessly. She had never witnessed anyone so emotionally involved with an animal, not even her mother. It was as if Noor really were a close friend instead of just an animal. She had always found people who found pleasure in killing them murderous cowards, but this kind of emotional bond with an animal was incomprehensible to her.

The heavy, persistent darkness that had enveloped and terrified Noor was beginning to lift. It was still hot in the room, but not as unbearable as it had been before. She heard Josh's voice close to her ear and felt his hand reassuringly firm on her neck. Her mouth was dry, and she longed to lap her tongue into a pool of cool water, but now she was having trouble even opening her eyes.

An unfamiliar voice. A female voice. Then a small hand touched her forehead. She had to open her eyes to see who it was. But when she opened them, all she saw was Josh's face very close to hers. His eyes widened, his mouth opened, but no sound came out. Josh turned to the female and said something to her, and she ran out of the room. Noor barely caught a glimpse of her. Josh was kissing Noor's head and saying her name over and over again.

When Josh's friend in the white coat came running in with the female right behind him, he took out his instruments and began to peer into Noor's eyes and her throat and pressed his hand on her chest. Why all the fuss? Why were they all acting so strangely? She vaguely remembered the pain in her stomach and how she had wanted to lose her food all the time. But the pain was gone now, and she hoped that when she woke up from just a little short nap, they would have a nice dinner waiting for her. She would have to find out later who the female was and why she was with Josh. For now, Noor was content to sleep without pain and, lifting one paw with much effort, she put it down on her master's arm and drifted off into a peaceful dream of wide-open places.

The door flung open into the cold, black night and Josh's voice blasted the silence. "Whooeeh!"

Rosemaria came out behind him with a wide grin that matched his own. If he hadn't had an arm in a sling, he would have liked to pick her up and whirl her around and around until his head spun, but he settled instead for an affectionate squeeze. Still holding her, he said, "I'm so fucking relieved, I could cry."

She patted his arm. "I'm glad you're happy about Noor but you better take it easy or she'll be keeping watch at *your* bedside."

But there was no calming him down. "Where's your car?" She pointed and he steered her in that direction. "You're the one who brought her back."

"Me? All I did was get you here."

"No. It was more than that. She responded when you touched her."

"Sheer coincidence, I assure you. Where are we going, by the way?"

"I'm starving. Let's go eat."

They found an all-night coffee shop on Riverside in Burbank. At 2:00 a.m., they were the only customers in the restaurant. Josh ordered an avocado sandwich and a huge mound of fries, and Rosemaria ordered a salad. They both became absorbed with their meals and only picked up their conversation when their hunger pangs were partially satiated. Josh did like a woman who knew how to eat heartily.

"I wish I could tell you more," he said with a mouthful of fries and ketchup. He pointed to his fries. "Want some?"

"I shouldn't, but since you offer." She grabbed some fries off his plate, dipped them in ketchup, stuffed them into her mouth, and spoke with her mouth full.

"I hope you don't think I was trying to worm my way into your confidence by doing this."

Josh shrugged noncommittally.

"That's not why I did it," Rosemaria reiterated.

He turned his attention away from his food and looked at her. "Why did you do it?"

"Because it offended my sense of justice. Because there was a life at stake and Hahn was pushing his weight around out of petty vindictiveness." She grabbed another fry, dipped it in his ketchup, and chewed it vigorously.

They ate in silence until Rosemaria spoke. "How did Noor get her name?"

"My first-grade teacher, Eleanor Hendricks. She convinced my mother I had talent and needed a guitar. Her husband called her Noor."

"That's nice. So, you always knew what you wanted to do?"

"Always."

"I wish I could say the same."

More silence as they sipped their coffee.

"Would you mind taking me back now? I want to be there when Noor wakes up." He patted his pockets and a mortifying thought struck him. "I ah, don't seem to ah..."

"My treat." She brushed off his embarrassment easily. "Let's get you back to Noor."

They drove back in silence. She stopped in front of the entrance. "Hahn can't touch you now, so don't worry about that and just concentrate on Noor."

He hesitated before opening the door. "I meant what I said earlier."

She looked at him questioningly.

"You got the magic touch, lady."

He was out of the car and limping away before she could say anything.

"Shit!" She slammed her palm into the steering wheel. There was no way she would allow herself to be attracted to this musician-animal-nut murder suspect. And there was no reason to feel guilty about what she had done tonight. None at all. She was still a cop and she was doing her job. But she had to face an obvious fact—Josh Sibley couldn't kill a fly.

CHAPTER SEVENTEEN

LOS ANGELES

Rosemaria was at her desk and Waite and Osborne were seated in chairs in her cubicle, intent on studying their laptop screens they'd set down on Coleman's desk. She had gotten home a few hours before dawn after dropping off Josh at 3:00 a.m. She couldn't get to sleep until 4:00, had to get up at 7:00 to be at this meeting, and now she was so tired she was breathing from memory. They were waiting for Coleman, who had been trying to track down Jennie Seger. Her eyes started to close, and her head was beginning to fall when a quiet voice woke her up. "Baker?" Oh, God, the Lieutenant. Her head snapped up. "Yes, sir."

"Report to me after you interview Mrs. Levy. Is she here yet?"

"No, sir, she should be here shortly."

He nodded briskly and walked back to his office, passing Coleman on the way, who stepped aside with a smile and let his boss pass.

Rosemaria looked at him through bleary eyes. "Any luck?"

"She's not at home and Ken says she hasn't been in the office since the shooting. He's worried about her."

"Well, we know she visited Josh in the hospital, so she's probably okay."

"According to Ken, she and Stan had something going, maybe platonic, maybe something else. Whatever it was, they kept it under wraps."

"Undoubtedly to avoid Lila's wrath." Rosemaria had a hard time keeping the sneer out of her voice.

"So, she's drowning her sorrows somewhere," Coleman offered.

Rosemaria looked over at Waite, still focused on his laptop. "Waite, you're good at finding people who don't want to be found."

"I'm on it."

"What'd you find out about Lila's murky past?"

Coleman chuckled as he sat down at his desk. "Does it have to be murky just because she's a gorgeous female you don't like?"

"Just when we were starting to become good friends."

Waite coughed to get their attention. "Not too difficult to find out about Lila. She was born in Salinas to a mother who worked in the office of a tractor company. The father ran off when she was six and disappeared off the radar. Lila graduated high school, worked part-time at Taco Bell, then moved to L.A. and lived with a photographer for a year, left him for a casting director, left him for Stan, who gave her a couple of small acting jobs and then married her."

"Rosemaria stood up and stretched her arms above her head. "Print out your report for me, will you? I want to go over it before we talk to her."

Osborne lifted his head. "Anything you want me to do?"

Rosemaria walked over to the printer and waited thoughtfully as it printed. She grabbed the report and read as she walked back to her chair. "Mother, Cassie Bauer, still lives in Salinas. Father, Ernest, works freelance construction, whereabouts unknown. Before we talk to the transportation captain and Jennie, we need to have a word with the mother. Will you do that, Osborne?"

"I'm on it. I can drive up to Salinas in the morning. Levy's funeral is in two days. I'll bet Jennie and Moe will be there."

"Wouldn't miss it. Not looking forward to the press being there, though." She absently answered her cell phone as she scanned the rest of the first page. "What's up?...What room? Thanks, Lonnie."

She looked at Coleman, who was already on his feet. "It's show time."

Rosemaria studied the woman seated across from her and had to admit she was everything any woman in her right mind would want to look like. Lila's beauty was of such exquisite perfection, there wasn't even any point in being envious. Who could compete with this? You merely admired it like any other piece of art. Even now, with tears streaming down her flawless face, there was no mascara running and no makeup caked at the sides of her mouth or under her eyes, all of which seemed to happen to Rosemaria if she even sniffled slightly at a sad movie.

Lila had her compact out anyway, dabbing at invisible imperfections. "Are you sure we can't get you anything to drink?" Coleman asked.

She answered in a tiny voice. "No, thank you."

Rosemaria had advised her of her rights but she agreed to talk to them before her lawyer came. She was either very naïve or playing them. Rosemaria bet on the latter.

"I know this must be very difficult for you," Coleman said.

Lila nodded and sniffed into her tissue.

"Do you have any idea of who could have done this to your husband?"

"No, he was a wonderful man. Everybody loved him."

"And the two of you got along? You were happy?"

"Very. He was going to put me in his movie. He had that much faith in me."

Rosemaria and Coleman exchanged looks.

"So, everything was fine between you that night?"

"Well…"

"Did you have a fight that night?" Rosemaria asked.

"No!...Yes! But it wasn't anything unusual!" Lila was going on the defensive.

"Where did this happen?"

"At home, in the afternoon, when he came home."

"And you left right after that?

"Yes."

"Was he expecting any visitors?"

"I didn't bother to ask."

"What was the fight about?"

"His cocaine habit! I hated it! It made him mean and not like himself at all!"

Coleman took over more gently. "That must have been a terrible thing to live with."

"It was. I loathe drugs and alcohol. He promised to stop and then he never did."

"Did it make you angry when he told you that you wouldn't be in his movie?" Coleman asked.

Lila looked up at him sharply. "How...I didn't..." She seemed stunned that he would know.

"You'd worked so hard and the recording was everything you'd hoped for, and yet they were going to give Joell the role you deserved."

Lila's face hardened and she looked down at her clenched hands.

"That must have been very frustrating for you. Of course, you needed to get away for a while. So, where did you go?"

"Yes, it was hard. What do you think? I put my heart and soul into that damn song." Angry tears sprang into her eyes.

"Where did you go?"

She snapped out her words and brushed the tears away. "I drove up the coast and slept in my car in a rest area. I was too exhausted from crying to even find a motel. Then I drove back down to Oxnard and checked into where you found me. I didn't even know what happened until the police-man came."

"And what time did you leave home?"

"I don't know. I was so upset, I just ran out of the house...maybe around four in the afternoon, something like that."

She abruptly changed gears and turned the full force of her helpless vulnerability on Coleman. "I didn't kill him. I couldn't have. He was every-thing to me. I would have stayed with him no matter what. Do you believe me?"

"Why would you lie? When you love somebody, you'll do anything for them."

Lila relaxed. "Yes, yes, that's true. That's how it was."

Rosemaria interrupted the love fest. "Do you think the murder had anything to do with his drug problem? Do you know where he got his cocaine?"

Lila turned to her. "No. I have no idea. I don't have anything to do with that world. Absolutely nothing. But I'm not an idiot. I know that people on the crew who want to get hired suck up to producers and directors by giving them drugs. Where Stan was getting his, I just don't know."

"He had been going at it for a long time. He had to have a regular supplier."

"That's up to you to find out. You're the cop." Lila really didn't like this woman. She put her teeth on edge. "Shouldn't my lawyer be here by now?"

Coleman smiled at her and took out his cell phone. "Let me check on that for you."

Waite and Osborne had been watching the interview on their laptops and looked up as Rosemaria and Coleman came back. Rosemaria sat at her desk and Coleman remained standing at the cubicle opening.

"Well, what do you think?" Rosemaria asked of no one in particular.

"Snake, liar, dangerous comes to mind," Waite opined.

"Lost, needy, frightened," Osborne offered.

"Beautiful, sexy, great body," Coleman added.

"Rosemaria groaned. "Coleman, you are so predictable."

Coleman smiled and lifted his fore finger. "Did you notice in Harvey's report that she left her cell phone at home? Wouldn't you take that if you're going for a drive, no matter how upset you may be, especially if you're an actor?"

Rosemaria's eyes narrowed. "So, no one would be able to track where she really was that night or when she really left the house."

Coleman walked toward his desk but leaned on Rosemaria's instead, wrinkling her papers on purpose. "And you thought I was just another pretty face."

CHAPTER EIGHTEEN
LOS ANGELES

Josh was so relieved and happy about Noor, he almost didn't care that he still faced assault and battery charges. Almost. He did care that Lila was still missing and nightmarish images kept running through his head of her being dragged out of the house by Stan's murderer and killed and dumped by the side of the road. But if that had happened, they would have found her by now, or maybe not. Maybe her body was rotting out in the woods somewhere. He needed a drink, but the cupboard was bone dry and he didn't feel like running out to the store. He ran his fingers through his hair in frustration but knew there was nothing he could do but wait. He was pretty sure that Sergeant Baker didn't suspect him of killing Stan, but her bosses might, and being under suspicion was something he couldn't dwell on or he'd end up at the bottom of a bottle.

After a night and day of sleep, he'd finally woken up with a melody running through his head and he decided to shut out everything else and concentrate on making some changes in his musical. For ten years, he had been adding to and refining the book and lyrics, trying to make it perfect. Until it was perfect, no backer would hear a note. If there was a way to make a musical rejection-proof, he would find it. Getting the boot from ad execs was one thing, but this musical was a part of him. The words and the music were his soul laid bare. Rejection of this musical would be a rejection of him, and he would rather rewrite it for the rest of his life than let insensitive assholes with ledgers for hearts invalidate his work. Ken and

Jennie both thought he was crazy, but so be it. It was the one thing in life he had control of and he was going to keep it that way.

Two hours later, Josh looked up bleary-eyed from the pile of yellow legal pads and charts all around him and had to laugh. He hoped the cops would never decide they needed to search his place because if they did and they threw his stuff all over the place the way cops do, it would take days for him to figure out what went where. He was still in his terry cloth bathrobe and ravenously hungry. He decided to make himself some spaghetti, do a little more writing, and then go visit Noor. He would think about lawyers and that whole mess tomorrow.

As he stumbled into the kitchen, his cell phone rang, and he bent down and desperately dug through his pile of papers before he finally managed to snatch it up. "Hello."

The soft, almost whispered greeting was what he had been waiting for. Josh felt pure relief surging through his entire body. "Lila!

"Can you come see me?"

"Of course, I can. Are you okay? Where are you, at your house?"

"No, I don't ever want to go back there. I'm at the Beverly Hills Hotel."

Josh suddenly had second thoughts. "I want to see you, Lila, but do you think it's a good idea?"

"I don't care what they think! I need to see you!"

Josh sank down on the couch, knowing what the cops would think if they found out he had met with Lila. On the other hand, neither one of them had killed Stan. They couldn't prove anything, so why should they sneak around as if they were guilty?

"Take it easy, Lila. I'll be there. What room are you in?"

After he clicked off, he showered, dressed, and noticed his arm was almost healed. He hit Sunset in record time. He wove expertly though Saturday night traffic in Billy Jordan's old red Camaro, which Josh was borrowing for a few weeks while Ken's son was visiting his grandparents. As a vehicle, it was on a par with his almost dead Mustang, hopefully to be revived by his ever-faithful mechanic at the Econo gas station on Hollywood Boulevard. But it was wheels, and right now he was especially grateful he had them.

He passed through the lobby feeling, like always, that he didn't belong anywhere near such a bastion of wealth and privilege and took the elevator to Lila's floor. He was anxious to see her but didn't even know how he was supposed to interact with her; she had just lost her husband and may be overcome with grief. Should he act like just a friend or let her know his feelings for her? As soon as she opened the door, she erased any ambivalence about how he should behave as she flung herself into his arms before he even closed the door.

"Oh, Josh, I'm so glad you're here!"

He led her over to the sofa and gently set her down beside him as she sobbed softly. She leaned into him and he wrapped his arms around her, a part of him knowing he was taking advantage of her vulnerability and another part knowing that this had been inevitable from the first time he saw her.

"Why did you stay away, Lila?"

"I didn't know anything about what happened until I heard it on the news. I didn't want to come back. I was so scared. I thought they'd blame me."

"Why didn't you call me?"

"I was so shocked when I heard, I didn't know what to do or where to go."

"You can talk to me whenever you need to. Promise me you won't make me worry like that again."

"I promise. You're the one person I trust over anybody."

She pulled back and stood up. "Give me a minute, okay? I've been crying and I'm a total mess. I'm sorry."

He heard water running in the bathroom and looked around the suite, noting that it wasn't anything special and hardly worth the amount of money it probably cost to stay here. Hopefully, Stan hadn't spent all his money on drugs and had left Lila well taken care of.

She came back out with a fresh face, free of makeup, and looking like a teenager. She stood by the window, looking out.

"I can hardly believe he's gone. Everything is so unreal."

"You need to call the police and tell them where you are. It's better than having them find you."

"Oh, I did that already. They found out where I a couple days ago."

"What?" Detective Baker had known where Lila was all along.

Lila saw the changed expression on his face and looked concerned. "Is something wrong?"

"No... nothing." He walked over to her and took both her hands in his. "When is the funeral?"

"Tomorrow. His brother from New York came out with his wife. He arranged everything and paid for a plot at Forest Lawn. Stan had told me his brother is rich, real estate or something like that, so I guess he can afford it...not that I could."

"Did Stan have insurance? Was the house paid for? He didn't leave you in debt, did he?"

Lila walked back to Josh and pulled him to his feet. "Questions, questions, I don't want to answer questions. I just need you to hold me." She pressed herself against him and his body reacted instantly. He wanted her so badly it made his teeth ache, but the thought of Stan's murdered body lying in the same house where he had first met Lila doused his libido and made it impossible for him to even think of betraying Stan before his body was even buried. He took her arms from around his waist and looked into her sweet face and realized he already loved her more than he had loved anybody in a long time. "Have you eaten today?"

"I haven't even thought about food."

"Well...you know what a hotel phone is for, don't you?"

"Room service?"

"Let's look at the menu and see what this hotel has to offer."

She gave him a peck on the cheek and walked over the desk. She picked up the menu and handed it to him.

"What is your pleasure, sir?"

"That's a loaded question, miss. Mind if I give it some thought?"

She studied him seductively, "Not for too long, I hope, I'm very hungry."

Reddening, he bent over the menu, knowing but not caring that he might be headed down a very slippery slope with this one.

* * * *

The sun was about to come up and smile on Hari in the twenty-four-hour market. Very much out of character, he was reading the Los Angeles Times with great interest. Even though Hari devoured The Enquirer, People Magazine, and other celeb gossip publications every day, he rarely looked at an actual newspaper. They had too much bad news, local and national, and who cares about the homeless problem in Venice or another bomb going off in some far-off country where people weren't happy unless they were blowing each other up?

However, this morning, he was reading the paper very carefully, sipping his coffee and contemplating his moves. The funeral for the TV director was today and all the actors who wanted to be seen and rub shoulders with producers and other big shots would be there. He bet that the wife would be playing to the reporters like crazy since, according to what he deduced from the scandal sheets, she was an actress who had yet to play a decent role even though her access to nepotism should have made it a no-brainer. If her own husband wouldn't hire her, she must really stink. But he, Hari, was the only person who knew that Miss Merry Widow had lied to the police about being out of town the night her husband was shot. He had seen her with his own eyes and so had the security camera above the door. This Levy case could be just the boost his career needed. The question was, should he go to the dead guy's wife (the market's owner had delivered a case of sparking water to her house once, so they had the address in the computer), or should he go to the police and get publicity as the man who helped break the case? The O.J. trial was way before his time, but he saw a special on it on TV and what stuck out for him was how Kato Kaelin was crucified by critics when he sucked up to O.J. and messed up royally on the stand. Hari wouldn't want that to happen to him. What good was publicity if everybody thought he was a self-serving little creep? He poured himself another cup of coffee. This would take some careful thinking and planning.

* * * *

From the hills of Forest Lawn in Burbank, the view of the valley was obscured by smog. Burbank was hazy and Glendale was even more so. To Lila, it all looked depressing and dirty and evoked an air of poverty and hopelessness. She was looking out past the grave of her husband at the industrial areas below, next to which thousands of people resided in their gray little houses and apartments. They were living inane, insignificant lives which were headed towards oblivion, never having made a contribution to this world and nobody caring whether they're dead or alive. She shuddered. She'd rather die right now than be like them.

She had made sure Stan's life insurance premiums had been paid. He had left her that much at least, and the house was almost paid for. She had some savings of her own and would make out just fine. Her only challenge was to keep the police off her case, and she knew, between her own powers of persuasion and her shark of a lawyer, eventually they would give up on her. There were people who needed to keep their mouths shut but even they couldn't incriminate her on anything. Nobody could prove she was in the house when Stan was killed, except one person, and he had completely disappeared. But not for good, of course. They had a lot of unfinished business to take care of.

She was standing next to Stan's brother, David, and his mousy wife, Ellen. If Lila had all that money, she sure would have owned a better wardrobe than Lila had seen Ellen wearing so far. Howard, who she needed to suck up to big time because he was her best chance to get some work out of loyalty to Stan, was standing next to them looking all teary-eyed as the Rabbi droned on and on. Stan hadn't been even a bit religious. This whole thing was such a farce. At least they had not insisted on sitting Shiva or anything over the top like that.

Josh and Ken were standing together, looking properly downcast. Jennie, next to Ken, was really crying her eyes out as if she had lost her best friend. What the heck was that all about? Olga was hunched over next to one of the other secretaries on the lot who Lila didn't know and looked like she could barely stand up. She had never been very nice to Lila, so screw her. On second thought, now that she worked exclusively for Howard, Lila might need Olga on her side later on.

As soon as the Rabbi finished his unending talking and carrying on, she would schmooze with the celebrities in attendance at the reception David and Ellen had arranged at the Smoke House. Only the most important people had been invited. Meanwhile, on the way to her limo, she would allow herself to be interviewed by the media, mixing proper grief and modest gentility, emulating her idol, Jackie Kennedy. She could portray just as much class as she did.

Oh shit! That bitch Baker and her sidekick, that drop-dead gorgeous cop whose name she couldn't remember, were making their way through the mob of reporters, rebuffing any attempts to interview them. Some other nondescript cop was with them as well. You'd think they'd leave her alone today, of all days! Of all the fucking nerve! They kept a respectful distance, not even looking at her as the Rabbi was winding down his talk. Mercifully, it ended, and Lila braced herself for them to approach her. But they didn't. One cop headed straight for Moe rat-whatever-his-name-was and Baker and her sidekick walked toward Josh, Ken, and Jennie. Lila couldn't see what happened next because she was immediately escorted down the hill toward the media with David on one side and Ellen on the other. She liked the optics of that—very Jackie Kennedy and Ted.

Coleman couldn't care less about talking to the media one way or the other. But he couldn't resist giving a couple of female reporters an appreciative eye just to annoy Baker as the three of them pushed their way through the crush of media. The reporters approached him hopefully, thinking that he would talk to them, but he continued past them without saying a word. For some reason, he enjoyed nudging Baker whenever he had a chance. She had really pissed him off in the beginning when she couldn't appreciate his jokes and harmless flirtation as if he was actually coming on to her. She was not his cup of tea in any way, shape, or form. He liked his women feminine and compliant—intelligent yes, strong, yes, but not anything like this major league queen bee with no sense of humor. And that story about her father and her boyfriend, that still grated at him.

Waite approached Radanovich, while Coleman followed Baker up the hill to where Jennie was walking toward them alongside Sibley and Jordan. He watched Jennie carefully as she came near and saw fear in her eyes that were red from crying. All his instincts told him this woman had something interesting to hide.

As Rosemaria walked toward Josh and the group of people who were with him, she felt an inexplicable pleasure at seeing him and smiled at him warmly, despite herself. "Hello, Josh. Sorry to intrude on everyone's grieving." He said nothing. Just glanced at her coldly, then looked away. Rosemaria wondered, "Now what the heck was wrong with him?!" She turned to Ken and held out her hand. "You must be Ken Jordan."

Ken shook her hand. "Nice to meet you. I talked to Detective... Coleman?" He nodded in Coleman's direction. "I don't know what more I can tell you, but I'll be glad to help you in any way I can."

"Actually, it's Ms. Seger we'd like to talk to." Rosemaria turned towards Jennie. "I'm assuming that would be you."

Jennie response was barely audible. "Yes."

"Would you mind speaking to us informally, at one of the coffee shops on Riverside?"

Jennie's voice was hoarse and shaky. "Sure. How about Patsy's. You know where that is?"

"I do. We'll follow you."

After a short drive into Burbank, Rosemaria, Coleman, and Jennie were ensconced in a booth and had ordered their coffees, with Coleman adding a cinnamon roll. They took off their coats and made themselves comfortable, Jennie facing Rosemaria and Coleman. Rosemaria had decided her partner would lead the questioning. She couldn't deny he had a certain effect on the opposite sex, even though she herself was completely immune to it. She had always made use of her partners' special talents.

"Thank you for agreeing to talk to us. I know this is a very difficult time for you," Coleman said gently.

"It's okay."

"We need to try and find out everything we can as soon as possible."

It didn't take Jennie long to warm up to Coleman, Rosemaria noticed. "I know. I've seen that on TV, the First 48 and all that."

He smiled. "Well, maybe not that fast but it would be preferable." The waitress brought their coffees and his cinnamon roll. He gave Jennie time to take a sip of her coffee and pulled off a piece of his roll, put it in his mouth, and chewed appreciatively. "This is good. Anybody want a bite?" No takers, so he continued affably.

"We've been trying to find you, but you haven't been home."

"I didn't mean to be hard to find. A friend has a place at the beach. I needed a shoulder to cry on."

"Well, that makes sense. I gather you were very close to Mr. Levy."

Jennie hesitated as if talking about Stan was unbearably painful. "We were friends. We met when I had just been fired from an assistant's job at the studio on another show—not his—before I started working for Ken."

"And you met where?"

"Outside the commissary. I was upset over losing my job and literally ran smack dab into him as he was headed inside. He took me inside and sat me down and talked to me like I was an actual human being instead of the nobody that I was. He told me when there was an opening on his show, he'd hire me. But after interviewing with Ken, I realized I really liked him and would have some stability for a while. It's worked out for me."

"But you and Stan kept in touch?"

"He was always nice to me." She broke down and wiped the tears off her face with her napkin. "He hired me for small parts on his show so I could get some experience and maybe somebody else would hire me, too."

"I didn't know you were an actress."

"I hardly ever work, so I can't say I'm much of one."

"Did Lila know about your friendship with Stan?"

"She knew we knew each other but he didn't tell her about when we met for lunch or anything. If she had known, she wouldn't have liked it much...even though, to her, I'm a total loser."

"I don't know that she has any right to say that. She doesn't exactly have her name up in lights, either."

Jennie looked at him gratefully. "She's beautiful and she was married to a director. It was just a matter of time."

"Don't underestimate your own looks, Jennie. You've got a lot going for you and you're young, you have plenty of time."

She grabbed another napkin as the tears started flowing again. "That's what Stan used to say."

Rosemaria let her cry for a few seconds, then, "Were the two of you more than friends, Jennie?"

Jennie blew her nose again, her face splotched red by grief. "No, I was more than willing, but Stan was faithful to Lila. She didn't deserve it, but he was."

Rosemaria's ears perked up. "Why, was there someone else in her life? Her maid mentioned there might have been someone."

Jennie picked up her purse. "I don't know. I don't know anything. Please, can we talk some other time? I just want to go home and be by myself. Please." She looked at Coleman, her eyes pleading with him to understand.

"Sure, we can talk some other time," Rosemaria said. "Just tell me before you go, do you know where you were the night Stan was killed?"

Her eyes grew wide. "You think I could have killed him? I was home! Home by myself, where I usually am." She grabbed her coat and purse and slid out of the booth. "I don't know how you could even ask me that!"

Coleman watched Jennie run out the door and down the street to her car. He glanced at Rosemaria as he took a money clip out of his back pocket and pulled out several bills. "Now there's a girl who's definitely hiding something."

Rosemaria reached in her purse. "You won't mind if we go Dutch?"

"Wouldn't have it any other way."

Her cell phone beeped, and she took it out and read the text. "Moe gave Waite the slip at the funeral. Said he had to get back to the studio pronto." She started texting. "I'm telling Osborne to get over there and nail him down. That slime-ball drug dealer will talk to Osborne or we'll haul him in. You and I will go to Howard's office and have a few words with him. Then you, Jimmy, and I can confab at the studio.

"What the hell is confab anyway?"

"If you have to ask, you're not really in showbusiness."

"Feeling the irresistible pull of glitter and tinsel, are we?"

"Cut out your tongue and grind it in the garbage disposal."

"Only if you say please."

Rosemaria grabbed the check and headed for the cash register.

CHAPTER NINETEEN
LOS ANGELES

They were in Howard Grossman's office, which was understated—no expensive furniture, just a long wooden table as a desk, shelves filled with books and scripts. There were no pictures on the wall with himself and celebrities, only a few family portraits with his wife and two teenage sons. Rosemaria liked that. He was a successful producer, but not self-aggrandizing. Howard was the one person she had eliminated as Levy's killer. As her mother used to say about solid, upstanding men—this guy was a mensch.

Rosemaria and Coleman were seated in front of his desk when Howard walked in and sank heavily into his chair facing them, a little harried and distracted. "Sorry I'm a few minutes late. We just broke for lunch. I've had so much to deal with—too many people to talk to about this show, the feature, backers wanting to know when and if production is starting, and I'm still reeling over Stan's murder." He stopped talking and sighed. "I'm sorry. You're Sargant Baker and Detective Coleman and I'm happy to do anything I can to help you find Stan's killer. I saw you at the funeral, but Lila insisted I come with her to the wake, which seemed more like a typical Hollywood party to me. Most of those people didn't even know Stan but Lila insisted on inviting them, and, of course they came."

"We know how busy you are, Mr. Grossman." Rosemaria assured him. "We'll just take a few minutes of your time."

"Ask me anything."

"We know from Detective Osborne that you and Stan had been friends for years, best friends even."

"I hired him as assistant director right out of USC film school on *Night Games,* a show about undercover agents that had a lot of action. When my second unit director had an accident with a crane, Stan stepped in, took over, and the rest is history. Unfortunately, there was a lot of cocaine flowing on that show—cast and crew. Lots of night shoots, people had to stay awake—at least that was their excuse, mine too, if you must know. Stan and I had some high times together, literally. Fortunately, my wife stuck with me and helped me get clean. Stan kept right on going."

Coleman's eyes lit up like a diehard fan coming face to face with Leonardo DiCaprio. "You did that show? I watched it all the time. I loved those two actors—what were their names?"

"Terry Kline and George Matthews?"

"Yeah, they were great together. What are they doing now?"

"Don't know. Prodding their agents to get them work, I suppose."

Rosemaria tried to get things back on track.

"Was Moe Radanovich on that show?"

"That son of a bitch. No. Stan connected with him at some party. I didn't know until a few weeks ago that Moe's cousin in Vegas was Stan's drug dealer. Moe will never work on my show again or any other show on the lot, if I have anything to say about it, which doesn't mean much considering how the Teamsters throw their weight around."

"How did you find out?"

"I caught Stan snorting that crap in his trailer on set. I almost fired him, but he begged and pleaded and swore he'd quit, so what could I do? He was my best friend. I was stuck with Moe till the season was over."

Coleman seemed distracted for a moment. "I was wondering about Lila."

"Worst thing that ever happened to Stan."

"Could be, especially if she had anything to do with his death."

"She'd never give up her meal ticket."

"But we understand that you told Stan that she was no longer in the feature."

"Joell wanted to do it. It was a no-brainer."

"That must have made Lila very angry."

"I witnessed her explosive temper a time or two. I wouldn't want to be the target of that tornado."

"Would that have made her angry enough to have someone help her kill him?"

"No, the two of them might have had a knockdown, drag out fight, but to wait and plot and have him killed, I don't see it. She's impetuous and can be coldly calculating but if she calculated for even a few minutes, she'd come to the realization that without Stan, she'd be just another pretty face in a town of pretty faces."

"Olga mentioned that you might know who brought Lila to the party where she met Stan."

"Oh, sure, that was Vanessa Sheridan—nice girl, good actress. I've used her on my shows a couple of times. She and Lila are no longer friends."

"And Moe's cousin, do you happen to know his name?"

"No. If I did, I'd call the cops on him as soon as he showed his face." Howard pushed back from the desk and stood up. "Is that about it? I need to get back to the set."

"I think we're done here. Thanks for your help."

Howard ushered them into the outer office, where Olga was sitting over her computer. She looked up at them briefly, gave them a weak smile, and went back to pecking at the keyboard as if she barely had the will to keep working. As they were going out the door, Howard turned to Coleman. "Say, would you like to come on the set for a visit? Sam Anderson is the guest star. He worked a lot on *Night Games*. You must know who he is."

Coleman was instantly interested. "Sure! I remember him as their main contact at the bureau." He looked over at Rosemaria who had a neutral expression on her face that he recognized as a no. "Sorry. Thanks for the invitation but we have a meeting in a few minutes."

Howard walked out and gave them a brisk wave. "Any time. You're welcome on any set of mine."

Coleman knew he was in for it. Rosemaria looked at him with barely disguised amusement. Before she could fling one of her famous insults at him, he defended himself. "For Christ sake, so I watch TV and like certain actors! Are you totally immune to anything that has to do with acting and show business?"

"As a matter of fact, I am."

"But not singers, I'll bet."

Rosemaria was about to shoot an angry retort when they both spotted Osborne sitting with Moe at a picnic table by a food truck set up for lunch outside Howard's set. They immediately made a beeline for the two of them and sat down, Coleman next to Moe, Rosemaria next to Osborne.

"I hope we didn't miss anything important," she said sweetly. "I'm Sergeant Baker and this is Detective Coleman. We're investigating Stan's murder, too."

Osborne, calm as ever, nodded toward Moe. "He tells me his cousin knows nothing about drugs or murder or Stan's addiction to cocaine. Says his cousin met Stan once and that was it."

"Really?" Coleman sensed that when Rosemaria was nice to a suspect, the outcome would not be good for him.

"That's so interesting," She looked straight at Moe, "because we heard otherwise."

"I don't know who'd say that." Moe, not very tall, muscular, and a face like a boxer who'd been hit in the face one too many times, was squirming under her intense gaze.

"We're Beverly Hills cops, Moe. Do you know what that means?"

"You like the Pointer Sisters' music?"

Rosemaria slapped her hand on the table. "Oh, ha, ha, you're referring to the movie soundtrack of *Beverly Hills Cop?* Very clever, Moe. No, actually it means that we know a lot of people: Hollywood people, celebrities, actors, directors, producers, Las Vegas entertainers. Some of them get into a little trouble and we help them out and they help us out. You know what I mean?"

"What does that have to do with my cousin?"

"We know he deals drugs to people in this town and that he was Stan's connection. We're looking to connect him to Stan's murder and if you know something and aren't telling us, that is obstruction of justice and a felony. You want to go to jail, Moe, or keep driving trucks for movie producers?"

"Wait a minute. My cousin wouldn't have anything to do with any murder. He drives trucks like me, like my uncle and my father. We've been Teamsters for generations. It's what we do."

Coleman looked at him contemptuously. "So, your cousin decided driving trucks wasn't lucrative enough and on his jaunts down to Mexico, he managed to smuggle in some drugs. Very risky, Moe. What is he, an idiot?"

"He's no smuggler!"

Osborne had his cell phone out and was studying it. "But he is a criminal. According to LVPD, your cousin, Sal Radanovich, was arrested on charges of consorting with the head of a burglary ring and was caught carrying stolen items from Best Buy on his way to California in his truck."

"Charges were dropped on that."

Coleman smiled. "With your uncle's help, I'll bet."

Rosemaria glared at Moe. "Your father and your uncle can't help you out of this one, Moe. We're going to have Sal extradited and you're going down with him."

Osborne intervened as the kindly voice of reason. "That's all so unnecessary. If Moe was merely an intermediary, then maybe he knows somebody else who might have sold drugs to Stan or maybe he has some other helpful information. What do you say, Moe? No need for everybody to get hard-ass about this."

"I say you can talk to my lawyer."

Rosemaria stood up. "You got it, Moe. Next time we meet will be in Beverly Hills, and I don't mean Rodeo Drive." Coleman and Osborne laughed and Rosemaria joined in. "He'll find out soon enough that the Teamsters' reach doesn't extend to where we live. But he shouldn't worry guys, right? Our interrogations are very gentle. So why do people always end up telling us what we want to know?" More laughter. "I think we can tell the Lieutenant we got this one solved."

The three of them headed toward the parking lot laughing and were not surprised to hear Moe's voice behind them. "Wait a minute! We can talk. Come on back." The three gave each other knowing looks and walked back to the picnic table.

* * * *

If Lila had to have lunch in the Valley, the Fleur de Lys was the only restaurant she would even remotely consider eating in. She had been dodging the press and even for her, it was getting to be a bit much. The media was speculating about her possible role in the murder—why she disappeared and where she had gone and all that. She thought she had dealt with it pretty well and thrown suspicion on mysterious drug dealers the way everybody else accused of murder did, but it was not working. She was getting nervous and wondering if she really should be meeting with Josh. But if they had conspired to kill Stan, would they be meeting in a restaurant where everybody could see them? At least it was in the Valley and, for now, she could relax a little. Besides, she needed a favor from him, and he could be useful in more ways than one. She turned her little red Mercedes SLK into the driveway and waited for the valet.

Even though she was in no hurry, she hated being kept waiting. Lila had taken great pains to be at least thirty minutes late, but Josh still probably wouldn't be there. He was the only man she had ever met who could show up for an appointment later than she did. She took the ticket from the valet and walked to the restaurant entrance.

She waited for the couple ahead of her to open the door and the unmistakable purr of a Rolls Royce demanded her attention. It was Dick Bernadette. A snicker escaped her lips at the sight of him. Dick was the star of a hit action-adventure series in which he had the audacity to play a swashbuckling, macho, ladies' man. What a laugh. A few years ago, when he had been a struggling actor and dating Lila's roommate, he couldn't get a hard-on to save his life. After three months of heavy necking, the furthest his and Vanessa's lovemaking advanced was to intense handholding. As a man, the guy was pathetic. She had never liked him. Lila always felt he was more interested in her dates than in her, and that could mean only one thing. Ladies' man? I don't think so.

The maitre'd was not at his desk, as she surveyed the front room for interesting faces. She smiled at Dick when he came in. "Hello, Dick. How are you?"

He looked at her blankly, which infuriated Lila. How dare he pretend not to know her! "Lila? Lila Bauer? Levy?" She reminded him sweetly between tight lips. He pretended not to have recognized her until that instant, and then flashed his blinding white chicklet caps at her. "Oh, yes. Vanessa's roommate, Lila," he said, all the while looking past her into the dining room. "You've been in the papers recently. Nice to see you again." Excuse me, I have an interview with People Magazine."

It was all Lila could do not to smack him in the face. But that would never do. Not with everything else that was going on. She watched him walk to a table in the front room and effusively greet the middle-aged reporter seated there as Lila fumed to herself bitterly. That poor misguided woman is probably creaming in her pants. How I'd love to tell her and everybody else in the room what a ten-carat phony he is!

"Who're you staring daggers at?" Josh sounded slightly amused.

Lila started at the sound of his voice but recovered quickly and gave him a peck on the cheek. "Just lost in thought, darling," she answered with effortless guile.

"I only have an hour and then have to get back to work. I got my job back, thanks to some friends, and now I can see Noor all I want."

Lila was vaguely paying attention to him. To her dismay, they were seated at a table right next to Dick Bernadette, so she was forced to avoid looking at him while she scanned the room for important people. But they wouldn't touch her now, not with her being a possible murder suspect. She'd have to get past that before anybody would hire her. Even Howard wouldn't meet with her in public. Everybody was walking on tip toes until they saw which way the wind was going to blow. They'd be sorry when she was cleared, and all her notoriety was bringing in loads of offers. She'd pick and choose and remember everybody who had snubbed her.

"You're looking better than I expected, Lila," said Josh, seated across from her.

The undertone of disapproval, which she thought she detected, irritated her. "I've been crying my eyes out since the last time I saw you. If I have a nervous breakdown right here and now, will that make you happy?"

"Of course not," he reassured her. He looked around the room uncomfortably. "I told you when you said you wanted to meet here that I don't know if I can do more than pay for my part of the bill here. It's way over my budget."

"I have plenty of charge cards. Don't worry."

"It won't always be like this. I know things will turn around for me eventually."

She squeezed his hand. "I know. I have faith in you."

A wave of calm swept over Josh. With this beautiful lady on his side, maybe he could finally forget the past and make something of himself.

Lila brought the subject back to herself. "I couldn't afford to stay at the hotel any longer and had to go back home. Do have any idea how hard it is to have to walk by the living room where your husband was killed? This is a terrible strain on me." Her painted lips quivered.

"I'm sorry." It felt inadequate for him to keep saying that and be helpless to change anything.

She ran her eye over the menu and ordered without looking at the waiter who had appeared at her side. He started to announce the specials of the day, but she interrupted. "I'll have the poached salmon. House dressing on the salad. Nothing to drink except water."

Josh handed both menus to the waiter. "I'll have the spinach salad. No bacon."

Lila reached out for Josh to take her hand. She saw the caring in his eyes as he responded. "I need you to be there for me, Josh."

"Anything. You know that."

"The police searched my motel room in Oxnard and even at the Beverly Hills Hotel. That horrible Sergeant Baker suspects me of Stan's murder, I just know it. I can't stand her. Why does she want to ruin my life?" Her grip tightened on Josh's hand.

Josh squeezed her hand and tried to dispel her worries. "She's just asking questions. We have to get used to it until this whole thing is over."

Lila studied his face. He seemed to be avoiding her eyes. "Have you talked to her again? Did she ask anything about me?"

"A couple of times, and yes, she asked about you."

"And you defended me, didn't you?"

"Of course, I did. Stop worrying so much."

The past week had made her anxious and insecure but how ridiculous to think that a boring, plain Jane like Sergeant Baker was any threat to Lila Levy. She had to get on with more important things. "I have something to ask you."

"Your wish is my command."

She smiled despite the hackneyed cliché. She seemed to have no patience for anything anymore. "About my career. With everything that's happened, to be frank, it's in the toilet. I can't get auditions—nobody will even meet with me—but if you know of any commercial Ken has coming up, maybe..." Her voice trailed off when she noticed his lack of enthusiasm. "What?" she said more harshly than she meant to.

"Don't you think we should wait a while?"

"I don't want to wait. I don't want to dwell on all this negativity. Can't you write your next commercial for a female singer?"

"If commercials came along for me that easy and often, we could eat here every day. They are few and far between, I'm afraid."

She tried to hide her disappointment. She didn't want to push too hard and maybe push him away. Although she doubted that was possible. Besides, there were other ways to get what she wanted from him.

Their salads came and Josh all but dived into his. Lila hated when people ate like they'd been starving for a week. She brought a small piece of lettuce to her mouth and chewed delicately and chatted amiably about inconsequential topics, avoiding all talk of Stan and murder. Josh seemed quiet, even though she was considerate enough to ask how his court case was going and saying she was sorry his sessions with Joell had been postponed until the feature went back into production, even though the subject was so painful it made her stomach hurt. She also remembered to ask about that big cat he treated like a person, a topic that bored the hell out of her.

She didn't mind hurrying through lunch, since no one of any significance was eating there today, and Dick Bernadette was dragging out the interview, forcing her to keep avoiding his insipid face. It was beyond her comprehension what he could be talking about. The guy was so stupid, it wouldn't have surprised her to find out he was clinically retarded.

Outside, she gave Josh a chaste kiss on the cheek and watched him walk down the street to where he had a beat-up Camaro parked by a parking meter. He was sexy as hell and would help her if he could, but God, was he poor! There was always the possibility that he would hit it big with one of his songs or that Broadway show he was always working on, but chances of that were slim to none. He was not future husband material but was useful for now. The valet brought up her own beautiful SLK, thankfully paid for and all hers.

As she waited for traffic to pass before pulling out into the street, her eyes suddenly clouded over with tears. Out of nowhere, she felt a dark depression settling over her. There were so many things to handle right now, not the least of which was the most important man in her life, who had vanished without a trace. It was all starting to overwhelm her. She angrily brushed the tears off her face. She had put up with a lot to get what she wanted. Nothing and nobody, not even him, was going to take it away from her.

* * * *

Officers Vera and Nicholson were parked in an unmarked car at the Standard Station near some fancy French restaurant. Fifteen-year veterans both, surveillance still never bored them. When they tired of reading the sports pages and eating, which was almost never, they enjoyed analyzing the lives and problems of the people they were following. Officer Vera had figured these two out just by what he read in the papers He watched Lila drive by and started up the car. "Here we go."

Officer Nicholson finished up the soggy falafel his wife had packed for him that morning and licked the grease off his fingers, hoping she'd get off her recent health kick, like yesterday. "How come we're following her instead of him?"

"You wanna ask Sergeant Baker why, you ask her."

"Would I dare question our trusted leader?"

"I hope she nails 'em."

They saw Josh drive by them in his Camaro.

"I guess he'll be trading that piece of shit in for a Tesla soon."

The possibility raised the hackles of Officer Vera. "Not if I can help it," he said and aimed the car up Coldwater Canyon, not too close behind Mrs. Levy.

CHAPTER TWENTY

LOS ANGELES

Rosemaria and Coleman were standing in front of the Lieutenant's desk, watching him scroll through their report on his computer. He was dressed immaculately, as usual, in a light gray suit, blue silk shirt, and matching tie. All cops reacted to the stress of their jobs in one way or another and the Lieutenant's was to become hermetically sealed. Rosemaria knew that he had spent his early years in the Rampart division a few years after a corruption scandal gave the division a bad name. He had worked hard as a rookie to prove cops were the good guys and was almost killed when a woman was held hostage inside a liquor store. He managed to sneak in the back door and surprise the robber but got himself shot in the process. After a few weeks in the hospital and a month recuperating at home, he went back to the job more determined than ever to build a name for himself. He worked his way up in the system and finally landed in Beverly Hills, as straight a cop as Rosemaria had ever known. He had given her a chance to prove herself and she felt guilty about leaving him for the courtroom, but until then, she would make sure she didn't disappoint him. "Moe convinced Sal to come in on his own tomorrow."

"No lawyer?"

"That's what he said. We'll see."

The Lieutenant was still glancing down at the report. "Mrs. Levy couldn't have done it on her own. Someone else would've had to have been there. What's your take on Sibley?"

Coleman spoke before Rosemaria had a chance. "He's so in love with Mrs. Levy, he can hardly see straight. We had officer Mira pose as a diner with officer Lloyd when Levy and Sibley had lunch yesterday. She said Sibley acted like a love-struck teenager the whole time, looked at her like she was a cross between Marilyn Monroe and the Mona Lisa—Mira's words, not mine."

"We can't indict him for being lovestruck." Rosemaria said, irritated at the pang of jealousy that shot through her.

The Lieutenant smiled. "We'll wait until we have the facts, then. We need the gun to prove it was Stan's. That would tend to link Lila to the murder. I'm inclined to believe if it was some sort of drug hit, which I find farfetched, they would have brought their own guns to the party. Stan was paying Sal good money on a regular basis—why kill the goose that was laying all those golden eggs? I'm inclined to go with Coleman's theory: somehow, Mrs. Levy is involved with this and you need to find out what would have motivated her to destroy her own cushy situation. Maybe there's someone else in Lila's life that we don't know about. Find him."

The Lieutenant looked up at Rosemaria, "By the way, did this small favor you did for Sibley help gain his trust?"

Coleman couldn't help himself and instantly regretted it. "Small?"

Rosemaria ignored him. "I think so. I think he's starting to open up to me."

Lieutenant Mandel pursed his lips. "Talk to Langston about the Laurel Canyon killings that he's working on. Not quite the same M.O. but the bullets were .38 Specials and the victim was a rich lawyer who also happened to be a heavy drug user. Could be related."

The Lieutenant opened his maroon Cartier briefcase and placed a thin spiral notebook in it. He liked to keep his paperwork to a minimum. "All four of you are doing a good job; your reports are very thorough. Right now, I have a lunch appointment with your father, Larry. It's been awhile since I've seen him. Is he doing well?"

"He is. They just got back from Barbados."

"If anything breaks, I want to know right away."

"Yes, sir." She turned to go, but the Lieutenant's words stopped her, and she turned back to him.

"Keep working on Sibley, Sergeant, but don't get too close, okay?"

"Don't worry sir, I know what I'm doing." Were her feelings that obvious? She needed to get herself under control.

She followed Coleman back to their desks and he sat on the corner of hers in his usual spot. She avoided putting papers there now. "So, who the heck is your father?"

"Stepfather. Commissioner Collins. I kept my real father's name."

"Wow. You could've told me."

"Didn't think it was important."

"Collins is really, really rich."

"That he is."

"That means you're really rich."

"Pretty much."

He jumped off her desk. "I think I'll call Langston and have him send over what they have on the Laurel Canyon killings. That okay with you?"

"Yeah, yeah. I'll see what I can find out about Vanessa Sheridan. We need to talk to her."

Rosemaria was starting to feel a slight but growing sliver of respect for Coleman. He had everything handed to him on a silver platter yet here he was, working a case, following leads, asking no favors, just like the rest of them. Well, well, well, will wonders never cease?

* * * *

It was an exceptionally hot December day and Lila's room was open to the full blast of heat. She hated the unnatural coldness of air-conditioning and rarely used it. But the beads of perspiration forming on her upper lip that she saw reflected in her dressing room mirror were not caused by the summery climate. She wiped away the sweat with her fingers. As her agitation grew, she pressed them down on the worry lines that appeared on her forehead, all the while focusing her attention on the voice at the other end of the cell phone that she held tightly to her ear.

"Why haven't you called before now?! I was worried sick!" she cried out. His answers angered her, and she threw herself down on the silk pink and yellow chaise lounge. "Why do you always have to put her first? I'm the one who needs you now!?" She sat up in panic. "No! You can't go now! I'm fine as long as you say you won't ever leave me. I love you. Do you love me? Say it!"

She hated the way he made her lose self-control, but she had long ago stopped fighting her need for him, even now after all that had happened. And if he stayed in her life, somehow, somewhere, she could dredge up the strength to fight the battles she had to fight in this lousy town. If only he hadn't destroyed her trust and allowed an invader into their lives, she felt she could do anything. She had asked him time and again to tell her who it was. She *needed* to know who it was. But Lila knew it was hopeless. He would never tell her. But, as she listened, his words calmed the doubts that clawed at her heart. She was Lila Levy...beautiful, talented, and she would find a way out of all of this.

* * * *

Martha had been very disappointed to find out that Gilbert had been taken back to the zoo. She had taken a special liking to the little cub and had treated him almost as lovingly as she treated Josh's plants. The crazy bird she could live without.

Josh had watched her that morning, fussing with his withering palm, wiping the dust from each leaf, lovingly bringing it back to life. He could see the remnants of her gentle soul, now bruised and battered, and wondered why life had forced her to find peace in a bottle of gin or if it was booze that had caused her downfall in the first place.

He checked his messages as he watched her work and was surprised to hear Lila's voice. She hadn't called him since their lunch two days ago, and even then she had seemed distracted and distant. He had hoped that she would turn to him even more after what had happened; instead, she seemed further away than ever. She wanted him to take her to a party tonight. Josh hated Hollywood parties, but at least this gave him a chance to see her again.

His lawyer had also left a message for him to return the call and said that they had drawn a judge who was a former prosecutor. Not good. Josh decided he had two days to avoid thinking about it.

After Martha had finished with his plants, he had escorted her to the door and paid her for her services. He would have liked to have given her more than usual, but he knew she would never allow him to pay more than what was fair. Martha would rather go through trash bins to find what she needed and, crazy as it was, he admired her cock-eyed sense of pride.

Now he sat beside Lila as she drove along Mulholland and watched her perfect profile, intent on every treacherous curve that plunged hundreds of feet straight down into the San Fernando Valley. Despite everything that had happened, just looking at her made him happy. He finally understood her dependence on Stan. Everyone needed a benefactor to make it in the business, someone important, whether it was a relative or a lover, but someone who cared about you and had clout and could get you in to see the right people. For Lila, that had been Stan. In Hollywood, lovers and users were hard to tell apart, but when it came to Lila, he admitted he didn't really want to know why she needed him. He only knew that she felt cast adrift, alone in a business where every actress was a bimbo or an over-the-hill nobody, until she was lucky enough to become a star. If stardom eluded you, you were nothing, a big fat zero. You spent life in a deep dark pit, struggling to crawl out, sometimes giving up and wallowing in your depression, then gathering up all your strength and willpower and struggling again. It was a curse and a mystery to him why, for a performer, living a normal obscure life was a deep dark pit, but Josh wanted to avoid that pit just as much as Lila did. He shook the morbid thoughts out of his head, and Lila reached over and patted his thigh.

"You okay?"

"Never better."

They rounded a curve and stopped in front of a house that was on the city side of the road. Please, let it not be one of those things on stilts. Josh always expected an earthquake when he was in one of those. The parking valet took charge of the Mercedes and Lila and Josh walked towards the house. He saw it was on stilts. That, combined with his dread of parties, made him even less eager to go in. Lila sensed his mood.

"Come on, lighten up. There's a lot of music industry people here. This could be good for your career."

"I don't need parties and sucking up to people to get ahead."

"Are you kidding? Your career is pathetic. It's in a nosedive to nowhere."

Her comments hit a raw nerve and he stiffened. She tightened her grip on his arm.

"Oh, for Pete's sake. It's not that you're not talented. Besides, if all goes well, you'll have a hit record with Joell and be looking at me in your rearview mirror." She brushed a kiss on his cheek.

It was too late to make a getaway now. Lila had rung the bell and the door was opening.

"Look happy," she hissed.

Their hostess, a fortyish blond with a tight face and big lips, led them into the living room and excused herself into the kitchen. Josh ordered vodka rocks at the bar over Lila's objections, and she placed a few raw veggies on her plate from the buffet table. A rhythm and blues ballad was blaring out of the stereo.

"They're playing Lonnie Sylvester's new album. Isn't it great? I've got to figure out a way to meet him."

"Why don't you just go over and talk to him?"

He accepted a carrot stick she handed him, and he nibbled on it, looking around the crowded room for a familiar face.

"I want to," Lila said hesitantly, "but I just can't. I wish I weren't so shy."

The absurdity of her remark made Josh choke on his carrot and Lila patted his back absentmindedly.

"Well, maybe," she considered. "I'll be back in a minute." She made a beeline for a black man surrounded by a coterie of admirers, and Josh thought he might as well take his drink out on the deck and see how far he would fall when the earthquake hit. Halfway across the deck, he could see it would be a long way.

"Josh." A familiar voice stopped him from turning around and going back to the relative safety of the living room. Ken was standing on the deck a few feet away, laughing at him. "You, at a party?"

Relieved to see a friend, Josh held out his hand. "How you doin', buddy?"

Ken shook his hand and slapped him affectionately on the shoulder. "The power of a gorgeous woman."

Josh looked at the deck floor, both self-conscious and proud that someone as beautiful as Lila might be interested in him. "We're just friends. She just lost her husband. I have to give her time."

"I understand."

"She said this party would be good for my career."

"No explanations necessary. You have a hearing in two days, don't you?"

"How about coming up with a job for me so I can pay my high-priced lawyer?"

"Who'd you get?"

"Public defender."

Ken shook his head. "Not a good thing, Josh. You need somebody good or you could end up in jail."

"You got no faith in the system, Kenny," Josh responded with a light-heartedness he didn't feel.

"Find an experienced lawyer, Josh. I'll bust my hump to get you a job. The Hines bread commercial has yet to be shot. The old man hated the rapper and we still haven't settled on anybody."

"I'm available." Josh downed his drink and Ken nodded his head in the direction of the living room.

"Got to go back inside and schmooze." He smiled and left Josh standing by himself on the deck, looking like he was trying to decide which was worse: staying outside where he expected the deck to give way beneath him or going back inside and talking to people he couldn't care less about talking to.

Ken wound his way through the crowd to the bar, worried as always about his friend being at a party like this. It had taken exceptional restraint to keep from asking Josh to take it easy on the alcohol. Josh never seemed able to take one or two drinks and leave it at that. He had to keep going till he ran out of booze or passed out. Whatever insecurities Josh was wrestling with seemed to be gaining on him, but even after eight years of friendship, they had never discussed what they might be.

The bathroom was occupied, and Ken leaned against the wall to wait, noticing Lila in action just a few feet away. It didn't take much perception to see that Lila was not the fragile, helpless flower Josh had described. She was flirting outrageously with Lonnie's publicist and one of his musicians. If Josh happened to wander out into the hallway and catch an eyeful, the results would be disastrous. But, he thought, as an attractive brunette came out of the bathroom sniffing and pulling at her nose, maybe that would be for the best in the long run. He went in the bathroom and came out just in time to see the musician place both hands firmly on Lila's behind as Josh rounded the corner from the living room. There was no use interfering. The result was inevitable—disaster.

Josh, his face set grim and hard, grabbed one of the musician's offending arms and pulled him away from Lila. He shoved the astonished man against the wall, pushing his forearm against his throat.

"You keep your fucking hands off her, or I'll shove them down your throat and pull them out your ass," Josh growled, inches away from the man's face.

The musician was trying desperately to nod in agreement, but Josh's grip was too tight for him to move much. The color of his face was changing from red to blue. Ken couldn't tell what Lila was thinking. She was standing still, fascinated by what was going on. A crowd had formed around them, and Ken finally moved toward Josh to convince him not to kill the man.

Josh let the man down before Ken got there, then grabbed Lila's arm and half dragged her towards the front door, leaving his hapless victim hungrily sucking in air to fill his oxygen-starved lungs.

Ken didn't bother following them. Josh's intensity would take a while to die down. Let Lila deal with it. That lady had a talent for getting into trouble and Josh was the perfect candidate for getting her out. He wondered how far Josh was willing to go to play knight in shining armor, and he hoped this little incident didn't get back to the cops.

"I'm not angry, Josh. You rescued me from a disgusting letch. I'm grateful."

Josh had insisted on driving and Lila hadn't argued. She tried to snuggle close, but the console made it difficult.

"I didn't ruin anything for you, did I?" he grumbled.

Lila could see he was still boiling, but his guilt would come in handy. "Of course not. Show business people love theatrics like that."

"I wasn't acting, Lila."

"Oh, I know, I know." Her voice was sweet and tender. She didn't want his temper flaring up again. "You know what I mean. Tell me more about what Ken said."

"It's just a possibility."

"But you will use me if—." He didn't let her finish.

"I told you. I'll do the best I can."

She put her lips against his cheek then murmured, "I know you will, honey, and that's good enough for me."

Officer Nicholson was frantically signaling Officer Vera to get in the car. Their suspects were taking off and his partner was shooting the breeze with one of the parking valets a few feet up the road. After the couple had passed the unmarked car by only a few inches and rounded the curve out of sight, he leaned out of the window and yelled for his partner to hightail it out of there. Officer Vera jumped in the car, cackling.

"You won't believe what just happened in there. That Sibley character is a wild man. Wait'll I tell Sergeant Baker about her number one suspect. We'll make her day!"

* * * *

They pulled into a parking lot behind a liquor store only a block from Josh's apartment. If Lila had had a choice, she would never have set foot in this filthy part of town. And this parking lot, in this neighborhood, littered with derelicts, empty booze bottles, and other garbage, was no place to leave her beloved red Mercedes. Josh assured her that the store owner would keep an eye out, and that he had always parked his own car there. Who the hell would have wanted his ancient pile of rust anyway? she thought but refrained from saying. Lila was not comforted by the sight of two dirty men sifting through the dumpster by the back entrance of the store, but she decided not to make an issue of the car. Tonight was too important. She had come up with the idea of having Josh pitch her recording of the movie song to Ken's friends at a recording company to convince them to sign her to a record deal, with Josh writing the songs. He would then teach her how to sing them and produce them as well.

"I'm ready, yes, I'm ready." A vile old man covered in corroding military medals, half sang, half spoke gibberish to them, and Josh actually had the bad taste to respond.

"How ya doing, General?" Josh asked absently, then hurried her along the sidewalk. If she hadn't been working him up to a full head of steam all the way home, she was sure he would have stopped and conversed with the demented old fool.

His apartment building was around the corner and not as bad as she had expected. The street was fairly clean but still in proximity to the slums nearby. The elevator was out of order and they had to walk up one floor to his apartment. She had a strong urge to run out and forget the whole thing. Keep your eye on the goal, she reminded herself, keep your eye on the goal.

Once inside his apartment, they had to step over piles of yellow legal pads and sheets with notes scribbled on them that littered the living room floor. Even when Lila had been dirt poor, she wouldn't have tolerated living in a pig pen like this. He led her toward the bedroom, passing a bird cage covered by a dark cloth. She saw at least the sheets looked clean. They undressed wordlessly in the dark. Lila slid out of her low-cut silk sheath and laid it carefully over a chair. Josh ripped off his jacket, shirt, and trousers and let them lay where they fell. She could see by the streetlight shining through the window that he was already fully erect. She had to slow him down or everything would be spoiled. Josh shoved the sheets and blankets aside and pulled her down on top of him. He caught her head from behind and pulled her mouth hungrily toward his. His body felt large and masculine, but his lips were surprisingly warm and yielding. The slight softness in his stomach and buttocks only made him feel more sensual and inviting.

He ran his hands lightly down her back, then lifted her forward until her breasts were over his mouth. He sucked on one nipple eagerly, manipulating the other expertly between his thumb and forefinger. Lila was horrified to find herself responding. The blood was pounding between her legs, and her resolve was getting weaker by the second. Only one other person was capable of evoking this kind of reaction from her. She was tempted to give in and luxuriate in the moment. Almost. She pushed herself away from his mouth and brought her face down close to him. Josh looked at her with eyes glazed over with desire and tried to pull her mouth down to his but she teased him with a brief kiss and slipped down his body slowly.

"Slow, Josh, let's go slow," she whispered, moving her lips and tongue down his chest.

"Do you love me, Josh?"

"Yes, yes." His eyes were closed, and his breath was harsh and labored.

"Tell me. Say the words." She flicked her tongue and nuzzled his chest and he shuddered.

"I love you, Lila."

She moved down his stomach, enjoying his need for her.

"I want you to say it in a special way, Josh."

She was kissing his thighs, then raised her head slightly.

"Will you tell it to me in a song?"

She could see the great effort he was exerting to hold back.

"Something really, really special?" She sounded more urgent now.

He took hold of her head with both hands and guided her mouth down between his legs.

"It would mean so much to me, baby."

"Yes, yes, I promise I'll write you a song."

"Tomorrow?"

"Yes, tomorrow."

She enveloped him and gave him what he wanted. He moaned as if in agony and came almost immediately. She gently released him and lay her head on his stomach. She smiled with satisfaction. She could have just made her request without the sex, she supposed. But this way it was ingrained in his entire body that he must write her a song, and if she had her way, more songs. This was just the beginning. She would give Josh a few minutes and then he could administer to her needs. Considering Josh's talent and her drive, she just might end up with a hit record, and fantasizing about her picture on the cover of Rolling Stone was sure to get her off tonight like gangbusters.

CHAPTER TWENTY-ONE

MARYSVILLE, WISCONSIN

The high-pitched scream echoed across the white fields and disappeared into the snowy mist. It was followed by a ripple of childish laughter and playful chatter.

"Again, again," Scott demanded. "Fun, lots of fun!"

"Follow me, then." Josh took Scott's hands and climbed slowly to the top of the slope, waiting patiently for him to take his small, clumsy steps, and half carrying him whenever his brother lost his footing and started to slide back down.

A snowfall two days before had covered the ground and reached just four feet below the eves of the tool shed in the back of the house. Josh had packed the snow so it created a small hill slanting down from the peak of the roof for Scott and him to slide down on an old innertube.

"Aaaaaah!" Scott screamed again as he slid down in the safety of Josh's arms. They were dumped out of the innertube at the bottom of the hill, covered with flying snow that snuck into their mittens and the tops of their boots. Josh hugged his brother in a sudden burst of affection, but Scott squirmed to be freed. Sullivan romped around in circles nearby and barked with excitement. He loved the snow, too.

"Again, again," Scott cried, and Josh complied. There was nothing more important to him than making his brother happy. Scott's first five years on earth had not been easy, and his future didn't hold anything much better.

It had only taken a year at the most after his brother came home from the hospital for Josh to realize that he wasn't developing the way he should have. The subject was never talked about, but he could guess from his parents' arguments that his father took it as a direct insult to his masculinity, and his mother perceived it as a failure on her part. His father never bothered to pretend that he loved Scott. He acted as though he didn't exist. His mother showed Scott some affection, but Josh could see the disappointment that was always underneath the surface of her emotions. After Scott was sent away to the special school, she was relieved to be able to go back to work almost full time, depending on how much she was needed on the farm.

Josh found it easy to love Scott. Despite his slowness, he was good-natured and no trouble to take care of—not at all like his friend Tim's cranky, bratty little brother. Every day, Josh had taken Scott with him when he did his chores after school. And when Josh had sung him to sleep every night, Scott rewarded him with a look of such peaceful contentment, Josh figured God had given him his musical talent just for the purpose of putting that look on the little boy's face.

After Scott had been sent away, Josh had felt as though his heart would break. He had let Scott down and there was nothing he could do about it. Now he realized it had been for the best. At least he was around people who really cared for him. A lady in Leroy had started a special school and home for children with special needs and with help from the state, his mother working, and his father working part-time at the feed store in Marysville, they could afford it. His father was willing to work twice as hard, going from plowing their small corn field in the morning, to the feed store in the afternoon, just so he wouldn't have to live with his own son.

The temperature had risen slightly, and the falling snow was coming down mixed with rain. Their clothes were getting soaked to the skin and Josh knew he better get all three of them inside before they caught their death. He hoisted a protesting Scott up on his shoulders and headed for the back door with Sullivan prancing at his heels.

"Let this Christmas go by without an argument," Josh prayed. His father's dark, sullen moods were preferable to open warfare, at least when Scott was home for Christmas vacation. Then the two brothers could spend hours in Josh's room, singing and playing games in peace. And, for a while, they could pretend that they were part of a normal, happy family.

CHAPTER TWENTY-TWO
LOS ANGELES

Outside the interrogation room in the back of the detective bureau, Rosemaria stood holding one Starbucks coffee and sipping another, waiting for Coleman to finish taking a robbery call at an empty desk that had come in a few minutes ago. An almost bare Christmas tree was visible in a nook between cubicles. Sergeant Marlon had brought it in and hung the lights that were twinkling on and off, but so far no one had found the time to decorate it. They had all decided that this year they would have a regular tree instead of the usual holiday battering ram hung with mostly broken ornaments that somebody had stored in a closet decades ago and got hauled out every year at Christmas. Maybe Rosemaria would throw on a few bits of tinsel before going home and wading through her law books tonight.

She had always loved Christmas and every Norman Rockwell cliché that came with it. But this year, with her father planning to be out of town for the holidays, she wouldn't bother with her own tree. She felt a brief pang of longing for the illusive husband and child that was missing from that Rockwell painting and, as her biological clock ticked away, they seemed less and less likely to exist anywhere but in her fantasies. She had vowed as a small girl that she would never be the clinging vine her mother had been, depending on her husband to support her as she followed her illusive dreams. As a result, Rosemaria denied the part of her that hungered for home and family. She sighed a rare, self-pitying sigh and comforted herself with the fact that soon she would be able to fight for what she believed in in the courts instead of out in the streets with a gun and badge, which, more often than not, proved to be futile and frustrating. These days, any piece of garbage she risked life and limb to apprehend could be back on the streets before she finished her report. Not that risking life and limb was an everyday occurrence in Beverly Hills—not like downtown where she started or Hollywood. In a way, she did miss the stress and tension of being undercover. Strange. Sometimes even she couldn't figure herself out.

Coleman came out of the cubicle and headed her way. He smiled when he saw the Starbucks she handed over. "Decaf, soy, mocha, as ordered."

He took a deep sip. "You are too kind."

"The robbery anything I should be concerned about?"

"I referred it to Marlon. It's the same rich widow who always complains her gardener breaks in at night and steals her crystal. Then we find it in her refrigerator or some other strange place and she gets flustered and embarrassed. Probably Alzheimer's. Marlon is good with that."

"Oh, God, if I start doing things like that, I hope somebody shoots me."

"Don't look at me."

"Why not? I'd do it for you."

"Just make sure first, okay?"

Rosemaria nodded toward the interrogation room. "Sal is in here and Jennie in the one up front. Which one do you want?"

Coleman pretended to be shocked. "You're giving me a choice, boss?"

"Don't be a smartass. Jennie was drawn to you last time. Maybe she'll open up to you when you're by yourself."

Coleman sipped. "Well, Sal is a Teamster, hardcore drug dealer, smuggler, and probably hates cops—sounds like he'd respond to some tough, macho, bullshit threats to scare the living daylights out of him—why don't you do it?"

Rosemaria gave him a look that was intended to pierce his brain with hot rays, except that he was used to it by now.

"On the other hand," he continued, "I think Jennie could use a little push from a less friendly type person who knows how to cut through her crap, while I convince Sal we're just mellow Beverly Hills types who are used to celebrities who need a little blow now and then and we mean him no harm as long as he tells us the truth."

Rosemaria considered all that for a couple of seconds. "Sounds good." She headed down the hallway toward the interrogation room up front, where Jennie was waiting.

The girl was much calmer than the first time they had talked to her, but Jennie's uneasiness convinced her that the lady was still hiding something.

"Thank you for coming in, Jennie, there's just a few things I'd like to clear up. Would you like something to drink?"

Jennie shook her head impatiently. "Will this take long? I'm supposed to be at a recording session right now."

Rosemaria brushed aside the question. "You said you met Stan at the studio. What made the two of you decide to take it further?"

"I...I don't remember...Did I say that? We just hit it off like...it was easy to be with him. He seemed, I don't know...lonely." Jennie's eyes threatened to well up and Rosemaria gave her a moment.

"And you went out on a date?"

"Not exactly a date. We agreed to meet at the restaurant next door to the studio after work."

"Did he tell you he was married?"

"No, but I knew it anyway. We just didn't talk about it."

"Why, if you were just friends?"

Jennie's eyes flashed with indignation. "That *is* all we were. But talking about his wife brought him down. She hated his smoking and drinking and nagged him about it constantly. He needed to unwind after all the stress he faced at the studio. She didn't understand that. He was a very gregarious person. He liked hanging out with friends and she liked parties with the A list crowd. Ironic, considering her past."

"How's that?"

"She didn't talk much about her childhood to Stan but I do know she was born and raised in Salinas dirt poor. He said she always became very upset when he asked about her family."

"Why do you think he married her if they were so different?"

"You've seen her. What man wouldn't want Lila?"

Rosemaria detected a note of rancor in her voice. "Yes, indeed," she was forced to agree.

"He thought he was marrying a helpless, fragile young girl. What he got was your classic iron butterfly."

"You sound like you hate her."

"I hardly know her. I saw her in my acting class once and at parties, that's it."

"Did she know about you and Stan?"

Jennie's face tightened and she looked at the wall past Rosemaria who wondered if Jennie's irritation was caused by guilt or anger.

"She knew we were friends and we really weren't much more than that."

"What does 'much more' mean?"

Jennie was trapped by her own words and she resigned herself to it. She heaved a big sigh. "We tried having sex a couple of times and it was very uncomfortable for both of us. He was unable to...perform, so we quit trying."

"And Lila never suspected that there was anything more than friend-ship going on?"

"I don't know what goes on in her head and I wouldn't want to."

"Could she have found out about the two of you and taken it out on Stan?"

Jennie was horrified. "You mean killed him because of me? No! Never!" She shook her head adamantly. "I honestly don't think she cared one iota for him. If she had found out it might have slightly wounded her pride but all she wanted was for him to find her work and make money."

"Did you ever ask Stan to help you get work?"

Jennie hesitated. "Yes."

"Did he ever get you a job?"

"Not too often."

"Did that upset you?"

"Yes."

So, it was evidently all right in Jennie's mind for her to use Stan but not for his own wife to do the same.

"Did you use cocaine with Stan?"

The accusation startled Jennie. "No. Absolutely not."

"Did you ever encourage him to get help?"

"Once or twice. But nagging someone to quit drugs doesn't work. They have to do it on their own and Stan was going to do it as soon as he finished the feature."

"And you're sure you were home the night Stan was killed?"

"Yes, I told you that."

"I know there's something you're not telling me, Jennie. You need to tell me now because I will find out sooner or later."

Jennie's distress was becoming more apparent. "I did think of something. I was really upset last time I talked to you...I know I was home that night because I was waiting for Stan to call me. He told me he had something important he wanted to talk to me about. He was going to call and tell me where he wanted me to meet him that same night."

"When you didn't hear from him, you didn't call him or go over?"

"I've never done that. I didn't want to cause any problems."

"So, everything was done behind Lila's back?" Rosemaria's voice was cold.

Jennie was on the verge of tears again. "I'm not the way you think I am. I'm really not."

"Oh?"

"My God, he needed some warmth and friendship in his life. Someone who accepted him the way he was and didn't make him feel like a degenerate." Jennie was pleading with Rosemaria to understand.

Rosemaria said nothing and picked up her cup and sipped, waiting.

"Alright," Jennie sighed, "I didn't want to bring her into this because she's a really nice person but if you want to know about Lila you need to talk to her ex-roommate, Vanessa Sheridan. Nobody knows better than Vanessa what Lila was really like."

Sal, stocky like Moe, younger, and with an unruly thatch of brown hair, was pacing and gesturing wildly while Coleman calmly looked on. "We were supposed to have a friendly conversation, you said! No harm, no foul, just wanted information! Now you're accusing me of killing one of my best customers and trying to get me tied to some other murderers somewhere else. This ain't friendly and I'm gettin' a lawyer!"

Coleman shrugged. "If that's what you want, you can call your lawyer right now. The two of you can keep coming back here as long as we're investigating the murder. Since you're a truck driver, I'm sure it won't be that much of a trip for you." Coleman stood up. "We'll make sure that the LVPD keeps its eye on you, so you can't cross any other state lines in case we need you."

"You can't do that! I make my living driving!"

"You said you wanted a lawyer. I can't talk to you anymore."

"I take it back. I ain't done nothin'."

Coleman pushed a sheet of paper at Sal. "Great. You just need to sign this." He handed Sal a pen, who then grabbed it and signed.

"See how easy that was? Calm down, Sal. Sit."

Sal stared at him, then plopped down in his chair. "I ain't done nothin'."

Coleman smiled. "That double negative you keep repeating says you did."

Sal's mouth fell open. "Huh?"

"I merely asked if you had ever been to Stan's house."

"You made it sound like I was there when he was killed, and I wasn't. But, yeah, I been there. We usually met at the studio somewhere or outside the restaurant next door, but one time he sounded desperate and needed me to come over."

"Lila wasn't there?"

"You kidding? She woulda killed us both. He blanched and hurried to cover. "I'm just sayin' that. Not that she really woulda. But she hated drugs worse than anything."

"When was the last time?"

"It was after Lila went berserk at the party when she saw him with a packet of coke. She blew up in front of everybody and I wasn't going to go anywhere near him after that. But I guess his other sources dried up, so he begged and pleaded, and I told him I was driving to L.A. anyway and would come by. I don't know the exact date."

"Who are his other sources?"

"Just crew, hangers-on, that type of thing. Nothing regular. Just me."

"So, Sal, I checked with your boss and he tells me he doesn't know where you were when Stan was shot because you were taking some time off."

Sal started to get worked up again. "There you go with that shit again! I told you I was with my uncle in Reno helping him work on his truck."

"Okay, I believe you, Sal. I'm sure your uncle wouldn't lie."

"Damn straight."

"Man to man, Sal, since it's obvious you had no reason to cut off a friend who pays on time. Is there any other reason you can think of that somebody who also might have been supplying Stan would want to kill him?"

Sal struggled to think on this. "Well, if somebody's payin' you, it means you got a good thing going so if they had a fight, say, it woulda been over somethin' else."

"That's good thinking, Sal."

Sal half closed his eyes to help him ruminate around his brain. "People on drugs, even rich ones, hang out with people who are the scum of the earth. Maybe some of them don't have a lotta money, maybe they're desperate, maybe they want what you have, and maybe you don't want to give it to them, so you argue and fight and somebody gets hurt. Could happen."

Coleman reiterated. "Somebody who Stan knows, might be an addict, or somebody who just needs money for whatever reason and sees wealth all around the house and desperate enough to kill to get it?"

"That's logical to me."

"To me, too, Sal. You just might help us solve this case."

For the first time since he got there, Sal smiled. "Can I go now?"

"Don't see why not."

Coleman followed Sal out into the hallway, shook his hand, and watched him go out the door. Sal didn't waste time with any amenities and just about ran down the stairs. Coleman walked toward his cubicle where Rosemaria was hunched over her computer and pulled up a chair next to her. "What's up?"

Rosemaria looked up and shook her head. "Now that I cleaned off my desk, you're not going to sit there anymore?"

"I heard about the little dustup Sibley had at a swanky party in the hills."

"That doesn't mean he could kill anybody."

"If you say so." Rosemaria ignored the barb so he continued. "And I'm pretty sure Sal didn't do it either. But maybe one of Stan's fellow snorters did, according to him."

"Did he have any of those?"

"Waite and Osborne are sifting through Levy's friends and people he worked with, seeing what they can find. What about Jennie?"

"Stan wanted to talk to her about something important the night he died. She had no idea what, or so she said. And she mentioned Vanessa Sheridan as someone who was close to Lila. I don't think she's hiding anything besides the fact she was madly in love with him." She scrolled through the reports on her computer. "I'm missing something and I don't know what it is."

Coleman bent down and saw what she was focused on. "Lila's childhood? Think there's any clues there? She came from poverty, used her beauty to get what she wanted, used a photographer and a casting director before eventually meeting Stan. Maybe they had a grudge."

"Are you kidding? This is how the town works; everybody uses everybody else."

"Not so different from any other business."

"It's worse. The stakes are higher. People are more desperate."

He kept reading. "Her father abandoned her when she was a kid. That may be why she thinks she has to have a man help her get what she wants. She's looking for her father. Deep down probably hates men. Maybe she hated Stan."

"One thing is for sure. We need to speak to Vanessa Sheridan. How would you like that assignment?"

"Does the Pope pee in the woods?"

"Maybe on a camping trip. And stop stealing my lines."

Coleman chuckled and went out.

* * * *

It had taken a week of chanting, meditating, and checking out his astrological sign before Hari could decide which way his karma was pointing him. Waiting on rich bitches every day, who treated him like scum, was making him feel like a loser, when he knew for a fact he was anything but. It was time to turn the tables and take advantage of one of them for a change. As soon as the part-timer, Rosie, came back from her dinner break, he intended to make a couple of phone calls. He knew her address and had a couple of actor friends who worked for the phone company. One of them should be able to help him out.

* * * *

Everything else had gone wrong for Vanessa that morning, so why shouldn't some nosy detective make it complete by coming over and asking the inevitable questions about Lila? She had mentally prepared herself for this moment, but she still dreaded it. Except for two mindless, idiotic indiscretions, all her connections to Lila had ended two years ago and that's the way she wanted to keep it.

She was curled up in her cozy little breakfast nook, sipping her third cup of coffee and getting more jittery by the minute. Her long, pink fingernails clicked impatiently on the waxed pine tabletop, inches away from the aggravatingly silent phone. At least she didn't have to deal with Rod anymore. For six horrible months, she would wake up to nagging: his socks were not aligned correctly in his sock drawer, his underwear was folded incorrectly, his clothes hung in the closet were touching. Charming, handsome Rod had turned into *warden* Rod as soon as she had given up her own apartment and moved into his luxury high-rise condo on Wilshire Boulevard in Westwood, or Attica West as she preferred to call it. After two months of lockdown, she had started saving her "getaway fund," and it had been slow going since she'd only had three acting parts in the past year. The role in the pilot hadn't come through, and she hadn't had an audition since. But at least she was free! She packed and escaped while he was at work at his big shot job at a crypto currency company.

Before leaving, she had considered doing something evil to his precious underwear, but she refrained and found comfort in knowing that when he came home and found her gone, he would have a heart attack, or worse, which could be the case since he hadn't bothered to call her since she left two weeks ago. Her conscience told her she should call and make sure he was okay, but the thought that he might seduce her back into his world of luxury and no money worries frightened her out of doing that. She'd rather be happy and poor than a slave in a million-dollar condo. Besides, there had never been anything wrong with his heart, at least physically.

So now she was back in a little apartment in Sherman Oaks not far from where she used to live, and, by God, be it ever so humble, there's no place like your own place minus a controlling jerk. But she needed to earn money because her residuals were growing smaller by the week and temping in an office would be a fate worse than death, as was asking her parents back home in Arizona for money. They were so proud of everything she had accomplished. She didn't want to seem like a failure to them.

That morning, Vanessa had swallowed her pride and called Dick Bernadette. He would do the best he could, he had said coldly in answer to her request, but he didn't have that much influence with casting and had to get back to the set. She had thanked him meekly and hung up in a fury, hating Dick and her own lack of pride. They had dated briefly a few years before, but a healthy, normal girl expects more from her boyfriend than brief, unsatisfactory groping sessions two times a month. He was handsome enough to attract her but had nothing else she wanted in a permanent relationship.

Three years ago, after she had broken off with Dick, he had come to her begging for a favor. A pilot was being shot that had a lead role he was perfect for. Would she please ask the producer, Jim Gerrard, who she had worked with and was an acquaintance, if he could come in and read? She called Jim at least three times asking for this favor until Dick was finally called in. He had won the part and hadn't contacted her since. In all the interviews he had given since the show became a hit, he had never mentioned her name, not even once.

It had taken her an hour of tub scrubbing and floor polishing after that phone call to calm her down enough to the point where she could even think of another person to call who might help her get a job. Then a truly rare event occurred while she was scrolling through her cell phone—her agent called. Vanessa was again being considered for the lead in a feature that she had auditioned for months ago. The girl they had cast had turned out to be pregnant and suddenly was as big as a house. Was Vanessa available to do the role? Very funny. He should know better than anyone that she was extremely available. Her agent said he would talk to the producers and call her back.

After that phone call, Vanessa had been so nervous and excited that she had almost jumped out of her skin when the phone rang again. It was the detective. She had quickly agreed to see him, partially to keep the line clear and partially to get the whole unpleasantness over with as soon as possible, so it wouldn't interfere with what she was sure would be the biggest break of her career.

The doorbell rang and she slid out of the booth and went into her tiny living room to press the buzzer and let him in. When he appeared at her door, she was pleasantly surprised to find Detective Coleman to be a very handsome, personable man. He was at least six feet tall, with dark hair and an unfeigning macho aura that had always been her downfall—one that she was determined to swear off forever after the Rod debacle.

She led him into the living room. "Please sit down and make yourself comfortable. Would you like some coffee? I have great lemon cake from Starbucks."

Coleman nodded and she disappeared into the kitchen. He sat down on the couch and looked around at the prints on the wall—reproductions, but nice. Romantic impressionists. Not his cup of tea but he instinctively knew they suited her. She was beautiful and charming. Too bad he was on the job.

She came out of the kitchen. "It's brewing." She sat in a chair next to him. Then, "I guess you're here to ask me questions about Lila."

"If you don't mind."

"Not at all. The whole thing is so unbelievable."

"The two of you were friends?"

"We were roommates for a while, but I wouldn't say friends. I don't think Lila had any female friends."

"Is that because women were envious of her?"

"Should *I* be?"

Coleman reddened. "No, no, of course not."

She leaned over and touched him lightly on his arm and smiled. "I'm just teasing. Lila didn't know how to be friends. Anyone she met served a purpose in her life. I served my purpose for a while. I didn't like being used and left."

"How did she use you?"

"I knew people she wanted to meet to get ahead. She was not subtle."

"Did you know Stan?"

"Only as an actress on a couple of his shows. He was a great director, very tuned in to what an actor needs to fulfill the obligations of the scene and the character. I learned a lot from him."

"You liked him."

"Very much."

"Did you know about his drug and drinking problems?"

"I heard rumors, but he was always sober on set." She stood up. "Almost forgot about the coffee. Anything in it?"

"Cream and sugar."

"You got it."

Coleman had seen Vanessa a few times on TV. Driving to her apartment, he had been afraid when he met her that he'd make a fool of himself because her fame would intimidate him. But he felt so comfortable with her, he almost forgot he was there as a cop. She was as beautiful as Lila, but had her own unique, pale blonde good looks. She was also as unassuming and open as Lila was self-centered and evasive. Vanessa's combination of appealing qualities made him abandon his usual take-charge role. No woman had affected him this way before. It was a relief to be able to relax with a woman.

Vanessa came back out with a tray holding coffee cups and two small pieces of cake and he jumped up to take it from her and set it down on the table. They served themselves in comfortable silence.

Coleman bit into his cake and chewed appreciatively. "Really good. I love everything Starbucks."

"Me, too. I practically live there."

Coleman hated going back to the subject of murder but there was no way around it. "I have to ask the obvious question: do you know of anyone who hated Stan enough to kill him?" He was studying her face carefully and suddenly, Coleman sensed a shift in her mood.

"No."

"Do you think Lila capable of it?"

Vanessa hesitated. She sipped her coffee. He sensed her mind was racing. "I don't like to think so."

"Was there another man in Lila's life who might have been jealous of Stan?"

"No. I told you, I didn't know either one of them very well."

Now he could tell she was lying. He had no idea of the veracity of his questions, but he decided to guess as he went along

"We know she's been seeing someone from her hometown. Did she ever mention any names when she was living with you?"

"No, she never talked about anyone like that with me." Vanessa set her plate on the coffee table with trembling hands. "She had boyfriends before she married Stan who were nuts about her, like her photographer, but I don't know anything about anybody she might be seeing now—just the musician I read about in the papers." Vanessa set her face in a neutral expression that was impossible to read.

Coleman munched on his cake and figured there was no use in badgering her. The open line of communication between them had closed. The wall had come down and there was no use beating his brains trying to break it down. Better to stay friendly and sympathetic and maybe later, after she had mulled things over, she might reconsider and let him in on what's troubling her. He strongly suspected that the mystery man, as he was starting to think of him, was from Lila's hometown, Salinas.

He polished off his cake and stood up. "I appreciate your help and hospitality and if you think of anything else you might want to tell me, you can reach me here." He handed her his card.

He smiled at her and held her eyes. He had a feeling she wanted to tell him something and it made him feel strangely vulnerable. This was the kind of woman who didn't make him feel defensive and force him to overcompensate and make an ass of himself, which was unavoidable around Rosemaria.

Vanessa held the door open for him and he turned and faced her again. "Remember what I said. Call me anytime."

Vanessa nodded politely before closing the door, relieved the interview was over. At first, she had thought that she and Detective Coleman were making a real connection beyond the obvious professional interest he had in her. She could tell he liked her. Then he had asked the wrong questions and all bets were off. How had they found out about Steve? Did the detective know more than he was letting on? Was he testing her? It was impossible that anyone knew, she reassured herself. Steve wouldn't tell anyone. Lila didn't know and Vanessa had never breathed a word of that incident to a soul. She decided to take a hot bath before her imagination ran away with her.

Living with Lila had been the worst mistake of her life, but she wasn't prepared to die because of it. With everything that had happened, she wasn't sure that Lila wasn't capable of killing her for what she had done.

CHAPTER TWENTY-THREE
LOS ANGELES

Josh opened the door to his apartment and looked out through bleary, hung-over eyes.

"Good morning," Rosemaria greeted him cheerfully, even though it was late afternoon. She walked past him into the living room and almost tripped over a pile of debris. Out of nowhere, an exotic looking bird swooped down past her head. She stifled a scream. Blasted animals! She looked at the bird, who had landed on his perch near the couch, and wondered what other creatures were lurking in the apartment, ready to pounce on her at any second.

"Behave yourself, Susie," Josh grumbled. He tightened his bath robe and hobbled towards the bathroom. "Be right out. Gotta take a shower."

Rosemaria looked out the window with its view of dingy apartment buildings and trees that were barely alive. A young Latina was pushing a baby carriage with three toddlers tagging along behind. What a place to raise kids. She glanced up at Susie on her perch gazing at her indifferently. She was determined to make the best of this situation. She hardly knew this man, and yet she found that she was jealous he had spent the night with another woman. It was totally irrational and totally un-Rosemaria-like. But after hours spent questioning his friends and business associates and reading the police report she had requested from Marysville, she felt she knew him better than any man in her own life except for her father, which she had to admit, wasn't saying much. Not only were men not high on her priority list, for almost two years they hadn't even been on it. The last man she had had a serious involvement with, a prosecuting attorney she had met while testifying in a robbery trial, had moved to Washington, D.C., and she had chosen to continue her career in Los Angeles over moving there with him. She had been convinced at the time that she had made the right decision, even though the pain in her heart had told her otherwise. Now, she wasn't so sure she shouldn't have listened. She wanted it all, and some-day, somehow, she would have it. If she didn't run out of time, she said to herself, catching a glimpse of herself in an old foggy mirror that hung on the living room wall. The woman looking back at her wasn't getting any younger.

She found a small space on the couch to ease down onto and leafed through some pages of lyrics that Josh had left scattered on the battered coffee table like so much trash. Sheets of poetry treated with little respect, the same way he treated his talent. After the police report had come back from Marysville, she had a better understanding of Josh's self-destructive-ness, but she wanted to do more than understand. She had a crazy impulse to fly to Marysville and follow a hunch and a couple of leads, but that was out of the question now. The bar exams were only a few weeks away in January and she didn't have enough time to study as it was. And it wasn't her responsibility to solve his personal problems. She also wasn't sure why she was there today, except that he was still a suspect and, to Coleman and the Lieutenant, a very viable one. She didn't agree with them, but it gave her an excuse to see Josh, so here she was feeling like she wasn't being honest with any of them. She heard him come out of the bathroom and go into the kitchen.

"Want anything?" he yelled.

"No, thank you."

He came out with wet hair, again wrapped in the terry cloth robe, holding a large mug. He settled into the stained, overstuffed chair by the couch, took a healthy swallow, and set the mug down on the table. It was filled with a clear liquid she strongly suspected was vodka. His blond hair was sticking out in all directions from being toweled dry. Not exactly the man of her dreams. On top of that, he was glaring at her.

"I'm sorry to come barging in. I thought you'd be up."

"Been up for an hour."

Cold.

"Have I done something?"

"You knew how worried I was about Lila but, you didn't bother telling me you knew exactly where she was."

"Oh."

This was starting great and it was her own damn fault. She might as well throw herself on his mercy and hope for the best. "You're right to be angry. It was thoughtless and inconsiderate of me, and I have no excuse. I had plenty of time to tell you after we knew Noor would be all right. I'm sorry. How is Noor, by the way?"

Her contrite response took the steam out of his anger and his response was almost friendly. "Forget it. Noor's fine. Now, what can I do for you this afternoon besides say again I did not murder Stan?" He took another sip from his mug.

She indicated the papers strewn around the room. "What are you working on?"

"A musical." He took the music chart that she was holding and laid it down. "Why did you come here today?"

She ignored the question. "A musical?"

"Yeah."

"For Broadway?"

"Hopefully."

"Will you please sing something for me?" She was surprised to find how eager she was to hear him sing.

"Please."

"It's a little early."

"It's four o'clock."

"As I said, it's early."

He reached back and grabbed his guitar from behind the couch. "This is why you came over?"

She leaned back and made herself comfortable.

Josh cleared his throat and tuned the guitar. "This isn't from the musical. It's something I was working on today. It's a little rough."

"That's okay."

His warm, raspy voice filled the room.

"They say it's wrong to need him.

They say it's wrong to cry

About those nights together

Before I said goodbye.

Was he the one who should have stayed
And filled this ache inside?
Instead I watched and waited
Until his love had died."

As he continued to the chorus, goosebumps stood out on her arms. Even though she knew it hadn't been, it was as if the song had been written for her. Everything she had been feeling lately about her life had been there in the song. He might as well have been reading her mind.

"That was wonderful!" she breathed when he had finished.

"Thank you."

"The melody, the words, your voice, everything."

"Lila asked me to write something for her to record. I'm still working on it."

Rosemaria felt like she'd been punched in the stomach. "For Lila?" she managed to get out calmly.

"Yeah. I hope she likes it."

What the hell was she doing here? This over-the-hill drunken bum was not her responsibility. Let somebody else figure out how to get him off his one-way trip to oblivion. She looked at him slumped down in his chair, hair spiked out in every direction, knobby knees sticking out from underneath his robe, and she felt her resolve begin to crumble. Even worse, she felt herself feeling motherly towards this creature. What on God's good earth was happening to her?

"I'm sure she'll like it," Rosemaria said confidently. "I don't understand why you're not singing in clubs and going after a recording career of your own. Your voice is wonderful." She searched for the right words. "Sweet, gentle, haunting even."

"Well, it's nice of you to say that. I tried for a while—sang in clubs where everybody's talking and nobody's listening. I hated it. Sent demos to different recording companies but never heard back. Then somebody gave Ken one of my demos, asked if I knew anything about writing commercials...naturally, I said I did, booked one, and there you are. I was headed in another direction."

"I hope you get back to recording your own songs someday."

"All I want is to make a living writing music. That's it."

"Okay. I get that. Do you mind if I ask you something?

"Go ahead." He set the guitar down behind the couch and picked up his mug.

"Josh, you've got two raps hanging over your head and you're ignoring both of them. Tomorrow you're going to be facing a judge who feels frustrated that he can't hang jaywalkers. What do you think he's going to do to you?"

"I never jaywalk."'

Rosemaria threw up her hands "Why do you have such a suicidal attitude? Your lawyer told me you had one brief meeting with him."

Josh was clearly irritated. "Who the hell are you to talk to my lawyer?"

"Your lawyer needs your help to prepare a proper defense. Don't you understand that?"

"Why are you sticking your nose into things that have nothing to do with you anyway? Compared to the murder rap you want to hang on me and Lila, this is nothing."

She had no answer for that and slowly got to her feet.

"Don't get me wrong, I'm still grateful for what you did for Noor. You get a lot of free passes for doing that. But Lila didn't kill Stan. I know that for a fact."

She opened the door and started out. She didn't know what more to say.

"Come after me all you want but leave her alone."

Rosemaria closed the door behind her and fought the urge to scream. She started down the hall and heard his door open.

"Want to take me out to breakfast?" He was standing in the doorway, bathrobe flopping in the breeze.

She put both hands on her face and shook her head. Who the hell could figure this guy out? She looked up at him. "Sure, but maybe you could put some clothes on first?"

* * * *

The entire contents of Lila's purse had been dumped out on the bed. Her long, perfectly manicured fingers searched frantically through the rubble of lipsticks, brushes, compacts, keys, two cell phones, and scraps of paper. The doorbell rang and she ran to open the door for the maid the service had sent. She motioned for her to come inside and directed her towards the kitchen. "Un momento."

Lila ran back into the bedroom and picked up one of her cell phones that was ringing. "Hello," she said irritated. "Yes, Laura, I know I'm a little late for my appointment." She shook her head back and forth in annoyance. "I don't understand. Why is it cancelled?" Lila's face puckered up with fury as she listened. "He's dropping me?" Lila paced back and forth from the bedroom to the bathroom. "So now that Stan is dead and I'm not cleared, yet, which I will be, Kyle is dumping me?!" She smashed her fist into the back of a silk-covered overstuffed chair. "Fine! When all of this is over and I'm more famous than ever, I'll find an agent who is worthy of me and Kyle can go straight to hell!" Unwanted tears welled up in her eyes as she clicked off the phone and threw it on the bed. She fumbled through the crumpled pieces of paper, looked at one, and snatched up her cell phone and dialed.

"Misses, can you please tell me..." Lila looked up and saw the maid standing in the doorway and tore into the unsuspecting woman, livid.

"Did I not tell you to wait in the kitchen?! You do exactly what I say, or you can get the hell out!" The maid turned away in terror and walked quickly down the hallway to the front door.

"Shit!" At hearing the front door slam, Lila let loose with a string of obscenities and vowed to make sure the woman who had sent that bitch to her was fired. She heard a message beep tone and snatched one of the phones up to her ear. She tried to keep the desperation out of her voice as she left her message. "There's no reason to be upset, Steve. Please, call me back. The musician means nothing to me. The papers are making it all up. I'll be there soon. Wait for me. We'll get through this. You and me." There's no reason to be upset. I love you."

Lila clicked off the cell phone and ran to her closet. She intended to knock herself out to make herself look good for him. Hopefully, he had gone back to Valley Inn, where he always stayed. She had to see him and explain that all was forgiven. She wasn't worried about the cops. Losing those two idiots who were following her would be easy.

* * * *

"It was recommended by a good friend of mine. I know what I'm talking about."

They were in a new pizza place on Vine Street that had sprung up since Rosemaria had worked vice in the neighborhood. One bite later and she was convinced.

He held out a piece toward her. "Have a bite of the vegan."

She pulled back but didn't want to offend him and took a bite. "Not much like real cheese, is it?"

"You get used to it." He attacked the piece with gusto, and she did the same with hers. "Let's walk." They both picked up their last slices of pizza and walked outside and munched as they walked down Hollywood Boulevard. Josh stopped her at the corner of Hollywood and Vine and pointed to the sign. "You know where we are now?"

"Since I arrested more than a few creeps in this exact spot, yes, I do know where we are."

He scoffed at her. "No, no. What this is, is the most famous corner in the whole world. When I first came here from Wisconsin, I thought that the center of show business was right here, and I wanted to live as close as possible. Capital Records right down the street. I thought I'd died and gone to heaven. Needless to say, I soon found out I was wrong."

"Why don't you move? You can afford better now."

"I'm waiting."

"Waiting for what?"

He pretended not to have heard. "It's crazy, isn't it? Millions of people dream of standing where we're standing right now."

Rosemaria stepped off the curb and continued walking. "I see a Starbucks on one corner and a parking lot on another. Big deal. Show business people are wacky."

He caught up with her in the middle of the street. "You don't believe in dreaming?"

She polished off her piece of pizza before answering. "You have to do more than dream to get what you want in this world."

"I agree."

Rosemaria felt at home on these streets. She noticed some familiar faces, eyes still vacant, faces older but no wiser. "My mother was a dreamer," she finally offered.

"Did hers come true?" Josh asked kindly.

"She was an actress and a singer, and no, they didn't come true. She died when I was twelve."

"I'm sorry."

"The doctors said it was cancer, but I say it was twenty years of rejection and a broken heart."

"Rejection is part of life."

"For her, it was almost all of it."

The sadness she had felt over her mother's final defeat had left her long ago. Now it was just a cold, hard fact. She spotted someone she used to know a block ahead of them.

"Excuse me, Josh!" she yelled, and followed the man who was dragging a girl into an alley. She arrived at the entrance of the alley and looked past the dumpsters and piles of refuse. She was right. It was Wilbur. The pale, pock-marked, slick-haired pimp had one of his girls backed into a doorway with one hand wrapped around her throat. She was wearing a micro-mini and three-inch heels, and not much else. The girl couldn't have been more than fifteen.

"I see you're still smelling up the streets after all this time, Wilbur."

Wilbur started at the sound of Rosemaria's voice and loosened his grip on the girl, her face smudged black with tears and mascara. She took her chance, pulled away, and disappeared down the dark alley. Wilbur affected a cocky stance and sneered at Rosemaria.

"Well, shit. What are you doin' back in town? And don't call me that," he whined as an afterthought. "The name's Rocco."

"Sorry, I forgot, Wilbur."

His half-lidded eyes glinted like a snake's. He walked towards her.

"Didn't your daddy tell you that little girls should stay out of dark alleys?"

Josh's voice threatened him from behind her. "Didn't your daddy teach you to be nice to little girls?"

Rosemaria dismissed his rescue attempt. "I can handle this." She took a step towards Wilbur. "I'd really love it if you gave me a bad time," she said softly, her full attention again on the pimp.

Wilbur looked uncertain and started to back away. "You're crazy as ever."

"Come on. Give me an excuse." Her adrenaline was pumping.

"I ain't touchin' you, lady."

"Don't be like that, Wilbur. Show me how you treat your girls."

By now, Wilbur had backed away several yards. "You got nothin' on me!" he yelled.

"Anything happens to that girl, I'll find you, you dirt bag!"

"I'm shakin', lady, really shakin'," he yelled before ducking around the first corner he came to.

Rosemaria joined Josh back on the sidewalk, chuckling to herself, and started chattering happily. She found perverse pleasure in rousting creeps that preyed on helpless girls. She intended to follow up with her former partner and make sure he kept an eye open for Wilbur. "I haven't seen him since I worked on the task force two years ago," she laughed. "I spent months undercover as a hooker right here on this street. Can you believe that? Working vice can really get addictive. Everything else seems dull after that. Always had trouble with Wilbur. He gets his kicks beating up fourteen-year-olds." She finally looked up at Josh and saw that his face was set in studied indifference. "What's the matter?"

"Nothin'." He pretended to be interested in the window of a tacky lingerie store.

"Nothin"? What's nothin'?"

He shifted his attention to the paraphernalia in an S and M gadget boutique. "Back there."

Rosemaria belatedly recognized a wounded male ego. "It was police business."

"I felt like a goddamn asshole."

"I appreciate your wanting to help me, but I don't need rescuing."

"I'm finding that out."

Now she was getting aggravated. "There's nothing wrong with that!"

"You're right."

She wished he would stop being so tight-lipped and just scream at her and get it over with. "Why do you have this incredible need to rescue everything and everybody?"

"I don't."

The calmer he remained, the angrier she became. "You do! Everything and everybody!"

He stepped out onto Hollywood Boulevard and glanced both ways. "Gotta get goin'. See you later." He dodged a slow-moving car and ran across the street.

"You're jaywalking!" She yelled after him. He ignored her and continued walking down Hollywood Boulevard to Cherokee. She put a hand up to her forehead, closed her eyes, and moaned. Why was she letting this screwed-up boozer get to her? This couldn't be happening. She had too much sense. Oh, well, why fight it? Tomorrow she would make a call to

Marysville. She had to know what happened that night eighteen years ago. There had to be a lot more to it than what was written in the police report.

An icy wind was blowing down the boulevard, but it wasn't nearly strong enough to penetrate the steamed up, boiling over, heat of Josh's aggravation. He had had it with that overbearing pain-in-the-ass. If he wouldn't let Ken practice his amateur psychology on him, he sure as hell wasn't going to put up with some female cop who thinks she's Dirty Harriet and probably wants to probe his mind for murderous tendencies and take pot shots at him.

He made it across Wilcox in a few quick strides and stood beside Kevin's car in the liquor store parking lot, hesitating before unlocking the door and trying to come to a decision. He made up his mind and took out his cell phone. He saw he had some calls but didn't recognize the numbers and made a note to check messages later. He started to call Lila, then remembered this was her afternoon at the fancy gym she went to. He got in his car and headed towards Beverly Hills.

He knew he had been lying to himself and everybody else about his court case that was now only one day away. He had assumed that the judge would understand that defending Katy and her colt had been the reaction of any decent human being. Now, doubts were nagging at him and the thought of spending time behind bars was no joke. It was finally penetrating his brain that the law didn't care about somebody doing the decent thing. It only cared about if you broke it, at least if you were poor and couldn't afford a decent lawyer. Or, like Josh, had no faith in his lawyer and hoped the judge would take it easy on him. He still had the option of postponing the hearing, but what was the point? He did what he did, and nothing could change the facts. He would tell his side of the story and hope for the best.

Rosemaria had stirred up insecurities that were better left undisturbed. He could hardly think of her now without seeing red. She had barged into his life, snooped around, interfered in his personal business, and then when she needed help and he offered it, she had left him standing with his dick in his hand. Better to be with someone warm and feminine who didn't feel the need to pry into his past and psychoanalyze his every move.

He saw the health club sign and drove down the street until he found a parking meter. He hurried up the street and entered the luxurious lobby where a fire was crackling in the fireplace. He asked the lady at the front desk to page Lila and peered through the glass walls at an aerobics class where women of every size and shape were waiting for their class to start, but he didn't see Lila among them. Sure, she was a little self-centered. Who wouldn't be who was that beautiful? He found himself wanting to do for her, to help her in any way he could. It drove him crazy that he could do so little. He might even clean up his act and stop drinking. There was no telling where all of this could lead, and he was almost afraid to hope.

After a few minutes, when Lila didn't show up, he went back to the desk and asked the lady to page Lila again, but she looked at him regretfully, "I'm sorry, I don't think she's here. I don't see her on the sign in list. I called the locker room, and no one's seen her."

Josh excused himself and walked over to the fireplace, sat down on a bench, and called Lila on her cell. He was sure this was her night to come to the club. She answered immediately.

"What is it, Josh?"

"I came to the health club to talk to you. Why aren't you here?"

"Why? Is something the matter?"

"Nothing much, just the police think we murdered your husband." He had felt an irresistible need to be blunt and regretted it instantly.

"Stop talking like that! We haven't done anything wrong!"

"Besides that, I have my hearing tomorrow," he reminded her.

"Oh, yeah, that's right. I guess I should say good luck."

"You guess? I could end up in jail." But sympathy from her was not forthcoming.

"I told you I'd get you a better lawyer," she said, almost annoyed.

"My lawyer's fine. That's not what I need right now."

"Honey, you know I'm here for you. You can count on that, okay?"

"Will you be there?" That pathetic pleading voice coming out of his mouth could not be his.

"I'll try, but I really don't think it's a good idea. You can see that, can't you? But, right now, I'm in the car on my way to an appointment so I have to cut this off. We'll talk tomorrow."

"Where are you—" but he was talking to dead air.

If Rosemaria could see him now. The rescuer begging to be rescued and going down fast. He had come here to feel better and now was leaving with a stronger sense of dread than when he came. He needed a drink.

CHAPTER TWENTY-FOUR

MARYSVILLE, WISCONSIN

The banging on the bedroom door was getting louder and more insistent.

"Hey, lovebirds!" It was Bud Johnson, the biggest defensive player on the football team and the most offensive when he was drunk. He was pretty tanked up at the moment.

"Stop having a good time in there and come out and join the party!"

Fat chance. Wild horses couldn't have dragged Josh out of that room. Connie had just pulled her tank top over her head and taken off her bra, revealing small, firm breasts that begged for his attention. He touched them tentatively as she unbuttoned his shirt. He couldn't believe this was finally happening.

The pounding on the door continued.

"We know what you're doing in there!" This time it was Jeff Constantine, the star running back.

"Come out now, or we're coming in."

More raucous laughter and Connie eyed the door. Josh was terrified she'd change her mind. "It's locked. Nobody can come in," he assured her.

He heard the voice of his best friend and captain of the wrestling team, Billy Swenson. "Come on, guys, leave him in peace. He's entitled to some fun his last night at home."

Josh heard some grumbling, more laughter, and then the music on the stereo turned up. Strains of Kenny Chesney's *How Forever Feels* came floating up from the living room. He loved that song, but he was focused on getting Connie back into a cooperative mood.

After two years of Josh begging in parked cars, Connie was finally coming through in her own parents' bedroom with a room full of people a few feet away. And he was determined she would not change her mind. Billy would keep his friends away, and Connie's parents were on a plane headed for Chicago and a three-day doctors' convention.

He knew why she had finally decided to let down her defenses. Tomorrow, he was leaving for Army boot camp and it would be the last time she would be seeing him for months. She was female enough to want to make sure he wouldn't be forgetting her with some bimbo his first night on leave. Blonde, rich, Connie Meyerhoff was jealous as heck, and he liked it that way. She had moved from Madison to Leroy with her parents during her freshman year. When she and Josh were both juniors, they had met after a football game where Marysville High had stomped all over Leroy High, with Josh having thrown the football all afternoon like it was a guided missile. Naturally, she was a cheerleader and, naturally, she had been impressed. Her loyalty to herself was stronger than her loyalty to her school, about which she cared not one wit. She drove her little Toyota into Marysville to see Josh whenever her parents would let her, and even sometimes when they wouldn't.

Still looking anxiously at the door, Connie pulled back the covers on the bed and they sank down on it together. It suddenly occurred to Josh that this was Connie's first time, but after a few minutes of mouth and hands exploring various places on their bodies, she seemed to forget about the people down in the living room and relaxed. After two years of necking, it's not like they were unfamiliar with each other's bodies, but totally naked like this, Josh was afraid it would all be over in minutes. He told himself, think about boot camp, think about ending up in Kuwait and getting shot at by Iraqis. That was enough to put a damper on his libido. The recruiter made it sound like it would all be over soon, besides which, going into the service had been his only hope of getting somewhere in life. He had wanted to go to college to study music, but his football scholarship hadn't come through, so he thought he'd let the military foot the bill for that once he got out.

His father's reaction to him signing up had been noncommittal and his mother had absently patted his arm and told him to be careful. Their reactions were what he had expected and not important to him. The only reaction that mattered was his brother's. Scott had made many friends at school and seemed happy there, but Josh was still the rock and center of his life. Now that Josh would be making decent money, he never had to worry about Scott not being able to stay at the school. He had tried to make his brother understand that even if Scott didn't see him for a while, he was coming back, and nothing could keep the two of them apart for very long.

Connie's mouth was traveling down his stomach and he realized where she was headed. He didn't even know that she would do anything like that. But he wasn't complaining. He knew he was about to explode and would have to take care of her later. But that was okay. They had all night to get it right.

CHAPTER TWENTY-FIVE

LOS ANGELES

The pizza had turned into a rock in her stomach. Despite being in agony, Rosemaria had gone home and hit the law books with a vengeance, determined to be ready for the grueling tests awaiting her in January. She would pass the bar if it killed her. She put all thoughts of Josh and the case out of her mind and read and studied till she thought her eyes would pop out of her head. Now, here she was, sitting on the toilet seat cover still waiting for the antacid to take away the pain. She couldn't get the nagging thought out of her mind that there was something in the report regarding Lila that she wasn't seeing. She couldn't help it. The case had become all-consuming. So, she hauled herself into the living room, sat down at the table, and opened her laptop.

She went through the report again. Lila's life had been turned upside down when her father, an often out-of-work construction worker, left them flat. Her mother struggled to pay the rent and keep food on the table. Ernest Bauer must have been a real prick to leave his family in the lurch like that, but guys like him were a dime a dozen. Single moms had become the rule these days, not the exception. It turned out that Bauer was wanted for a robbery that happened at the time he left home, so it wasn't just that he didn't want to pay child support, he wanted to avoid jail. Osborne said the mother was pretty but frail and needy. She had had relationships with a few men, one in particular—Stephen Beaumont, who was making a decent living as a roofer and was apparently staying with her off and on. The whole scene depressed Rosemarie to no end. No wonder Lila would do anything to escape her mother's fate.

Her cell phone startled her out of her ruminations. It was Sergeant Kowalski.

"Ernie, what's up?"

"I hate calling you when you're off duty, but the lady insisted."

"What lady? Ernie, what are you talking about?"

"A lady named Vanessa Sheridan called and said she had to talk to Sergeant Coleman tonight. She sounded desperate. I couldn't get ahold of him, so I thought I better call you. Can I give you her number?"

"Sure, thanks, Ernie."

Rosemaria wrote down the number, clicked off her phone, and went to the bathroom to survey the damage. Her curiosity was piqued but the pain in her stomach refused to lessen. She quickly ran a comb through her hair and grabbed a clean sweatshirt from a drawer to replace the ripped tee shirt she had on. The older she got, the less her stomach liked the foods she was addicted to. Maybe she should become a health food nut. Or maybe not. No need to get desperate yet. She couldn't dredge up the energy to put any paint on her face, so Vanessa the TV star would have to take her as she was.

She called Vanessa, who answered after one ring, and explained that she was Coleman's partner. After what seemed like an initial reluctance, Vanessa asked if she could come over to Rosemaria's apartment right away. She didn't want to be seen in public talking to a police officer. Rosemaria agreed and gave Vanessa her address.

Instead of second-guessing what Vanessa had to say, she sank down on the toilet seat cover and concentrated on getting rid of the pain. She thought it might help, and also lower her stress level, to think pleasant thoughts. So, she thought about passing the bar, quitting the force, and working her way up to becoming the district attorney in a large city, preferably on the west coast so she could be near her father. She saw herself in a crowded courtroom where a mass murderer was on trial, with four lawyers by his side who had dressed and groomed the defendant to the point where he now looked like a helpless Sunday school teacher. She faced a judge just aching to find an excuse to acquit the scumbag in spite of the testimony of some poor bastard cop with a wife and three kids who had barely escaped getting killed arresting the creep, instead of saving the taxpayers a fortune and blowing him to kingdom come.

Rosemaria had been tempted to do that more than once, but she had no desire to sink to the level of the slime they hunted. She would never let the hatred take over. It had nothing to do with decency, honor, or high-minded morals, just survival of mind and spirit as well as body. She was a defender, not a killer. She saw herself in the courtroom again, defending society with the law, dotting every *i*, and crossing every *t*, leaving no loop-holes for the criminal to crawl through. He would get the maximum sentence, the appeal would fail, the four lawyers would start thinking about their next case and, most important, the poor bastard cop would not have risked his life for nothing.

She continued on with her pleasant fantasies until her head fell on her chest and she almost nodded off. The doorbell rang and she awoke with a start and went to answer. She opened the door and saw that Vanessa looked just as beautiful as she did on TV, but was obviously very tense, and her thin nylon jacket was pulled tightly around her. At Rosemaria's invitation, she walked nervously into the living room. "I'm sorry for disturbing you in your home."

"Think nothing of it," Rosemaria said. "Would you like something to drink…coffee, tea?"

"No, thank you."

"Have a seat, then."

Rosemaria grabbed her notebook from the little writing desk by the door and joined Vanessa, who was sitting on the couch. She still had her jacket wrapped around her and looked as though she would spring up and take flight at any second.

Rosemaria sat with her legs folded underneath her at the opposite end of the couch and attempted to put Vanessa at ease. "I know this room isn't all that comfortable. I have no flair for decorating whatsoever, not to mention law books taking over the dining room table."

"You're studying to be a lawyer?"

"If I manage to pass the bar."

"I wish you well on that."

"Thank you. I admit I don't watch too much television, but I have seen you a couple of times and enjoyed your performances."

"That's nice of you to say."

"I mean it."

Vanessa cleared her throat and breathed in deeply while looking as though she were being forced to swallow something bitter and distasteful.

"I'm not sure this was such a good idea anymore. I'm starting to feel a little silly that I'm making such a big deal out of this."

"Whatever it is, I'm here to listen. Would you like some water?"

Vanessa shook her head. "I wanted to tell Detective Coleman when he came, but I really didn't think it had anything to do with the case, and if Lila found out, I was afraid of what she might do. I realize now that you'll probably find out everything anyway, and I wanted to ask you if there's anything you can do to keep me out of it."

"I can't promise anything like that."

Vanessa bit her lip. "I figured you'd say that, but you have to understand, I'm truly afraid of Lila. I don't want her to find out I talked to you. She really terrifies me."

Rosemaria had to control her excitement. Finally, she was going to hear about the other side of Lila Levy, which she had always suspected existed below the surface of that helpless veneer. This was what she had been waiting for.

"Go ahead," she said calmly.

"This is about the man Lila is involved with."

Rosemaria didn't like where this was going.

"You mean Josh Sibley?"

"Josh?" Vanessa seemed momentarily perplexed by the name. "The musician? No, of course not. I'm talking about the man she's crazy, out-of-her-mind obsessed with."

Rosemaria almost fell off her chair. "She has another man in her life?" Coleman was right. The clues were there all along.

"He's the *only* man in her life as far as she's concerned—Stephen Beaumont."

Rosemaria's mouth fell open. "Her mother's boyfriend?" she whispered.

"Sick, isn't it?"

Wow. She hadn't expected this. "But how does that affect you in any way?"

"Can I tell you from the beginning?"

Vanessa finally loosened her hands from her jacket and sighed. "The night it all started, Lila and I had had a big blowout. We fought all the time in those days, just before we went our separate ways, usually because she was so damned selfish. All she ever thought about was herself. I'm sure the only reason she wanted to be my roommate was because I happened to be a working actress and might be able to help her career. We met at a swank show business party in Bel-Air. I guess she thought I knew all those important people and decided she wanted me to become her best friend. Friend?! What a laugh. She doesn't know the meaning of the word. I was more like a glorified dating and chauffeur service because she couldn't drive for a while because of a DUI."

"Could we please get back to the man in question?"

Vanessa shook her head and clenched her hands tightly in her lap. "I'm sorry. I guess I'm still angry that I allowed myself to be used by her. I usually have more sense than that, but Lila could be very persuasive."

Rosemaria nodded and waited patiently. Vanessa needed to talk and Rosemaria was feeling generous. The hard lump in her stomach had not come back and there was no feeling quite as good as the absence of pain.

"I was so angry with her that night! I used to..." Vanessa realized she had raised her voice and stopped mid-sentence. "I think I'd like that drink now, if you don't mind?"

"Sure. I don't have much of a selection. There's water, soda, some brandy, I think."

"Brandy is fine."

Rosemaria went into the kitchen and came back with a half-filled bottle of brandy and a glass. "No snifter, sorry."

Vanessa smiled and waved her off.

Rosemaria poured brandy into the juice glass. "I'd join you but my stomach's been a little off."

Vanessa unabashedly took a big gulp of brandy.

"Why were you so angry with Lila that night?"

Vanessa smiled a humorless smile. "As I started to say, I used to take Lila to every single party I was invited to. I introduced her to all my friends. I was the one who introduced her to Stan at a wrap party, to my everlasting regret. I never let her sit home alone while I was out. But Lila sure the hell wouldn't do the same for me." Her words came out harsh and bitter. "One night, she was invited to a party at the home of a director I was dying to meet. I had been trying for weeks to get an audition with him for his next movie because there was a part in it that I was perfect for. I wanted so badly just to get a chance to read for him. I was thrilled when she was invited to a party at his house. I just assumed we would go together. But you can't assume anything when it comes to Lila."

Vanessa paused as she tried to control the anger she still felt. "She regretfully informed me that only *very* close friends were coming to this party and she certainly wouldn't want to annoy the director by dragging along someone who would pester him about a job." Vanessa shook her head in amazement. "Can you believe it? As if Lila were a close friend of his, as if there aren't more business deals made at parties than at the studios, and as if she didn't have every intention of expending every ounce of energy in that conniving little body towards getting *herself* hired by somebody at that party. And not only did she refuse to let me go with her, she had the colossal nerve to expect me to drive her there. It's incredible."

Rosemaria had to laugh. Lila did raise egomania to new heights.

Vanessa smiled in acknowledgment, as if reading her thoughts. "Yeah, I know. Anyway, when I refused to take her and she couldn't find anyone else to drive her, she was furious that she had to spend money on a cab. I finally couldn't take anymore and started screaming back at her. That was the beginning of the end. I couldn't live with her after that." She took a sip of her brandy and stared off into space.

Rosemaria tried to bring her back. "I totally understand that."

"About five minutes after she left, Steve showed up."

"Her mother's boyfriend."

"*Him.* Her one and only true love. I'd met him once before for a few minutes and thought he was an okay guy: middle-aged, in great shape, fairly attractive, nothing special. But that night, in the mood I was in, he suddenly looked better to me than George Clooney. We talked, had a few drinks, and ended up in bed, right there in my room in that apartment. He wasn't bad in that department either. To be honest, it was incredible. We met a few times after that in various motels, but I was too nervous about Lila finding out to keep it up, and I couldn't really see a future with an itinerant construction worker."

"Lila with a blue-collar guy?" That was impossible to believe. Rosemaria was starting to think Vanessa was weaving fantasies.

"It's true. She would've killed both of us if she found out, and I'm speaking literally."

"Forgive me if I'm being dense, but what does all of this have to do with Stan's murder?"

"I haven't seen him or talked to him in a long time." She forced herself to continue. "That is, a year before the day of the murder."

"You saw him that day?"

"No. Steve called me that night." Vanessa said, her voice cracking. "He told me he was leaving town and wasn't coming back. He said Lila was getting out of control, had threatened to tell her mother about them and he was afraid for the woman's safety." She sat the glass down on the table and clasped her hands together again.

"Good lord." Vanessa thought Lila would hurt her own mother? "So why was it so important that you talk to me tonight?"

"I knew from the questions Detective Coleman was asking me about Steve that he knew more than he was telling me. I thought if I told you first what had happened, that you'd be able to keep me out of the investigation as much as possible."

"Tell me everything, Vanessa."

"She saw me coming out of Steve's hotel room last year. She was supposed to be at a screening. I had just broken up with my boyfriend."

"Never mind all that."

"She came off the elevator just as I was coming out of his room. She only saw my back as I headed for the stairwell and ran down the stairs. I didn't know it was her, but in case it was, I ran. She didn't know who to go after first, Steve or whatever woman he had been with. She picked him. They had a huge fight and she stabbed him with a letter opener and almost killed him. He ended up in the emergency room. They both said it was an accident and the hotel was only too happy to cover it up."

"And he went on seeing this maniac?!"

"He's half afraid of her. She's evil to the bone."

"The only way she'd find out it was you, is if he'd tell her. Would he do that?"

"No! But she still hasn't given up finding out. She tried to get ahold of the hotel video from that floor that same night, but she wasn't able to. If this goes to court and I have to testify, she'll find out it was me and she won't rest until I'm dead."

Vanessa stared at Rosemaria as she sat quietly processing everything Vanessa just told her. This was as tangled a web as any show Stan had ever directed, but it was all too real.

Vanessa was desperate. "What can you do?"

"Don't talk to anybody about this, and I suspect that's the last thing you'd do. I will share this with Detective Coleman and no one else for now. And I promise you, we will protect you. Lila will not harm you. You can trust me on that, okay?"

Vanessa's voice was shaky. "I trust you, and Detective Coleman as well. He's – he *was* very nice to me."

"I agree. He's a very nice man."

Vanessa reddened slightly and Rosemaria recognized the improbable beginnings of a genuine crush. She could see why other women might find Coleman attractive, even if she didn't. Stranger things were happening in this case than that.

After Vanessa had expressed her gratitude a few more times and left in much better spirits than when she arrived, Rosemaria decided to forgo the law books and go to bed early and sleep on all the new information she had just gotten. Sometimes, her brain would keep nudging her as she slept, and she would wake up with solutions to whatever was troubling her. And sometimes, her brain would just go to sleep along with the rest of her and still leave her with no answers in the morning. She sank into her bed and turned out the light. Tomorrow would bring whatever it brought.

* * * *

Daylight was beginning to filter through the curtains, but Larry was already awake at 5:45, his usual time to go down to the gym. But today, for whatever reason, he didn't feel like it. He got out of bed and walked to the sliding glass doors that faced the marina. As he drew the curtains aside, his eyes rested automatically on his boat, The Duchess II, nestled safely in her berth just a few feet outside of his apartment. Forty-five feet long, his 450 Sundancer was his pride and joy. When he spent a day out on the open sea with The Duchess and maybe a friend or two, he was reminded that there was more to life than killers and thieves. Although he suspected Rosemaria thought he wasn't up to it, he knew he could handle whatever was dished out to him in the way of cases. He had been spoiled and protected most of his life, and grit and grime were repugnant to him, but he still had that innate sense of justice that most good cops had. He'd never worked undercover or vice like Rosemaria and wasn't as enthusiastic about slamming perpetrators up against the wall and screaming obscenities at them, but he could do it if he had to. He suspected she had enjoyed working the streets in Hollywood a lot more than she did Beverly Boulevard. He would do what he had to do to move up the ladder and follow in his stepfather's footsteps. No reason it shouldn't happen twice in a family.

His eyes were drawn back to The Duchess and he decided, when they closed this case, he would go to Catalina. It had been a while since he'd been there. Too bad there was no one special to take with him. He opened the sliding door, went out on the balcony, and breathed in deeply of the fresh sea air.

The first Duchess had been a sailboat. His father had named it after his mother's nickname, and when the shimmering white hull of that twenty-five-foot sailboat had cut through the waves, she more than lived up to her namesake. He remembered his father's affectionate laugh as he watched his nine-year-old son scamper around the deck obeying his father's instructions—his easy-going father, who had been too busy enjoying life to properly run the large computer firm he had built up from scratch. If he hadn't crashed his own plane into the San Bernardino Mountains, the company would probably have gone bankrupt in five years, instead of being the huge success it became under his mother's capable hands.

She had gone from having lunches at The Bistro and getting facials and manicures at Elizabeth Arden, to running a major business without chipping a nail. She made it all look easy—she was calm, cool, and just as charming as she had been as her husband's hostess. Except now, she was charming businesspeople who never suspected this sweet, lovely lady knew both her business and theirs up one side and down the other. After being widowed for three years, she had married the brother of her best friend, who happened to be a cop she had known for years. After falling in love with him, she found out he had inherited a publishing company and was even richer than she was. Larry had ended up in the middle of a bonanza and could have spent his life a wastrel, but that was never an option for him. He had grown up watching his mother work her butt off to have what she had and throwing all her money down the drain was the last thing he wanted to do.

After an initial reticence and resistance, Larry had sought the love of his new father, but there wasn't much to be found. His parents lived their lives in a whirl of social activity and work, and there wasn't much time to spend with a little boy except for a few trips to visit his stepfather at the Hill Street precinct (just like on TV!), which caused Larry to decide that being a cop was the manliest job there could be.

His life had played out pretty much the way he had planned, but there was still something missing. He could barely admit to himself, let alone anyone else, that he rarely felt the confidence and strength his stepfather exuded, and only acted out these traits in empty gestures.

He never talked about his money and connections with his fellow cops. He didn't need the kind of grief that would get him. Not even Rosemaria would have known if the Lieutenant hadn't mentioned it. But on this particular morning, he was very glad she had found out. The guys at the station all thought he was out getting laid every night when he wasn't working, and he didn't say anything to change their minds. In reality, he felt uneasy around women who were tough and aggressive, but after a couple of nights with the kind of social-climbing bimbos he found at his mother's parties, he would get bored and avoid their phone calls. Until he met Vanessa Sheridan, he didn't think he'd ever find what he was looking for. But who knew what it would take for her to take an interest in him. He stepped back inside and slid the door closed, considering going down to the gym after all. The landline rang as he was walking toward his closet. "Coleman."

"You answer your home phone like that?"

The dulcet tones of Rosemaria first thing in the morning. "Isn't it a little early to be handing out abuse?"

"I need to see you and I'm on my way over."

"What?"

"Get up, get dressed. I've got news about the case."

"Why not meet at the office?"

"No, it needs to be there."

"You know where I live?"

"I'm a detective, aren't I?" And she hung up.

Half an hour later, she burst through the door all energy and enthusiasm, laptop and black folder in tow, then stopped short and looked around his place. "This is some swell digs you got here, detective."

"Please, can you call me Larry now? I think we know each other well enough."

She gave his apartment a fast going-over and then sat herself down at his glass dining table and opened her laptop.

"You won't believe this, Coleman."

Larry rolled his eyes. "Let me hear it."

"Vanessa came to see me last night and told me a few things that jogged my brain loose. It had all been there, but I didn't see it. She had wanted to see you, but Kowalski was on the desk and couldn't find you."

"Why did she want to see me?"

"She wanted to tell you Lila is having an affair with her mother's boyfriend, Steve Beaumont, and ask for your protection. But never mind that, first things first."

"What?! Are you kidding?! Her mother's boyfriend?! But why does Vanessa need protection?" Damn! He had to have picked last night to join friends at his favorite seafood joint in Venice and forget to bring his cell.

Rosemaria continued as pictures popped up on her screen. "Waite called me first thing this morning and told me the computer matched some fingerprints in Lila's car to a robbery suspect up in Salinas. The fingerprint expert went over them and he came up with a 90 percent match."

"Who?"

"Ernest Bauer."

"Lila's father? What the hell was he doing in Lila's car? He hasn't been seen or heard from in decades. He came back to kill Stan? That doesn't make any sense."

"I asked Waite to send me pictures of Bauer and Beaumont, Lila's mother's boyfriend. All he could come up with was Bauer's booking photo and Beaumont's driver's license photo from years ago." Rosemaria took two pictures out of her folder and laid them on the table. "This is Bauer back then and this is Beaumont's driver's license photo from three years ago."

Larry studied the two pictures—Bauer was a lot younger, dark haired, and handsome. Beaumont had mostly silver hair, was slightly heavier, but still a good-looking guy. They were the same person.

"Jesus God in heaven."

"Yeah. We're all going to need a long vacation after this one. I thought Waite was going to throw up."

"I can't handle this town. I need to move to New Zealand."

"Can't move away from evil, or incest either."

Larry felt sick. This was almost worse than the murder. After a moment, he looked at Rosemaria, puzzled, "What does Vanessa have to do with this?"

"Now, don't judge her before I tell you everything."

"What? What do you mean?"

"Vanessa dated the guy."

Larry felt instant repugnance, disappointment, and betrayal overwhelm him. The woman of his dreams with this piece of garbage. He stood up and started pacing.

Rosemaria saw the look on his face. "Now, don't judge her too harshly. All she knew at first was he was Lila's boyfriend. He didn't tell her for weeks that he was Lila's mother's boyfriend and shortly after that, she cut it off."

"So, she knowingly had an affair with somebody else's boyfriend?"

"I know what you're thinking. But if you knew the whole story, you'd be more understanding. Lila treated Vanessa like dirt, they had a big fight and—there was Steve standing in the doorway, handsome and more than available. She didn't know anything about him then."

"Then?"

"A year ago. Vanessa broke up with her boyfriend and she hooked up with Beaumont again. Still not knowing who he really was, or who she thought he really was, okay? Apparently, Lila caught Vanessa coming out of his hotel room, didn't see who it was, and tried to kill Steve…almost did. Now she's still trying to find out who that woman was. If we nail Lila and Steve on this, and we will, Vanessa will have to testify. Meanwhile, Vanessa will need protection. I'm thinking a safe place might be your boat."

This was too much for Larry to compute.

"She likes you. She trusts you. I promised her we'd keep her safe. Please don't hold this mistake against her."

"She said she likes me?"

"Not in so many words, but almost. She's a decent person, Larry. Don't let one mistake define who she is for you."

"She must be scared as hell."

"It calmed her down when I told her we would keep her safe. Can I count on you, Larry?"

He went to the window and looked out at The Duchess. Yeah, he would do this for Vanessa. "Sure."

Rosemaria sighed with relief. "Okay, then. I'll ask the Lieutenant to assign someone full time and you and he can take turns at night, if that's okay with you?"

"Why not a hotel?"

"This is much safer. No one to spot her and blab to the media."

"You did this for me as well as her."

Rosemaria made a face.

"If you want a favor, you don't need to bribe me with Vanessa. You can just ask."

"Okay. I was thinking you could talk to your stepfather about Sibley. You can tell him we're about to solve the case and Sibley is absolutely out of the picture and that he's a great guy and blah, blah, blah, you know what to say."

Larry still stood by the window, looking out. "Okay, I'll try."

* * * *

"Josh!" A man's voice whispered through the bars. "Josh, are you in there?"

Noor came to the edge of her compound and saw the white-coated human who had been there when she thought she would die. She thought that this human had much to do with bringing her back from the edge of the darkness she had been afraid would claim her. He had been there through it all. Noor looked back at Josh, partially hidden by brush. He had come to her last night and spoken words that she knew were sad. She had sat beside him and tried to bring him comfort but he had brought his bottle and knew that soon he would sleep, so she had lain beside him all night to keep him warm. Now she went to him and softly touched his face.

Josh felt the pressure of Noor's paw and slowly roused himself awake and sat up, Noor's face a foot away from him, her yellow eyes boring into his. He suddenly felt an overwhelming sense of sadness that he was letting her down, was letting himself down and disappointing every person who believed in him. Now fully awake, he saw Jerry standing outside the bars gesturing angrily. "Josh, for Christ's sake! You've got to get out of there now! You have your hearing in an hour!"

Every muscle in his body ached. He couldn't move without causing excruciating pain. Noor was nudging his face. "I'm up, I'm up."

"I'll meet you in the clinic. You can wash up there. I have a shirt and jacket for you."

"I don't deserve you, Jerry."

"Tell me." Jerry turned away in disgust.

As Josh exited the elevator, he saw that the corridor of the seventh floor of the Van Nuys Courthouse was bright and clean and nothing like the packed courthouses seen in movies. A few defendants, cops, and lawyers paced the hallways, waiting their turn. Others sat on benches staring out the floor-to-ceiling windows facing the mountains. Josh found the department number of his courtroom and started to sit down nearby but changed his mind, deciding he needed to keep his mind off his upcoming hearing. Maybe listening to someone else's problems would help.

He opened the door to another courtroom that was almost empty of spectators and sat alone in the last row of benches. A man who looked like he would just as soon slit your throat as breathe was accused of breaking and entering, and the prosecuting attorney was summing up the case against him to persuade the judge that they should go to trial. Josh kept eyeing the door as he listened. He was anxious for his lawyer to show up and get this over with. He expected Lila to arrive soon, too. He had left a message telling her what room the hearing would be in.

The prosecutor finished and the defense attorney stood up. Josh listened, fascinated, as the lawyer proceeded to tear apart the seemingly airtight case the prosecution had presented. He reminded the judge of discrepancies, witnesses' doubts, and inaccuracies, and wormed his way through every loophole he could find to the point that Josh wondered why they had even bothered to have the hearing.

Someone tapped him on the shoulder. It was Leonard Weitz, his lawyer. Josh followed him out into the hallway.

"You're absolutely sure this is what you want to do?" Leonard took off his glasses and rubbed his eyes hard.

"Yes."

"All right. It's your funeral."

They waited a full hour before they were called. His lawyer spent most of that time on his cell phone and Josh kept anticipating Lila every time the elevator doors opened. He had only one short-lived panic attack during that hour. If the lawyer in the burglary case could make that ten-time loser look innocent, then Lila's high-priced lawyer could surely have done the same for him. Too late now. He dismissed the thought from his mind. He liked getting things over with and whatever the hell was going to happen, would happen, no matter what anybody did.

As they entered the courtroom, Josh saw the three boys who were the instigators of all this drama walking just ahead of him, their gang tattoos partially hidden by high necked t shirts and long sleeves. As Josh passed them, they smirked and sat themselves down on a bench near the front. After the usual preliminaries, Josh said his nolo contendere and waited for the judge's verdict. The judge, a balding man in his sixties with a no-nonsense attitude wasted no time in getting to the point.

"I have read the report which details the origin of this incident, including the fact that your actions were precipitated by three hoodlums' unconscionable attacks on helpless victims. While I deplore what the three young men were doing, and they shall answer for their behavior, your response was overzealous and might have caused great bodily injury to one of the young men if not for the fact that you yourself were then brutally attacked. That this incident took place where we should expect animals to be provided with absolute security is something my office will take up with zoo officials. I do not believe that you are any risk to society, and as it has been recommended to me by people for whom I have the highest respect, that you should not face any criminal charges. I hereby dismiss this case and warn you to keep your wits about you should you be faced with anything like this again. Control your urge to act on your own and avoid at all cost a reappearance in this courtroom. Let security officers do their job. That's what they're there for. Next case."

Josh was dumbfounded, his lawyer looked dazed, and the prosecutor's mouth was hanging open. Josh turned around to look at the three hardened gangbangers and they practically had tears in their eyes, they were so shocked and angry.

Josh followed his lawyer out into the hallway, passing by the now hangdog teens. He didn't bother saying a word. Out in the hallway, the lawyer looked at Josh. "What the hell happened in there?"

"I don't know, but if I'm dreaming, don't wake me up."

"Your guardian angel is working overtime, Mr. Sibley. You must have built up a lot of good karma to pull this off."

Josh could think of no response.

"Whatever connections you have, and they must be damn high up, please let me use them some time." He looked down at the cell phone in his hand. "I gotta meet another client in a few minutes. I can brag about how I just got somebody off in thirty seconds flat." He walked toward the elevators shaking his head.

Josh waved goodbye to his lawyer and sat down on a bench in the lobby. Yes, he did have an angel. And he had her phone number. He dialed his cell phone.

"It was you, wasn't it?"

She recognized his voice and asked anxiously, "How'd it go?"

"Charges dismissed."

"Yes!"

"It was you, wasn't it?" Josh repeated his question.

"You're not angry, are you?"

"I'm not that much of an ungrateful jerk. I'd just like to know how you did it."

"I'll have to tell you later. Right now, I'm running out for an appointment."

"Can we meet tonight?"

"It would have to come under the heading of an investigative interrogation in my report."

"I don't care if you call it a ride on a ferris wheel. What's your address?"

Rosemaria told him and clicked off. She knew she couldn't let him know he was completely off the hook. He was still under Lila's spell, so she didn't dare share anything she knew with him. Maybe soon all that would change.

The call from Bill Swenson in Marysville had come just as she was running out the door for her lunch appointment with Howard Grossman. It had shaken her so badly, after hanging up, she had run to the ladies' room to cry, grateful that no one had seen her or they would have razzed her within an inch of her life. But her instincts had been right. The police report was one thing and what really happened in Marysville that night was quite another. Only three people still alive knew what had happened, and Josh's old friend was one of them. She hadn't known that when she saw his name in the records, but something in his description of the events of that evening hadn't rung true. She had followed a hunch and had gotten very, very lucky.

Mr. Swenson had been uncooperative and distrustful when Rosemaria first began to question him, and it had taken all of her persuasive powers to open him up, but once the story was out, he had seemed almost relieved. The horror had been eating Josh up alive all these years. It explained a lot.

But she had still another hunch to follow—someone else in Marysville to talk to—and if that lead panned out, she would be able to do a lot more for Josh than just sympathize.

A long stretch of Coldwater Canyon was being paved and it was slow going over the hill into the Valley. She was impatient to get to the studio and talk to Howard and Jennie. She just needed a little more information before she sprang her trap for Lila, and with a little luck, it would work. Josh had been eliminated as a suspect, Sal would be indicted in Las Vegas for drug dealing (she'd made sure of that), and the bullet casings from the Laurel Canyon case didn't match the one at Stan's house, so that connection was slim, at best. No, she was betting on Lila, and not just because she couldn't stand the evil conniver, but because every instinct she had told her she was right.

Howard had left a pass for her, so Rosemaria drove through the gate with no problem and without having to flash her badge. She parked in a green zone right inside the main gate and tried to remember the directions to stage twelve. She looked at the people rushing down the streets and sidewalks and thought how her mother had longed with all her heart and soul to be a part of all this activity. To Rosemaria, this was just a place where people made make-believe and were lucky enough to get paid for it. To her mother, this had been the pot at the end of the rainbow—hell, it had been the whole damn rainbow, her very reason for breathing.

She turned right and walked to the end of the street. She assumed that the flashing red light outside the stage door was a signal not to enter and waited until it went out before opening the door. The sign had said "Closed Set," but no one approached her as she walked through the cavernous stage from one dark deserted set to the next. Finally, at the far end of the building, she found an area that was heavily lit with several people milling about, seemingly not doing much of anything. A young girl, made up to the teeth and most likely an actress, was seated in a director's chair doing needlepoint. The girl pointed out Howard standing a few feet away, engaged in conversation with a woman who was making notations in a heavy, leather-bound notebook.

Howard looked surprised to see her as he shook her hand. "Sergeant. I didn't think you were going to make it. I expected you at lunch."

"Sorry, I was held up," Rosemaria said, without offering any explanation.

"Sergeant Baker, I'd like to you meet Sandy Casem, our script girl—I mean, our continuity person," he added playfully.

Sandy gave Rosemaria a look that told her she was used to his chauvinistic jokes and shook her hand. "It's very nice meeting you. If you'll excuse me now, I need to share some notes with the star of this turkey. No offense, Howard."

Howard laughed and nodded his head in the direction of the girl doing needlepoint. "Girlfriend of a network vice president. We have to baby sit her through the whole shoot. At this rate, we'll only be two weeks over schedule. I had to get another director up to speed after Stan was killed."

He guided her to an adjacent set that was so dark, she could barely make out the colors of the couch they sat on. Once her eyes gradually adjusted, she noticed that this set was about a hundred times better decorated than her own, very real, not a little bit tacky living room.

"I don't have much time before they relight."

"This won't take long. I've been talking to a few people about Lila and another man she was seeing. Do you know anything about that?"

"Another man? She flirted with anybody she thought could do her any good, but I don't know of anyone in particular."

"There was no one in her past—someone Stan might have found out about?"

"No. But Stan might not have shared that with me. It would have been more than a little humiliating."

"All right. I won't keep you any longer. But if you think of anything in the next couple of days, please call me."

"You know, I don't know what this would have to do with anything, but she did humiliate Stan once in front of a room full of people at a party. She saw somebody slip a packet of cocaine into Stan's pocket and went ballistic. She dug the coke out of his pocket and started pounding on his chest yelling, 'You bastard, you fucking bastard!' Everybody came running outside to the patio to see what was going on. Lila always liked to act like she had so much class, but this time she let it all hang out. She opened the plastic packet and threw the powder in Stan's face. He was so mortified, he couldn't move. She took off in their car and, after he recovered, he got a ride home. From what I hear, he kicked the door in when he got there and beat the shit out of her. A typical day in tinsel town."

"And you still chose to work with this man? He should have been arrested."

"You're right. But he was a friend and I just couldn't do it to him. You don't know how sorry I am now."

"If Stan knew about another man in her life, what do you think he would have done?"

"He probably would have been relieved."

A bearded young man appeared out of the darkness to tell Howard that they were almost ready to go. Howard thanked him and told him he'd be right there. "I don't really have to be on the set, but the director needs a little coaching for the first couple of days. I can tell you, I really miss Stan."

He excused himself. Rosemaria made a few notes in her notebook and started to make her way through the dark stage again, avoiding tripping on cables and running into walls that popped up where she least expected them. A hand came out of nowhere and touched her on the shoulder. Startled, she turned around. "Jennie!"

"I'm sorry," Jennie whispered, "I thought you saw me."

"Let's get out of here before we get yelled at by somebody."

They both shielded their eyes to protect them from the harsh sunlight that greeted them as soon as they stepped outside.

"Ken gave me the morning off to be here. Howard and I waited for you in the cafeteria, but you didn't come."

"I'm sorry." She indicated a picnic bench next to a food truck. "Let's just sit for a few minutes."

Jennie sat and looked at Rosemaria like she was about to face a major inquisition.

"Relax. I just have a couple of questions and you can get back to work."

"Did you talk to Vanessa?"

"I did and she really couldn't tell me much other than Lila is a real piece of work."

"That's one way of putting it. Oh, and I heard that you kept Josh from going to jail. I can't tell you how much that means to me."

"All in a day's work. But I have a question for you. When Stan called you the day of the murder, are you sure he didn't say anything about a man Lila might have been seeing?"

"No. I'm sure he didn't. He suspected there was someone, but he couldn't bring himself to hire a private detective to follow her."

"You do know Stan was not the nice man you make him out to be. He was a violent drug addict." Rosemaria looked at Jennie, a soft smile on her face. "You can do better than that, Jennie. You don't have to settle."

Jennie became defensive. "He wasn't always like that. Lila drove him crazy. I know he overreacted once or twice to her nagging and complaining. But he wasn't a bad person. He didn't deserve to die because he was a bad judge of women."

Jennie denied knowing about Steve or who he really was. Rosemaria had her doubts about that but decided not to push. "Thanks, Jennie, enjoy the rest of your day."

Jennie stood up and stared hard at Rosemaria. "Don't let her get away with it. Make her pay."

CHAPTER TWENTY-SIX

LOS ANGELES

For a couple of hours, at least, Lila would be able to forget about her personal problems and concentrate on her much-neglected career. Howard had left a parking pass on the lot for her so, thank God, she didn't have to park across the street. Considering how many people would be at the screening, she took that as a sign that her luck was changing, and good things were in store for her. After a lot of cajoling, Howard had agreed to getting her an invitation, even though he had nothing to do with the show. It was important for her to be there to show she had absolutely no worries of any criminal charges because she was as innocent as a newborn babe, at least that was the image she intended to project. A couple of network vice presidents might even be here tonight, since it was a pilot for a series.

Lila shivered with excitement as she quickly parked, walked out of the garage and up the street to the screening room. She saw Howard walking up ahead with Olga, but she didn't bother trying to catch up. She wanted to see who else was there before she got stuck sitting with people she already knew. Rumor had it that the president of the network himself might be there, and it was common knowledge that his marriage was on the rocks. He was pretty much of a toad but with all his power and money, who cared? Sitting next to him could be the start of a whole new phase in her life and career.

She felt a tap on her shoulder. "Lila."

Dammit! It was Cary, an assistant director, who was barely out of his teens. She'd met him on the set of one of Stan's shows and his infatuation with her was extremely annoying. She sure as hell didn't want that nobody glomming on to her all evening.

"Hi, Cary," she said as coldly as she could muster without being downright rude. You never knew where he might end up one day. He was too crazy about her to notice.

"Lila, I'd like you to meet my mom."

Lila nodded at the plain, middle-aged woman who dressed like she had bought her outfit at the Salvation Army.

"This is her first Hollywood screening."

"It's nice to meet you," the woman said shyly.

Cary took his mother's arm and grabbed Lila around the waist and pulled her along with him as he began walking toward the theaters. "We better hurry up or we'll miss the opening credits."

Lila groaned inwardly. This was absolute disaster—her reward for always being late. But it was cruel and unusual punishment, even for someone with her record.

The lights were already down as they entered the screening room, and the only empty seats they could find were in the fourth row. Lila sat trapped between Cary and his mother and fumed. Would anything ever work out for her?

She had thought this screening would get her mind off all her fears and insecurities for a while, but her anger grew as the opening credits appeared, and she directed all her frustration at Steve. It was his fault that Lila was the way she was.

When he had left her the first time, she had been devastated. His return had been the real beginning of her life. Without him, she might as well stop breathing. He was her life. Three years ago, when she had found out that Steve was cheating on her, she had lost control and had wanted to kill herself as well as him. She never found out the identity of the woman, no matter how desperately she begged him to tell her. She had her suspicions, but they seem too absurd to consider seriously. Who could compete with her? Not her pathetic mother; she was no threat. But who would Steve prefer over Lila? She couldn't keep prying and acting jealous, though. Lately, she had felt him slipping away from her. That might push him away for good.

After that horrible night, she was both terrified she would lose him and determined to make him pay for his indiscretion. But how could she live without him? It was all too confusing and painful to dwell on. She sank down in her seat and tried to concentrate on the movie. It suddenly hit her that she had forgotten to call Josh to find out what happened in court today. He'd get over it. Right now, she had more important problems. Like how to dump Cary and his mother before the post-screening party in the commissary.

* * * *

Josh was driving Rosemaria east on Santa Monica Boulevard, and feeling a hundred pounds lighter than he had that morning. Possibly because the weight of a jail sentence had rolled off his shoulders.

"So, how did you do it this time? Your father and the mayor again?"

"The mayor wouldn't have enough clout."

"I guess you're not going to tell me."

"You guess right. And there's more good news. The civil suit was dropped. The D.A. said if they insisted on going ahead with suing the city, he'd have to go ahead with a few charges of his own, so why clog up the court calendar with the end result being they'd spend time in jail?"

"So even with all the bad publicity about Lila and me, people in the system are sticking up for me? It doesn't make any sense."

Rosemaria's eyes narrowed, "You're not going to give me a bad time for getting you out of this, are you?"

"I'm not that much of an asshole. I'm damned pleased. But why all the favors? And don't take my head off! I got the feeling you believed in law and justice and fair play and all that."

"I do believe in all that," she answered matter-of-factly, relaxing again. "I don't believe you're guilty of anything. You would have to have lived in a cave all your life not to realize that the law and justice are rarely the same thing. If Ed Hahn wants to use his influence to burn you, I'll use mine right back to make sure he doesn't."

The tension that had been building up in him the past few weeks was beginning to drain out. "So, where do we go to celebrate?"

She put a finger up to her lips and thought for a moment. "How about your place and you can sing some of your songs for me."

Josh hesitated. He didn't want Rosemaria to get him trapped in his own apartment and start acting like a psychiatrist again. The whole evening would go right down the toilet if that's what she had in mind. He stopped at a red light where Fairfax crossed Santa Monica and studied her happy, contented face. Josh decided she didn't look like she was in the mood to inflict any more of her homemade therapy on him tonight. "Okay. We can stop at the liquor store by my house and load up on supplies."

"Juice for me. I'm on a health kick as of a couple of nights ago."

"Me, too. I believe in drinking a lot of alcohol to kill all the germs in my body."

"Is it working?"

He puffed up his chest and sat straight. "I leave that to your appraisal."

"Don't push your luck."

Josh expertly wove in and out of the traffic up Highland and along Hollywood Boulevard where the Christmas decorations looked, as always, out of place and out of time and failed miserably to evoke the spirit of the season. Josh needed snow and crisp, cold weather to get him in a holiday mood. But Christmas also reminded him of bittersweet memories that would never be recaptured and were better left forgotten.

In ten minutes, they were in front of the liquor store. "I'll meet you at your place. Any and all brands okay?" Rosemaria asked, getting ready to jump out.

He had the urge to kiss her, and he pulled her close and did just that. To his surprise, there was no resistance and her lips melted softly against his. They pulled apart slowly and she met his eyes with a steady gaze. "Any and all, then," she said and was gone.

Josh sat there thoughtfully for a few seconds, then pulled around back to his usual parking spot. The lady cop was growing on him. He had never known such a feisty, independent broad in his life. Sure, he had met plenty of loud, aggressive women in the music business, but they were all ego-oriented: me, me, me, success at any cost. Rosemaria was just the opposite. She asked very little for herself, and he knew there was nothing he could offer her that she couldn't get or do for herself. Not like Lila, who needed a man to start breathing in the morning. Rosemaria was just so damn irritating sometimes. He made up his mind to enjoy the evening and let happen whatever happened. He wasn't getting engaged. It was just an evening. He would play her a few songs, get a little mellow, forget about Lila—who hadn't even bothered to call to ask about his hearing—and maybe get laid.

Josh got out of the car, and as he passed the dumpster that leaned against the wall, a thought flashed through his mind that the parking lot seemed unusually dark that night. He looked up to see that the light on the wall on the back of the building had been broken and before a warning light could go on in his brain, an arm shot around his neck and the point of a knife was at his throat. The man pulled him out of sight behind the dumpster and a second man's voice whispered softly, "We've been waiting for you." He came around to face Josh. It was the oldest of the punks he had fought at the zoo, Manuel Guerrero. "You really fucked us over good, man," he said, twisting his face into an ugly snarl. "We were sure we could get a whole lotta cash for our trouble. You must have some friends in high places. They're not going to help you now."

The sweat was popping out on Josh's forehead and drenching his armpits. These two thugs were crazy, and he was as good as dead if he didn't do something fast. "You brought it on yourselves, dickheads," Josh said with a calm he didn't feel.

Guerrero stuck his face closer to Josh's and a knife materialized in his hand. He held it up to Josh's eye. "My friend Raul here doesn't agree with you. You broke his little friend's face and that hurt him a lot." The knife was an inch from Josh's cornea. Guerrero's pitted face looked paradoxically moronic and insidious at the same time, and his foul breath assaulted Josh every time he opened his mouth.

"Now, we got to do something to your face. It's only fair, don't you think?" He took a couple of steps backward and smiled. "I'm glad you understand. Friends have to stick together, right?"

Josh didn't bother answering. He knew they would kill him in the next few seconds if he couldn't get the drop on the guy behind him, and then maybe—and it was a slim maybe—he would have a chance. Guerrero backed up against the dumpster and eased over to the far edge. "Too bad your friends aren't here now," he said, just before peering around the corner of the dumpster to check out the parking lot.

Josh was half a second away from stomping down on Raul's instep when he heard a loud thwack behind him, and the knife at his throat clattered to the ground. Guerrero turned around just in time to have Rosemaria's Springfield Armory forty-five stuck in his face. "You want to argue with this, mother-fucker?" she said as cold and hard as any voice Josh had ever heard.

* * * *

The evening had been a disaster for Lila. Cary and his mother had stuck to her like glue at the reception, and even walked her back to the parking lot afterwards. None of the network execs had shown up, not even any of the low-level types from the studio. The pilot stunk and everybody knew it. Lila would have to go back to plan A and rely on Josh's songs to get her into the spotlight, get a new agent worthy of her, then build her acting career from there.

She heard her landline ringing as soon as she walked through the door. She couldn't imagine who was calling on that phone. Most people used her cell and Steven only used the throwaway she had bought just for the two of them. She picked up and the voice on the other end was unfamiliar. "Yes, this is Lila. Who's this?"

She felt the blood draining out of her face as she listened to the reply and let her coat and purse fall into the chair beside the phone table.

"All right—No! We can't meet; I'm being followed. I'll think of something. Call me tomorrow."

Lila sagged against the wall and fought back the despondency as she had all her life, and, as always, she steeled herself, gathered her strength, and renewed her determination. She knew she could do it all herself like she always had, but she didn't want to anymore. No more. No more. No more. Please, no more. She needed Steve. It was late and he hated to be disturbed once he had gone to sleep, but he owed her. Dammit, he did. With a resentment that hit her out of nowhere and began to build, she grabbed their special cell phone and clicked the speed dial.

* * * *

"I don't understand your attitude." Rosemaria was at her desk, typing the report into her computer. What she really wanted to tell Josh was that he was an ungrateful son-of-a-bitch, and that she'd like to give him a swift kick in the pants. She had just saved his life, and now he was sitting there glaring at her as though she was the one who had tried to kill him.

"I'm sorry," he said insincerely, "I was just thinking how you're Carrie Nation, the cavalry, and the U.S. Marines all rolled into one."

Rosemaria shot him a look but didn't stop typing. "I'll take that as a compliment."

A friendly voice boomed out a greeting at the door and Rosemaria looked up to see Sergeant Kowalski come in the room.

"Good work, honey." He grabbed her shoulders from behind and gave her a gentle, good-natured shake. Her mood brightened considerably. He was the only man in the world, besides her father, who she would let get away with making her feel like a helpless female.

"All in the line of duty," she said.

Kowalski pulled up a chair and glanced around at the empty cubicles. "Everybody else keeping banker's hours again, huh?"

She shrugged. "What do you expect? This is Beverly Hills."

Kowalski grinned and looked at Josh. "And this must be the lucky guy who didn't get his throat slit." He held out his hand. "Kowalski, Ernie."

"Josh Sibley. Good to meet you."

Kowalski refocused his attention on Rosemaria.

"Any problems with the arrest?"

She clicked off the report and pushed her chair away from the desk. "None." She smiled at Kowalski. "Josh called for a squad car while I cuffed the unhappy young men. Two officers took them downtown, where one of them will wake up with a nasty bump on his head. If we're lucky, they'll be off the street for one whole night. Now..." She rubbed her hands together enthusiastically. "Enough business for tonight." She stood up and looked pointedly at Josh. "Which one of you wants to take me to dinner? I'm having a Pink's attack."

Kowalski jumped up and helped Rosemaria on with her coat. "I'm on duty. Count me out," he said with obvious relief. "I've seen the results of your Pink's attacks."

"I owe you one," Josh said. Then added, "I thought you were on a health kick."

"Arresting creeps makes me hungry. Besides, I need to talk to you about something." She knew by the look on his face that it had been a mistake to say that as soon as the words were out. She was tired of walking on egg-shells around him.

Without much conversation, they drove to Pink's outdoor fast food stand on La Brea, where Rosemaria ordered a hot dog with everything. They sat at one of the outdoor tables, and Rosemaria opened wide to accommodate the drippy, messy concoction. Josh watched her in disgust.

"Do you have any idea of the crap that's in those things? All the ground up animal parts they put in there?"

Rosemaria chewed contentedly on the poisonous hot dog. "I know, but it tastes so good."

"Pure shit. And I mean that literally."

"Stop nagging." She took a long drink of her root beer.

"Speaking of which, what did you want to talk to me about?"

He was starting to irritate her again. "Will you stop acting like some spoiled little kid? I bust my ass trying to help you, and all you do is sulk!"

"No more lectures, okay?"

"How do I get through to you?" The hot dog felt like it was caught in her chest.

"Why would you want to?" She studied the cars going by La Brea.

Rosemaria wrapped what was left of her hot dog and threw it in the trash can.

"I know about your father."

He was stunned. "How the hell–"

"I'm sorry. I wasn't prying. It was part of my job to check you out like I check out anybody who might be involved in a murder."

"It's not your job to butt into my personal life."

"I just want to help you, Josh. There's no reason for you to blame yourself for your father's death. What happened wasn't your fault. I know that you only did what you did to defend–"

Josh slammed his fist into the table. "You don't talk about him!"

"I know you don't have to go on paying, for God's sake! It's alright for you to be happy."

Josh slid off the bench and strode purposefully to the car. "Get in. I'll take you home."

"You don't have to let the past ruin your life."

"What about you?" He turned on her. "You think people in show business are lower than shit because your mother loved *it* more than you."

"That's a lie!" Rosemaria shouted back at him. "You're great at avoiding the subject!"

He yanked open the car door. "Get in the car!"

Rosemaria jumped to her feet, trembling with anger. She could hardly get her words out. "How the hell can someone so talented...and... intelligent, be so, so, incredibly stupid!?"

"Get in the goddamned car or I'm leaving you here!" his voice boomed out at her.

"I can take a fucking cab!" Rosemaria was yelling at the top of her lungs.

By now, people had gathered, and Sam, the man behind the counter at Pink's, was watching the action, fascinated, but Rosemaria was beyond worrying about public decorum.

Josh got behind the wheel and slammed the door shut. He yelled through the open window. "Your language is lousy!" He blasted away from the curb, tires screeching.

She screamed after him. "So's yours!"

Her next shout was almost a sob. "So's your car!"

She dragged herself back to Pink's stand, oblivious to the stares of a couple of other customers, her hand resting tenderly on her stomach. It was screaming out in agony. She had to start listening to her body before she killed it. No more hot dogs, ever. She reached up for the glass of Alka-Seltzer Sam had prepared for her. He had come to know her stomach better than she did.

CHAPTER TWENTY-SEVEN
FORT MCCOY, WISCONSIN

If there was anything Sergeant Tillson hated, it was being awakened in the middle of the night for no damn good reason. It made him feel cranky and out of sorts for the whole next day, but there were a few smart-mouth assholes who had told him they could hardly see the difference between that and his regular mood.

When the phone rang at zero one hundred, Sergeant Tillson was on the verge of blowing a whole mess of ragheads to hell and back, but instead, the irritating jangle interrupted the most fun he'd had in months. Reluctantly, the Sergeant pulled himself out of his satisfying fantasies and the comforting warmth of his bed and stumbled over to his desk.

"This had better be good," he warned whatever idiot had the balls to call him at this hour, then picked up the phone.

"Sergeant Tillson here."

It was Captain Hubbard.

Tillson listened for thirty seconds. "Yes, sir, Captain, right away."

He made his way yawning and scratching, thinking how great it was going to be a few months from now when he retired. After forty years, he would get full benefits and he could sleep as long as he wanted with no interruptions. He made his way into the barracks room and down the row of bunks until he got to Sibley's.

He looked down at the poor schmuck sleeping like a baby and thought that it was too bad that a guy who tried as hard as him, had such a weird, pain-in-the-ass mother. This was her second mysterious "life or death" phone call in less than two weeks.

"Hey, Sibley." he shook Josh's shoulder. "Wake up. You gotta call your old lady."

Sibley woke up instantly and hauled ass into the office. By the time the Sergeant got there, he had already dialed and was shifting nervously from one foot to the other, waiting for an answer. The Sergeant leaned against the doorframe and shook his head. What in the hell could be important enough to interfere with training to serve God and country as a soldier? Life and death, my achin' butt, he thought. This time, Sibley looked shook up as all get out, though, and he could already tell, the man was no coward.

"Ma, what's going on? You okay?" Sibley's voice was shaking with worry.

He sank down heavily in the chair by the desk as he listened to what-ever the old lady was telling him. Josh raked his fingers through his hair and spewed curses into the phone. "Oh, shit! Goddamn it. Oh, shit!" He leaped to his feet again. "Don't do anything, you hear me? I'll come. I'll talk to the Sergeant and see what I have to do. But don't you go. I'll come take care of it." The kid looked like he was about to have a fuckin' shit fit. "Don't cry, Ma, okay? Don't cry."

He hung up and the Sergeant seriously considered that he was losing his own mind. "Be back by morning or you're AWOL."

"Thank you, sir. You can count on it." And Sibley was out the door.

The Sergeant was getting soft in his old age. He figured he better go back to sleep and fight war in his dreams. It was probably the only place he was fit to fight it these days.

CHAPTER TWENTY-EIGHT

LOS ANGELES

J osh had driven halfway home with the urgency of someone being chased. Around Highland and Sunset, he finally slowed down and thought rationally about what Rosemaria had said. He could live with her knowing what had happened that night, but he couldn't live with her constantly trying to tie up all his problems with a convenient little ribbon and pinning it on something he rarely even thought about anymore. There were a lot of reasons why you failed in this business, and it wasn't necessarily that you were trying to sabotage yourself. Hell, nothing would make him happier than to be able to send his mother a truckload of money and get her out of that run-down beauty shop where she washed hair and swept up the floor every day.

He noticed the blinking light on his ancient answering machine as soon as he opened the door. It had been days since he last checked it. He splashed some vodka into a coffee mug and sat on the couch to listen.

"You said you'd call me, Josh." It was Cherie of the soft and breathy voice. "It's been weeks since our night together. You said you'd never forget it. I sure haven't. Call me, okay? You know the number. Bye."

Cherie had been his last foray into the world of the beautiful but brain-dead. It would be awhile before he got that drunk again.

"It's Ken. I'm working on something for you. I'll let you know what happens in a day or so. Heard the good news. Keep your nose clean."

A message of hope. He decided to brew up a pot of coffee and work all night. He shuffled through the stacks of papers on the coffee table looking for a clean yellow pad and got his guitar out from behind the couch. He listened to the next message. It was Lila. Probably wanted to tell him how sorry she was she couldn't make it to court. Fat chance.

"There's no reason to be upset, Steve."

Steve? Who the hell is Steve?

"Please, call me back. The musician means nothing to me. The papers are making it all up. I'll be there soon. Wait for me. We'll get through this. You and me. There's no reason to be upset. I love you."

The tears that sprang into his eyes were unexpected, like the pain in his gut. She was in love with someone else—whoever she had thought she was calling. Lila had lied to him from the beginning. With a surge of anger, he swept the answering machine and phone off the table and sent them crashing into the wall. "Damn you, Lila! Damn you!" The unescapable thought flashed across his brain—he never knew her…she might be capable of anything, even killing Stan.

* * * *

Jennie found him cleaning up in the chimpanzee compound as the monkeys scooted up and down their trees and along the branches, barely paying attention to Josh. She watched him through the fence and saw how intent he was, concentrating on his work and whatever else was going through his mind—probably Lila, always Lila. She hoped that she could put an end to that as soon as they talked. A musical genius, cleaning up monkey poop for a living. So unfair. She called his name and he squinted out at her.

"Jennie? What are you doing here?"

"Can you come out and talk to me for a few minutes?"

"Is something wrong?"

"No, I just need to tell you something."

"Okay." He picked up his bucket and broom and made his way to the inner doorway. He came out in a few minutes and sat down on the bench beside her.

"What's so important that you're interrupting my very important executive board meeting?"

Jennie smiled. "Well, there's something I should tell you that I've known for a while but figured…" She hesitated. How could she hurt him like this?

"Get it out. It's okay."

"Lila is having an affair."

"I know."

Jennie was surprised. "You do?"

"Yes."

"What do you know about it?"

"Not much. What do you know?"

"Just that it has been going on for a long time. Stan suspected and was waiting until the feature wrapped to ask her for a divorce."

"But he didn't find out who it was?"

"No. I don't think he cared. He just wanted to be free of her."

Josh sat still, looking off into the distance.

"What is it, Josh? Are you okay?"

"I'm just thinking of the first time I met her. I thought she was the most exquisite creature I had ever seen."

"It was just a façade, Josh."

"I guess so." His sadness broke her heart.

"Don't feel so downhearted, Josh. I also wanted to tell you that Ken may land a major account with Statewide Insurance and if it comes through, which seems very likely, Ken is pushing you to write and sing the commercial. It looks good, really. You know I wouldn't say that unless it were true."

He finally turned and looked at her. "I know, Jennie. Tell Ken I appreciate it." He stood up to go back to work. "You know where to find me."

She watched Josh walk away and felt a deep abiding hatred for the woman who had broken her friend's kind, gentle spirit. She prayed that Sergeant Baker would make sure Lila was locked away for the rest of her life.

* * * *

Waite walked up to the front of the room to the whiteboard. The rest of the team—Rosemaria, Coleman, and Osborne—were seated around the table in the conference room, waiting for Jimmy to speak his piece. The pictures on the board showed Lila and Bauer/Beaumont in the center and pictures of Josh, Jennie, Sal and Moe off to the side. Waite pinned a picture of Hari on the board beside Lila. "Okay, so this guy gave off weird vibes that made me a little suspicious. Harry O'Shaughnessy. He calls himself Hari Suma. That's his professional name. He's an actor."

"Naturally. Isn't everyone in this town?" Coleman asked.

Rosemaria looked up from where she was making notes on her legal pad. "Go on."

"So, I checked out all the businesses and homes near the 405 on-ramp where Lila most likely would have gotten on the freeway coming from Bel Air, heading for the Ventura freeway and Oxnard. Some of the businesses had cameras and most save their recordings for several months before recording over them. I have copies of and looked at these videos, hoping to find what time Lila drove by in her car, assuming it was after the murder and not before, as she alleges. Do you have any idea of how many Mercedes SLKs drove by that night?"

"Probably at least ten," Osborne piped up.

"You know because I told you."

"Get on with it." Rosemaria was impatient.

"But at the gas station, this guy Harry seemed surprised and not too happy to see me. He told me the camera didn't always work very well, which I checked out later with the owner, who said that wasn't true. And when I looked at the video, an hour was missing from about nine to ten, which would have been soon after the murder. He's either an idiot or he wants to be a suck-up like another Kato Kaelin and just wants publicity."

"Who was also an idiot." Rosemaria said. "Okay, we'll get back to this. Thanks, Waite. Osborne?"

Osborne, with his laptop in front of him, began his report seated. "I followed Vera and Nicholson who were following Lila..."

Coleman was confused. "Wait a minute. You were following the followers. Why?"

Rosemaria admitted a bit sheepishly, "Actually, I had told Vera and Nicholson to be a little obvious so Lila could ditch them and think she wasn't being followed and let down her guard."

Coleman looked slightly put out. "I like it. But you could tell me these things."

"Sorry. Didn't think it was important. Go on, Osborne."

"I followed her to the Valley Inn in Sherman Oaks, which is courtyard style. She went into room 203, which was occupied by one Byron Talbot, who looked exactly like Steve Beaumont and, in fact, is him. Stays there on a regular basis one or two months every year since Lila moved here for a week or less, pays in cash, and is no trouble. He must have an alias or two from his wandering around days. Couldn't see what was going on in the room but she left after about two hours, a little more disheveled than when she came. I put the fear of God into the manager that he will not mention a word of my being there or be liable for obstruction of justice and a few other crimes. He won't talk."

"Now all we have to do is find the murder weapon with the prints of the killer and we'll have them dead to rights," Coleman said sarcastically.

Rosemaria smiled. "Actually, I have a hunch about that."

Coleman couldn't resist. "I thought only old-timers had hunches."

Rosemaria looked at him askance. "Be kind to your elders, Larry, you'll be one someday."

"She called me Larry! You all heard it. I think she's starting to like me!"

"Baker, I'd like you to come into my office, please." None of them had noticed the Lieutenant standing in the doorway.

"Yes, sir." The Lieutenant turned away and walked quickly into his office. Rosemaria shot a mystified face to her cohorts and stood up and followed him.

"Your team is right up to the minute in their reports. I appreciate that," he said as he put his briefcase on the desk.

"Thank you, sir."

"This is some sordid muck we're having to wade through. Even for the fly-by-night Hollywood crowd."

"Yes, sir. It took us all by surprise."

"So, the one witness we have to Lila's infatuation with her...father..." Mandel could hardly get the word out, "is this Vanessa Sheridan."

"Yes, Vanessa is the only one who saw him and was close to him."

Mandel sank into his chair and looked up at her. "So to speak."

"She didn't know who he really was, sir. She still doesn't. She's going to need protection once we arrest Lila. Lila's lawyer will undoubtedly get her out on bail..."

"Who's her lawyer?"

"Solly Geller."

"Yeah, he'll have her out."

"And when she finds out that Vanessa is going to testify against her, I have no doubt she'll want Vanessa dead."

"Mrs. Levy is that deranged?"

"Absolutely."

"Do I have your permission to put Vanessa into protective custody after we arrest Lila?"

"Yes, of course, but detective, we're getting way ahead of ourselves here. We have our suspicions, but that's all we have. You know perfectly well we need a lot more than what we have to move forward on this."

"I have a hunch about how to get that, sir."

"A hunch?"

"Yes, sir, and I need a warrant."

"I can't get a judge to issue a warrant on a hunch."

"If you have any outstanding favors out there, this is the time to use them, sir. Give him all the circumstantial evidence and make your case. She's outsmarted herself and we can turn it against her. I know it."

Mandel studied the photographs on his wall showing him smiling with every kind of bigwig in town and beyond. Rosemaria could tell he was mentally going over what she had told him and who the hell owed him a big enough favor to get this done. He finally looked at her.

"You'll have your warrant. Now, I want details."

* * * *

Vera and Nicholson walked up the stairs to room 203 at the Valley Inn. They stopped outside the door, exchanged smiles, and shrugged on their most officious and intimidating law officer personas. "Ready?" Vera asked. Nicholson nodded and pounded on the door. "Police! Open up!"

After a few seconds, the door opened slightly and a thin, wiry man in his late forties with gray hair and ruggedly handsome features—Steve Beaumont—stood in the doorway and peered out at them, surprise and fear on his face. "What's wrong?"

Nicholson handed the man a warrant. "Ernest Bauer, AKA Stephen Beaumont, AKA Bryon Talbot, we have a warrant to search your room."

"I... I'm not Beaumont. I'm Bryan Talbot. You have the wrong room."

Nicholson held up the photo ID he had of Bauer/Beaumont. "Is this you?"

"I... Yes."

Nicholson and then Vera brushed past him on their way into the room. "You may stay here, but do not interfere with our search."

Bauer stood by the door, stunned as Vera and Nicholson began to go through his belongings. He slowly regained his composure and made his way to a chair by the small, round dining table and sat down, watching the two detectives expertly search his luggage, dresser drawers, and closet and behind various pieces of furniture. "Can you at least tell me what this is all about?"

"It's all in the warrant, sir," Vera said coldly.

Bauer looked down at the warrant he was holding and started to read. His face turned white. He looked as though he might become ill. Vera noticed, but kept going about his business.

The two cops moved into the bathroom, lifted the toilet seat, and removed the tank cover, thoroughly searching every inch. Vera's cell phone rang. He took it out and clicked it on.

"Vera...Yes, sir." He looked at Bauer and halfway closed the door. "I'll tell him, sir." He and Nicholson moved close to the partially open bathroom door and Vera whispered, "That was the Lieutenant. He says that a tip came in that sounds legit and they're sending out the cadets to search by the freeway entrance tomorrow morning. We can wrap it up here."

Bauer, who had heard every word, his face a stony mask, looked at the two cops heading for the front door. "Find anything?"

"Thank you for your cooperation, sir, we're done here," Nicholson said politely and the two went out the door.

Outside, as the two reached the ground floor, Vera asked Nicholson, "Think he went for it?"

"We'll find out tonight."

"I hope he doesn't watch too much TV."

"Why?"

"They've done this a million times on *Murder She Wrote*."

"Never heard of it."

"I bet the Sergeant has."

* * * *

It both excited and frightened Lila to be the target of Steve's rage. No one else could turn her on with just the touch of his hand. She had known she wanted him as soon as she laid eyes on him when she was sixteen. It had been a challenge to seduce him. He had all sort of reasons why it was wrong, why they shouldn't, but she hadn't given up. What was wrong with what she wanted? She hadn't known him when she was little. He was just like a stranger, just like any other man she met for the first time. Eventually, he'd given in and they became addicted to each other. Her idiot mother, who obviously knew nothing about hanging on to a man, never suspected a thing. Lila still couldn't understand why Steve insisted on keeping up the charade of living with that woman and catering to her wishes. Guilt, she supposed; ridiculous, annoying guilt.

She drove into the parking garage at the Sherman Oaks shopping center and onto the top floor where few cars were parked, except for Christmas and black Friday. She had driven all the way to Westlake and back, driving on deserted roads, looking behind her every other second to make sure she wasn't followed. She saw him leaning against his rented car and seeing his face and his flashing dark eyes filled her with so much desire, she wanted him then and there.

She parked beside him and quickly got out of her car and threw herself into his arms. He pushed her away angrily. "What did you do with the gun? Did you get rid of it like you said?"

Lila stiffened and stepped away from him. "Yes, of course I did. No one will ever find it."

"Well, think again. Someone told the cops they saw you walking near the Bel Air on-ramp that night and the cops are starting a search there tomorrow morning."

Lila's eyes widened in fear. "No! How did you find that out?"

"They came to my room with a search warrant. I overheard a phone call."

"What if it's not true? What if they just made it up?"

"You want to take that chance?"

"I don't know." She felt confused. Everything was falling apart.

"What did you do, Lila? Is it somewhere they could find it?"

"No, I hid it really well. They can't possibly find it."

Steve was livid. "Hid it! Why did you hide it?! Why didn't you get rid of it?! Throw it off a pier where it could never be found?!"

"I... didn't think of that."

His eyes narrowed suspiciously. "You did wipe off the prints, didn't you?"

"I did! How can you ask me that?"

He stared at her. She was capable of anything. "You need to get it tonight."

"What if they follow me?"

"They obviously followed you to my motel. I suggest you do a better job of losing them or we're screwed."

"They didn't follow me here. I can assure you of that." Lila considered her options and smiled.

He looked at her like she had lost her mind. "This is amusing to you?"

"I know exactly what I'm going to do. Everything will be just fine."

She moved toward him, lifting her mouth to his, desperately needing and wanting him. But he pushed her away and looked at her hard. "I need to leave. We can't be seen together." He opened the car door and sat in the driver's seat.

"You better not disappear," she said so coldly it caused a shiver to run up his spine.

"I won't. Just get the gun to me and I'll make sure it's never found." He slammed the door and started the car.

Lila watched him drive away. He wouldn't treat her like that for much longer. She still had the upper hand. Midnight tonight and all would be well. Meanwhile, she had to mend fences with Josh.

* * * *

One of the rich-bitch regulars brushed by Hari, knocking his cell phone right out of his hand and sending it crashing to the floor before he had even clicked it off. He bent down and picked it up and went back behind the counter where she was waiting impatiently for him to ring up her sale. He watched the old battleax walk outside, rip open her bag of corn chips, stuff a few into her mouth, nonchalantly hop into her Rolls Royce as if it were nothing more than a beat-up old Volkswagen, and drive away into the unimaginable pleasures of those hills.

He had been a little shook up when the cop came by yesterday asking questions and wanting to look at the video footage from the security camera. Fortunately, he had deleted the incriminating footage after copying it to his own laptop and told the cop it must have been a computer foul-up. Hari had put his acting talent to good use, and he was sure the cop had bought it hook, line, and sinker. "It shouldn't be long now," he whispered to himself.

CHAPTER TWENTY-NINE

LOS ANGELES

Harry's Bar, slightly seedy and dark with high-backed booths where one could nurse one's wounds in relative privacy, was Josh's favorite watering hole. It was located on Hollywood Boulevard, west of Highland, so the clientele wasn't quite as down on their luck as the Hollywood and Gower crowd. It always attracted a few stray tourists, who wandered in after visiting the glitz and glamour of Mann's Chinese and all the rest of the tourist trap hoopla that existed on the intersection of Highland and Hollywood Boulevard. They usually wanted to know where the heck were all the movie stars they had come all the way from Nebraska to see.

Ten years ago, when Harry first opened the bar, he used to get so fed up with all the kvetching, he'd either give them impeccable directions to East L.A. or tell them to go back to Podunk where they belonged. Nowadays, he was inured to all the complaints and just rattled off the directions to Rodeo Drive for about the millionth time.

Ken signaled to Harry from the back booth that he was ready for his check, and turned his attention back to Josh, who was strumming the last few chords of a song on his guitar. He looked sober and confident.

"Better?" he asked Ken, as if he already knew the answer.

"It's good. The other changes will fit in with that, too."

"I'm working on the song in act two. I haven't quite figured that one out yet."

"Harvey has to be in New York tomorrow for a backers' audition for Jud Wessel's show, so you have time." Ken saw Josh's panicky look but didn't give him a chance to indulge in his insecurities. "Harvey won't like it. Don't worry. The book is long and boring and will put Harvey to sleep before intermission."

Harry put the check on the table and Ken waved off Josh's offer to pay. He peeled off a few bills and put them on the table, then stood up and smiled. "We've got a good chance at this, and I think you're getting the commercial, too. I'll let you know in a couple of days." He grinned at the strangeness of seeing Josh in a bar drinking straight coke. "By the way, I don't know what happened, but I like it."

He left Josh strumming his guitar and thought how great the timing had been in all of this. Josh was miraculously getting his act together, and Ken had stumbled upon Harvey Honnigbaum by pure accident. He'd run into Harvey at LAX on his way to New York two months ago and found out that he had a secretary who wanted in the worst way to be a Broadway star, and then Mrs. Honnigbaum, in that order. Harvey, being short, fat, and bald, was eager to please his young, almost attractive girlfriend. Wonder of wonders, a couple of weeks later, Ken had found out that the woman could actually sing when Harvey invited him to hear her at a piano bar on Ventura Boulevard, and that love-struck Harvey was even richer than when they'd shared joints at political protests at Berkeley after Harvey had inherited the family fortune. The girlfriend loved Josh's demo tape and was chomping at the bit to start working out the deal. But Harvey, forever the prudent businessman ever since he turned in his protest signs for a gold-plated sign on his corner office, wanted to check out a couple of other possibilities before making a final decision.

The heady smell of success on Broadway lit up Hollywood Boulevard with a pleasant glow and Ken sailed through traffic, until a car sped through a red light at La Brea and would have hit him if Ken hadn't slammed on the brakes, thanking God no one was behind him. As he waited at the light, he happened to look in the rear-view mirror at the entrance to Harry's and saw Lila enter the front door.

"Aw, shit!" he said aloud, before honking horns forced him to move ahead.

When he looked up and saw Lila coming toward him, Josh steeled himself. Her beauty always hit him with the impact of a skyscraper falling on his head and turned his brain to mush. He wasn't about to let it happen this time.

He didn't invite her to sit down, but she slid into the booth opposite him anyway.

"I know you're angry with me. I wanted to be in court but...well..." Her voice drifted off.

Not this time, baby, he thought coldly.

"Why are you looking at me like that?" she asked, looking like a lost twelve-year-old.

It might have gotten to him except that, knowing what he knew now, when Lila was twelve she was probably seducing her neighbor's husband.

"I finished writing your song."

"You did?" Her response sounded unsure.

Josh strummed his guitar and spoke the words to the song as they came into his head.

"There once was a whore named sweet Lila,

Whose body was filled with desire.

She always had pick

Of any man's dick

But I'd rather fuck a spare tire."

Lila sat immobilized, her eyes riveted on his face. Not a muscle in her face moved for several seconds. Then, slowly, her eyes began to fill with tears and spill down her cheeks.

Josh continued to stare at her dispassionately. His icy composure was too much for Lila to bear and she began to cry. He felt his resolve starting to crack. She put her head down on her arms and sobbed as if her heart was breaking. Josh couldn't handle this. He had wanted a bit of revenge, but he hadn't reckoned on getting a reaction this strong. He felt small and mean, and he signaled Harry.

"Whiskey. Two glasses."

It was obvious Harry was not at all happy about this development, but he reluctantly brought the glasses anyway. Josh ignored the filthy looks.

Josh held out a glass to Lila. "Drink. Don't argue."

Lila lifted her head and looked at him. Half her eye makeup was dripping down her cheeks. She blew her nose on the cocktail napkin and took a small sip of her drink. Her total unconcern about her face made Josh suspect she wasn't faking this time. No matter how upset she had gotten before, she never failed to make sure she looked like a *Cosmo* cover. Right now, she was a mess. Josh felt himself sinking again into her abyss.

"It was you that got the phone message, wasn't it?" she asked, avoiding his eyes.

When he didn't answer, she went on. "Will you let me explain?"

"You don't have to. Jennie filled me in."

"Jennie?"

"Stan told her he suspected something."

Lila looked so confused, Josh had to wonder if she really didn't know about the two of them.

"I don't know what he told her, and why would he discuss my personal business with her anyway?"

Josh was not about to throw Jennie under the bus. "They were friends. He needed someone to talk to."

Lila waved away the comment. "I knew that. Neither one of them had a clue what I was going through."

"Which was?"

"I wanted to tell you, Josh, but I was afraid of what you'd think, that you might leave me."

Suddenly Josh was tired of all the drama. His reply was remote and robotic. "So why don't you just tell me the truth?"

"It started when I was sixteen."

Josh waited for her to continue.

"He was my mother's boyfriend."

Lila paused, expecting a reaction from Josh. There was none.

"It was horrible. So horrible, you can't imagine. I was terrified my mother would find out. It would have broken her heart, or probably she would have blamed me. I felt helpless."

At sixteen, you were helpless? Josh almost asked but took a sip of his drink instead.

"I was very young and naïve for my age," she said defensively. "He said he would blame me if I told my mother, and she would hate me." Lila was working up to more tears. "She depends on him. He takes care of her. I didn't want to destroy her life!" She calmed down and continued. It was hell for two years. I left as soon as I could get some money together and found a place to live. I despised the sight of him."

"That phone message wasn't meant for somebody you despise."

"You don't understand. My mother asked him to come down to help me take care of things after Stan was killed because she was sick and couldn't come herself. If I don't act nice to him, he might tell her out of spite. I can't hurt her like that."

Josh felt like he was drowning in bullshit. "What about those other times he's come down?"

"I'd only see him long enough to ask him to please leave me alone. I didn't want to aggravate him." She reached across the table and grabbed his arm. "You have to believe me!"

"In that case, the next time he hassles you, call me. I'll take care of that son-of-a-bitch."

"You can't!" Lila panicked. He'll go to my mother!"

"Do you want him out of your life or not?"

"Do you think we could get another drink?" She was becoming inexplicably submissive. "It's making me feel better."

Josh signaled Harry again, who looked at Lila with undisguised loathing before setting the drinks down on the table. Josh ignored him and drank.

*　*　*　*

He was drunk again. In the inner recesses of his brain, for the umpteenth time, he experienced a profound disappointment with himself. In an equally profound way, but of more immediate concern, he felt like he was about to vomit up his guts.

Lila had managed to get him in and out of her car and was carrying his guitar case and supporting him with her other arm, steering him towards his apartment.

He didn't see the General until he was standing almost directly in front of them, but before he had a chance to launch into his usual singsong garble, "I know, I know. You're ready, General, right?" Josh asked.

"Yes, I'm ready."

"What the hell are you ready for? You wanna tell me that?"

Josh wanted to stay and get an answer to his question once and for all. It was very important. But Lila kept dragging him forward and forced him to have to crane his neck around in order to yell at the General, who was walking away down the street.

"What the hell are you ready for, General?"

Lila took a firmer grip on his arm and yanked him so hard he nearly stumbled and fell.

"It's driving me crazy! I gotta know!"

He wasn't sure, but he thought he heard Lila say, under her breath, "Oh, for Pete's sake!" as she kept steering him towards home. She didn't look like she was having a good time. That he was sure of.

It seemed like an eternity, but they finally made it to his building, through the front door, and up the steps. She searched his clothing for his key and helped him inside. By this time, the whole world was spinning like a carousel, and he had to reach down and hold his bed still before he could lay down on it. He mumbled his thanks to Lila, who seemed strangely hard and cold.

"I can't understand what you're saying, Josh," she said harshly. "What do you want?"

He concentrated on enunciating his words, but they still came out like overcooked mush.

She was struggling to take off his trousers and had no patience.

"All you want to do is drink yourself to death."

"No, I don', I don'."

She finally yanked off his pants. "Just go to sleep."

"But the General. I gotta find out about the General."

She grabbed a corner of the blanket and pulled it over him up to his neck. "Will you shut up about the General. If you must know, he's auditioning."

She took some tissue out of her purse and went over to the dresser mirror and started wiping off her makeup.

What was she doing that for, vaguely went through his mind.

"Martha told me this afternoon when I stopped by." She went on talking nonsense. "The General knows you're a song writer and he wants you to make him a famous singer. He's trying to sing *Are You Ready for Love*, but his mind is too far gone to remember all the words so he just sings the same words over and over."

Josh tried to sit up, but his elbows slipped out from beneath him and he fell back on his pillow. "That's crazy. I'm the only one he talks to because he likes me."

"He doesn't like you." She was intent on her face and didn't bother looking at him as she spoke. "He wants you to make him a star."

No, no. It couldn't be. Josh turned his face into the pillow in anguish. Was it possible that even an old, demented Hollywood derelict was a show business user? This was too much too handle. He needed more booze to dull the pain.

Lila turned away from the mirror and looked at Josh in revulsion. If she didn't need him to help her with her career, she'd never lay eyes on him again. But right now, she had to focus on ditching those two idiots who were following her so she could do what needed to be done.

CHAPTER THIRTY

MARYSVILLE, WISCONSIN

"Mmmm," Connie sighed contentedly. "You didn't forget me." She snuggled closer to Josh, who knew for sure he had died and gone to heaven after six weeks of pure hell.

He had called Connie from the bus stop, and they had practically raped each other in her car before they even got to the motel. Two hours and three comes later, he finally felt satiated enough to relax and just hold her close. He stroked her blonde hair and let himself sink into the pleasure of feeling her smooth, silky skin next to his. Tomorrow morning, he would pick up Scott from school, and then he would have fourteen whole days to divide between him and Connie. The only hitch was his father, who had taken up drinking again with a vengeance. The last thing he wanted to do was to spend his leave breaking up barroom brawls, like the one the old man had started three weeks ago.

The revolver his father had waved in his mother's face was tucked in the belt of his trousers as he tried to trade punches with another drunk as unsteady on his feet as he was. Jimmy had been at the bar and called his dad, who had gotten help in putting Josh's father in his truck and then had driven him home. By then, Josh had made it home and all of them had helped get his father in the house and into bed. Jimmy's dad had taken the gun, but that wouldn't stop Josh's father from getting another one and shooting somebody, if that's what he wanted to do. Despite all that, his mother refused to leave and there was nothing that Josh could say or do to convince her otherwise.

He ran his hand down Connie's back, and it brought his mind back to thoughts of more pleasant pursuits. She moaned deeply in appreciation. Jimmy's voice and the pounding on the door stopped his hands from roaming into warmer, moister territory. "Yeah, Jimmy, yeah. What do you want? Hold your water!" He staggered out of bed and went to the door; one look at Jimmy and he had his answer.

"Get dressed fast. Your mom just called looking for you. She said your dad's acting real crazy again, but she doesn't want to call the police 'cause she doesn't want him put in jail."

Josh was already hopping into his pants, and Jimmy looked over at Connie, who was sitting up in bed with the sheet tucked under her chin. "Sorry, Connie."

She ignored him and said to Josh, who was pulling on his jacket. "Be careful. You know he's not right in the head. He could hurt you."

Josh kissed her forehead. "Keep my place warm?"

Her face was etched with worry and concern, "He could hurt you."

Josh followed Jimmy, who had already run out to his truck.

He hadn't remembered the distance between Marysville and the farm being this far. Jimmy had the gas pedal pressed to the floor and his eyes peeled to the road. "I hope to God the trooper isn't manning the radar trap tonight. If he catches me going this speed, he'll have my license suspended till I'm forty."

That's nuts. He works for your father, for Christ's sake."

"You're right. He'd just lock me up and throw away the key."

Josh was too worried to keep up any good-natured sparring. "We're almost there. The turnoff's just a few miles further."

"I know. I've been there before."

When they came closer to the house, Jimmy turned off his headlights and coasted to a stop.

His father's brown truck was in the driveway.

"Do you want to go in alone?"

"Yeah, wait here unless I call you."

Josh padded silently across the front lawn and avoided all the creaks and groans on the steps and front porch. Through the gauzy front window curtains, he could see his mother and Scott huddled together on the couch facing his father, not visible except for the back of his head over the top of his easy chair. A cold hand wrapped around his chest, and fear paralyzed him with indecision. From the look on his mother's face, he was sure his father was holding a gun on them. It was too late to go back and call the police. He had to do something. Despite the cool night, his shirt was damp with sweat. He wiped the moisture from his upper lip and made his decision. He ran back to the truck where Jimmy was waiting and explained the situation.

"Stay at the front window and when you see me touch my mom's shoulder, open the door."

Jimmy nodded his assent without hesitation. Josh crept back to the house and, taking a deep breath, went inside.

His father knew who it was without turning around. "Come in, Josh." His voice was deadly calm. He was very drunk.

Scott tore himself out of his mother's arms and threw himself at Josh, who hugged his brother tightly, murmuring assurances into his ear.

"Sit down!" His father's voice boomed out. "Everybody sit down!"

Josh didn't hesitate to do as he was told, and he took Scott back to his mother and sat down on the arm of the couch beside her. Was there any use in reasoning with this madman? He had to try. "Dad..."

"Shut up!" His father's hands tightened around the shotgun. "Shut up! I'm the only one who does the talking around here!"

There was no point in waiting. Josh put his hand on his mother's shoulder, and when Jimmy saw the signal through the window, he opened the front door. His father instinctively turned around and Josh leapt across the few feet between him and his father and knocked him to the floor.

Jimmy snatched up the shotgun as soon as the old man fell, and looked down at Josh, who had his father in a hammer lock. "Shit, man. You've gotta do something before he kills somebody."

CHAPTER THIRTY-ONE

LOS ANGELES

Vera and Nicholson were parked in an unmarked car on Wilcox with a clear view of the entrance to Sibley's apartment building. They observed, without much interest, an old bag lady enter the building, then went back to the business at hand. Nicholson had opened the calendar section of the paper and was resting it on the steering wheel as he tried to read the movie pages by the dim light of the streetlamp. Vera kept his eyes peeled on the building as he took bites of his Hostess Twinkie.

Nicholson glanced down at what he was eating. "You shouldn't be eating that crap."

"I'm packing my own lunch now. I get to eat whatever I want."

"It's shit and you know it."

"Who cares? It tastes good. Angie got a promotion at the bank and says she's too busy. I asked my daughter to do it and she just laughed. Can you believe the lack of respect?"

They both spotted the old bag woman coming back out. A couple of inches of silk black back dress hung down below her coat. She hurried up the street towards Franklin.

"Wanna bet who that really is?" Nicholson started the car.

Vera smiled. "You think I just fell off the turnip truck?" Then added, as they slowly cruised by the building…"There goes Sibley!"

"Forget him. We're supposed to follow Mrs. Levy. Very discretely this time, the Sergeant said."

Vera looked back at Sibley coming up the street behind them. The guy could hardly walk, he was so drunk. Vera gave silent thanks that he was a cop and not in show business.

They followed the woman along Hollywood Boulevard to Highland and stopped the car when they saw her sit down on a bench near the bus stop.

"She's taking a bus?" Nicholson turned off the motor and they settled in to wait a block down behind a parked car.

A half an hour and two busses later, they decided it was time to investigate, especially since the woman had made herself comfortable by lying down on the bench.

They stood beside the bench and looked at the reclining woman. Her coat was pulled over her head.

"Ma'am?" Vera tapped on where he thought the woman's shoulder probably would be. "Ma'am, it's not safe to lay here at night like this."

The woman pulled her coat down off her face and spoke to them with not a little authority. "The name's Martha, and please stop bothering me. I merely stopped here for a short rest." With that, she dismissed them by promptly pulling the coat back over her face.

Nicholson spewed out curses Vera never knew existed and led the way back to the car to report that they had lost Mrs. Levy.

Rosemaria slammed the phone down at her desk and jumped to her feet. "They lost Lila, dammit! We need to get over to the 405 now."

Coleman, Waite, and Osborne looked ready to go as they checked their holsters and headed for the door.

"I thought you told them to really follow her this time and not be conspicuous." Coleman said as they followed Waite and Osborne down the hall.

Rosemaria frowned. "I did. She outmaneuvered them."

"Then let's return the favor."

She saluted Coleman and smiled her way out the door.

Coleman pulled the car up to a curb a short distance away from the 405 Bel Air on-ramp. Rosemaria opened the passenger door and walked back to where Waite and Osborne had pulled up behind them. Waite rolled down the driver's window and Rosemaria leaned down. "We'll stay here. You two drive up past the on-ramp and wait there."

"Think she'll show?"

"Who knows? Can't wait to pounce if she does."

Waite smiled and Osborne gave a thumbs-up that Rosemaria returned. She walked back to her car and got in the passenger seat.

"So, here we are." Coleman observed.

"Very true."

"Because you have a hunch."

"That I do."

"Care to share now?"

"Why not?"

Coleman turned and looked at Rosemaria, waiting.

"My theory is this." She paused to think. "The night of the murder, Beaumont or Bauer or whatever his name is, threatened to leave Lila. He had had it with her and wanted to cut ties. From what Vanessa told us..." She smiled at Coleman. "How's she doing, by the way?"

"Locked up snug as a bug in a rug on my boat with one of our best officers as protection. I have no worries about her. So, you were saying?"

"As I was saying, I think Lila was enraged, terrified of Bauer leaving, desperate to hang on to him, and whatever else a woman like her feels at the thought of being abandoned. So, she decided to call him, crying hysterically, claiming Stan was beating her again and begged him to come over. So, Bauer comes over, Stan is surprised to see him there, says he's not doing a damn thing to Lila. Lila cries and plays the victim. Stan and Bauer get into a shouting match, Stan gets out his gun, they fight over it, and Stan gets shot, falls on the table, and bleeds to death while Lila and Bauer take off."

Coleman mulls this over. "Could Lila have spilled the beans to Stan about Bauer and Lila? Maybe that enraged Stan and caused the fight to get out of control."

"We don't know. But at that point, maybe Lila didn't care if Stan lived or died because maybe he told her he was going to divorce her, and if she could convince us that some lunatic drug addict killed him, she would be free and clear to have her affair with her father." Rosemaria screwed up her face and swallowed hard. "I can't believe I'm saying those words."

"Okay, all that is possible. But why are we here?"

"I think Lila told Bauer to leave the murder scene, said she'd wipe the prints off the gun, but didn't. That way she'd have a hold on him if he threatened to leave again. She decided to drive up the coast so she could say she wasn't home when the murder went down but needed to put the gun somewhere close where she could get her hands on it whenever she wanted. And, of course, she wouldn't want it found in the car if, for some reason, she was stopped by highway patrol."

"And she left her cell phone at home so we couldn't trace her movements that night."

"Exactly."

They sat quietly for a few moments, pondering the untold depths of the machinacious mind of Lila before Coleman finally spoke. "You really think she's that sneaky evil?"

"I do."

An hour later, Coleman's eyelids were at half-mast and Rosemaria was pinching herself to stay awake. She looked down at her watch—twelve thirty. She looked up and saw someone walk out of the convenience store, look furtively up and down the street, and head up to where Waite and Osborne were parked—Hari! She nudged Coleman, who sat up abruptly and looked at her with eyes half-closed, "Wha'?"

"It's Hari what's-his-name from the convenience store!" she whispered. "He looks like he's up to no good."

She clicked on her walkie-talkie. "Hey guys, Hari's coming your way!" She heard Waite say, "Who?" She answered back, "Hari, the actor who works at the convenience store. He's walking your way. Keep your eye on him."

Coleman looked at her expectantly. "What do you want to do? Follow him?"

"No, he might see us."

"You think Lila somehow..."

"She can talk any man into anything."

Coleman looked hurt. "Please, not all of us are putty in the hands of a beautiful woman."

The radio came on with Waite's voice whispering. "He's walking up a driveway between two houses...Now he's walking to the back of the lot up to a garden shed. He just disappeared behind the shed...Now he came back out holding a plastic bag with what looks like it could have a gun in it."

"Yes!" Rosemaria was ecstatic. "Don't stop him. We'll follow him to wherever he's going." She clicked off and started the car. They saw Hari come walking back down the street and, looking both ways, get into his car.

Coleman laughed. "Could he be more obvious? He looks so suspicious, my Aunt Mary would think he's guilty of something."

"He's watched too much TV. Do you really have an Aunt Mary?"

"Yes, believe it or not, I have a life."

Hari's car pulled out of the parking lot and headed for the onramp. Waite and Osborne followed several yards behind him and Rosemaria followed them onto the 405 freeway north.

"I do believe we will find gold at the end of this rainbow. If all of your hunches pan out."

"Us old-timers live by our hunches."

"I aspire to have them myself, someday."

Rosemaria gave him a look. "I don't know what I did to deserve you."

"Years from now, you'll remember me fondly."

Rosemaria laughed. "If you're not careful, I'll call you Larry again."

Hari was driving in the slow lane, heading for the Ventura Freeway. They followed him onto the 101 and stayed several cars behind Waite and Osborne, all of them driving fifty miles an hour. Nearing the Laurel Canyon exit, Hari put on his blinker and slowed down before going down the off-ramp and turning right onto Laurel Canyon. At two o'clock in the morning and hardly any traffic, the cop cars had to stay far behind not to be noticed by Hari, who seemed unconcerned about being followed. But after crossing Ventura Boulevard, he turned left onto a winding road, seemingly making his way to the summit, driving up narrow, twisting roads before finally ending up back on Laurel Canyon. Rosemaria and Waite hung back far behind. Obviously, Hari had become concerned with being followed, probably having been given advice on eluding cops by Lila, but Waite was up to the task and all Rosemaria had to do was follow him.

Waite allowed a car that conveniently came along to follow Hari up Laurel Canyon and continued to stay far behind as Hari turned left onto Mulholland. After several miles, the walkie-talkie crackled. It was Osborne. "He just pulled over and parked at the top of Runyon Canyon. We'll drive by and pull up a ways ahead. You should stop where you are and walk the rest of the way."

"Okay. We'll walk towards the entrance to the canyon. You stay in the car."

Rosemaria turned to Coleman. "Shit. She could be in a car, in some-one's driveway, on foot, anywhere along the road. How the hell do we stay unnoticed?"

"I say, drive close to the entrance of the canyon, pull into someone's driveway as if we live there. Go to the back door, explain to the residents why we're there, creep down to the road, and wait for her in the bushes."

Rosemaria considered this. "I like it. Let's go." She informed Waite and Osborne on the walkie talkie what they intended to do and started the car. Unfortunately, every driveway near Runyan Canyon had a remote-con-trolled gate and their plan seemed doomed. She stopped a good block before the entrance to the Canyon, trying to figure out her next move, when a car passed her and pulled up into a driveway and the gate opened. "Hallelujah!" she whispered to Coleman and followed the unsuspecting homeowners through the gate.

Waite clicked back on as the mystified, frightened, elderly homeowners got out of their car and stared at Rosemaria and Coleman. "Hari's coming back to his car. He must've left the package somewhere near the entrance to the canyon...He's starting his car...He just passed us. We're off the road and it's too dark for him to have seen us."

Rosemaria and Coleman jumped out of the car, flashing their badges at the wide-eyed couple.

Lila stood a few yards down the path from the entrance to the Canyon. She knew lots of celebrities walked their dogs there. She had thought of getting a dog herself, so she could maybe meet someone who she could befriend so they could help her with her career. But it didn't take living in this town very long to figure out actors don't help other actors, and since she was already married, she couldn't exactly throw herself at some rich actor who she could snag as a husband. Now that Stan was gone, she might be willing to walk up and down the mountain a few times to check out the possibilities. Of course, that meant getting a dog and who needed that kind of aggravation?

One car had gone by just after Hari parked fifteen minutes ago and two cars pulled into their driveway and went inside. So far, no sign of anybody lurking anywhere in the vicinity. All she had to do was get her hands on the gun and figure out a better place to hide it. Tomorrow, the police could search all they wanted but they wouldn't find what they were looking for. Idiots. She was always one step ahead of everybody.

She finally had what she needed to keep her hold on Steve for as long as she wanted, and Stan was conveniently gone. Steve had been getting too restless lately and maybe it was almost time to let go. But she wasn't ready yet. Not yet. And she had to have the upper hand. She would figure out how to deal with Hari. People desperate for fame could be handled. She waited another fifteen minutes and not one car had gone by.

She hadn't heard a single sound except for what must be little animals scampering around in the underbrush. The dark didn't scare her. She felt absolutely all-powerful. She stepped out of her hiding place behind the bushes and walked toward the fencepost, where she had instructed Hari to leave the gun. Yes! It was there. She picked it up, smiled, and put it in her bag. She peered down Mulholland left and right, saw no cars coming, walked down the road to her rental car and clicked it open.

"Hello, Lila." Rosemaria said quietly.

Lila whipped her head around, shocked to see the bitch cop walking toward her. She reached for the door handle, but another cop appeared behind Lila and grabbed her arm. She tried to twist away but he grabbed her other arm and her purse fell to the ground. She watched with horror as Rosemaria picked it up.

"Well, well, lookie here, Waite. What is this?" Rosemaria took the plastic bag with the gun inside out of Lila's purse and held it up. "A .38 Special, just what Stan was shot with. I'm thinking we're going to be able to match some fingerprints. What do you think, Coleman?"

Lila whipped her head around and saw that the handsome, cop bastard partner of the bitch was giving her the once-over. Another cop was standing behind him. Lila knew they all thought they had her cornered, but she was far too clever for these morons.

"I have a hunch you're right." Coleman said.

"I haven't done anything wrong and I want a lawyer."

Waite took out his cuffs and locked Lila's arms behind her back. "You're not under arrest for now, just a material witness. We want to make sure you don't go anywhere, in case you remember you have another appointment."

"Lila's cold stare was so filled with contempt, it could have withered his very soul if it weren't for the fact that like every good Catholic, Waite wore his crucifix around his neck at all times to protect him against evildoers, even blood-sucking vampires like this scarier-than-hell broad. "Let's go, lady. You'll find our accommodations aren't all that bad."

* * * *

Guerrero could not believe his luck. He had just won fifty bucks in a poker game, and now he had found that piece of shit, Sibley, passed out in his car in the same parking lot where he and that smart-mouth female cop had gotten lucky. He nudged his friend, Kelly, who he had met during a brief stay in county jail. They walked over and peered in at Josh, who was slumped over the steering wheel. Guerrero knew he was going to kill the bastard, but first he wanted him awake so the asshole could worry about it for a while. He told Kelly what he wanted to do.

"You go get your car and follow me a block over in front of the school. It's nice and deserted this time of night. We'll do it there." He opened the driver's door. "Help me shove him over."

Kelly was more than willing to help. "Fuckin A, man." He walked around to the other side and opened the passenger door.

In the back seat, Noor stirred from underneath the blanket that Josh liked to cover her with when he took her out of her surroundings that, Josh somehow knew, sometimes threatened to suffocate her. She looked forward to those occasional nights when he drove her to wooded places where she could run free, if only for a short time. She always came back to him when he called. They had a bond nothing and no one could ever break, even though, more than once, he worried her. Like now, when he was slumped over and not moving for a long time. When the doors opened, her ears went flat against her head and a low growl rumbled from her throat. Strangers were not allowed near Josh in her presence. Especially not at night. Especially when he was helpless. She lifted her head and saw them coming into the car from both sides. Instincts bred in her since time immemorial told her they were there to harm Josh, and she would kill them before they even came close. One stranger yanked Josh's head up from the steering wheel and the other grabbed his arm and started to pull.

All the combined wildness and rage that had been passed on to her from her ancestors exploded in Noor's brain with the force of ten tons of TNT. No one had ever dared touch Josh like that in all the years they had been together. She raised up and put both paws on Josh's shoulders and emitted a sound so full of passion and fury, it echoed through the parking lot and filled the night air for blocks with her anger.

The two men froze. She saw moisture pop out on their faces and their eyes grow large and round with fear. She growled again, her incisors gleaming ruthlessly in the ambient light. Both men began to shake uncontrollably and make unintelligible sounds. Noor knew she needn't waste much more energy on these two. She glared at them, her eyes narrowing with pure hatred, and hissed. In slow motion, they began to pull away from Josh and ease out of the car. Sweat was pouring down their faces. She hissed at them again and made a move as if to pounce, then watched as they slammed the car doors in perfect unison and went running down the sidewalk screaming.

Noor gave Josh's face a gentle nuzzle and tried to wake him up. The cowards wouldn't be back, but more might come. Josh's head stayed slumped on the back of the car seat and he refused to be awakened. Noor lay back down, staying alert, fearful of more strangers who might come.

* * * *

Waite and Osborne stood inside the observation room and looked at the scene on the other side of the one-way window. Waite had a folder tucked under his right arm. They had taken Lila to the interview room in the jail section of the third floor to see if that would scare her into telling them some semblance of the truth.

Lila was seated at the table, doing her best imitation of a put-upon victim. Rosemaria was standing in a corner looking at Lila dispassionately, and Coleman was seated with half his butt on the table, doing his best to show disrespect and irritate Lila into saying something stupid.

"I'm not saying anything, and you can't make me," Lila said in as nasty a tone as she could muster.

"Who's asking you?" Coleman said casually. "You're not under arrest, remember? Until they get the prints off the gun, and forensics compares the gun to the bullet, all we know is you hid a gun and had Hari go get it for you. Could be you and Hari were just playing treasure hunt in the middle of the night."

"Then what?"

"Then what, what?"

Lila looked at him with undisguised contempt. "You're an asshole."

Coleman flung his hands to his chest. "You hurt me. You really, really hurt me! He looked at Rosemaria. "Did you hear what she called me? That's low. I don't deserve that, do I, Sergeant?"

"You sounded just like Sally Fields at the Academy Awards when you said that." Rosemaria observed.

"Coleman protested, "Sally didn't say 'hurt me,' she said, 'you *like* me, you really *like* me.'"

Rosemaria looked up as if mulling this over. "Whatever. I've heard you called worse, and by a better class of people, too."

Lila exploded. "Where the hell is my lawyer?! Are you keeping him waiting somewhere so you can play your cop games with me?!"

"Sorry," Coleman said, "but he's not here yet. Maybe he's involved in something more important...at four o'clock in the morning."

Rosemaria nodded towards the observation window and Waite smiled at Osborne and left the observation room with the folder in his hand. He entered the interrogation room and, with a knowing look at Coleman, handed him the folder.

Coleman slowly slid his butt cheek off the desk, much to the aversion of Lila, and walked over to Rosemaria, where they both proceeded to read what was written on the reports inside.

"I already know what it says, okay?!" Lila burst out angrily. "You don't have to act smug like you know it all, because you don't!"

"Oh, I think we do. Stand up." Coleman took out his cuffs and snapped them on Lila's wrists. "Lila Levy, you're under arrest for the murder of your husband, Stan Levy."

Lila was incensed, "I did not murder Stan!"

Coleman continued. "You have the right to remain silent. Anything you say or do can be held against you in a court of law."

Lila was seething.

"You have the right to an attorney. If you cannot afford one, one will be provided for you. Do you understand these rights?"

"You can't arrest me. Those aren't my fingerprints on that gun."

"We can't talk to you now, sorry." Rosemaria said. A uniformed officer entered the room. "Take her to a holding cell, please. We're waiting for her lawyer."

"I will sue you for false arrest! Every one of you!"

The officer took her out and closed the door. They could still hear her yelling as she was escorted down the hall to a cell.

Rosemaria was relieved but knew they had trapped a wildcat in a bag and she would come out fighting. "What do you want to bet I had the scenario just about right?"

"I'd bet on that and I'd bet she's capable of anything."

"You have Vanessa tucked away safe?"

"That's a bet you can take to the bank."

Rosemaria was taken aback by Coleman's uncharacteristically serious response.

"Since we're done here for now, I think I'll go check on her."

"It's a little early."

"I'll bring breakfast."

His eyes revealed a profound sadness that Rosemaria had never seen before.

"I have to tell her about Bauer before she hears it on the news."

On the drive to the marina, Coleman remembered yesterday afternoon and was overwhelmed at how one woman and a few precious minutes could change a life—namely, his. He had picked Vanessa up at her apartment and she acted nervous and worried—how long would she have to be in hiding, how would she get to her interviews and her acting jobs, and would she be a burden on him and the department?

For about an hour, he had reassured her that she would be safe on his boat; she would have the best protection the department had to offer throughout the hearings and the trial, and neither Lila nor anyone she might hire to harm her would get near her. She seemed to respond to his reassurances and eventually started asking about him and what he wanted in life and then, more shyly, about the women in his life. This made him think she'd like to know if there was anyone special. He didn't hesitate to let her know there was no one and that he had been relatively alone for quite some time. He noticed this made her smile and he felt himself opening up to this woman, this actress, this person who he had just met and wanted to get to know much better, and yet feeling like he had known her all his life.

And why was that, he asked himself. And the answer was obvious. The way she talked and looked and moved—she was the woman he had imagined but never knew existed. When that realization hit him with the force of a tsunami, he had to smile at how quickly and unexpectedly his entire future had just landed in his lap with a resounding thud. He knew he didn't deserve it, but here it was and he was taking full advantage. Vanessa had asked him why he was smiling. He told her he was happy. And that was the truth. Now he had to break her heart.

* * * *

Josh was convinced he would never walk again. He lay sprawled across the console, twisted into a human pretzel. He tried to recall when last night he had been run over by a full army battalion, but his head was stuffed so full of cotton, he was having trouble remembering his own name. He pushed himself up into a sitting position and grimaced in pain. Noor was sitting up in the back seat looking at him as if she had seen it all before. Unfortunately, she had. Too many times.

"I can't keep doing this," Josh rasped. He tried to smooth down his spiked-up hair and looked around the deserted parking lot. It was still dark out, thank God. "I've gotta get you back to the zoo before it gets light, and then I gotta go see a lady." He tried to reach back to scratch Noor's head, but his body wouldn't move that way. She leaned forward and he kissed her black face. "I don't know what I'd do without you, my best friend." Noor sensed what he was saying. Little did he know, she thought.

* * * *

Larry and Vanessa were standing in the galley of the Duchess II where Larry had just placed two bags from Starbucks on the counter. She looked up at him, sensing something was wrong. He hated having to hurt her and was terrified that everything they had would come undone. "I have something to tell you that you can't share with a single soul. But you must understand you did nothing wrong." He held her at arm's length and studied her face, seeing her growing confusion and uneasiness. "Promise me, you'll remember that."

Vanessa pulled back. "What are you talking about? What have I done—or haven't done? Tell me."

Coleman approached her but she brushed him off impatiently. He kept his voice gentle and calm. "Please sit, okay?"

"No, I will not. Get it out whatever it is."

"Beaumont's real name is Bauer. He's Lila's real father."

"Her real father? What do you mean? That can't be true."

"As sad and abhorrent it is, I'm afraid it's true, Vanessa. Lila felt him slipping away from her and she was desperate to have a hold on him. She left the fingerprints on the gun so she would always have that to threaten him with if he tried to leave her."

Vanessa choked back a laugh. "That's the most diabolical thing I've ever heard. You must be joking."

"No, I'm not."

"Jesus, God in heaven. What kind of a person was I living with?" Then her mouth opened in horror as the impact of what Larry had told her hit her without mercy. "I was sleeping with a child molester, a loathsome pervert?!"

Larry reached for her, but she stood up and began pacing. "NO, no! What have I done?!"

"You haven't done anything. You didn't know. You couldn't have known. Not even her mother knew, and it happened right under her nose in her own house."

Vanessa stopped pacing and stood still, staring out the porthole at the water lapping against the pier. "Lila was obsessed with him even after she came here—and it went on and on and on…"

Vanessa's anger melted into tears and she brought her hands up to her face and sobbed. "How can you stand looking at me?"

"This doesn't change anything between us. Please understand that."

She let him come to her and hold her again. The love and concern she heard in his voice overwhelmed her with gratitude. "Thank you. Thank you."

Larry breathed a sigh of relief. "I believe that's my line."

* * * *

Kowalski, at the front desk, told him that Lila had been arrested, and Josh couldn't say he was all that surprised. The coldness he had felt from Lila last night still gave him chills. He walked upstairs as he ate his breakfast of Doritos and peered through the glass outside the detective's area at a woman at her desk typing into a computer. She recognized him and told him she'd check if Rosemaria was here. He sat down to wait and absently chewed on a Dorito, barely tasting it. He was taken aback when Rosemaria came out of the elevator with Coleman and suddenly stood glaring down at him. "How much more of her punishment can you take?" She shook her head and walked around the corner to the detectives' entrance.

Josh was taken so off-guard by her vehemence, it took him a couple of seconds to respond. "Wait a minute," he called after her. "I came here—"

Larry stepped in front of him and blocked his way. Josh finished his sentence under his breath, looking into Larry's not-too-friendly face. "—to see you."

Larry stared him down. "You have any business here?"

Josh made a move towards him and reconsidered doing anything that stupid. He crumpled up his bag of Doritos and headed back down the stairs to the exit. He would eat a decent breakfast for a change. And then he would call Sam Loggins, a musician friend he hadn't seen in two years. Maybe he could talk Sam into letting him stay in his cabin up in Arroyo Grande for a week. He needed time alone. Away from Lila, away from Rosemaria and all the chaos and confusion that was engulfing him. No booze, no TV, no phone. Just fresh air, his guitar and nobody to talk to except deer and rabbits. He had to clear his mind and think about where he was going from here. The path he was on was unsustainable. He would tell Jerry he needed a week off, and he, more than anyone, would understand. He would tell only Noor where he was going and reassure her, as much as he could, that he would be back. All he knew was, he had to get the hell outta Dodge.

CHAPTER THIRTY-TWO

LOS ANGELES

Steve figured he might as well blow his brains out right then and there. He stood at the window of his motel room and looked out at the traffic on Ventura Boulevard. He hadn't heard from Lila all morning. She should have brought the gun to him last night, but she never called and didn't answer her prepaid. Something must have gone wrong…as if his entire life hadn't been wrong, except for a few short years alone, free to do exactly as he pleased. That all ended with Lila. He was tired of it all. He turned away from the window and went to the closet to get his clothes and get dressed. Lila had always ignored his feelings about their relationship. She never experienced a moment's guilt about what they were doing, while he couldn't remember when he hadn't been ridden with guilt since the day they started. What they were doing was wrong and he knew it, but he couldn't stop.

He had been on his way from San Diego to San Francisco that day and gave in to an impulse to stop in Monterey and call Cassie. Time had expired on that robbery warrant and he was free to come and go as he pleased without fear of getting arrested. Cassie had been his first love in high school and he had never found anyone who was as kind and loving as she was, besides being the prettiest girl in school. He had wondered if there was any chance for them again. If not, if she told him to get lost, he would keep driving north to where another construction job was waiting. Right after they got married, when Cassie told him she was pregnant, he knew he couldn't handle having to take care of a kid. It just wasn't his thing.

When the baby was born and started bawling and puking and soiling her diapers, and Cassie started looking like any other harassed housewife who didn't give a damn about her looks or sex or anything but looking after that mewling little shit, he'd had enough. He took off and never looked back, until that fateful day on his way to Salinas.

Cassie had welcomed him back without hesitation. She didn't lay guilt and didn't complain or ask too many questions about his life on his own. Lila had been in San Francisco with friends on a post-high school graduation trip and he and Cassie had five whole days to get reacquainted and decide if he would live there again for as long as he wanted. He had driven into Carmel to apply for a job laying tile on the roof of a remodel and Lila had been hitchhiking home from the bus station in Monterey when he picked her up, not having a clue as to who she really was.

She had been a baby when he left and with her died black hair, piercings in her nose and ears, and hoody over her head, she didn't look anything like Cassie. But later, when she cleaned herself up before moving to Hollywood, he could see the strong resemblance. He had lectured her on the dangers of getting in a car with strangers and she had laughed and joked and asked what he was going to do to her. All the while, Lila was getting friendlier, touching his thigh, and making him uncomfortable. He asked her what neighborhood she lived in and when she told him, he finally had the presence of mind to ask her name. He almost choked when she told him but said nothing until he drove her to her door without her having to tell him the address. She stared at him. "You knew where I lived."

"I used to live here, too."

Her mouth opened but no words came out.

He stared back at her, then nodded.

She got out of the car, then leaned back in. "This should be interesting."

Knowing it could be the worst mistake of his life, he decided to stay for a while and see how everything played out, even though every instinct in his mind and body told him this situation spelled disaster. He told them both he had to go by the name Steve Beaumont because that was the name on his work history now.

Around Cassie, Lila treated him as if she couldn't be happier to have her long-lost father back. She constantly hugged and kissed him in front of Cassie, who was genuinely happy father and daughter were getting on so well. But to Steve and Lila, the chemistry between them was unmistakable—Lila's kisses were not those of a daughter and the way she touched him made his heart beat faster and terrible thoughts entered his head. This couldn't go on. It was sick and completely unthinkable. He couldn't do this to Cassie. He had put her through enough. He had just about decided he better get the hell out before he did something really stupid when, as if she were reading his mind, Lila snuck into his room one night when Cassie was working nightshift and he was forever doomed.

He had known it was inevitable that Lila would leave for Hollywood. It was all they ever talked about when they did talk, and he hoped that the distance would give him the guts to end it. Instead, the relationship grew more intense, and every time she called, he came to her. His only way of maintaining his pride was to control her sexually and make her want him more. She had drained every ounce of will and ambition out of him. All he had possessed was that power over her, and now he was certain that was irretrievably gone.

It had all started with Vanessa. He had known at the time that she only went out with him to spite Lila. But compared to Lila, she was like a breath of fresh air, much too good for him, but physically they had connected and enjoyed each other for a while. They both knew that continuing was much too risky, so had agreed it had to end. He was sorry to lose someone who helped him feel close to being a normal human being, but he was sure Vanessa was relieved to never have anything to do with him or Lila again.

His relationship with Vanessa, hopeless though it was, helped him see that it was possible for him to live without the constant revulsion he had for himself and for Lila as well. She had clearly felt him drawing away in the last few months and when he told her he was leaving her and leaving Cassie for good, she had called and told him Stan was beating her—her one last life-condemning lie.

Sirens drew him to the window, and he looked down at the cop cars pulling into the parking lot. Yes, she had truly fucked him over for the last time now.

* * * *

The four detectives were gathered in Mandel's office, sitting in chairs facing his desk, waiting for Celia Mathison, the Assistant D.A., to arrive. Rosemaria studied the faces of Coleman, Waite, and Osborne, reflecting on their strength of character and work ethic. She felt proud of her team.

In reality, the case had not been so much of a who-done-it as much as a case of nailing the person they knew was responsible for Stan's death. She still wasn't sure if Lila would pay the price for her crimes. Celia, who she had worked with before, would fight for the maximum penalties, but had no way of proving exactly what happened that night.

Lila had hired Solly Geller, notorious lawyer of the rich and famous, to work his magic on judge and jury while painting her as the victim of an abusive husband in the minds of the public. But if they knew the truth about the depths of her malignancy, none of them would hesitate to lock her up and throw away the key. Bauer, on the other hand, had to settle for Nick Wagner, a public defender. Lila refused to pay for his lawyer and was making it obvious she was about to leave him up the creek without a paddle.

"Hi, everybody, sorry I'm late." Celia Mathison breezed into the room like the successful, confident prosecutor she was. Still in her twenties, African American, tall, attractive, with perfectly groomed, straight, shoulder-length hair, she had zoomed to the top of the ladder. She had a 100 percent conviction record and, on the rare times when she was willing to make deals with defendants, she made sure the sentences were as harsh as she could manage and still get the deal made. She put her briefcase on Mandel's desk, then greeted them all by name.

She sank into the chair beside the Lieutenant's desk and didn't waste any time. "I've been conferring with Geller and Wagner, hoping I could reach a deal with both parties, but so far, no go. Somehow, Bauer managed to dig up enough money for bail but must wear an ankle monitor. Vanessa, however, is free as a bird." She looked at Coleman. "I'd like your assurance that Vanessa is still under your protection. I don't trust either one of those two."

"All taken care of," Coleman agreed.

"Even though this is a preliminary hearing, I want to hit them with everything we've got. To get a murder conviction on Bauer, I need to show that he had malice in his heart, wonton disregard for human life, and that this was not a sudden passion killing. He had plenty of time to cool off and plan what he was going to do on the way over to Lila's. Lila could very well have told him where the gun was, Bauer grabbed it out of the drawer, and when Stan saw him pointing it at him, he fought for his life. To get a manslaughter conviction for Lila, again, I have to show wonton disregard for human life, because she let Stan bleed to death. Everybody in this room knows she most likely plotted this whole scenario for her own unfathomable reasons, but I have to get her to admit that on the stand."

"Both their clients admit that Stan was shot while he and Bauer were fighting over the gun, then Stan fell and hit his head, and bled out. I pointed out that Lila had called Bauer and instigated the fight and I was willing to let her plead to involuntary manslaughter. But Geller turned me down, saying she was a victim of domestic violence and in no way responsible for Stan's death."

Coleman was shaking his head. "And Bauer?"

"Bauer's prints were on the gun, his DNA under Stan's fingernails. He has admitted they were fighting. I contended he went there looking for a fight, shot Stan, and did nothing to help him when he saw him bleeding on the floor. If it was an accident, why not call the police? Why not call an ambulance? He's facing prison time. I'll make sure of that."

Rosemaria asked Celia what they all were thinking. "But when the jury hears about the incest and listens to Vanessa, who will testify the relationship was voluntary on Lila's part, they'll understand how despicable she is, how she's capable of just about anything, and throw the book at her, right?"

"Geller asked the judge to disallow any testimony about the incest on the grounds that it would be inflammatory and neither of them would be able to get a fair trial. The judge said he'd make a ruling on that before the hearing. And that means, for now, we are forbidden to say anything about the incest to the press."

Rosemaria was outraged. "But I'm sure she told Stan the truth that night! That's why he was out of control. It fueled the fight between him and Bauer. She did that on purpose. The judge has to allow that in!"

"Calm down." Celia turned a cool gaze toward Rosemaria. "We'll just have to wait and see what happens with that. To convince the judge at the hearing that Bauer should be tried for murder and Lila with voluntary manslaughter, I have to prove Bauer planned to kill Stan, and Lila conspired with him. They're planning on testifying at the hearing, so I have to get that out of them while they're on the stand. I'm sure Geller isn't happy with that, but I get the feeling stopping Lila from doing what she wants to do is like stopping The Beast Mode from crossing the goal line back in the day."

Coleman perked up. "You a football fan?"

"Isn't everybody?"

Coleman surveyed the room. "Yeah, of course."

"So, you know what they say."

Rosemaria bit. "What's that?"

"The best defense is a good offense."

Coleman didn't get it. "Geller always has a good defense, and it's usually very offensive."

"Possibly, but when the star player for the defense is a complete wacka-doodle, she might as well be playing for the offense...that'd be us."

She picked up her briefcase and grinned, "Just sayin," and stood up. "Good work, everybody. The D.A. is happy, and he's arranged a press conference. As soon as the judge gives us the go-ahead, we'll charge them and throw their asses in jail." She smiled, "After a trial, of course." And she was gone.

"We don't have to get in front of the cameras, do we, Lieutenant?" Rosemaria asked, after Celia had left. Her brow furrowed until she had deep creases between her eyes that looked like inverted railroad tracks.

Mandel laughed. "Try not to look quite so eager, Baker. Share the limelight with your partners."

Rosemaria grumbled under her breath.

"What was that?"

Rosemaria forced smile. "I'm all about sharing."

"Good. You'll want to spend some time coordinating your testimonies tomorrow, so I'll leave you to it. Celia wants us to give the judge just about everything we have at the hearing. If we're lucky, we may not even go to trial. You can let yourselves out." With that, he picked up his briefcase and went out.

Rosemaria looked at the three others. "Who has a quarter? We'll toss for which one of us gets to crucify Lila on the incest angle."

* * * *

Josh drove up Cahuenga Pass on the 101, past Universal Studios, heading toward Van Nuys and the courthouse. He had come home late last night, after going by to see Noor and making sure she was okay, and then fallen into bed without checking either land line or cell phone for messages. After a week spent in semi-wilderness by himself, he felt almost cleansed of civilization and all the demons chasing him that he had spent his life avoiding.

He was determined to keep going along that same path and would start tomorrow by going to AA. He knew there were meetings in a Presbyterian church right off the freeway near his apartment and, after years of denial, he was going to sit in a room full of people and admit he was an alcoholic. Not easy. But he was going to do it.

When he had finally listened to his phone messages that morning, he heard nothing especially important, but he did have one message from Lila asking him to be at her hearing today. Funny how she couldn't be bothered to come to his hearing but sounded like she expected him to be there for her. At first, he dismissed the thought of going, having no desire to see Lila ever again. She meant nothing to him anymore. But curiosity got the best of him. Some perverse instinct to see how all of this was going to play out got him showered, dressed, and out the door and heading toward the freeway in his trusty Mustang that seemed to be running better than ever. If Lila expected anything of him he would waste no time in setting her straight. On the other hand, he didn't know what he'd say to Rosemaria when he saw her, but he'd figure that out when the time came.

* * * *

Coleman watched Vanessa, seated on a bench a few feet away from him where she was waiting to testify, nervously clasping her hands together in her lap. He wanted to wrap his arms around her and comfort her, but that would hardly be an appropriate thing to do in the empty courtroom where they'd been allowed to wait, with Officer Sanchez looking on. Sanchez, six feet two and a glowing testimony to constant workouts in the gym, had been staying on the boat with Vanessa. He alternated with two other officers who had been personally vetted by Coleman as the most qualified protectors the force had to offer. They also had been with her on a few auditions, but no luck yet. They had bonded with her so quickly and intensely, they were almost as disappointed as she was when she was told the pilot she had counted on booking didn't materialize.

Vanessa saw him studying her intently. "I'm all right, Larry. Honestly, I'll be fine. If I have to do it, I just will. I'll pretend I'm onstage playing a part."

"I have to go out for a few minutes, but I'll be back as soon as I can."

Coleman looked up at Sanchez, who was standing by the door. "Don't let her out of your sight, even when she goes to the ladies' room. Clear the room before she goes in."

Sanchez let out a sigh and nodded. Coleman shook his head and sighed. "I'm sorry. You're doing great."

Sanchez held up his hands, palms front, "Hey, I've got this. Go do what you have to do. They won't be calling her for a while."

Coleman moved toward Vanessa as if wanting to touch her, then backed away. "I won't be long." Giving her a smile, he reluctantly walked past Sanchez and went out.

Rosemaria had asked Coleman to go on ahead upstairs with Vanessa and Sanchez while she waited outside the courthouse. She assumed Josh would be with Lila when she showed up, knowing Josh's penchant for punishment.

She paced nervously back and forth in front of the entrance, trying to compose exactly what she wanted to say. It wasn't easy for her to admit when she was wrong, but Coleman was right. She had been demanding and obstinate. Nobody was perfect, least of all her, and she had gone ahead and fallen in love with a guy who tipped the scales heavily in the direction of not perfect. But she was stuck on the guy, and if she had to swallow her pride to help him, that's what she would do.

She glanced up and saw Coleman walking toward her, looking like he wanted to rip somebody's head off. She was afraid to ask what was wrong. "What's the word?" came out of her mouth anyway.

"I just talked to Celia. She and the two defense lawyers are meeting with Judge Harvey again this morning. Geller called him and convinced him he has a new case law and hinted at appeals and the judge being overturned by the appellate courts. That's because there is no way to keep the incest out of the media if our side brings it up at the hearing, even if it *is* closed to media."

"Shit! No! That's not fair!"

"Tell me."

"If she squirms out of this, I'll go stark, staring, raving mad!"

"They'll get her on depraved indifference. That's murder two. They've got to. She let Stan bleed to death."

"In her case, depravity is a minor flaw."

A limousine pulled up and stopped in the restricted driveway. The back door opened, and Geller got out. Rosemaria's heart started beating wildly. It was crazy to be this nervous, she told herself. The worst Josh could say was thanks, but no thanks, and she'd live through it. Kind of. Then she'd give him the papers and he could do with them as he chose.

"I'll join you upstairs, okay, Larry? I need to talk to Josh."

Coleman looked at her and then at Geller. He was about to object but changed his mind. He indicated his disapproval with a shake of his head and walked back inside.

Geller held his hand out to help Lila out of the limo. She spotted Rosemaria immediately and glared at her. Then she and Geller walked past her and through the entrance without Lila giving Rosemaria another glance. But where the hell was Josh? Rosemaria had been so sure he would come to the hearing with Lila. She hadn't heard from him in over a week, ever since he'd shown up at the station and she'd given him the cold shoulder. Now she wondered if something had happened to him but asking Lila if she knew anything was out of the question. Rosemaria had so much wanted to talk to him before the hearing and give him the information she had managed to dig up from her sources in Marysville. Maybe he would still show up. After all, he was always late.

She waited outside the glass doors until she saw Lila and Geller catch an elevator, and then followed them upstairs. If there was any justice in the world, Lila would get locked up as soon as the hearing ended, but since Justice was blind as a bat and wouldn't recognize fairness if it hit her smack in her big fat face, there was slim chance of that happening.

Upstairs, Coleman came out of the elevator and walked through a motley group of people standing impatiently waiting for a hearing on a kidnapping case to be over. The court watchers were eager to get good seats in the courtroom so they could personally experience the ugly secrets of the Hollywood elite. They were practically salivating as they waited for the principals to arrive. As Coleman looked around for his partners, the elevator doors opened and Geller came out first, with Lila, hanging on Geller's arm. The press was waiting for them but before they or the human vultures could surround Lila, Geller pushed them aside and a bailiff appeared to lead Lila and Geller into another empty courtroom down the hall from where Vanessa was waiting, and shut the door.

Coleman noticed Bauer waiting with his lawyer in a far corner, unnoticed and anxious. "May you burn in hell," Coleman whispered to himself as he joined Waite and Osborn, who were seated on benches by the windows waiting for him.

Wagner, having noticed Lila and Geller's arrival, stood nervously beside Bauer and wondered if he should knock on the courtroom door where, unlike him and his own client, they had been allowed to wait in privacy. Then, to his relief, he saw Geller come out and head straight towards him. Geller looked at Wagner like he was an insignificant worm. "We'll be meeting with the judge in chambers in a few minutes. Follow me." And, without waiting for a response, he headed down the hallway.

Bauer grabbed Wagner by the arm as he passed him. "The reporters are looking at me. They'll be coming down the hall any second."

Wagner pulled his arm away. "Go hide in the men's room, lock the door, do whatever." He hurried after Geller, wishing he could do a better job of hiding his revulsion for his client. He knew if he stayed a defense lawyer, he would have to deal with even worse garbage than this. He'd have to get used to it. Geller had been rolling in the mud with the worst of them for years and now he was richer than God. It was something to aspire to.

Bauer saw the reporters beginning to stare at him and whisper to their camera people. He knew there was no way in hell he could handle talking to them. He looked around and saw an elevator door open and ran toward it and jumped inside just as the door was closing. He took the elevator to the first-floor lobby and, trying to avoid being seen by any stray reporter, quickly walked toward the snack shop and slipped inside. He stood unnoticed in a corner just inside the doorway and again, considered suicide, but again, admitted he was too much of a coward. Who knew what he would face on the other side, if there was one. No, he could wait for that. Maybe in prison, he could somehow make up for what he had done. Maybe he could make amends and find redemption. Maybe. All he had left was hope.

Rosemaria and her three cohorts sat side by side on benches at the far end of the hall, waiting to hear what they were sure would be bad news. They all knew Geller wouldn't have asked for another meeting with the judge unless he had solid legal precedence or a solid gold bluff.

Rosemaria chose to remain calm. "Okay, let's go over it again. We know Lila was obsessed with Bauer and terrified that he would leave her. So, in order to keep her hold on him, she called Bauer and told him to come over because Stan was beating her, which he wasn't. Before or during Stan's confrontation with Bauer, she told Stan the truth about her relationship with her father in order to fuel his rage. Stan must have gone completely ape shit hearing what she had to say, and that's exactly what she wanted. She probably took the gun out of the drawer herself and handed it to Bauer, who had not come over there with the intention of killing Stan, no matter how much Lila egged him on. Stan, to his horror, must have finally understood that he was to be Lila's victim and not her savior, and grabbed for the gun. He and Bauer struggled, and the gun went off. Lila must have been plenty relieved when she saw it was Stan who went down. Her sickening scheme would have been for nothing if it was Bauer who got shot." She paused. "How's that?"

Waite, who was as determined as any of them to see Lila punished, sounded almost resigned. "She probably thinks she'll get away with it, too."

They sat in silence until Coleman finally spoke. "If nothing gets in about the incest and Vanessa isn't able to testify about Lila's obsession with her own father, and the jury doesn't get to figure out the lengths she'd go to hang on to him, she will get away with it."

Osborne was not so sure. "Lila is ruled by emotions and her narcissism and grandiosity. That's usually a formula for disaster."

Rosemaria's cell phone rang and she quickly clicked it on. There was nervous apprehension all around as she listened. She clicked off. "The incest is out."

Vanessa glanced up from where she was seated as Coleman walked in the door. His smile told her everything. She jumped up from her chair and threw her arms around him. "Thank God!"

"I thought you were okay about testifying, just an acting exercise," he teased.

"I lied. But I don't understand. What's going on? Why don't I have to testify?"

Coleman nodded at Sanchez. "Can we be alone for a few minutes?"

Sanchez shrugged. "I'll be right outside."

After he was gone, Coleman explained. "The defense considers the incest angle as inflammatory. The judge has decided not to let it in during the hearing. He may allow it to come in at the trial, which may never happen if Celia offers the defense lawyers a deal their clients find acceptable."

"What happens now?"

"Now, the hearing starts. I'll have to testify, and Sanchez will wait with you until he thinks it's safe to sneak you out."

"Will you stay with me awhile?"

"I'm all yours." And for the first time in his life, he meant it.

Bauer was waiting for his lawyer in the snack shop. Wagner had called him with the news. Now that his relationship with Lila would be kept out of the trial, he had hopes that maybe his sentence would not be so long. Maybe there was a chance he could start his life over again. The door had permanently closed on his relationship with Cassie. He could only imagine what she had gone through when watching reports on the news about him and Lila. She didn't deserve the heartbreak she must have felt. Then again, he had never been fair to her from the get-go. He had followed his own fucking self-centered path and abandoned her without a backward glance.

There was no such thing as a fresh start for him, ever. His self-revulsion would stay with him for the rest of his life and color everything he did a drab and ugly gray that he would never escape. A black wave of despondency washed over him. No matter what happened in court, his life was over.

Wagner looked at him from the doorway of the snack shop. "Come on. We're starting in a few minutes."

Bauer followed him toward the elevators and warily looked around for reporters. When the elevator door opened on their floor, he panicked when he saw a female reporter heading down the hallway towards him, a mini recorder in her hand. He thought to himself, "To hell with Lila, she can put up with me for two minutes till this thing gets going." He grabbed Wagner's arm, pushed past the surprised sheriff's deputy, opened the door to the courtroom, and pushed Wagner in ahead of him. Lila had her mirror out and was working on her face when she saw him. She bolted out of her chair in fury.

"You can't be in here!" Lila hissed vehemently. "Get out!"

Somewhere in the back of his brain, he knew there were people right outside who could hear him, but he was past caring.

"Now you want me to get out?! After you made my life a living hell?!"

Rough hands grabbed him and dragged him to the open door where the reporter was waiting, recording this unexpected welcome spectacle. Bauer struggled helplessly to free himself of the two sheriff's deputies who had their hands wrapped around both of his arms. He glared at Lila, who by now was standing directly in front of him and said with more intensity than he had ever felt in his life, "I've never hated anyone as much as I hate you. You're a pathetic, sick old man!"

With the help of the deputies, his lawyer managed to guide him out of the doorway and down the hall. But Lila was just getting started. She followed Bauer while Geller came running towards them. "You deserve everything that's happening to you! You murderer! I wish I'd never met you!" She was out of control and didn't give a damn about the scene she was creating.

Inside the room, Vanessa and Sanchez were listening to the ruckus outside. Sanchez made a move to open the door, but Coleman indicated for him not to. "Sit tight, not our fight."

Out in the hallway, Bauer's face cracked into an ugly sneer at Lila's words. "You fucking whore," he spat at her.

In desperation, Wagner opened the door to the other empty courtroom and shoved Bauer inside, but Lila was right behind him, her mouth opened to let fly with a string of obscenities. But what she saw froze her words before they could take flight. Vanessa, standing in front of the judge's bench, and Bauer, in the doorway, were staring at each other so intensely, everyone in the room stopped moving. The recognition and intimacy between the two was unmistakable and no one saw that more clearly than Lila. For once, she was dumbstruck. Geller grabbed Lila and pulled her from the room while Bauer continued to stare at Vanessa.

Coleman moved to Vanessa's side and said sharply, "Sanchez!," whereby Sanchez firmly took Bauer by the arms and handed him over to the two sheriff's deputies who were in the doorway and closed the door behind him. Out in the hall, the two deputies, sheltering Bauer from the salivating press pack, moved him into the other empty courtroom and barred the press from entering. Bauer leaned against the wall and put his face into his hands, weeping. Wagner stood helplessly beside him, wishing he could have drawn a nice, simple DUI instead of this fiasco.

CHAPTER THIRTY-THREE

LOS ANGELES

Geller, living every moment of his life accepting that his talent, skill, and charisma were unmatched in the legal world of Los Angeles and maybe even the country, was frustrated that he had not managed to convince the judge, for now, that the two cases should be severed. Lila was a battered wife who was merely a witness to a crime, if it was a crime, while Bauer was the obvious shooter. He would keep working on that and was certain he could make it happen by the time they went to trial, unless the D.A. came up with an acceptable deal assuring Lila of no jail time. While surveying the courtroom, Geller happened to glance at the spectators seated behind the prosecutor's table and was certain he recognized Cassie Bauer. He leaned forward and whispered to Lila, "Isn't that your mother back there?"

Lila turned around and immediately spotted Cassie at the same time she looked over at Lila. Lila immediately resumed looking straight ahead. "Yeah, so what?"

"I thought she wasn't coming. We may have to call her as a witness at trial."

"Forget it."

"But she could testify that—"

"That pathetic old hag has nothing to do with this. Forget it."

Geller didn't bother to argue. Lila had turned to ice after that little drama between Bauer and Vanessa. He drew the obvious conclusion that Lila had not known before of that possible romantic connection and he was grateful the judge had ruled in favor of keeping the incest out. Lila was difficult and unpredictable. Geller usually handled his clients with ease and they did as they were told. Not Lila. A deal was definitely a possibility.

Bauer had noticed Lila and Geller glancing at someone across the aisle and he was stunned to see Cassie sitting two rows behind the D.A. She had unpredictably welcomed him with open arms when he shown up at her house what seemed like just a few years ago. He had done his best to make her life easier and watched her blossom and become the girl he had fallen in love with. But the illicit relationship with Lila hung over them like a black cloud, always reminding him of the betrayer that he was.

He had tried from time to time to stop what was happening, but the urge for them to be together was too strong. He had abused Cassie's trust and now she had come to witness the fate of her husband and daughter, neither one whom had given her the slightest consideration. Her face was etched with pain and defeat. He couldn't bear to keep looking at her. And he couldn't help wondering why she was here.

The chill at the defense table was felt by anyone who even glanced at Lila and Bauer. That they despised each other was so apparent, Wagner was certain that any minute one of them would leap over him and try to strangle the other with his or her bare hands. He had heard prosecutors refer to defense attorneys as being on the "dark side" and had always resented that. Now, he knew for a fact that it was true. These two clients were scumbags he could barely stomach. Geller, on the other hand, looked perfectly at ease, probably wondering to what luxurious resort he would fly his own plane after he got Lila off with a slap on the wrist. Dark side or not, he hoped some of Geller's magic would spill over to his own client.

Celia was still seething over her loss of motive but was convinced she could make both defendants see jail time. She had the irrefutable physical evidence and with that would win justice for Stan and for his brother and wife who now sat behind her, barely able to contain their loathing for Lila. If she had ever felt more overt hatred pervading a courtroom, she couldn't remember when.

She called her first witness, Sergeant Harvey, the first officer on the scene. After he described what he saw and the steps he took to protect the crime scene and begin the investigation, Celia was done with him. Geller had one or two questions for him, then let him go. Next, the pathologist, Dr. Lowell, recounted the physical evidence: fingerprints on the gun, Bauer's DNA under Stan's fingernails, the subdural hematoma caused by the blow to the skull as Stan fell on the coffee table, and the approximate amount of time it would have taken Stan to bleed to death.

Geller had a few questions for him. "What did you find out about the deceased in the autopsy?"

"In reference to what?"

"In reference to the fact that Mr. Levy was a heavy cocaine user."

"Mr. Levy's septum was severely damaged, and he probably would have needed surgery to keep it from perforating, should he have lived. He also had lung tissue damage and advanced cardiovascular disease, possibly associated with cocaine use."

"Is inexplicable rage a symptom of excessive use of cocaine?"

"Dramatic mood swings would not be unusual."

"Now, about Mr. Levy's condition after he had been shot and hit his head on the edge of the coffee table. Might it not have seemed to anyone who saw Mr. Levy laying on the floor, passed out, blood pouring from a wound in his chest and one from his skull, that he was already dead?"

"I think anybody looking at him would have known that he was severely injured and to call 911 immediately."

"But a person could believe that, with two serious wounds, he was already dead and there was no point in calling 911."

Celia stood up. "Dr. Lowell is a forensic scientist, not an expert in reading the minds of perpetrators."

Geller nodded at her and smiled. "I'm finished with this witness." Facts were facts and there was little he could do about it, but he knew he could twist them in his favor. He was also counting on Lila to work her charms on the jury. After knowing her for only a few weeks, he sensed she could manipulate people to do just about anything she wanted them to do. But, he was worried about her present demeanor. Something was simmering under that cold exterior and it was worrisome.

Josh came off the elevator and made his way through a throng of reporters, realizing he might not be allowed inside the hearing room after all. He saw Rosemaria talking to some other cops further down the hall, but he quickly walked to the door of the courtroom making sure she didn't see him. He wasn't ready to talk her yet and wanted to do it away from the courthouse. Since no one stopped him, he entered the courtroom and found a place to sit in the back. He saw Lila seated beside her lawyer at the defense table. Two other men were sitting at the opposite end of the same table. One of them looked to be in his twenties and a little overweight. The other man was gray haired and had to be Steve Beaumont, Lila's lover. She obviously wasn't looking around the room for Josh so apparently didn't miss him. He hoped the hearing wouldn't last long. He was looking forward to this chapter in his life being over.

Celia called Ryan Meeks, the head criminologist, and had him go over in detail the condition of the living room, the scene of the murder—furniture upended, broken vases and dishes, smashed mirrors and photographs—indicating a fierce struggle had taken place. Celia managed to portray, through the words of Meeks, that Stan had fought for his life against a much stronger Bauer.

Wagner painted a different picture of Bauer as the victim of a husband's rage and Geller, during his time with the witness, portrayed Lila as being too terrified to intervene.

As he listened to the testimony, Josh was confused. Why were they talking about this guy Ernest Bauer? It didn't make any sense. Why weren't they talking about Steve Beaumont who was sitting right there? What had he missed while he was gone? Josh suddenly felt dizzy, his ears filled with a hissing sound and he leaned forward to keep from passing out. His brain did not want to accept the obvious. No, no, no! Beaumont was Bauer and Bauer was Lila's father. Josh wanted to bolt out of the hearing room and find some fresh air to breathe. He needed to stop the noise in his head and the pain in the pit of his stomach. But something kept him glued to his seat. A perverse instinct made him stay and listen. Rosemaria was right. His obsessive need to rescue broken wings had led him into this horror show. He was going to see it through to the end.

Waite and Osborne testified regarding their investigations into other possible perpetrators before finally concluding that Lila and Bauer were the most likely suspects. Coleman outlined their rationale in suspecting Hari of being complicit with Lila in getting the gun back to her, and then described trailing Hari to where he left the gun for Lila to pick up. Coleman forced himself to hide his personal satisfaction at finally nabbing Lila holding the gun, and he managed to sound totally dispassionate as he described her arrest and that of Bauer.

Neither Geller nor Wagner challenged much of what the detectives said. After all, it was all factual and already known to most of the country through the news media. And when Rosemaria took the stand to fill in the details, everyone was already chomping at the bit to hear what the two defendants had to say for themselves.

As Rosemaria came back down the aisle after testifying she was startled to see Josh sitting in the back row. He nodded at her, solemn and unreadable. She nodded back and went out into the hallway. He *had* come! But why wasn't he sitting behind Lila, supporting her like always? She sat down on a bench next to the wall and pondered the question. He must have figured out by now who Bauer was. She wondered what else he knew.

A terrified Hari Suma testified that Lila had asked him to get the gun for her at the vacant lot, in return for introductions to some very important people in show business. He had seen her come into the twenty-four-hour market many times and had noticed her getting gas the evening of the shooting. He was sure she couldn't have shot her husband and he felt sorry for her, but he had nothing to do with the killing. Nothing. Nothing. His voice trembled and his body shook uncontrollably. Geller couldn't challenge his testimony that Lila was still in the area right after the shooting because Hari had managed to find the missing video footage that clearly showed she filled her car up with gas after the shooting had taken place. Lila had admitted she was present when Bauer shot Stan, but Celia never left a stone unturned.

As soon as Coleman was off the stand, he had gone straight to Vanessa's room to see if she was still there. She wasn't. Sanchez had managed to smuggle her out, hopefully without being noticed by the press. Coleman had told her she still needed to go back to the boat with Sanchez and wait till the hearing was over to see if the case would be carried over to trial. Besides, he wasn't ready to have her move back to the valley. He thought of spending the rest of his life with Vanessa, and as he visualized all of the things he wanted to do for her and share with her, it made him feel more alive than cutting through the water on his Sea Ray on a perfect summer's day.

The moment had finally arrived. Geller had insisted that Bauer testify first, and he was nervous as hell. All he had to do was tell the truth. He hadn't wanted to kill Stan. His only intention was to get him to stop beating Lila and let him know he'd be back if Stan as much as laid a hand on her again. He had never owned a gun and never wanted to. He had never even shot a gun until Stan. But he did have to tell one lie. Stan hadn't taken the gun out of the drawer. He and Stan had been wrestling all over the room and Stan had gotten his hands around his throat. And by the determined look on Stan's face, he wasn't going to let up until he choked the life out of him.

Stan slid backwards on spilled water from a cracked vase and Bauer managed to fight free and back away toward Lila. Suddenly, she thrust a gun into his hands and he barely knew what to do with it. He fumbled with it for a moment, giving Stan a chance to lunge back at him as they fought for control of the gun. It went off and Stan fell back and cracked his head on the edge of the coffee table. But that was not what he would say now.

Josh watched Bauer get on the stand and was surprised to find he had no impulse to run up to the bastard and kill him for what he had done to Lila. No, there was no one to defend here. Neither of them was a victim of the other. Lila was as guilty as Bauer. Josh continued to listen and could only imagine the fear and pain Stan had suffered while slowly dying.

Wagner was looking intently into Bauer's face. "Describe exactly what happened when you arrived at Lila's house."

"Lila heard my car drive up and she was hysterical. She came running out of the house and said Stan was out of his mind with rage from the cocaine and had slapped her and was threatening to kill her."

"Why didn't you just grab her and get out of there?"

"Because she always ended up going back to him. I needed to let him know that I was her father and I was going to protect her."

"Where was her mother in all of this?"

"Her mother knew nothing of what Lila was going through. They never spoke."

"So, you went inside. What happened?"

"I tried to talk reasonably to Stan, but he wouldn't listen. He ranted and raved about how he knew Lila was cheating on him, even though she wasn't. He said she didn't give a damn about him and was just using him to get ahead in the business. I told him that if he ever laid a hand on her again, he would deal with me, but that only set him off even more. He came at me and shoved me in the chest hard, saying, 'You think you're tougher than me? You think you intimidate me?' And I shoved him back. He took a swing at me and I grabbed him, and we wrestled around the room, trading punches when we could. At one point, he staggered over to the sideboard, pulled out the drawer, took out the gun, and pointed it at me. I didn't know what to do. Lila was screaming for him to put it down. I grabbed his wrist, we struggled for the gun, and it ended up in my hand. The gun went off and Stan fell."

"Did you have any intention of killing Stan when you went over there?"

"Absolutely not! I hate guns. I hate violence. It was an accident. I never meant for it to happen. I only wanted to protect Lila."

"Thank you." He smiled at Celia. "Your witness." Wagner nodded his approval at Bauer and sat down at the table.

Celia stood up and surveyed the room as she spoke. "You considered yourself Lila's protector, did you not? Her only family except for her hapless mother."

"I wouldn't describe Cassie that harshly," Bauer said, "but yes, I was pretty much her only family."

"Lila had told you before, hadn't she, about Stan's vicious temper and how he used to slap her around?"

"Yes, she had told me."

"So, you had known about him abusing her for quite some time."

"Yes, she'd told me about it."

"But you did nothing."

"I'm not proud to say it, but no."

"You were supposed to protect her and yet you did nothing about her being abused by her husband. How did that make you feel when she called you to say he was beating her again?"

Wagner stood up. "I think we can assume he had the feelings anyone close to Lila would have. There's no need to rehash painful feelings."

The judge stared at Wagner. "That's why we have hearings and trials, son. To rehash painful things." He turned to Celia. "Go on."

"So, how did that make you feel, Mr. Bauer?"

"I was not happy with what he was doing."

"Not happy? He was beating your daughter on a regular basis and all you felt was 'not happy?'"

"Of course not. It was more than that."

"Then what did you feel?"

"It made me angry."

"I should think it would make you a lot more than angry. This was your family, your little girl, you were supposed to be protecting her and you weren't."

Bauer knew she was baiting him, but her words struck home in a way that caused him unexpected pain. "I know I wasn't. I would have like to have been there for her all that time, but it wasn't possible."

"But that night you were. You were able to take all that anger toward Stan and finally do something about it. You were finally able to take action to protect her. You must have thought about that on the long drive to Bel Air from Sherman Oaks. You must have looked forward to finally acting like a man for a change. Isn't that right? Isn't that what you were feeling?"

Geller stood up to object, knowing exactly where Celia was going, but the judge overruled him.

"Tell us, Mr. Bauer, isn't that what was going through your mind?"

"Well, that night, I was there when she needed me."

"And you would have done anything to keep her safe."

"Yes, I would have."

"Anything."

Bauer hesitated. He knew she had sucked him in. "No, I wouldn't have killed anyone."

"Even to protect Lila, even though this was finally your chance to put an end to it?"

Geller objected again and again was overruled. "There's no jury here, counselor. I'll judge the evidence for myself."

"You had plenty of time to formulate what you would do when you got to Lila's, didn't you? You must have come up with something."

"Not what happened, no, not that."

"Stan's death meant the end of her suffering, didn't it? Not a bad outcome for both of you, was it?"

Geller shot out of his chair.

"Your honor!"

Celia walked back to her chair. "I'm through with this witness."

Outside the courtroom, Rosemaria was looking in the window at Bauer on the stand. "He looks done in. Now he's getting off the stand."

"Did you hear anything?" Waite was standing beside her.

Rosemaria eyed the sheriff, standing a few feet away, giving her a warning look. She moved away from the door. "We're not supposed to. It's not allowed, remember."

"Now Lila gets to put on her big show," Coleman said. "I wish we could be in there for that award-winning performance."

"I can only imagine how she felt when Vanessa and Bauer locked eyes." Rosemaria shuddered, then glanced over at Coleman. "Sorry." He shrugged and Rosemaria went on, "Lila hates Vanessa now more than she hates me, and that's saying something."

Osborne stared past them thoughtfully. "All that hatred has to be directed somewhere." He turned back to his friends. "She may yet surprise us."

In the courtroom, Geller gently leaned over and spoke to Lila. "I know you're probably very nervous, but all you have to do is speak the truth and tell us exactly what happened that night."

She walked up to the witness stand, promised to tell the truth, sat down and looked timidly up at the judge and then at Geller, who had walked up to stand a few feet away from her.

As Lila took the stand, Josh wondered about all the terrible accusations against Stan. That was not the man he knew and had worked with. He had heard of defense teams smearing the dead victim to try to get their clients off. Now he was watching it play out in front of his eyes. Josh stared at Lila long and hard. He no longer found any beauty in her face. All he could see was a mask that hid the ugliness underneath. He looked at the other side of the courtroom and saw Jennie sitting behind the prosecutor and thought of all the grief he had put her through. No more. He had to make amends and she was at the top of the list.

"Where do you want me to start?" Lila asked in her little-girl voice.

"You can start with what happened that afternoon between you and Stan."

"Okay."

She looked so young and helpless, Josh figured every acting class she ever had was being put to good use for that moment. She should have gotten way more acting jobs, he thought bitterly; her performances had always been convincing to him.

Lila began. She described how Stan had come home, drunk, obviously having taken a few hits of cocaine somewhere along the way. He started attacking her about the money she spent on clothes and how she had married him for his money and what he could do for her career. The same old accusations he always leveled at her. She tried to escape but he grabbed her and wouldn't let her go. She got angry and yelled at him and he slapped her in the face. She backed away from him and he tried to grab her again, but she ran to her room to call her father. She told him he needed to get over to her house because Stan was angrier than she had ever seen him. She stayed in her room while Stan pounded on the door and then went back downstairs. Finally, her father showed up and she ran downstairs and out the door to meet him, begging him to somehow get Stan out of the house.

Celia objected to nothing in Lila's story, making notes, biding her time.

"When Stan saw my father, he wanted to know who the hell he was and what he was doing in his house. I told him he was my father and I'd called him to protect me from him. That made Stan go ballistic. He looked at my father like he wanted to kill him." Lila stopped, her eyes wildly searching the room, her mouth open; she seemed to stop breathing. "Because...because..."

Geller sensed disaster. "Judge, I think my client needs a..."

"No!" Lila interrupted. "No, I have to say this!"

Bauer froze in place. Somehow, he had known she would do this.

"Because I had told Stan a long time ago that my father had molested me when I was a child."

Outside the door, Rosemaria had pushed it open a crack and motioned the others to quickly come over.

Inside the courtroom, there was a collective gasp and everyone, including Josh, was wondering what was coming next.

"...and had been for years." At that last part, Lila aimed her cold blue eyes at Bauer with the full force of an arctic storm. He recoiled as if hit.

Geller was on his feet. "Judge, this was ruled inadmissible. You have to stop this."

Celia jumped to her feet as well. "He can hardly say this is my fault, judge. This is his client saying whatever she wants to say."

The judge turned to Lila. "Do you understand that none of this was to come out at the hearing?"

Lila ignored him. "I'll say whatever the hell I want to say." She spoke directly to Geller. "And you can't stop me."

The judge shrugged. "It's your funeral."

Geller tried again. "Lila, we can go into the..."

"No! I'm getting all of this out now! I've been waiting years for this! That man," she pointed at Bauer, "seduced me when I was a child. He drove me out of my own home because I was terrified my mother would find out."

Bauer glanced over at Cassie. Her face and body were rigid. She hardly seemed to be breathing. This was killing her.

"I called him that night so he would help me, protect me. But after Stan found out who he was, Stan went crazy and started screaming threats at my father. They started shoving each other and fought all over the living room, knocking over furniture. You have to understand, I was terrified. I begged them both to stop but they ignored me. Somehow the drawer to the hutch flew open and my father saw the gun and grabbed it. Stan tried to wrestle it away from my father, but it went off and Stan fell and hit his head on the coffee table. My father gave me the gun and told me to wipe off the prints and not to call the police. I didn't know Stan was still alive! I swear it! My father left me with Stan's body, and I didn't know what to do. I was afraid I'd be blamed. I took the gun and hid it! Later, when I told my father I forgot to wipe off his prints, he went crazy and told me I had to get it back. That's the truth. I swear it!"

Josh felt like he had been crawling around in a sewer for weeks and been covered in slime. But he had no doubt Lila was going to talk her way out of this entire sordid mess.

Geller sank back down into his chair at a loss for words. He avoided looking at his client as he asked, "Is that all?" Lila nodded and the judge moved a box of tissues close to her so she could wipe the tears off her face. Geller looked at Celia, barely able to get the words out, "Your witness."

Out in the hallway, the four detectives were openmouthed with shock and surprise, except for Osborne. "I had a feeling."

Waite went back to the door and opened it a crack to listen. A woman pushed open the door and stumbled out, walking haltingly toward the elevators. Rosemaria stared after her. "Do you know who that was?"

Coleman was staring as well. "Lila's mother. Why would she subject herself to this kind of public humiliation?"

Rosemaria watched Cassie walk toward the elevators. "She didn't know Lila would actually spill the beans, I guess."

"I think she expected it," Osborne observed. "She wanted to be there when it all came out."

Back in the hearing room it took a moment for Celia to pull herself together but after a few seconds, she stood and walked a few steps closer to Lila until she was only a few feet away. "You say your father started molesting you as a child. Isn't it a fact that he didn't come back into your life until you were sixteen?"

Lila was defiant. "I was a very young sixteen, very naïve and inexperienced."

"Would it surprise you to learn that we have several witnesses from your hometown in Salinas that could testify to the complete opposite of that assertion."

"They're lying if they say that."

"And your mother never noticed a thing? You never went to her and complained about what your father was doing?"

"It would have hurt her too much."

"And you care deeply about your mother."

"Yes."

"How often do you go see her or ask her to visit you here?"

"She doesn't like leaving Salinas."

"How often has she visited your home?"

Lila said quietly, "Never."

"Never. This mother that you'd sacrifice your well-being for has never been to visit you and you have never visited her in Salinas since you left home."

"So what?"

"But your father has visited you many times. Your roommate can testify that you were madly in love with him, addicted to him, so crazy about him when you found out he had been with another woman, you made it clear you'd do anything to keep him."

Geller stood up. "Your honor, none of this was allowed to come in."

The judge was not moved. "You opened the door, counselor."

Celia continued her attack on Lila. "We will provide evidence that you were so obsessed with him, you were even willing to kill to keep him tied to you!"

Geller jumped to his feet. "Your honor..."

Celia walked back to her desk. "I'm through with this witness."

Rosemaria was grinning ear to ear and her cohorts moved away from the door down the hall, barely refraining from jumping up and down in celebration. "Go, Celia!" Rosemaria whispered. The reporters at the end of the room started to move en masse toward the courtroom as people poured out, chattering excitedly. The four detectives observed the chaos, grinning from ear to ear. Rosemaria saw Josh headed toward the elevators and went after him.

Josh felt nauseated. Lila was worse than anything he could have imagined. Now she would go on trial and then make a deal and worm her way out of any punishment. He managed to squeeze into a packed elevator and the closeness of other people made him feel claustrophobic. Stan was dead and she didn't give a damn about him. She wanted vengeance on her father for whatever reason and for that she was willing to throw herself off a cliff. If Lila ever came near him again, he didn't know exactly what he would say to her but whatever he said, he would make damn sure she stayed away from him for good. He wanted to talk to Jennie and tell her how sorry he was that she had to hear about Stan fighting for his life, and even worse, that he could have lived had either Lila or Bauer given a damn. But not now. Now, he didn't want to talk to anyone. He came out of the elevator into the lobby as Rosemaria stepped out of the one across the hall. She moved toward him, but the noise of excited conversations made it made it impossible to hear what she was saying to him.

They walked down the hallway away from the crush of people and Rosemaria spoke quietly. "I'm sorry about what happened upstairs. It must have been hard to hear."

"You knew, didn't you? You knew everything."

"I couldn't tell you. I'm sorry. Will you please listen to me, just for a few minutes? I have something to show you. Then I'll let you go."

He walked to a bench further down the hallway and sat, exhausted and emotionally drained. He didn't need this now. His brain was on overload and all he wanted was to be alone. She followed him and sat beside him. "There's something I have to tell you."

Rosemaria knew it was now or never. She had to tell him how she felt about him, and he could take it or leave it. She was about to place her heart on her sleeve and hoped he wouldn't yank it off and stomp on it.

"Josh!" It was Lila, with Geller, trying to move her out the door with a mob of determined reporters in their wake. "Josh." Lila called to him plaintively.

He waved to her and yelled. "Wait for me by the limo."

Rosemaria was appalled. "Even now?! Even now you're going to let her keep using you?"

"Calm down. You don't know what you're talking about."

"You're the one who doesn't know! People aren't like the helpless animals you bring home all the time. They can be evil and selfish and hurt you badly."

"I know that now, Rosemaria. Obviously. Not everybody is like you."

"Like me?" She choked back tears. "Like me?" Fine...that's just fine!" She saw the confusion on his face and it only made her feel angrier and more frustrated. She took an envelope out of her purse and shoved it into his hands. "I doubt if this will do any good, but here is a medical report from your father's doctor in Marysville. He didn't tell anybody about this, not even your mother. The reason he went crazy and started drinking was because he found out his body was practically eaten up by cancer and he didn't have the guts to fight it or do himself in. He manipulated you into doing it for him. One hell of a father! Really worth ruining your life over!"

She stood up and was backing away into the crowd seeing the questions forming in his mind, but she didn't have any more answers for him. All she felt for him now was hatred. Hatred for his stupidity, his self-destructiveness, his rejection of her, and for letting Lila win and humiliate her. Let him solve the mess of his life by himself. Let him have Lila. They deserved each other.

"Go on being a coward!" she yelled. "Be just like him!"

"Rosemaria!" He stood up and took a step in her direction, but Lila moved from behind him and firmly clamped a hand down on his arm while the press swarmed around them.

"Go to hell!" Rosemaria yelled, before running across the lobby to the opposite exit. She had vowed after her last argument with Josh that she would never make an ass of herself in public again, and here she was making a total fool of herself in front of every reporter, crook and lawyer in the county. Coleman and the others could testify at the trial if there was one. She just wanted to get as far away as she could from everything and everybody.

Josh released Lila's hand from his arm and Geller yanked her away out the front entrance. Lila looked back at Josh angrily as Geller guided her through the crowd. Josh noticed Lila's mother pushing her way through the crowd to where the limo driver was holding the door open for Lila and

Geller. He saw but couldn't hear the woman say Lila's name. Lila turned to the woman and they stared at each other for one millisecond before the woman landed a resounding slap on Lila's face. Geller tried to grab Cassie as Lila fell against the car, but she was too fast. She disappeared into the avalanche of reporters who were recording every delicious moment. *If it bleeds, it leads…*and this story was just getting better and better. Josh saw the icy malevolence Lila directed at the disappearing figure of her mother, and he knew he would never speak to her again. He glanced at the papers Rosemaria had handed him and stuck them in his jacket pocket. Nothing was as it seemed, or ever had been.

CHAPTER THIRTY-FOUR
MARYSVILLE, WISCONSIN

It was Saturday night and Billy's Bar and Grill was packed to the rafters. The country music coming out of the stereo speakers was not too loud, and above all the chatter, people were still able to hear themselves think and talk. The furniture and fittings were old and worn but nobody cared. Billy's was all about comfort and the familiar and feeling like, no matter what, their world wouldn't change, and life would go on the same in Marysville even if the whole rest of the world blew up. Jimmy and a couple of Josh's other buddies were tucked away in a corner playing poker, just for pennies, nothing illegal that would get Billy in trouble.

Josh, George Constantine, and Randy McAveety had reconnoitered to a booth to contemplate what the future held for them the next few years. The table was littered with beer bottles and they weren't done yet, as they acknowledged their futures were still less than certain. Josh was home on leave and hadn't been told where he'd be stationed. George was set on moving to Chicago and learning all about computers, even though his parents thought he was crazy to leave the security of the family farm. Randy had gotten his realtor license and was going to make millions as soon as he saved enough to move to Madison, where the market was booming, or so he had read in the money magazines he subscribed to. Neither of them thought Josh was fit to be in the U.S. Army but never had the nerve to tell him that the few times they'd seen him since he enlisted. Sure, he was fit and strong, even more so after basic training, but everybody knew he couldn't kill the smallest living thing, let alone a human being.

"What are you going to do when they ask you to start shooting people?" George asked, the beers having loosened his tongue. "Sooner or later, you'll have to do it."

"I've heard rumors we'll be going to Somalia," Josh said. "On a humanitarian mission."

Randy frowned, took a good gulp of his beer, and shook his head. "That place is a powder keg. They murder U.N. peacekeepers, for God's sake. It's on the news all the time."

"People are starving. They need food and protection from both sides."

George agreed with Randy. "I don't think you can kill anybody, even to protect people."

Josh spoke softly and thoughtfully. "I'll find out, won't I?"

Randy wouldn't let up. "Why the hell did you run off and enlist, anyway? You never said a word to anybody, even us."

Josh's face was an implacable mask as he set his beer down on the table. "I think that's it for me if I'm going to be able to drive home."

Randy knew he should have kept his mouth shut as he watched Josh stand up and take a few bills out of his pocket. He and George decided they'd had it, too, and reached for their wallets. Josh, feeling a little woozy, steadied himself on a post by the booth before getting his bearings and heading for the front door. He was almost there when Jimmy walked up behind him and slapped him on the shoulder. "Just the man I need."

Josh rocked back and forth dizzily. "What? Need for what?"

"We just lost Kevin to his nagging wife. We need another hand at the table."

"Sorry, gotta go home." He stumbled toward the front door.

"Hey, you gonna be okay?"

"I'm fine."

"You shouldn't drive like that." Jimmy looked at Randy and George for help.

Josh waved them all off. "I can drive."

Jimmy was reluctant to let him go. "Don't forget, we're supposed to take Connie and Marlena to the carnival Saturday. Scott can come, too."

Josh was at the door. "I'll pick him up from the school in the morning." He started to go out the door when Jimmy said, "He's not there. I saw him in your dad's truck an hour ago. They were headed towards your house."

Josh stared at Jimmy, suddenly stone cold sober. He banged through the door and ran towards the parking lot where the ancient pile of nuts and bolts he had bought for a song was waiting. He prayed that it would start. It did, and Josh screeched out of the lot and hit the highway full speed, which wasn't too fast, considering the old heap he was driving struggled to get to forty miles per hour. He pushed the gas pedal to the floor and still it seemed the car was barely moving.

The drive home was interminable. If anything happened to Scott, it would be his fault. His brother trusted him, and he had let him down.

He promised God his life, his future children, should he have any, and everything else he could think of, if his morbid premonition was wrong, but as soon as his house came into view, he knew his prayers had been in vain. The nightmarish scene on the lawn was dimly lit by the light from the porch. His father was holding Scott at arms' length, pointing a shotgun to his head. His mother was on the ground a few feet away, sobbing hysterically. Old Sullivan was barking frantically and straining against the rope around his neck tied to the truck's front bumper.

His father saw Josh and shouted, "Don't come near me, you son-of-a-bitch, or I'll blow this retard's head off!"

If he was going to get Scott out of this alive, he would have to distract his father. But how? He couldn't make his brain work right. The drunken old man was so itchy-fingered and jittery, the gun could go off any second by accident or on purpose.

"Let Scott go. He hasn't done anything."

"Hasn't done anything?!" The words seemed to drive him into a new fit of frenzy. "He's a fuckin' idiot, is what he is! He ain't got the brains to do nothin'!"

"He's your son—"

"Shut up! Just shut up! This retarded piece of shit ain't no son of mine!" Suddenly, the old man's eyes glazed over and the muscles in his face seemed to slacken into an expression of total apathy. He shoved Scott to the ground and took aim. Josh dove desperately for the shotgun, but it went off before he could reach it. What was left of Scott fell backwards, a bloody heap on the ground. His mother's sobbing erupted into an agonized wail as she threw herself on her son's body. Josh picked up the shotgun and aimed the handle at his father's face as the old man came staggering toward him. He caught him under the jaw, and with a loud cracking sound, slammed it halfway up his face. The bastard was dead before he hit the ground.

Sirens sounded in the distance. Jimmy must've called his father and told him to get out to the farm. But Josh didn't give a fuck. Let them do whatever they wanted to do to him. He watched the lights from the cop cars come up the road and heard the sirens come screaming toward him. As he stood over Scott's body and his mother, draped over him, drenched in blood, he thought he wouldn't have to worry anymore about killing anybody in Somalia.

CHAPTER THIRTY-FIVE

LOS ANGELES

Josh had waited a week before attempting to contact Rosemaria, but by then, it was too late. He got nothing out of Larry except that she had decided to retire from the force a few weeks earlier than she had planned, and why didn't he just leave her the hell alone? Finally, after a week of begging, Kowalski took pity on him and told him he'd ask Rosemaria's father to give him a call. Kowalski wouldn't say where she had gone, only that she was with Mr. Baker, skiing up in the mountains somewhere. Kowalski took down Josh's cell phone number and assured him he would try to get him to call.

Josh had no choice to but to be patient and wait, work at the zoo and spend time with Noor. He had his musical that he probably would be working on from now until doomsday unless Ken's old friend came through for him. Ken had told him he should be ready to come in with something in case the bread people decided they liked him after all. Howard's movie still hadn't gone into production and his hopes were fading that it ever would. He looked around at the mess on the floor and decided he would finally straighten things out. He got the trash can out of the kitchen and started picking through the pile—what to keep, what to throw away. He picked up a newspaper and glanced at it—definitely trash.

Josh, against his better nature, had followed the blow-by-blow descriptions in the media of the results of the hearing. The judge decided that there was enough evidence to go to trial on first degree murder for Bauer and voluntary manslaughter for Lila.

Lila and Bauer, to Wagner's relief and Geller's disapproval, both took the deals the D.A. offered instead of going to trial. The publicity from the hearing was already so toxic, even Lila had chosen discretion over valor. Josh predicted that she would try to somehow put a positive spin on everything, making good use of her hereto unsuspected acting talent and never-ending machinations. She had decided to accept Celia's offer of involuntary manslaughter and would be serving two to four years in the county jail. Josh had no doubt she would never serve the full four and would probably try to go one better than Martha Stewart and turn the whole thing into a reality show. Why not? There was no shame in anything anymore, not even incest and murder.

Celia had offered Bauer voluntary manslaughter and he must have been grateful to accept. Three to eleven years in state prison would have seemed like a reprieve compared to what he would have gotten for murder.

Josh tossed away more newspapers and organized his music sheets and papers the best he could, then straightened the rest of the room as well. He found old clothes he didn't remember having worn in years and put them aside to hang up. He sat down and picked up his guitar, thinking he should tackle the kitchen and bedroom as well, now that he was in a rare cleaning mood, but first he strummed a few chords and hummed a melody that had been floating through his head as he cleaned. For a few days, he had been trying to find the music to match some lyrics in the musical and it wasn't coming. The more he pushed, the more he hated everything he wrote. He stood up from the couch and put his guitar aside and paced. He couldn't lose his music. It was all he had left. He paced until a worried Suzi landed on his shoulder and gave out a squawk that made his ears ring. He smiled at her and she flew back to her perch.

No, his music wasn't all he had. He had his AA meetings that were keeping him sober. And he still had his good friends Ken, Jennie, Jerry, Martha, Suzi and Gilbert. They were important pieces in the brand new puzzle that was his life. But Noor was his heart. Her welfare and happiness were foremost in his mind and he was determined his dreams for her would become reality. Some people, including Rosemaria, might think his love for Noor was highly unusual, even extreme. But animals had always been his touchstone, and his empathy for them was something he had been born with. He thought of his faithful dog Sullivan who had given Scott his love and devotion for the entirety of Scott's short life. What Sullivan had done

for Josh, he had done for Scott as well, shown them both what uncondi-
tional love was all about when the world seemed to be crumbling around
them. He hoped that soon he would be able to think of his little brother
and remember only the good times.

Sullivan had died peacefully in his sleep before Josh had moved to L.A.
Then Noor came into his life and filled the empty hole that his best pal
had left there. There was no doubt that Josh had much to be grateful for
and, one day at a time, he was learning to accept that. He sat down and
picked up his guitar and resumed strumming and humming. The melody
was there, somewhere.

His cell phone rang, and he panicked. With all his cleaning, he had
misplaced it. He started throwing papers everywhere and messed up everything he had just organized until finally finding it under an old sweater. He
clicked it on. "Hello," he said, his voice shaking.

"Hello, Mr. Sibley?" The voice was not unkind, which could be a good
sign.

"This is he. Mr. Baker?"

"It is. Sergeant Kowalski gave me your number."

"I appreciate your calling."

"She *is* with me."

"Please let me talk to her."

"Sorry, but I can't do that. I think it's best that you do not try to contact
her for a while. This is the first vacation she's taken in ten years. She seems
to be needing time to herself. I know that girl. The only hope you have of
making her do what you want is to let her decide to do it herself."

"That's not easy."

"Maybe not, but you don't have any choice. Good-bye, Mr. Sibley."

The line disconnected and he dropped his phone on the couch. Mr.
Baker was wrong. For the first time in his life, he did have choices.

CHAPTER THIRTY-SIX
NEW YORK

J osh dug fifty cents out of one of his many pockets and handed it to the flower vender. With careful deliberation, he picked the most beautiful rose in the vender's collection and handed it to the lady by his side. "For the best new assistant prosecutor in New York City."

"Thank you, but you shouldn't be spending your money on me," Rosemaria admonished.

"On you, I would gladly spend my last penny," Josh said theatrically, with a gallant bow from the waist.

"Oh, Josh!" Rosemaria looked stricken with guilt.

"I'm just kidding," Josh assured her. "You don't have to worry about me. I'd rather hear about you."

He could see she was much too concerned about his situation to want to talk about herself, but she did as he asked. "All right, well, my father loaned me the money to survive for a few months, and since I decided to move here to…well, to get a new start, I skipped the California bar exams, crammed like crazy on New York state law, and took the bar exams here." She rushed through the explanation and turned her full attention on him as he started slowly walking down the street. "I've been so busy, I haven't really kept in touch with anybody from L.A., except talking to Larry a couple of times. I do know he and Vanessa are very happy. And, of course, I heard what happened to Lila and her father. Hardly seems fair to Stan, just a slap on the wrist for both of them. Other than that, I've been buried in work, learning from the best, and trying to put my share of criminals in jail. I'm sorry if what I found out was hard for you. I thought you needed to know." Her voice trailed off as she touched his filthy clothes and tears came into her eyes. "I was so confused. I'm so sorry."

Josh grabbed her hand and held it. This was going all wrong. "No, I'm grateful for what you did. I called Jimmy and he told me he was the one who did some leg work for you up there and found my father's doctor. What made you suspect, anyway?"

"Just the normal, suspicious, paranoid mind of a cop. Jimmy was your best friend but even he didn't know what the report said until he dug it up for me. But, back then, he did ask his father to make sure you weren't prosecuted and got an honorable discharge from the Army."

"I always had more friends than I deserved."

"What about Noor? Is she all right?"

"Still the same. She'll be moving to a sanctuary soon, along with Gilbert."

Rosemaria's mouth flew open. "Oh! That's wonderful! How'd you manage that?"

"Well, I managed to meet a very rich woman who in exchange for certain favors, invested in the sanctuary. Then, Jennie and Vanessa plotted to get Larry to talk to his dad to talk to Hahn, and the rest, as they say, is history. I'll have a place to stay near the sanctuary when I visit Noor, which will be often."

Rosemaria stopped, took his arm and stood in front of him. "What are you talking about? What woman?" The idea that any woman, let alone a rich one, would be willing to help this rag-tag-looking bum made no sense. And what the hell was he doing wondering the streets of New York City?

They were nearing forty-fourth street on Broadway and he had no choice but to tell her now. He handed her the brown bag that held his bottle. "Have a drink, Rosemaria."

She looked at him like he'd gone crazy. "No, thank you."

He held it up to her. "Go ahead, take a drink. Please."

Rosemaria took the bag, not bothering to hide her repugnance, and brought the bottle to her lips. Her nose wrinkled in anticipation of the taste of hard liquor as she took a small sip. Her eyes opened wide. "It's soda water!" She took the bottle out of the bag and stared at it. "Why are you drinking soda water out of a vodka bottle?"

"I cleaned up my act."

Considering the dirty rags he was wearing, it wasn't surprising that she looked at him like he had just landed from another planet. She saw something past his shoulder and gasped. "You're not going to believe this, but I just saw Ken go around the side of that building. What an incredible coincidence!" She made a move to go around him, but Josh stepped in front of her. "I want to catch him before he disappears into the crowd," she insisted.

"He won't disappear," Josh said calmly.

"But there's hundreds of people on the sidewalk..." Her voice trailed off. "Oh, my God, I feel like I'm in the middle of some weird dream. Will you please pinch me?" She held out her hand and he took it in both of his.

"Don't get mad, Rosemaria."

Her eyes narrowed and the familiar furrows appeared between her eyes. "Why should I get mad?"

This was supposed to be the happy moment he had dreamed of for over a year, and now it could all go wrong in an instant.

"Tell me," she said impatiently.

"It's very good. You're going to like this."

Her eyes lit up. "Josh, is it the show? You and Ken got the show on Broadway?! Is that it?!" She looked at his clothes and her excitement vanished. "But then why would you...?"

"No, it's not the show. That didn't work out, but I haven't given up. Come on." He led her to the end of the block and around the corner.

At first glance, it looked as though they were back on the lot at Universal. Cameras, lights, trucks, crew, actors, and police clogged the street and sidewalks. In the middle of all the confusion, Ken and Jennie were talking to several people gathered around a movie camera as the cinematographer looked through the lens at actors positioning themselves, getting ready for a scene.

"Ken's rich friend Harvey had a girlfriend, now his wife, who decided she wanted to be in Ken's movie instead of my Broadway show. I'm doing the score, Ken's producing and directing, and Jennie's assistant director, and they gave me a little part just for the hell of it. I was doing a little research into my part when I ran into you."

She was staring at him with a frozen expression he couldn't make out and he figured he better talk fast while he had the chance. "I found out where you worked from Kowalski and I was going to look you up anyway. It just happened sooner than I expected."

She seemed to have stopped breathing. He was in an absolute panic. "Are you upset?"

"You're in a movie?"

He still couldn't tell by her face how she was taking it. "I should've told you right away, but I was so happy to see you I, ah...then, I thought I'd surprise you." When she finally reacted, he knew he was in deep shit.

She exploded. "You mean I went through all this hell...all this guilt... thinking I... for nothing?! For *this!*" She waved her arm in the direction of the movie set and enunciated the last word with utter disdain.

"I thought you might react this way."

"How could you do it?! How could you do this to me?! You did this on purpose, you inconsiderate, selfish, rotten, son-of-a—!"

He grabbed her and clamped his hand over her mouth. "It's a relief to know you cleaned up your language."

She pulled away and looked around at the people who were now staring at them instead of shooting the movie. "I can't believe this. I told myself that without you, at least I wouldn't be doing this anymore. Now look at us." She gestured at the gawkers staring at them. "I could scream, just scream!"

He clamped his hand over her mouth again and pulled her close. "I love you," he whispered.

She stopped struggling and looked at him as though she hadn't heard right, and he took his hand off her mouth.

"Yeah?"

"Yeah."

"So that means that I'm supposed to forgive you for everything? "Yeah."

"And I'm supposed to give up my job here and start all over again in Los Angeles?'

"You can take the bar there, too, and we'll be bicoastal."

"Forget it."

She loosened his hold on her and walked over to Ken and Jennie, who had by now, along with everybody else on the street, noticed them.

He waited a few more minutes before heading in their direction. He had some heavy-duty persuading to do. On second thought, maybe it wouldn't be so difficult. She was still hanging on to the rose.

* * * *

Noor's legs ached. She had been lying on the same ledge every day for a long time, waiting for Josh. She raised her hind end high in the air and stretched her front legs luxuriously, then sat back on her haunches and gazed over the hill to the path that was visible only from the ledge she was sitting on. She slept most of the time now, so she wouldn't have to feel the loneliness and uncertainty that was always with her when she was awake. Josh had never been gone this long before and she was beginning to think he would never come back. It had become difficult to keep her food down and some days, just walking about her cage was an effort.

It was early in the morning, much too early for people to be walking down the path toward her compound. But she was sure she had seen someone. Her heart beat fast. It was a man with light hair like Josh's. She concentrated her entire being on that one spot until the man was visible again. It was him! But someone was following close behind and holding his hand. A pang of jealousy shot through her. It was the female that had touched her when she had been sick.

Josh and the female disappeared from sight behind the hill, and for a second, Noor panicked and was afraid she had imagined them both.

They became visible again at the crest of the hill and began running when they caught sight of her. Noor jumped down off the ledge and ran to the fence, rubbing hard against it. Now her heart was beating so hard, she felt it would explode through her chest. The relief she felt at seeing Josh again was so overwhelming, she couldn't remember when she had felt such joy. It put her in quite a generous mood. Let him have this female if that's what made him happy. They would both belong to her.

THE END

AUTHOR'S NOTE

Many thanks to Sergeant Sean Smollen, who gave me a tour of the Beverly Hills Police Department, shared his considerable knowledge with me, and patiently answered my questions. Thank you, also, to Senior Forensic Specialist Clark Fogg, who showed me his lab at the Beverly Hills Police Department and explained fingerprint analysis in detail. I learned much more from them than I was able to use in this book, but I deeply appreciate their kindness and hospitality toward me. Any mistakes I have made regarding police procedure are completely mine.

ABOUT THE AUTHOR

Britt Lind is an actress, singer, and writer who has performed in television shows and movies and on stage in Los Angeles, New York, and Vancouver, B.C. She has written several screenplays and was runner-up in the Washington State Screenwriting Competition for her screenplay *A Light in the Forest*. Britt lives in Thousand Oaks, California, with her husband, Nick Alexander, a screenwriter, and their three feral cats—Teeny, Toughie, and Baby Hughie—who used to live a hardscrabble life in the cold and rain in the frozen north of Washington State and now enjoy a life of luxury in the sun, as is their due. Britt is also president of a nonprofit, People for Reason in Science and Medicine (PRISM), a pro-health, pro-environment, anti-vivisection organization. Her inspirational memoir, *Learning How to Fly*, a winner in the 2019 Beverly Hills Book Awards in the Performing Arts Category, is available on Amazon. Her website is www.brittlind.com.

To find out more about PRISM, please go to
www.peopleforreason.org and www.facebook.com/gotoprism
Follow PRISM on Twitter @gotoprism